"I'm sure we're fine."

How deeply she wanted that statement to be true.

A strong hand closed around her upper arm. "I may have snoozed in the car, but I'm wide-awake now," West said quietly, steel underlying his tone. "You and Baby-Bug are safe with me."

A bicycle whooshed past, the rider snaking out a hand and grabbing the stroller's handle. The sheer force of the bicyclist's speed ripped the stroller from Cady's fingers.

"Livvy!" Cady cried as bicycle and stroller veered onto a dirt path leading kitty-corner through the park.

West's hand grabbed hers, and they surged forward in pursuit. A fist gripped Cady's heart. They *had* to reach Olivia! She was slowing West down. He was practically dragging her along as those military-grade legs ate up the ground.

Cady jerked her hand from his. "Go, go!"

Jill Elizabeth Nelson writes what she likes to read–faith-based tales of adventure seasoned with romance. Parts of the year find her and her husband on the international mission field. Other parts find them at home in rural Minnesota, surrounded by the woods and prairie and four grown children and young grandchildren. More about Jill and her books can be found at jillelizabethnelson.com or Facebook.com/jillelizabethnelson.author.

Books by Jill Elizabeth Nelson

Love Inspired Suspense

Visit the Author Profile page at Harlequin.com.

THE BABY'S DEFENDER

JILL ELIZABETH NELSON

LOVE INSPIRED SUSPENSE
INSPIRATIONAL ROMANCE

LOVE INSPIRED® SUSPENSE
INSPIRATIONAL ROMANCE

Recycling programs for this product may not exist in your area.

ISBN-13: 978-1-335-72164-8

The Baby's Defender

Copyright © 2020 by Jill Elizabeth Nelson

This edition published by arrangement with Harlequin Books S.A.

For questions and comments about the quality of this book, please contact us at CustomerService@Harlequin.com.

Love Inspired
22 Adelaide St. West, 40th Floor
Toronto, Ontario M5H 4E3, Canada
www.Harlequin.com

Printed in U.S.A.

A father of the fatherless, and a judge of the widows,
is God in his holy habitation.
–Psalm 68:5

To our courageous and dedicated military service men
and women and to their equally courageous
and dedicated families.

ONE

Cady Long bent her neck and kissed the top of her baby Olivia's head. The peach fuzz of her daughter's hair tickled her nostrils, and she suppressed a sneeze. It wouldn't do to startle the child wide-awake at four o'clock in the morning. Livvy had just finished nursing and had fallen fast asleep again in her mother's arms. The normal routine that had finally developed in this sixth week of her baby's life consisted of at least another two to three hours of precious sleep for them both before they started a new day.

Yawning silently, Cady rose from the rocking chair and placed Olivia in her crib. A tiny sigh fluttered from the infant's lips and expanded Cady's heart like a balloon. How could she contain the love bursting inside her for this blessed child? Olivia was her legacy with her soldier husband, Griffon, who had given his life on a foreign battleground before he even had a chance to know he was going to be a father.

A dull ache that never totally went away throbbed deep inside her as she tiptoed from her daughter's room and headed up the short hallway toward her own. The rich smell of old woodwork newly refinished teased her nostrils. She'd recently inherited this nineteenth-century home in Glenside, a suburb of Philadelphia, from her great-aunt Anita. Memories of visits to this house featured as bright spots in a childhood deeply marred by parental alcohol and drug abuse. But as much as she treasured this priceless piece of history passed down through her troubled family, especially when she had desperately needed a place to live and raise her daughter, she would trade the massive Gothic Revival house in a heartbeat to have Griffon back alive.

A bittersweet smile flickered on her lips at the thought of how he would have delighted in his daughter and, in order to provide the best for her, would have thrown himself into the restoration projects this old home required. At least now she had West Foster, her husband's former sergeant, as well as Darius Creed and Brennan Abernathy, two other former army buddies, helping her gradually make repairs on this place without violating the conditions of the will and the preservation restrictions attached to such vintage structures.

Her soft pillow beckoning, Cady reached for her bedroom doorknob but a faint yet distinct thump from somewhere downstairs halted her abruptly. The breath froze in her lungs. That noise was not among the catalog of natural creaks and groans this old house often made. Had someone broken into her home? Stock-still and holding her breath, she continued to listen for unusual noises aside from the accelerated drumbeat of her pulse in her ears.

A click followed by a scrape carried to her from somewhere directly below her feet. Cady's heart leaped against her ribs. Someone *was* in her house!

Sharp prickles ran up and down her body as heat bloomed in her chest. Was she afraid or angry? Both sounded about right, but she wasn't about to react like those idiot heroines in the movies and head downstairs to investigate on her own.

Gritting her teeth against a shiver, Cady continued through the door into her bedroom. Her phone was on the charger atop her bedside table, and the gun Griff had given her and taught her to shoot was in the drawer beneath. In smooth, tandem motions, she snatched up her phone and yanked open the drawer. With the cool metal of the firearm cradled in her palm, she thumbed her phone awake and tapped in the number for emergency services. The call rang through in one ear while she strained with her other ear to catch any further sounds from elsewhere in her house. No more foreign noises. But that didn't mean the intruder was gone. At least the old staircase was not emitting the telltale creaks that would signal someone ascending toward the bedrooms, which meant she could be thankful the person seemed to be confining his or her activities to the downstairs.

The emergency operator answered, and Cady whispered her situation and address into the phone. The operator started saying something about staying on the line, but Cady put the call on hold and tapped the shortcut button for West Foster. Sure, she wanted the cops to show up, but they were strangers. West, she knew and trusted. Her body began to shake uncontrollably. She was going to need a friend by her side at this moment, and West's apartment building was only a couple blocks away. Besides, if the recently discharged Army Ranger got here before the law, any intruder would take one look at all that solid muscle and power and flee like his pants were on fire.

"Hello, Cady." West's tone was sharp and clear even though she had to have awakened him from sleep. More evidence of his military training—instant awareness.

"Come quickly." She shivered as if a chill breeze had wafted over her. "An intruder is in my hou—"

Something hard crashed against her skull, and Cady's brain went woozy. She fell forward onto the bed, face-planting onto her pillow. The phone flew from her hand, but the hard bulk of her handgun pressed against her belly where it was sandwiched between her body and the mattress. A weight leaped on top of her middle back, as if someone were sitting on her. Hands shoved her face into the pillow, robbing her of the ability to breathe. A pair of sturdy legs trapped her arms against her sides, rendering her helpless. The weight on her back was a boulder. Clearly, her assailant was larger than her.

Cady kicked and thrashed, pajama-clad legs scissoring the air fruitlessly, but her attacker only increased the pressure that forced her face into the pillow. Seconds passed like minutes, minutes like hours, and even though her attacker grunted with the effort of holding her, no matter how she wriggled she remained trapped. She was being suffocated! Her natural petiteness offered no advantage in the situation.

Pulse roaring in her ears, her heart hammered against her ribs. Her lungs ached for oxygen. She was going to die.

What about Olivia? Who would look after her?

Cady's heart wept for her orphaned daughter as consciousness faded.

West charged up Cady's sidewalk, his bare feet slapping the cool cement. Cady was in trouble! That's all he'd needed to know to send him running without wasting precious time donning his lace-up utility boots or even buttoning the shirt he'd thrown on over his jeans. He'd grabbed his gun and run.

Behind him and closing in fast, a siren sounded. Cady had called the police too—smart girl—but their proximity wasn't going to slow him down when seconds might count. West took the porch stairs in a single leap and the heavy, ornate front door loomed before him. Cady had given him a spare key since he and his buddies had been coming over to help out with the household projects this old place demanded. He thrust it toward the lock just as the screech of skidding tires and the siren's blare caught up with him.

"Stop! Police!" A male voice bellowed behind him.

Without a backward glance, West turned the key and burst into the spacious foyer.

"Cady!" His voice echoed back at him from the vaulted ceiling.

No response. The home was silent except for the countdown beep of the home security system that would soon blare if he didn't enter the access code. He couldn't afford the noise when the ability to hear evidence of human presence might be critical. He punched in the code as his heart beat a tattoo in his chest. This massive place was a house and half. Where would Cady be this time of night? Upstairs, most likely. West flipped on a light and took the steps two at a time, calling her name. A soft moan drew him to the second door on the right.

Readying his pistol for action, he burst into the room. His line of sight located no one except a pajama-clad figure, lying facedown, gasping and stirring on the bed. He swept his gaze and his gun to the left and then right. Unless someone was hiding in the closet, only he and Cady occupied the room.

"West?" She croaked at him as she rolled over, panting for breath, and sat up. "I can't believe…you came…so fast." A hiccuping sob cracked her voice. "The attacker ran off…when you yelled, and the siren closed in. The person was trying to suffocate me. I thought I was going to die!"

Fighting an impulse to run to her and gather her in his arms, West edged over to the closet door and popped it open. Nothing and no one inside except clothes and shoes and a few storage boxes.

He turned toward Cady. "What happened? Are you okay?"

"Drop the gun and get your arms in the air." The authoritative voice from a husky man in a police uniform cut off any response she might have made.

West complied instantly. He slowly bent and lowered his weapon to the carpet. He had no reason to resist when Cady no longer appeared to be in danger. *Thank you, Jesus.*

"That's not necessary," Cady said. "This is my friend." She motioned toward West. "I called him right after I called for the police, and you both came quicker than I believed possible."

"My partner and I were in the area, ma'am,"

said the cop as a female officer entered the room, also with gun extended.

"Please, put the weapons away." Cady's tone went a little shrill. "I've had enough of a shock this morning."

"You're holding one, too." West kept his voice gentle and even.

Her body visibly trembled, and her skin was pale as chalk. Those symptoms, plus her rapid breathing, betrayed the potential onset of shock. The enlarged pupils of her amber eyes were not a good sign, either.

Cady's gaze fell toward her lap where her hand rested, clutching her firearm. "Oh!" she gasped out and dropped the gun. It thudded to the floor. "Much good that thing did me when I needed it."

The police officers also lowered their weapons.

The female uniformed cop pulled a small notepad from her pocket. "Would you tell us, please, what happened here?"

West silently echoed the question. Something terrible had gone on in this room to strike such terror into this strong woman.

"Someone attacked me," Cady said. "The person hit me over the head with something, and while I was dazed, he tried to suffocate me with a pillow. Whoever it was tried to kill me!"

"I'm going to search this house from top to bottom." West's fists clenched as his words came out in a low growl.

"No, sir," said the male officer. "Leave that to the professionals."

"I *am* a professional. The army trained me to search dangerous territory and expose hostile elements."

The officer shook his head. "But—"

"Stop!" Cady's voice sliced the air. "Whoever it was has to be long gone. I need to check on my baby in the next bedroom."

West's gut twisted. Someone had infiltrated the house and attacked a new mother with her infant sleeping next door. How low could anyone get?

"There's a child here?" said the female officer. "Better let one of us do the checking."

"All right." Cady's mouth quivered beneath her wide gaze. "My attacker didn't have a spare second to do anything to Olivia, but I still need to be assured of her safety."

"Understandable," West said. "Hang in there. We're all here for you now."

"Thank you." She rose to her five-foot-two-inch height and squared her shoulders, her whole countenance firming. "But please be as quiet as you can as you go into Livvy's room. If she's slept through this commotion, I'd like her to stay asleep…at least for a while yet. Could you all leave for a moment? I'd like to put some regular clothes on."

"Sorry, ma'am," said the female officer. "You'll need to stay as you are right here until the crime scene investigators and EMTs arrive. The CSIs will need to collect the pajamas as evidence and be on hand while the EMTs check you out physically so that they can collect any evidence from your person. They will also collect items like your pillow for examination."

Cady slumped, her face losing color again. "I can't believe this is happening."

"Do as you're directed," West told her. "It's for the best. I'll look in on Baby-bug and then maybe Officer Harmon—" he filled in the name from the pin on the male officer's uniform "—and I can search the premises. Whoever attacked you didn't leave by the front door because that's where these officers and I came in."

"Sounds like a plan." The female officer, whose name tag dubbed her Andrews, shot a frown at her partner who was staring at West with a mulish look on his face. "I'll stay with you, ma'am, until reinforcements arrive."

Cady nodded silently and subsided into a seat on the edge of the bed. West's heart twisted. Just when it looked like a modicum of peace and contentment was peeping through Cady's bereaved sadness, something like this happened to send her back into dejection with an added heaping helping of old-fashioned fear. Whoever had done this had better hope he didn't find them before the cops did.

Jaw tense, West went with Officer Harmon into the hallway. He headed for the next bedroom, but Harmon brushed in front of him and slipped inside. Scowling, West waited in the hall, mindful of Cady's request for quiet in checking on Olivia. Not that he wouldn't rather have given Officer Grouch an earful. That baby was like a daughter to him, a sacred trust to look after in Griffon's stead.

Harmon soon returned wearing a small smile. "Cute kid," the cop whispered. "A-okay and sound asleep. The room is clear."

West swallowed a chuckle. Apparently, babies softened grumpy cops, as well as hardened soldiers.

"What do you know about what took place here?" Harmon asked.

"No more than you do. When she called me, Cady barely had time to tell me she had an intruder when I heard her cry out, followed by a thump and a grunt. Then the phone went dead. I just moved to town, and I'm without a personal vehicle at the moment, so I raced over here from my apartment two blocks away as quickly as my feet could take me."

The officer stared down at West's bare toes peeking from beneath the hem of his jeans.

"Fast feet," he said with a grunt. "From your military background?"

"Army Rangers. Discharged a week ago."

The officer nodded. "Let's go scour this house for any sign of the intruder or how he got in or out. That's got me curious, especially when the security alarm wasn't tripped. Is there any other way to get up to the second floor but those front stairs?"

West pointed into the dimness farther up the hallway. "There's an old servants' stairway at the far end, but the doors at the top and bottom are locked and boarded up for good measure, since the steps aren't safe anymore."

"We'd better check them out, anyway."

West popped his head into Cady's room and let her know Livvy was fine, then he and Officer Harmon set off on their search mission. By the time they'd checked out the servants' stairway, top and bottom, to discover it was still locked and boarded up at both ends, the EMTs and CSI personnel were arriving, a plainclothes detective with them. Everyone went about their business with calm efficiency while West and Officer Harmon finished scouring the premises.

They'd wound up in the spacious but old-fashioned kitchen when Cady walked into the room wearing a pair of black leggings and a floral-patterned, long-tailed blouse. Her medium-length blond hair had been pulled back in a ponytail. She held her athletic figure erect, chin high, but her eyes wore shadows.

"Did you find out how the intruder gained access to my home?" Her wide gaze shifted from West to the officer and back again.

"Sorry." West rolled his shoulders in a tense shrug. "Everything appears locked up tight and in order." It was beyond frustrating that they hadn't been able to discover the way the attacker got in or the method he used to slip away.

"There's no sign of forced entry anywhere, ma'am," Officer Harmon added.

Cady appeared to wilt. "I don't understand what's going on."

West stepped up to her and placed a hand

on her arm. She lifted those expressive amber eyes to his.

He offered a small smile. "Let me make you a cup of tea while law enforcement finishes up here."

"Tea sounds wonderful," Cady answered with a hint of enthusiasm.

Harmon nodded toward them and vacated the room.

"Pick a seat and I'll wait on you." West motioned toward the chairs around the kitchen table. "No argument." He forestalled her objection with a wagging finger, then turned toward the stove and flicked on the gas flame under the traditional kettle Cady always kept on the burner ready to heat.

"Now, let me see where this creep hit you." He stepped around behind her, and Cady sat still while he gently parted her hair. The light-colored strands were soft between his fingers, and the pleasant scent of her fruity shampoo wafted up to him. "There's a red mark, but not much swelling."

"Yes, the medical personnel told me I should be examined by a doctor once the clinic opens, just to be safe, but they doubt I have a concussion."

"That's one good thing." He moved in

front of her. "Did you get any kind of a look at your attacker?"

"Not a thing. The person was behind me or sitting on me the whole time. The detective asked me the same thing, but the best description I could give was that, judging by weight, the intruder could have been a small man or a large woman."

"A woman?" West let out a soft growl. "I hope they can find some sort of forensic evidence in the bedroom or somewhere in the house to give us a clue who did this."

"You and me both. Frankly..." She stopped speaking and tucked her lower lip between her teeth.

"What is it?"

"The detective seemed a little skeptical about my story."

"Why do you think that?"

"He kept asking me if I was sure about the details I was reporting, and he was really bothered about the fact that the intruder didn't set off the house alarm. Then when they found a couple strands of my hair in the carved woodwork of my bed's headboard, he asked if I might have hit my head on it."

West huffed. "Implication being that you caused your own head injury? How ridiculous."

"I'm not sure what he was implying, but he seemed to take everything I said with a grain of skepticism."

"Maybe it's just his way of being thorough." West went to the cupboards to hide his scowl from her. He didn't need to upset her further with an anger spike, but maybe he needed to have a personal talk with that detective about his crime-side manner.

He pulled out a pair of mugs, equipped with infusers, from the cupboard where he'd seen her store them last week when he'd been here fixing a leaky faucet. A tea canister sat next to the mugs, still with its plastic shrink-wrap seal. West broke the wrap, opened the lid and took a whiff of the dried roots and leaves inside.

"New flavor," he said. "Unusual. Smells faintly of celery."

"When it comes to tea, the odor and the flavor can be quite different. The canister came in the gift basket I received from the neighborhood watch committee when I moved in, but I wanted to finish my Tuscan herbal lemon variety before I opened the new container."

The kettle whistled and West turned off the heat. The shrill noise faded while he added several scoops of the new tea into the infuser baskets. He poured the steaming water over the exotic-looking dried herbs, then set a cup in front of Cady.

With his own mug he took a seat at the table opposite her. "I'm glad you called me at the same time you called the cops. Your trust means a lot to me."

Probably too much. His growing attraction to the widow of one of his squad members made him more than uncomfortable. What was he to do with feelings that seemed disloyal to his courageous buddy and were certainly too soon for him to look for reciprocation from his widow? West shook off the internal dilemma and gave his full attention to the woman across the table from him.

"I'm ashamed of the way I depend on you and the guys." Cady wrapped her hands around her mug, as if her fingers were cold, and stared at the brew inside.

"Are you kidding me? It's our duty and honor to watch over you and Baby-bug."

She glanced up at him, those wonderful eyes moist. "I can't tell you how much I appreciate that. The three of you even moved to Pennsylvania because I decided to come here and live in this place that I inherited. I know Griff would want you to keep an eye on me, but I almost feel like *my* choices are dictating *your* choices. You have your own lives to figure out now that you are civilians again, especially when you're gearing up to start your own business together."

"You think we're too busy for you?"

"Not exactly." She lifted her mug and started to bring it toward her mouth, but then set it down again. "I mean I don't want to be a burden. I want—no, need—to stand on my own two feet. Eventually."

West studied her as he took a sip from his mug. Pleasantly sweet, not vegetable-flavored in the least. Cady was right about the taste being different from the smell.

"Independence is one thing," he said. "We understand and respect your boundaries, but things changed radically tonight."

Cady visibly shuddered. "I'll tell you something I didn't tell the cops because it makes me sound off-my-rocker paranoid. Over the past six weeks or so, I keep getting this creepy sensation at odd moments—like something slithering up my backbone—as if I'm being watched."

West's nostrils flared. He'd experienced the sensation on many missions and learned to listen to it. Someone was spying on Cady? The same person who'd tried to kill her? A logical deduction.

If he gripped the tea mug any tighter, he'd break it. "Consider yourself the Triple Threat Personal Protection Service's first client. Pro bono."

Cady lifted a hand, palm out. "I couldn't take advantage of your new company like that. I need your services, but I need to pay like any other client." A distinctive baby howl blasted through the monitor on the kitchen counter. "Excuse me." A soft smile spreading her lips, she rose gracefully. "Her highness has awakened quite ravenous."

She left the room, and West sat nursing his tea and brooding. In the middle of a sip from his mug, he winced at a tearing sensation in his gut. The room began to waver and wobble as if the walls were breathing. West gripped his head and attempted to stand up, but another abdominal pain—like a KA-BAR knife twisting in his stomach—bent him double.

The strange tea!

Did Cady drink any of it? He didn't think so, but his mind was spinning. He couldn't remember for sure.

Please, God!

The world dissolved around him.

TWO

Cady paced the hospital waiting room floor, bouncing a fussy Olivia in her arms. What on earth had happened with West? A sudden attack of appendicitis? But appendicitis didn't cause seizures, did it? The minutes waiting for an ambulance to arrive had been horrible, watching West suffer. The EMTs who'd checked out her head bump had long left the premises, but one of the CSIs finishing up evidence collection had known to clear the area of anything sharp to keep West from injuring himself. Then, as he was being loaded into the ambulance, he seemed to become aware and he kept moaning, "The tea. It was in the tea." So, feeling a bit foolish, Cady had sent the tea canister along with the EMTs to the hospital.

The clomping of two pairs of booted feet quick marching alerted her that Brennan and Darius had arrived and were headed up the hallway toward her. She'd called West's business partners, aka former squad brothers, and apprised them of the situation even before the ambulance arrived at her house. The men burst into view, buddies sharing a level of trust that only comrades in arms can achieve. Darius—of the dark eyes, umber complexion and five-foot-nine-inch package of pure muscle—grabbed her close in a quick squeeze. The moment she was released from the breath-stealing hug, Brennan, a six-foot-tall, lanky and pale Kentuckian, plucked Olivia from her grasp and began tickling his honorary niece.

What a relief not to feel alone in a crisis anymore. Cady's leg muscles went weak, and she sank into a nearby chair. Darius perched on the edge of a seat beside her, as if ready to charge into action at any moment. Cady understood. Soldiers hated to sit still when one of their own was in danger. Even Brennan, the more laid-back of the pair, betrayed hyperalertness in the cool blue gaze that kept skimming the waiting room and up and down the hallways, even as he made goofy faces at Livvy, who kicked and cooed in appreciation. Unfortunately, at this moment, there was nothing any of them could do but wait for a report from the medical team working on West.

"Heard anything more?" Darius asked in his baritone voice.

"Nothing yet." Cady's fingernails dug into the palms of her hands as she struggled against tears.

How could she bear it if West were stolen from her life, too? *God, You wouldn't be so cruel as to allow that, would You?* Cady thrust the question from her mind. Griff's death had shaken her confidence in God's care and protection.

She only knew that in a very short time West had become like an anchor in her personal storm. Ever since Griff was killed in action, West had phoned regularly to check on her—no matter where he was in the world—visited in person when he was on base and acted as a sounding board for the many decisions she'd had to make. She'd never forget how he and the guys had obtained temporary leave to help her move three months ago when she suddenly inherited her great-aunt's house. That she received the life-changing bequest while she was in her third trimester of pregnancy was hardly convenient, but the stipulations of the will required her to move in immediately or lose possession. Sure, she talked big about independence, but was she ready for it? Certainly not by losing someone else she cared about.

Darius touched her arm and Cady jerked out of her dark meditations.

"Sorry." He lifted his hands, palms out. "Didn't mean to startle you. Was there some sort of emergency that brought West to your place so early?"

Rubbing the sore place on her skull, Cady launched into the harrowing tale of her personal attack. If thunderclouds could actually appear on someone's brow, Darius's head was wreathed in them, and Brennan's complexion all but burst into flame as she wrapped up her account of events.

"You're our first client, for sure," the Kentuckian bit out.

"That's what West said." Cady shrugged her shoulders.

"Then it's settled," Darius rumbled. "But right now, you're going to follow the EMTs' advice and head down to the ER to have your head examined—literally."

Cady grimaced. "More than one person in my lifetime has recommended such an exam to me."

The quip drew gentle smiles from the pair of ex-soldiers.

An hour later, she'd received a clean bill of health from a physician, provided she continued to exhibit no signs of concussion. Now she was back in the waiting room, her chest full and tight, like an invisible fist held her in its grip. Why was there no word yet on West's condition?

Darius and Brennan did their best to provide distraction by showering attention on Olivia, insisting on keeping Cady—the nursing mother—hydrated with good, old-fashioned H2O, and pestering the desk nurse for updates, which were not forthcoming. Finally, a tired-looking fortysomething man wearing a doctor's coat and a stethoscope stepped into the waiting room and called Cady's name.

"Here!" she cried, leaping to her feet.

He motioned her over, and Darius and Brennan followed close on her six, as her military exposure had taught her to refer to the area directly behind her.

"I'm Dr. Horton, Emergency Medicine Specialist," he said, eyeing the tough-looking pair looming in her wake. "These two must be Westley's army buddies and business partners. He said he figured you guys would show up 'loaded for bear,' as he put it."

"West is all right?" Cady's words emerged through a constricted throat.

"I wouldn't call him all right yet." The doc grimaced. "Full recovery from cicutoxin takes time, but he's out of danger now. It was a close call. If you hadn't sent that tea canister along so we could quickly identify what he'd ingested, I doubt I would have good news for you at this moment. Frankly, we would have spent too much time ruling out reasons other than poison for his seizures and gastrointestinal distress. With cicutoxin, there is no outright antidote. Prompt and proper treatment to mitigate the effects on the body is critical."

"What exactly is cicutoxin poisoning?" Darius folded thickly muscled arms over his barrel chest.

"*Cicuta* is the Latin name for water hemlock," the doctor answered. "It's a highly toxic plant native to wetlands in North America."

"Cowbane," Brennan inserted, face washing pale beneath his tan. "My family has lost livestock to that deadly plant. 'Course, cows just eat whatever's growin' out of the ground and tastes good, but people who should know better sometimes confuse the plant with wild

parsnip and have cooked it up in their frit-
ters—with fatal results."

Darius scowled. "So, this plant is something common that anyone could obtain if
they were knowledgeable about what to look
for."

"I'm afraid so," the doctor said.

"Can we see West now?" Cady cut in.

All this talk of poison sent her head spinning and her heart rate stuttering. The only
route to regaining any semblance of calm
would be to see him, talk to him, touch him.

"One at a time," Dr. Horton said. "And
only briefly. He needs to rest while his body
works to flush out the remnants of the poison. We're continuously monitoring his brain
activity with an EEG, though the seizures
seem to have abated. As far as prognosis, in a
strong specimen like him we can hope for recovery to be fairly rapid. Hopefully, we won't
need to keep him longer than overnight."

Cady exhaled a long breath. "Thank you,
doctor."

Shortly, Cady stepped into a small hospital room that smelled faintly of floor wax
and antiseptic. West's strong form filled out
the narrow hospital bed. An IV bag dripped
a clear substance into a prominent vein in
the back of his hand. Immediately, his head

swiveled toward her, disturbing the variety of wires which appeared to sprout from his scalp. Of course, he'd heard her soft footfalls over the beeping from the machine connected to those wires. Her heart tripped over that broad Dennis Quaid smile of his.

Though the edges of her lips wobbled a bit, she managed to grin back. "You look like a wonky science experiment."

"You mean my new antennae?" His chuckle warmed the last vestige of chill from her bones. "Doc says I have to wear these EEG gadgets until the last chance of a seizure has passed. I don't recommend having one of those to anyone. Did a number on me. A kitten could wrestle me into submission."

Cady amazed herself with a laugh. A few moments ago, she couldn't imagine expressing any semblance of mirth, but leave it to West to bring humor's cleansing perspective into a frightening situation. She touched his tanned arm, bare beneath the short sleeve of his hospital gown, and found it as much of a rock as ever. Not that she'd had much cause to know what West's arms felt like—other than the occasional casual friend hug when the squad had gotten together socially between missions—but Griff's had been like that, too. The sensation was like connecting with something familiar. Safe.

"Where's Baby-bug?" West asked.

"Darius and Brennan are in the waiting room competing for her attention. Of course, I guarantee if her diaper needs changing, each will be eager to let the other call dibs on her."

West's grin appeared again. "I'd like to be a fly on the wall for that face-off."

"I can't stay long. She's going to be hungry again soon, and there's nothing either of those lugs can do to remedy that problem. Besides, the doc said you need to rest."

"Rest is overrated." His brown eyes lost all trace of humor. "I need to get out of here and get on duty."

"Duty?"

"This time, you saved *my* life. I need to get on with protecting you—and little Livvy."

Cady's cheeks heated. "*I* saved *you?* Hardly. I think it's more like you already started protecting me. The tea was meant for me, but you drank it."

"Yes, but I served it to you. *Not* good on me that you neglected to drink it. I almost killed you!"

"Not you. Whoever packaged deadly poison as tea and slipped it into my gift basket did that. I'm pretty sure I'm going to receive more attention from law enforcement now."

"I'm not willing to leave your safety to them. They can't offer round-the-clock protection. We can, and we won't accept a dime. Not from you."

Sucking in a quivering breath, Cady wound her fingers together. "I won't argue about that offer anymore. I'm grateful."

"Good." West seemed to relax into his pillow.

"Do you know the creepiest thing for me about this situation?" She gazed into his sober eyes. "I've deduced that whoever attacked me this morning got tired of waiting—like a patient spider in a web—for me to drink that cowbane concoction and die, so they took direct action and tried to smother me."

West's hand wrapped around hers, spreading warmth up her arm. "We're dealing with evil here. But God promises never to leave or forsake us. We need to trust Him for guidance and protection."

Cady bit back the hot retort that sprang to her lips. Where was that guidance and protection when her husband walked into an ambush during some top-secret operation at an undisclosed location in the Middle East?

Instead, she forced a tight-lipped smile at West. "With all my heart, I trust you and your guys to keep me and Olivia safe."

"You need to trust us with Mrs. Long's safety, Mr. Foster," Detective Rooney said to West. He'd been the one on scene at Cady's home.

Rooney had strolled into West's hospital room only an hour or so after Darius and then Brennan had been in to see him. The pair had been more than willing to accompany Cady and Olivia home and commit to staying with them indefinitely. So far, the detective had taken West's statement and had him sign a release to law enforcement of his medical records pertaining to this incident. Now, the investigator was trying to get him to back off on watchdog duty, like West and his men's presence was somehow going to mess with the police investigation.

West scowled at the detective. "Are you prepared to assign officers to guard her and her premises 24/7?"

"There was no sign of forced entry at the house." The detective scowled back. "Is Mrs. Long prone to vivid nightmares? She could have been thrashing around and banged the

back of her skull against that massive headboard on her bed."

"Is that what you people are speculating
now? That Cady dreamed of being attacked
this morning?"

Did the detective know something that he
wasn't willing to share?

Cold iron stiffened West's spine. "If Cady's
imagining things, how do you explain the
poison in the tea that was certainly meant
for her?"

"The poison was present in Mrs. Long's
tea container, which implies danger to her,
but you say she never drank from her cup,
even though it sat in front of her for many
minutes."

"Understandable. She'd just been attacked
in her home, and we were talking over serious matters. She was too distracted and agitated to care about drinking tea."

"Yet you weren't?"

"I told you how things happened. Stop
trying to make something sinister out of it.
Are you saying she put the poisoned tea in
her own cupboard? That she knowingly let
me drink it? To what end? I've known this
woman since her husband was assigned to
my Army Ranger squad almost four years
ago. She may be hurting right now. Who

wouldn't be? But she's as solid as they come, a genuinely gentle and caring person."

The detective smirked. "I hope you're right, Mr. Foster, but you may not know Cady Long as well as you think."

"What is *that* remark supposed to mean?"

"Just a word of caution that I probably shouldn't be offering."

"You think *she's* behind an attempt on my life?" West sat bolt upright in bed. The EEG lead wires attached to his scalp yanked painfully at tufts of hair. He ignored the minor irritation and the light-headed swish in his brain. "You're out of line, Rooney." He jabbed a finger in the detective's direction. "I don't know how you've come up with such a ridiculous theory."

The man shrugged. "Take it easy, Mr. Foster. We'll get to the bottom of what's going on. In the meantime, you and your guys need to stay clear of our investigation. You don't need an obstruction charge on your record before you've even gotten your bodyguard business off the ground."

West ground his teeth. If steam could shoot out his ears, the room would be fogged. The detective had done some fast homework on *him*, as well as Cady.

"Is that some kind of threat, Detective Rooney?"

"Not at all." The man offered a bland smile beneath cold eyes.

West snorted. "My team and I can protect Cady and Olivia. You can't—or won't. You and your people should concentrate on catching the monster who's trying to kill her. We'll do our job and you do yours." He clamped his mouth shut, not about to let this law enforcement officer know that he and his partners would be conducting their own investigation on the down-low.

"You can count on us doing our job, Mr. Foster." Tight-lipped, the detective jerked a nod and stalked out of the room.

West got busy yanking the wires off his head and the IV out of his arm. Naturally, those actions sounded alarms and brought medical personnel rushing in, but he bulldozed their objections to his departure. At last, the doc arrived just as West was buttoning his shirt.

Dr. Horton, looking more tired than ever, shook his head and wagged a small piece of paper at him. "This is a prescription for a generic form of diazepam. Fill it and keep the medication with you at all times." He swiftly outlined specific directions for using the drug. "But only administer it if a seizure or signs of one occur. Instruct your friends on its use, because you might not be able to perform the administration. Then get back to the hospital immediately. Understood?"

"Understood." West took the prescription paper. "Here's hoping I won't need this stuff, but I can't be sidelined right now."

"All right, but keep in mind that your best hedge against a seizure is not the drug but keeping yourself hydrated as your body continues to purge itself of toxins." Dr. Horton frowned. "I gather from reading between the lines of the police inquiries that this was an attempted murder, but you may or may not have been the intended victim?"

"You got that right. Let me ask you, Doc, what would have happened had it been someone a little over five feet tall and maybe 105 pounds who ingested that poison and not a big goof like me?"

The doctor's frown deepened. "The truth? Survival would have been extremely doubtful. Water hemlock—what your friend calls cowbane—is one of the most toxic plants in the northern hemisphere. You pulled through purely because of your size and the fact that you received swift and accurate medical attention."

"Thanks for your frankness. That's pretty much what I thought."

An ice block formed in the pit of West's stomach. Only a few sips of tea would have rendered Olivia an orphan. What would have become of Baby-bug then? If she lost her mother, who would take her in and raise her? Through close comradeship with Griffon, he knew that Griff had come out of the foster care system and had no known relatives... and Cady had admitted she had no siblings, but she'd been stingy with further details about her background. Over time, West had gleaned hints that her parents were still alive, but out of the picture for some unspecified but strong reason. Since Griff had mentioned once that his own foster care situation had been a walk in the park compared to the dysfunction of Cady's upbringing, those particular grandparents didn't sound like a promising option for custody of Olivia.

West shook himself mentally. He couldn't allow himself to pursue any what-if scenarios. Cady's life had been spared—twice. The only conceivable future was one in which Cady and Olivia survived, and even thrived. That's where he and his Triple Threat team came in. Brennan and Darius and he were forming their personal protection service to help keep people safe. It was their honor to take Cady and Olivia on as their first clients. Failure to protect them was not an option!

Within the hour, West had taken a taxi to his apartment where he put on socks and shoes and retrieved his wallet. Then he went to a drug store. Now, prescription filled and bottled water in hand, he climbed out of another taxi in front of Cady's house. He stepped up on her porch and knocked on the front door of dark hardwood and vintage leaded-glass. This home she'd inherited was a historical prize, being one of the few remaining residential dwellings in the Philadelphia area designed by the famous architect Frank Heyling Furness in the late 1800s. She'd been offered big money to sell it. However, not only did the terms of the will prohibit her from selling the property, but Cady admitted she had always loved this redbrick Gothic Revival home, as it featured fondly in her memories from visits here during her young childhood.

Darius opened the door, shaking his head. "I figured you'd show up sooner rather than later. We've got everything under control here, Sarge. You should have taken a little more R and R."

"You know I couldn't do that."

"I know." Darius grinned.

West followed his business partner and former army buddy into Cady's living room. The furnishings in soft browns and greens were thoroughly homey, but also as vintage as the rest of the place. Cady had inherited everything, even the old-fashioned crocheted doilies under the lamps perched on the small tables flanking the long sofa and the easy chair near the front window. The terms of the strange will required her to keep the decor as is for the first year of ownership; then and only then would she be free to update one room per year, within the restraints specified by the historical society. West figured she might not make many changes, unless it was modernizing the old-school kitchen. Cady liked antiques. She currently occupied a genuine Renaissance Revival armchair designed by famous cabinetmaker Daniel Pabst, a detail West knew only because Cady had told him when he and the guys helped her move in.

Her head was bent over a large book in which she was writing. At his entrance, she lifted her pen and frowned up at him. "West, what are you doing—"

"No scolding," he interrupted her. "My strength is returning in leaps and bounds.

This is where I need to be. What are you writing?"

She held up the book. The cover featured a cute cradle in the center with a variety of infant toys around it. "Filling in Olivia's baby book. She's developmentally on track with holding her head up, cooing and turning toward sounds. And Brennan is convinced that this afternoon he stimulated the first real, non-gas-related smile out of her. I'm inclined to agree." She sent a grin in the Kentuckian's direction, and the man's chest noticeably expanded.

West laughed. "Careful there, Bren. You'll pop buttons. Where *is* Baby-bug, by the way?"

"Napping," the three responded in harmony.

"We need to talk strategy." West took a seat at one end of the high-backed sofa. "First off, one of us will be with you at all times, no matter where you go."

Cady pursed her lips. "Having a perpetual shadow is going to feel totally weird. What about nighttime?"

"Whoever is on duty will bunk here in the living room, but no sleeping allowed. This creeper has apparently discovered how to get into the house regardless of locks and bolts.

We need to be alert and waiting. Further, we need to search this house from top to bottom for any means of access that haven't been considered."

"Darius and I already did that," Brennan said.

"Then we're going to do it again. It's a priority to figure out how the intruder got inside and put a stop to any future occurrences. But we've got another pressing problem."

He didn't see any way around leveling with everyone about what the police were thinking. Forewarned was forearmed, after all. Hating every word that spilled from his mouth, he told Cady and his crew about Detective Rooney's insinuation that Cady had deliberately not drunk the tea because she knew it was poisoned, as well as the detective using a nightmare to explain Cady's attack in the wee hours of this morning.

"The man has lost it!" Darius bellowed.

"You got that right." Brennan snorted like an angry bull.

West turned toward Cady to find that she'd gone so pale he reflexively put out an arm to catch her if she fainted. She didn't, but if she looked any more crushed, she'd be a speck on the floor.

"Why would the police suspect me of

imagining a violent attack on myself *and* trying to kill a man I value and trust?" The words quavered from her lips like leaves fluttering in the wind.

"They don't know you like we do. Besides, they're paid to be suspicious. I have no doubt the detective is soon going to look mighty foolish for suspecting you of anything more underhanded than flipping those awesome chocolate chip pancakes of yours."

She sent him a weak smile, but her eyes shone with moisture. "I can't believe this nightmare is really happening! I thought I'd left this sort of thing far behind me."

"What are you talking about?" West drew his brows together.

She shook her head and clamped her lips closed.

Should he press her for an answer? Now, when she seemed so fragile, might not be the time. But maybe he *didn't* know her as well as he'd thought.

THREE

Cady's heart seized in her chest. How should she answer West's question? How much could she divulge about her family past without losing the respect of these men she admired or, worse, inviting them to suspect her as a bad apple that hadn't fallen far from the tree, the way the police seemed to be doing? Her tragic family history featured a neglectful alcoholic father who had disowned her, as well as a mother with her mind so destroyed by drugs that she barely knew her remaining daughter's name. Both parents were incarcerated for widely different but truly awful reasons. Would her past ever simply stay in the past?

Even Griff had never known the full story, and thankfully, he'd never pressed her for more than she wanted to share. One of the things she'd loved most about him was the way he loved her in the here and now, just the way she was, without analyzing or judging. She'd done her best to return the favor where his own painful past was concerned.

West's steady gaze sifted through her. Did his eyes narrow ever so slightly? Cady resisted the impulse to squirm.

"Let's get to our house search, then," he said at last, turning his dark brown eyes toward his business partners. "This is a big place and may have surprises for us."

"Yes," Cady confirmed. What a relief that he seemed willing to forego his line of questioning about her past. "Victorians, especially Gothics, are known for their nooks and crannies, possibly even hidden entrances or exits."

West sent her a sharp look. "How about secret passages?"

"Possible."

"Do you have a copy of the architectural plans for the house?"

Cady shrugged. "Not to my knowledge. But who knows what's stored up in that attic? It would take days…maybe even weeks to go through everything up there."

West frowned. "I don't think we can waste that much time digging around. Would the local municipality or the historical society have a copy?"

"It's possible. Let me call and ask." She laid the baby book on a side table and picked up her phone lying next to it.

"While you're chasing down leads on the plans," West said, "the guys and I can start canvassing the property."

"No way, Sarge." Brennan sliced the air with his hand. "Your color still isn't right, so you need to sit there and suck down some H2O while we do the legwork."

"And if we go anywhere, I'm going to drive." Cady shot him a stern look.

West raised his hands. "I yield to wisdom."

"Wise man," Cady said, and everyone laughed.

West turned eagle eyes on his buddies, who grinned and offered mock salutes as they exited the living room. Cady motioned for him to keep drinking from his water bottle as she began to look up the needed phone numbers. By the time she was speaking to someone at the township office, West's head had relaxed against the high back of the sofa and his eyelids were drooping. Cady's stomach clenched. She'd come so close to losing him. He shouldn't be up and about, but she had no clue how to make the endearingly stubborn man back off on taking care of *her* when he should be taking care of *himself.*

A short time later, Cady stepped over to the sleeping soldier and studied the clean lines of his face, vulnerable in a rare moment of repose. Not classically handsome but striking in its strength, with a bold brow and a generous nose that had clearly been broken more than once. The firm jawline and the square mouth declared *trust me*, and she did. With all her heart.

She touched one broad shoulder and he jerked upright with a gasp. A small cry left her lips, and his wide gaze riveted on her. The guy looked ready to leap off the sofa and pounce on any threat. *Sergeant Westley Foster, reporting for duty.* A small grin unfurled on her lips.

"Sorry. I didn't mean to startle you." She sobered. "You must need the rest. Are you sure you want to charge around the countryside in search of house blueprints?"

"I'm good. Did you get a lead on the plans?"

"A slender one. The municipal office was a bust. No record of ever having the blueprints. But the person at the historical society said that, while they don't have them either, I should check with the lawyer who handled the estate, so I called Mr. Platte and bingo! Well…" her enthusiasm faltered "…at least a partial bingo. He happens to have an incomplete set of drawings, not actual blueprints, in my great-aunt's file."

"When does his office close?"

"'Promptly at 5:00 p.m.,'" she said in a stuffy voice. "That's pretty much a quote from the guy and in just that tone." She let out a small laugh. "His office is in the neighboring suburb of Wyncote near Robinson Park. I only met him once to receive the house keys and sign the compliance papers for the inheritance. He's nearly as old as my great-aunt was and he runs a one-lawyer operation with a paralegal and a secretary. He struck me as a stickler for order and detail. I have no doubt he'll lock the doors exactly when he says he will."

West consulted his watch. "Then we'd better not be late. If we head out soon, we should have plenty of time."

The infant monitor chose that moment to register Olivia's awakening cries. "We'll have to wait until Livvy is fed and changed, then bring her with us."

A half hour later, Cady strapped her daughter into the car seat in the rear of her Chevy Blazer while West settled into the passenger seat. He was wearing his side arm, which comforted her for the protection it offered and repelled her that a firearm was necessary. He'd suggested she bring her gun in her purse, but she'd firmly declined. Accessing it to defend against a home invader was one thing, but armed-and-dangerous-pistol-packin'-mama-in-public-with-a-baby wasn't an appealing persona for her. West was protection enough.

Pausing beside the driver's door, she scanned the area. Goose bumps prickled up and down her arms even as a pleasantly cool, early fall breeze ruffled her hair and the small branches on a red oak tree in her spacious yard. Was someone hiding in the shadows, watching her every move? The quiet neighborhood of stately older homes, most of them brick, seemed peaceful, not another human being in sight—though the pungent odor of burning charcoal betrayed that somewhere close by, someone had lit their grill. Was this outward serenity a facade like the stillness of a lake's surface concealing a monster in its depths?

Shaking herself free of macabre speculations, she opened her car door. They needed to get going if they expected to make the lawyer's office before closing time. Cady backed the car out of the driveway, leaving Darius and Brennan still searching every inch of the house. Her skin crawled at the idea that someone might have unfettered access to her home through a hidden entrance or passageway, but at least if the guys discovered one, they would have an explanation for how someone was getting in and they could seal it off. What a comfort that would be!

She glanced over at her adult passenger to find West's head drooping toward his chest and his eyes closed. He really *had* left the hospital too soon, but apparently his call of duty overrode good sense. She'd let him sleep, perchance to snore. The thought drew a grin on her face. He'd be so mad at himself when he woke up.

Mere minutes later, she cruised along the edge of the small but attractive Robinson Park. The area, featuring many trees, a pond, a fountain and a gazebo, was sparsely populated this late afternoon. A young couple strolled along a path, hand in hand, and a middle-aged woman sat on a bench tossing crumbs to the pigeons. The law office came up on her right, across from the park, but signs prohibited curbside parking and the small, three-space lot next to the office was full. Sighing, Cady drove on for half a block and turned into the park's paved area for vehicles. They could walk from here.

As she stopped the Blazer, West's head came up with a jerk. "You let me sleep?" The question sounded part accusation, part astonishment.

No doubt the astonishment was at himself over the fact that he'd drifted off in the first place, and the accusation was divided between himself and her.

"Will wonders never cease?" She laughed. "Westley Foster is human, after all!"

West scowled, evidently not mollified by her attempt at humor. "Have you kept an eye out to see if we were followed?"

"Ugh, no. I should have considered that possibility." Cady's pulse quickened as she glanced from side to side. Could one of the cars cruising up the street contain a threat? Impossible to tell, which only increased the temptation to be anxious.

West muttered something in an angry tone under his breath. "It's okay. My fault, not yours. Some protector I am!"

"Don't beat yourself up. It takes a while to recover from being mostly dead."

This time her humor had the desired effect, and he chuckled. As he'd shared with his squad members and their families that his mother had been enamored with the film, *The Princess Bride*. She'd named him Westley after the hero, who spent a few pivotal scenes being "mostly dead" and undergoing a hilariously incredible recovery process to ultimately save the day.

As they emerged from the vehicle into the fresh air, that icky-itchy sensation of being watched threatened to overtake Cady again. Was she imagining things because West had suggested they might have been followed, or was her subconscious picking up clues her outer awareness hadn't registered?

West's head swiveled back and forth, gaze alert. "No one in the cars rolling past on the street seems to be paying attention to us or even slowing down. But that doesn't mean they aren't being smart in their tailing. I have no way of knowing if any of them followed us from your neighborhood. If only I'd—" He clamped his jaw shut and didn't finish scolding himself, though he was probably completing the job in his head.

"No point indulging coulda-woulda-shoulda," Cady said. "I'm sure we're fine."

How deeply she wanted that statement to be true. But how unlikely that it was—not when someone had tried to smother her and then to poison her and ended up nearly killing a dear friend instead. What a helpless feeling to know someone wanted her dead, but not to have a clue who it might be or why.

One step at a time, she told herself. They were on a mission to the lawyer's office up the block and across the street. Hopefully, said mission would yield helpful results. They really needed to get answers about what was going on.

They started up the sidewalk that skirted the park with Cady pushing Livvy in the stroller they'd retrieved from the rear of her SUV. West strode beside her. Livvy gurgled and cooed and batted the balmy air with her tiny hands, apparently enjoying the sunny-day outing.

Since their arrival, several more pedestrians had entered the park—a family group with a slouching teenager and two small children who ran in the grass, as well as an elderly man walking along the path with the help of a cane. Nothing and no one appeared the slightest bit out of the ordinary or in any way a threat. Cady's shoulders relaxed marginally.

A strong hand closed around her upper arm. "I may have snoozed off in the car, but I'm wide-awake now," West said quietly, steel underlying his tone. "You and Baby-bug are safe with me."

A bicycle whooshed past, the rider snaking out a hand and grabbing the stroller's handle. The sheer force of the cyclist's speed ripped the stroller from Cady's fingers.

"Livvy!" Cady cried as bicycle and stroller veered onto a dirt path leading kitty-corner through the park. The elderly man scurried to the side with his mouth agape as the cyclist sped past.

West's hand grabbed hers, and they surged forward in pursuit. A fist gripped Cady's heart. They *had* to reach Olivia! Cady was slowing West down. He was practically dragging her along as those military-grade legs ate up the ground.

Cady jerked her hand from his. "Go, go!"

He glanced back at her with wide eyes, even as they continued to run. The man faced a cruel decision. Leave Cady to her own devices or rescue the baby.

"Go!" she screamed at him again, waving him on.

Decision made, he charged ahead like a juggernaut in pursuit of that cyclist and the stroller's precious cargo.

Cady stepped up her pace, but someone leaped from a clump of bushes and knocked her to the grassy turf. The breath left her lungs in a high whistle.

A stocky figure wearing a sweatshirt with the hood pulled up over the head pinned her arms and torso to the ground, much like this morning's attacker had rendered her helpless. Only this time she was facing her assailant, but the person's face was completely in shadow. A gloved hand pressed hard against her face, swallowing her screams. Something stung the tender flesh in the fold of her elbow, and the world faded quickly away.

Only two more strides and he'd be able to snatch the stroller from that diabolical bicyclist. From behind, the guy appeared to be a slightly built male with the hood of his sweatshirt pulled up over his head. West and his quarry had nearly reached the end of the park. Who knew where the kidnapper would go with his precious cargo next? He pushed himself into greater effort, ignoring the unaccustomed weakness in his limbs and the tingling in his extremities that could signal an impending seizure. No time for that nonsense. If sheer willpower could hold one of those off, he was going to do it.

Suddenly, the cyclist released the stroller even as he executed a 90-degree turn. West dove forward and grabbed the baby's carriage. Olivia's terrified wails wrenched his heart, though she appeared to be uninjured. She was still securely strapped into her seat of the style that snapped in and out of the stroller's frame for convenient infant transportation.

Breathing harder than this exertion would usually cause, an eerie detached-from-body sensation pressed in on West. He fumbled for the anti-seizure medication in his pocket and finally managed to pop one into the space between his cheek and gum where his body would rapidly absorb the medicine.

Forcing himself to focus, he scanned the area for any sign of the man or his bicycle, but they were gone. Not that he'd be free to chase after the kidnapper, anyway. Olivia was his first concern and Cady a close second. He scooped the squalling, kicking child into his arms. Baby-bug began to quiet immediately as comforting human contact cradled her. Those tear-wet amber eyes, so like her mother's, blinked up at him as she wrapped her tiny fingers around the thumb of the large hand that held her close.

Sirens began to close in on the area. Evidently, someone had called the cops. He couldn't stand in place and wait to be questioned. He had to find Cady. She'd be worried sick about Olivia. He was a little amazed she hadn't caught up with him and her daughter by now.

Retracing his steps, his gaze searched the park grounds for any sign of Livvy's mother. Her svelte figure, crowned by golden hair, was nowhere to be seen. A cold fist began to close around West's heart. He walked faster, retracing his steps.

A scream sounded from the vicinity of the pond. Cuddling Baby-bug close, West raced toward the spot. Several people stood at the pool's edge crying out and pointing at something in the water. As West neared the location, a teenage boy, clad in jeans and long-sleeved T-shirt, waded in, grabbed a limp wad of clothes and started dragging it out of the water.

Not a wad of clothes.

West's pulse stalled and then skyrocketed. He knew that floral blouse paired with black leggings.

West reached the teen and his precious burden in time to employ a free arm to help him pull Cady from the water and lay her on the grass. Her pallor and bluish lips did not bode well.

Please, God!

West knelt beside her still form and felt for a pulse in her neck. There was a faint one, but that wouldn't last long. She wasn't breathing. His insides went still and cold, senses sharpened, like he'd entered the combat zone. Gently, he laid Olivia on the grass near her mother and went to work performing CPR.

Thirty chest compressions, two rescue breaths.

Thirty chest compressions, two rescue breaths.

Thirty chest compressions, two rescue breaths.

He was an automaton, focus absolute, registering nothing and no one else. Saving this woman—if she could be saved—was all that mattered in his world.

Suddenly, Cady's body convulsed and water spewed from her mouth. Her lungs gasped in a rattling breath. Coughing spasms wracked her as her eyes popped open and fixed on his face.

Thank you, God!

Her wild gaze darted everywhere as she strove to sit up.

West pushed her back down. "Olivia's fine. She's right here beside you."

Moments later, they were swarmed with emergency personnel. Quicker than West thought possible, he was back in a hospital bed with more IV fluids being pumped into him to accelerate the final flushing of the poison, and Olivia and Cady were in another room just up the hall. On preliminary examination, it appeared that Cady had been injected with something that knocked her out and was then thrown into the pond to drown, but that was as much as he'd gleaned in all the kerfuffle in the ER before they were separated.

West stared in disgust at the needle in his hand. How long did he need to be sidelined again? And which people were going to arrive first, demanding answers about what happened, answers that he dearly wished he possessed? His teammates or the cops? Within a minute of his speculation, both groups of people nearly collided in his doorway.

"Badges first," Darius said, motioning toward Detective Rooney and a thirtysomething woman of average height and build who was probably his partner.

Rooney grunted and took the invitation with a scowl, trailed by the female detective, who at least wore a pleasant expression. Darius sauntered in after them. West wasn't fooled. Tension radiated from his teammate's muscular shoulders and sharp gaze. He was itching for a fight but had no target. Yet.

"Is Brennan on guard outside Cady's door?" he asked Darius.

"You got that right."

"Good call."

The two of them exchanged wolfish grins. It was great to work with a pair of guys who didn't need direct orders to know what to do next.

"Fill us in on what happened." Rooney's sharp tone inserted itself like a knife into the taut atmosphere.

"Do you mind if we record this session?" his partner asked, producing a handheld recorder. "I'm Detective Leticia Grace, by the way."

The woman certainly had a better manner with witnesses than her older partner. Even her surname inspired trust. Rooney, on the other hand, was probably within spitting distance of his retirement, and if West had ever seen burnout, he was looking at it in the graying detective. The guy was putting in his time with entrenched cynicism and no heart in the job.

"Okay by me," West answered and delivered his account in terse, no-frills phrases as if reporting on a military mission.

Despite the recording, Rooney was taking written notes on a small pad. He paused in his scribbling, lifted his pen from the pad, and speared West with a narrow-eyed gaze.

"Let's summarize. You're saying some joker on a bicycle snatched the baby buggy and raced off with it. You and Mrs. Long gave chase, but Mrs. Long got left behind. The baby-snatcher released the buggy at the end of the park, and you recovered the baby. The cyclist got away, and you have no description of the suspect except the impression that he was a young male dressed in jeans, a sweatshirt with the hood pulled up over the head and cross-trainers."

"That's correct. Bystanders at the park may have seen the rider's face, but I did not."

"How about a description of the bicycle?"

"It was blue." West shrugged. "One of those commuter bikes with wide tires and upright handlebars. Common as dirt. I wish I could think of something distinctive about it."

"That's all right," said Detective Grace. "Uniformed officers are continuing to interview witnesses at the scene. Hopefully, we'll glean more details."

"Will you share them if you do?"

Rooney's amused sneer communicated a

negative answer loud and clear. "What do you know about how Mrs. Long ended up in the pond?"

"Nothing. What do *you* know?"

The detective's face went stony. "She says some guy pounced on her and injected her with something. She doesn't remember going into the water."

West sat up in bed and met Rooney's hard-eyed gaze. "Then you owe her an apology for suspecting her in the poisoning incident and for 'dreaming up' her attack in the night. Outside forces are at work here."

Rooney's too-bland smile sent a tingle down West's spine. "We don't have all the facts yet. *You* don't, either. Nor do we have any witnesses who corroborate her story."

There the detective went again, implying that there were things he didn't know about Cady's past that were pertinent to the situation. He was going to have to press her for answers about the issue that he hadn't pursued this afternoon. He and his guys needed to know if Cady was guarding some dark secret that could contain the key to keeping her and Olivia safe, not to mention catching and stopping people who clearly didn't balk at endangering an infant in their quest to eliminate Cady.

"Ri-i-ght!" West's tone oozed sarcasm. "She arranged for her own baby to be snatched and then injected herself and threw herself into the fountain pool? How ridiculous!"

Rooney opened his mouth, but his phone rang and he left the room with his ear to his cell. Detective Grace excused herself politely and followed her partner.

West locked eyes with Darius. "What is going on around here?"

"That's the million-dollar question." Darius crossed his arms over his barrel chest.

"We'd better find out then. Did you finish your fresh canvas of the house and property?"

"We did, but with the same result as before. I think we need those house plans ASAP."

"I'm sorry Cady's and my expedition was derailed."

"Perhaps that was a secondary intent of the attack."

"You mean, other than eliminating Cady?"

"Yeah, that," Darius said with a deep growl.

Rooney strode back into the room, grinning like a cat with a mouse's tail under its paw. Grace strolled in behind him, her smile more muted but definitely of the pleased variety.

"The bicyclist just turned himself in," Rooney said. "We're off to interrogate him now. I expect to have some answers to our questions very soon."

The detectives hurried from the room.

"All right then." West settled back against his pillow.

Maybe he could snatch some rest for a bit and shake off this lethargy and the fog that seemed to encase him. If only he could shut down his thoughts. Why would the bicyclist turn himself in? Something was off about that behavior. Yet the odd stroke of conscience in a baby-snatcher ought to be a good thing for Cady. The bicyclist's statement could lead to the identity of the attempted murderer or, at the very least, redirect the detectives' suspicions away from Cady and onto a third party.

West's eyes drifted shut as if the lids were attached to weights. Sometime later, a commotion out in the hallway roused him from a fitful sleep, and he raised himself up on his elbow in bed, ears perked. Cady seemed to be lashing out at someone—so out of character for her. Though he couldn't make out the words, her shrill, almost hysterical tone ratcheted West's heart rate into overdrive. He sat up and started to throw off his covers, but Cady marched into his room, clad in a hospital gown and robe and cuddling Olivia to her chest. A scowling Brennan followed directly in her wake. If storm clouds could have a face, it would be the expression on Cady's at that very moment. A stocky, middle-aged woman in a gray pantsuit entered, frown lines bracketing lips pulled tightly together.

Cady turned and pointed a finger at the woman in the suit. "This person—" she pronounced the word *person* like it tasted rotten "—from Child Protective Services thinks she needs to take custody of Olivia while *I* am taken into custody."

"Custody?" West's gaze flew from Cady to the other woman and back again. "What does that mean?"

"It means," pronounced Detective Rooney, crashing the party, "that we need Mrs. Long to accompany us to the station for questioning, and we need appropriate care for the child while the mother is with us, whatever length of time that may be."

"Are you arresting her?" West glared at the detective.

"Not yet." The man indulged his trademark smirk.

West's hands closed into fists. "If you're not arresting her, then why does CPS need to be involved?"

Rooney met West's gaze with a too-bland expression. "I have no doubt an arrest will soon be made. Our baby-snatcher claims Mrs. Long hired him to do it."

FOUR

Cady forced herself to sit still in the uncomfortable plastic chair inside the police station's interrogation room. She'd been given something at the hospital to counteract the drug that had been injected into her against her will, so her mind was clear, but the spot where the needle had stabbed her ached when she moved her arm.

The rank odors of stale sweat and bad coffee assaulted her nostrils. But she would not give Detective Rooney or his partner the satisfaction of seeing her squirm or so much as wrinkle her nose. At least she could take comfort in the fact that Child Protective Services had found no grounds to take Olivia when all three of the Triple Threat Personal Protection staff members stepped up and said they would look after the child. As a mother who had not been deemed unfit by the court system, Cady's permission for the guys to look after Livvy overrode any claim by CPS. *Thank you, Lord.* Now she simply needed to convince the authorities that she was not complicit in any of the horrifying events that had taken place.

Simple? Hah!

"How long have you been a drug user?" Rooney demanded.

"I've never used any drugs that weren't lawfully prescribed to me and in the correct dosages."

Rooney opened a file folder and glanced at a paper inside. "You tested positive for opioids in your system."

"Excuse me, but someone injected me with the drug against my will. How else do you think they were able to simply throw me in the pond and walk away?"

"How do we know you didn't inject yourself with a little too much of the drug and wandered into the pond by accident?"

Cady leaned toward the detectives. "First of all, I would never, ever endanger my daughter in any way, regardless of what some baby-snatcher claims about me. Second, as you well know from your access to my mother's records, I watched her fry her brains on drugs over a period of years. I vowed then and have kept that vow that experimenting with drugs was taboo for me, and that goes, too, for the alcohol that wrecked my father and cost my sister her life."

Detective Grace's expression softened, but Cady's words appeared to have no effect on the granite-faced Rooney.

"We understand your family has experienced more than its share of tragedy," Grace said, "but addiction seems to run in families, so we have to ask, especially in light of the drug test results from the hospital. Considering those results, together with the testimony of the bicyclist and your family history, you can see why we might have reservations about your claims of someone out to get you."

"Nevertheless—" Cady looked the woman square in the eyes "—that is the truth. I am the victim here—or, at least, the intended victim of a determined killer—and yet I am being treated like a suspect. You can see why I have little to no confidence in law enforcement's commitment to uncover what is really going on, much less to protect me and my baby."

Rooney grunted. "We can agree to disagree on the point of confidence in our abilities. Now, how about you tell us where and when you met Jason Green?"

"Who is Jason Green?" Cady blinked at the detective.

Rooney showed his teeth in a cold grin. "Come now. Don't tell us you never knew the name of the man you hired to lure Mr. Foster from your side by pretending to make off with the baby so you could have an opportunity to feed your addiction."

Fire flowed through Cady's middle. How could anyone believe she would endanger her child or follow in her parents' tragic footsteps after what happened to her sister, Tracy, and those other people in the crash that her drunken father had caused? But how could she defend herself against these charges when people looked at her background and assumed the worst? And why was this Jason Green person lying about her? Had the real perpetrator hired him to make false accusations, just like they hired him to snatch Olivia?

Angry words on her tongue, Cady opened her mouth to lash out, but a sharp rap on the door stalled her outburst. Detective Grace went to the door and opened it a crack. Cady couldn't quite catch what was said in a whispered exchange. Then the detective flung wide the door and motioned someone inside.

"Your lawyer is here," Grace announced.

A mature woman of medium build dressed in a skirt suit stepped into the interrogation room.

"My lawyer?" Cady asked.

"Deborah Treach," the suited woman said, extending a business card, which Cady accepted. The card proclaimed the woman to be a criminal defense attorney.

The lawyer stepped around to Cady's side of the table. "A man named Westley Foster called Reginald Platte about your situation. But Reggie handles only estate law, so he gave Mr. Foster my number, and here I am. Don't say anything further to these people." The woman placed a firm hand on Cady's shoulder and gazed sternly at the two detectives. "Are you charging my client with anything?"

Rooney pursed his lips like he'd sucked on something sour and crossed his arms over his chest without a word.

Grace shook her head. "Not at this time."

"Good," said the attorney. "Then we're leaving."

Prompted by the lawyer's nod, Cady got up and headed toward the door.

Treach held it open for her and turned toward the cops. "I understand you only have the preliminary lab report, indicating opioids in Mrs. Long's bloodstream. But you don't yet have the doctor's notes. I possess both. You might be interested to know that the medical opinion is, and I quote, 'there is no physiological sign of long-term opioid use,' so if you're trying to make a case for addiction being the motivator for alleged bizarre behavior by my client, that theory does not hold water. And if you continue to single-mindedly pursue Mrs. Long as your suspect in these dangerous occurrences, you won't like how it looks in court that you are persecuting the widow of one of our esteemed Army Ranger combat veterans. Especially because you insist on dredging up ancient family history, rather than considering Mrs. Long's personal clean record and exemplary life to date."

Gloating might be in bad taste, but Cady didn't bother stifling the small smile that spread her lips. She did, however, restrain herself from performing a fist pump. Her smile faded as she and her lawyer left the interrogation room and headed up the hallway toward the exit. West had to have done some fast work to get a lawyer down to the precinct to spring her so quickly. And the lawyer had to have done some fast work to get herself up to speed on Cady's history—past and present—as well as obtaining the medical documents. Did this fast work mean that West had also become privy to the dark details of her childhood? Her heart squeezed at the thought.

"Your friend is waiting for you in the lobby," Deborah Treach said.

"Which one?"

"Westley."

"He's out of the hospital?"

"Can't keep a good man down, I understand."

Cady halted and turned toward the lawyer. "Thank you for what you did for me in there."

"My pleasure." The woman smiled. "I have all the respect in the world for an abuse survivor."

"You're one?"

The light in the woman's gaze dimmed as she nodded. "Ex-husband, not parents."

"Pleased to meet you, Ms. Treach." She stuck out her hand toward her new friend.

The woman took Cady's hand and pressed it between both of hers. "Call me Deb. I would be very surprised if the cops don't back off from their interest in you now and do some wider digging, as they should have done in the first place."

"That would be so wonderful."

"Agreed, but I'm still your lawyer. Call me immediately if they try to talk to you about anything at all. I want to be present."

"You have my word. I don't want to go through that again all by myself." Cady shuddered.

They continued a short way up the hall and then entered a foyer where the front desk was located. Cady's heart leaped as West rose quickly from a seat against the far wall. His gaze searched her as if assuring himself that she was all in one piece.

Cady forced her lips upward into a smile. She was glad to see him. Oh, yes! But she dreaded the conversation she needed to have now. She owed it to him to explain the story of her life that had landed her, undeservedly, on the suspect list, but she hadn't the first clue how to rip the cork off the noxious brew and pour it out into the open.

West's heart ached at Cady's determination to hide stress and fear behind a brave smile. The woman had as much guts as any soldier he knew. She was concealing something big and bad from her past, that much was clear. But he also understood she must have her reasons, which made the necessary violation of her privacy that much more repulsive. However, he and his guys needed to know whatever it was that the cops knew, especially if it had any bearing on the attempts on Cady's life.

"Hey," he said, opening his arms to her.

She walked straight into them and allowed him to enfold her in a hug. Her slight body shuddered and relaxed against him as tension slowly ebbed from her. Bad idea for him to hold her like this—at least as far as his own heart was concerned. But she needed someone to lean on right now, in every sense of the word. If that person could be him, he was honored to serve. She stirred and West released her.

"How is Olivia?" she asked, gazing up at him.

"A text from Brennan a few minutes ago said that she's napping, but he figures she'll wake up howling to be fed pretty soon, so we'd better get you home." West turned toward the lawyer and held out his hand. "Thank you for whatever it was you did in there. You got quicker results than I thought possible."

The woman smiled and shrugged, accepting his handshake. "Detective Rooney is like a bulldog with a juicy steak when he gets a certain idea in his head, but he can be redirected if given a solid reason. I like to think I gave it to him."

West grinned. "Glad to have you in our corner."

"Call me if you need me." Deb waved and headed out the door.

With a hand on the small of Cady's back, he urged her in that direction, too. She went with a head-lowered docility that betrayed exhaustion. Or perhaps dread. She had to realize they needed to have a difficult conversation.

Outside, the sun had drifted toward the horizon, and a cool breeze stirred Cady's ponytail. "It's been a very long day." She sighed.

"It has," West agreed. "Darius is waiting up the street with your vehicle. He'll drive us to your place. When we get there, as soon as you feed Baby-bug, I want you to hit the sack. We'll look after her."

She glanced up at him. "You'd better mind doctor's orders and get some rest also."

He grimaced. "I'm getting tired of hearing that, but I'm also just plain tired, so I suppose you're right. Brennan has volunteered for the first half of the night watch, and Darius will relieve him at zero one hundred, so we've got it covered."

They came in sight of the Blazer parked at the curb not far ahead. Darius stood, leaning his back against it with his arms crossed, as if he were at ease, but the regular swiveling of his head let West know that his buddy was on high alert. Good on him.

Cady stopped and touched West's arm. He halted as she gazed up at him with shadowed eyes. "Could we save the soul-baring until morning when at least you and I will be fresh?"

West brushed her tense cheek with his fingertips. "I think that's a wise idea. And just so you know, there is nothing you could tell me that could possibly make me think less of you."

She whirled away and took jerky strides toward the vehicle. "Don't make promises you can't keep."

Her words drifted to him over her shoulder, and his heart shriveled. How bad could her secret past be that she doubted the steadfastness of friends who had already walked through deep grief and loss together?

The next morning around 7:00 a.m. found West seated at the kitchen table with a steaming cup of coffee in front of him. At least for the moment, tea had lost its appeal. Darius, just coming off night duty, and Brennan, fresh from six hours of shut-eye, shared the table with him. For a time, they sipped their brews in grim silence.

"We made it through one quiet night," Darius rumbled.

Brennan scowled into his coffee. "But we're still no closer to finding out how an intruder got into the house. I asked Cady yesterday, while you were still in the hospital, if someone else could have a key from before she got the place, but she told me she had the locks changed right after she moved in, and she updated the security system as soon as she started having that uneasy 'watched' feeling she told us about."

Frowning, West sat back and stretched his long legs out beneath the table. He deeply appreciated Cady's listening to her instincts and taking precautions, but he hated that such a thing had been necessary. Unhappily, rekeying the locks hadn't stopped the mystery intruder.

"We have a lot of investigating to do," West said, "above and beyond protecting Griff's widow and daughter. Here are our assignments for today—I want Cady to lay out anything else that was in the gift basket from the neighborhood watch committee. It will all need to be examined for threats, and whoever packed the basket will need to be interviewed at some point today. But the interview can wait until after Cady and I make a second run at getting those house plans. This time, we have to succeed. I'm feeling fit this morning, so I'll be hard to take by surprise. Darius, grab a few winks and then dig into this Jason Green character. He's our link to the enemy behind all this."

"Negative, boss," Darius said. "You know firsthand that in the field I've operated many times on far less sleep for far longer than this. I'm looking into Green immediately."

West grinned. "No argument here. Keep us updated. First, find out if he's still in custody, then work from there—who he is, what he's into, where he hangs out, his contacts, everything and anything you can find out."

"What about me?" Brennan sat up straight.

"You're guarding the house while the rest of us are on our missions. Make yourself useful tapping on walls and poking into the most unlikely places for any hidden passages. *We* know our Cady didn't dream up that attack in her bedroom."

"Amen to that," Cady said as she strolled into the room clad in jeans and a T-shirt and carrying her wide-awake daughter. "Knowing you guys were on duty, I slept like the proverbial log—well, except for when this little peanut decided she was hungry." She bounced Livvy in her arms and bestowed a smile upon them all.

West's mouth went dry. Who knew a woman could be so appealing with a faint pillow crease still marking one cheek?

Cady stepped up close and handed Baby-bug off to him. "Entertain her while I whip up some of my famous chocolate chip pancakes with sides of eggs and bacon. I assume you soldier-types are fans of rib-sticking breakfasts."

"You know it." Brennan grinned from ear to ear.

"A woman after my own heart." Darius chuckled. "Er, I mean, stomach."

The pair of guys laughed heartily, but West barely managed a faint guffaw. He ducked his head and focused on dandling Livvy on his knee. It wouldn't do to let anyone see how very much Cady *was* a woman after his own heart. If anyone were paying attention, his growing feelings must be written plainly on his face. He had to get his wayward heart under control. Too much was at stake to be distracted by inopportune thoughts of romance. He clucked at Baby-bug, and the infant blew cooing bubbles as she waved fisted hands at him. A genuine smile grew on West's lips. If only he didn't long to take this tiny cutie under his wing as his daughter for real.

The clatter of kitchen activity and the soft hiss and enticing odor of cooking bacon spread a relaxing, homey atmosphere around the room. Maybe they could enjoy a simple breakfast in peace before continuing to address the threat that loomed over this household.

The sudden clang of the doorbell shot a chill through the atmosphere. Everyone froze in place. Firming his jaw, West rose and handed Livvy to her mother.

"Brennan, stay here on guard duty. Darius, you come with me. Let's see who is at the front door so early in the morning."

West's gaze locked with Cady's. Her amber eyes were wide, and her throat visibly contracted as all three Triple Threat agents pulled handguns from the holsters at their sides. Heat ripped through West's gut. No one should have to live in terror in their own house. They needed to get to the bottom of what was going on—and fast!

FIVE

Cady held her breath as West and Darius glided from the kitchen on stealthy feet. Seconds later, the latch clicked, followed by West's voice in soft tones, and then an unknown male's in equally benign timbre. Not a threat then. Cady allowed herself to take a breath and return to her cooking.

Shortly, West and Darius reentered the kitchen. West held a brown manila envelope in the hand where his gun had been a couple of minutes ago. The firearms were out of sight again.

West waved the envelope at her. "This came by courier from your estate lawyer. Apparently, he has suddenly become extremely accommodating after yesterday's brouhaha. It's copies of whatever house plans he had in his files."

Cady let out a small laugh. "Probably feels

bad about what happened on our way to his office."

West snorted. "Or he doesn't want us bringing any more trouble near his doorstep."

She shrugged. "Either way. Our outing has been canceled."

"One of them," West said. "You and I need to go see the neighborhood watch block captain and find out who packaged your welcome gift."

Cady winced. "That could be a touchy question. It might seem like we're accusing someone."

"It has to be asked. Number one, I would hope the block captain is just as interested as anyone else about getting to the bottom of who might have planted poison in one of their gift baskets. Number two, if the police haven't already asked about it, they'll be asking soon, so the captain better get used to giving an answer. Where are the other items that came in the basket?"

"I'll assemble everything as soon as we've had our breakfast," she said, thrusting a stack of plates in his direction.

"Give me the house plans," Brennan said, taking the envelope from West. "I'll comb through them with a magnifying glass, if necessary. My dad and brothers and I built a house together from the basement to the attic, so I'll know what I'm looking at."

"Breakfast first," Cady said firmly. "I don't know about you guys, but my stomach is in serious doubt about whether I remember how to use a fork."

Everyone laughed and Cady's spirits lifted. At last, with the plans in hand, they seemed to have some hope of progress, and West had laid out a sound game plan for pursuing an investigation. With the Triple Threat team on duty, maybe the worst was behind them. Determined to enjoy her breakfast with a contented Olivia, who sat in her baby seat and batted at the mobile hanging above her, she ignored the tiny pessimistic voice in the back of her mind that wanted to insinuate maybe it wasn't.

Once they had eaten, Darius volunteered to load the dishwasher and Brennan retired to the study to go over the house plans. At Cady's insistence, West enjoyed another cup of coffee while she rounded up the items that the watch committee had delivered when she moved in. The coffee, she assured him, had been purchased by her at the local grocery store and was not among those items. By the time she returned to the kitchen, Darius had headed out on his assignment, so West remained her only audience.

"Here we go," she said as she laid out the array of items. "One copy of a recent issue of *Philadelphia Magazine*. One partially used tube of scented skin lotion, apparently poison-free since I've noticed no bad effects, only softer elbows and heels. An unopened package of slipper socks, which, for all I know, are lubricated to ensure I fall down the stairs." West cocked a brow at her dark humor. She snickered and went on. "A cell phone holder with an advertisement for an auto repair shop etched on it. A brochure for a home security system sold by a local business, along with a pen from said business. Better check the pen out for a bomb." Another snicker escaped her lips.

What was the matter with her? She sounded half hysterical. Backing away from the table, she hugged herself. West rose and laid his strong hands on her shoulders. The compassion in his gaze undid her. She leaned into him and buried her face in the soft T-shirt over his solid chest. His masculine, woodsy odor filled her nostrils. All of those sensations combined to strip away her defenses and make a mockery of her talk about independence. She was so pitifully *depen-*

dent. She'd depended first on parents who betrayed her trust at every turn. Then she'd depended on Griffon, until he was suddenly ripped from her life, calling into question the trust in God she'd begun to develop under her husband's urging and example. Now, she was allowing herself to lean on another man, and it felt too right to be right.

She moaned and pulled away from West, who dropped his arms and turned quickly away from her toward the items on the table.

Cady's heart gave a little jump against her ribs. What had she glimpsed on her friend's face? Disappointment? Hurt? Those emotions couldn't possibly have anything to do with her, could they? Of course not. She was being silly. West was grieving his buddy as badly as she was grieving her husband. No wonder they shared a special bond. That was all there was to it.

"What do you think about that stuff from the basket?" she asked.

West looked over his shoulder at her, his expression neutral. "These things look pretty benign, but let's take the pen apart, just to be thorough."

A lopsided smile quirked his lips, and the last vestige of awkwardness fled the room.

Cady smiled back at him as he twisted the pen and ejected the contents onto the tabletop.

"Nope, just regular pen guts. Is this everything?"

"Wait! I just remembered there was this small but lovely figurine of a Victorian couple. It was cheap, hollow glass, but so cute, and it suited my decor, so I put it on the mantelpiece in the living room."

"Show me," West said.

She led him to the fireplace. "Aren't they charming? They're dancing together."

Wearing a frown, West brushed past her and picked up the item.

"What are you doing?" she asked as he ran his fingers over every dimple of the figurine.

Suddenly, he let out a grunt. "There's something not right here. This thing's been cracked open and almost seamlessly glued back together."

He knocked the statuette against the stone of the hearth, and Cady cried out as glass broke. She started to kneel in front of the wreckage, but West grabbed her arm and pulled her upright.

"Still think it's charming?" he rumbled like a growling bear and pointed toward a strange object lying amongst the shards of painted glass.

His tone sent a shiver through her. Her gaze riveted on a black object about as big around as a dime but as thick as one of her pancakes.

Her insides turned to ice. "Is that what I think it is?"

"What do you think it is?"

"Someone's been listening to everything going on in this house." An oily sensation slithered through her insides.

"Whoever set up the attack on you yesterday didn't need to tail us from this house to the lawyer's office. They knew where we were going."

Cady's heart jumped in her chest. She gazed up at West. "When is this all going to stop? Who could possibly be so desperate to hurt me?"

"Bren!" West bellowed.

Cady backed away from him. He was scaring her. Frankly, he was scaring himself at the depth of his ferocity.

Eyes wide, his buddy trotted into the room. "What's up, Sarge?"

"Did you acquire that gear we discussed for our business? And I'm not your sergeant any longer."

Brennan offered a slight smile. "You'll always be Sarge to me, Sarge. And, yes, the gear is at our still-waiting-to-be-set-up office."

"Would you go get the bug-sweeping equipment? Hostile ears have been monitoring this place for weeks." He pointed toward the little black bug on the hearth, resisting the urge to lift his foot and squash it. Doing that he might destroy a fingerprint or some other clue.

Brennan let out a low whistle.

"I'll call the cops," West said. "They'll need to process this thing."

"Won't *they* have bug-sweeping equipment?" Cady asked.

"Immaterial," West said. "We'll do our own sweep throughout the house and your vehicle, as well. Every day until this situation is resolved. This little critter may not be the only one of its kind around here, since, evidently, someone is accessing the house from an unidentified quadrant."

"I'll go grab the gear," Brennan said, "but I'll have to take a taxi. Darius has the company pickup truck."

"Take my Blazer." Cady darted into the kitchen and returned with her keys and Olivia, who had begun to fuss in her baby seat. "Guess who's hungry and needs a diaper change."

West nodded toward Cady "You take care of Baby-bug. I'm going to prowl around a bit while we wait for Bren to return and the cops to show up."

With a long, somber look in his direction, Cady headed toward the stairs to go to her daughter's room. West watched her leave until she was out of sight and then walked Brennan toward the door.

"Did you see anything useful in the house plans?" he asked softly enough that he doubted the exposed-but-still-active bug could pick up his words.

"Not yet. They're frustratingly incomplete," Brennan answered in equally hushed tones. "More like sketches, really, than full plans, but I'm not done studying them. If there is a clue to be found, I promise I'll find it."

"I trust you," he told his friend and business partner.

"I know. I won't let you down."

"Good man." West nodded, beyond thankful for guys he could count on.

As soon as Brennan closed the door after himself, West locked up and called the cops. The next half hour crept past as West crept around in similar silence, checking doors and windows that had been examined multiple times and rapping his knuckles against paneling or drywall in various rooms. But banging his head against said walls would have been as productive as this random search. Just as he returned to the living room, the doorbell rang. Must be the police, since Bren would have simply used the house key on Cady's key chain and let himself in.

West peered through the door's peephole and discovered the top of a bald head ringed with a fringe of salt-and-pepper hair. Who in the world? West pulled the door open but left the chain on. A ferret-faced man wearing a stern expression and standing, shoulders square, to every inch of his no-more-than-five-foot-eight-inch height.

"Hello," the man said in a surprisingly deep voice. "I'm Donald Milcombe, the neighborhood watch captain. I understand there was a break-in at this residence yesterday. It's a part of my duties to keep myself apprised of such occurrences in our neighborhood. Do you mind if I come in and ask a few questions?"

A chuckle slipped between West's lips. How was that for irony? The very man they wanted to interview wanted to interview them.

West unchained the door and Donald stepped

inside with a military bearing that would have put some soldiers to shame. The guy clearly took his position very seriously.

Managing to keep a straight face, West motioned toward the living room. "Come in and have a seat. The owner of the house will be down shortly. She's looking after her baby."

"And you are?" The watch captain lifted sparse brows.

"West Foster. I and my two colleagues are Mrs. Long's personal protection detail."

"Oh, dear." The man sank onto the sofa. "Am I to assume then that the break-in was not a robbery, that the intruder was after her?"

"Assume away."

"Ex-boyfriend? Ex-husband? We really don't welcome these domestic violence situations into our neighborhood."

"Now you have assumed too much." West loomed over the man, and Donald paled as he cranked his neck backward to gaze up at him. "Mrs. Long is a soldier's widow, and her would-be assailant is an unidentified creep who seems to have access to the house without breaking and entering. Have the police been to see you yet?"

"Why would they?"

"Because the tea in the watch committee gift basket contained a deadly poison that Mrs. Long almost drank." No point in giving this guy information about his own close shave. The police could do that if the man were ever charged with anything.

The watch captain gasped and folded his hands together. "How awful! Tea, did you say? Our gift baskets don't contain tea."

"Do they contain small Victorian figurines?"

"Certainly not! We don't go in for anything so froufrou."

"I'd like a list of anything that *should* have been in the basket, and I need to know who packs these baskets and who has access to them at any time before or during their delivery."

"Of course. Of course. This is most unsettling. Most unsettling."

If the situation were any less serious, West's heart would go out to the fellow. He seemed unnerved to the point of wringing his hands and repeating himself. Despite his pseudo-military bearing, West had difficulty imagining anyone less threatening. However, he and his men had plenty of hard experience in learning that appearances could be deceiving. Did this guy have anything to do with the home invasion and the attacks on Cady?

"I'll supply that information now," Milcombe said. "Do you have pen and paper?"

"No need." West took out his phone and accessed his notepad app. "Tell me and I'll type it in."

"Wait!" Cady hurried into the room, minus Olivia, who had no doubt succumbed to her morning nap. "I'll get pen and paper." Cady nodded significantly toward the bug on the hearth, then locked gazes with West.

"Smart woman." He grinned at her.

A short time later, Milcombe took his leave, still as flustered as ever. No doubt the watch committee would soon be abuzz with shocking information, but at least they had the name of a person to interview—Mitch Landes.

West closed the door after their guest and turned toward Cady, who hovered nearby in the foyer. Her whole countenance radiated tension. He hated to add to her unease, but answers wouldn't be found unless more questions were asked and answered.

"I think it's time we had that hard talk. We should—" The ringing of the doorbell interrupted him. Had Milcombe thought of something he'd forgotten to share?

West checked the peephole. It was the police this time—the same two officers who had answered the original early morning callout when Cady was attacked in her room. He let them inside, and he and Cady proceeded to give their statements. The patrol officers assured them that someone would be by later to sweep the house for other clandestine surveillance devices. By the time the uniformed pair took the bug away in an evidence-collection bag, Olivia was waking up from her nap. Cady went upstairs to feed her while West put together some lunch for the adults.

Brennan returned to the house with the equipment to do their surveillance sweep and joined him and Cady for soup and a sandwich. West made a point of keeping the conversation light as they ate, and Cady shot him several grateful looks that warmed his heart, but her reprieve would come to an end soon enough. Once Olivia went down for her afternoon nap, there would be no more delay.

Until then, West busied himself helping Brennan with the sweep, which exposed no other surveillance devices, and the installation of additional security measures such as outdoor motion sensors on the porch and perimeter of the property. However, if they were dealing with someone accessing the home through a secret passage, the sensors might be useless, a chilling thought.

About mid-afternoon, West left Brennan testing the new installations and went in search of Cady. He found her coming down the steps without Olivia. Her face paled a bit as she spotted him, but she offered him a thin-lipped nod as she led the way up the hall into the kitchen.

"Livvy is sleeping." Her words and tone confirmed her understanding that the time had come.

His phone chose that moment to ring and, frowning, he palmed his cell. "It's Darius. I'd better answer this."

Grim-faced, Cady nodded.

"You're not going to believe this," Darius said. "Check that—you'll find it all too believable, considering what's been going on."

"Sitrep now," West clipped out in military terminology demanding a situational report.

"I found out that Jason Green is a known druggie who will do just about anything for his next fix, but someone bailed him out of jail early this morning. He skedaddled and disappeared, eluding a police tail."

"He's in the wind?"

"Not anymore." Darius's tone went darker

than midnight. "He was just found dead behind a hole-in-the-wall bar he used to frequent. Looks like an overdose, but the timing is suspicious. He won't be telling us or the police anything useful."

SIX

As the color receded from West's tanned face, the bottom dropped out of Cady's stomach. More bad news? Had to be. This man never looked taken by surprise.

"What is it?" she asked as West pocketed his phone.

He told her and Cady's knees went weak. Her stunned reaction must have showed on her face, because West took her elbow and guided her to a seat at the kitchen table.

Cady rested her head in her hands. "How very sad for this man, but that stunt he pulled with Livvy was inexcusable. Now, we'll never know who hired him, and I'm going to *stay* on the suspect list."

"Never say never. We'll expose this culprit one way or another."

She lowered her hands and glared at West. "But every step forward seems to end with a step backward. We still don't know how the intruder got into the house to attack me."

"Answering that question remains first and foremost on our list. But now, after this setback, we need more than ever to understand if something from your past has bearing on today's danger."

"I know." Cady stared at the wood grain of the tabletop. "I can't stand the thought of you or any of Griff's buddies knowing my background."

"Whatever it is, you can rest assured that none of us will blame you or look down on you."

"We'll see." She sniffed. "Do you suppose we could get out of the house, maybe just take a walk around the neighborhood while I talk? I need the fresh air."

West pursed his lips, then nodded his head. "Our nemesis attacked you in the park yesterday because he knew where we were going to be. Now, his listening ear has gone deaf so a short walk may do us both good."

Cady let out a long breath. "Thank you. Brennan is here if Livvy should happen to wake up." She squared her shoulders. "I refuse to hide in my house when it's clearly not a haven as long as this creep can get in at will."

"I'll let Bren know we're going out for a bit."

He left the room, but all too soon for Cady he reappeared in the kitchen doorway with his light jacket over his arm. "Let's take that walk now."

As if moving through thick sludge, Cady rose and headed for the back door. In the mudroom, she grabbed a zip-up sweatshirt and shrugged it on.

"Let's slip out this way." She stepped onto the back stoop, and crisp autumn air filled her nostrils with a reminder that winter lurked around the corner. Would she still be alive to see the first snowfall?

West joined her, closing the door behind him.

She turned in his direction. "I don't care to talk to anyone else but you right now, and frankly, I'm not all that excited about talking to you either, considering the proposed topic. No offense."

"None taken."

He stood quietly beside her, not pushing or urging anything from her. How she appreciated this man!

Cady surveyed her spacious fenced-in backyard. A utility shed stood in the far right-hand corner. Several mature trees, turning color with the season, waved their branches at her. In the middle of the yard, a faint depression outlined where her water or sewer line must be installed. One of her upcoming projects would be to install a swing set and playground equipment in the backyard.

"This will be a great play area for Babybug when she gets a little older." West's mellow voice echoed her own thoughts.

She offered him a small smile. "Our minds often work alike. I was thinking exactly that. It's a wonder I'm even capable of contemplating plans for the future when my life is in danger."

"Your spirit is nothing if not resilient." He took her hand firmly in his and led her down the steps.

Cady yielded to his guidance and walked quietly across the lawn to the gate that led into the back alley. West released her hand to open the gate and the loss of the warm, welcome touch sent a pang through her. If her heart had healed from the loss of Griffon, it would be in serious danger of capture by this man. She thrust the unsettling thought away as they stepped onto the gravel of the alley road. They fell into step beside each other.

She hauled in a deep breath. "Can't put this off any longer, then. The whole sordid thing starts back a long way, so be prepared to exercise patience as I get it all out into the open. I'm not sure I'll want to discuss it any more after this."

"No reason to do so if it has no connection with what's going on now."

"I don't see how my family history could possibly be a contributing factor."

"As an objective third party, I might be able to judge that better than you."

"Maybe so." Cady released a hard-edged laugh. "My earliest memories, believe it or not, are happy. My parents adored each other—or seemed to—and they doted on me. Then, when I was five, my dad lost his job and my mom got pregnant with my sister, Tracy, at the same time."

"You have a sister?" West slowed his pace and lifted his eyebrows at Cady.

"*Had* a sister."

"Ah." West stepped up the pace again as they crossed a paved road and entered the alley in the next block. His head kept slowly swiveling as he continually cased the area. "Go on," he prompted.

"That's when my parents' arguments started, and my dad began drinking daily. Then Tracy was born, and my mom started popping pills and sleeping every spare moment. With adult insight, I understand that she was experiencing postpartum depression. Probably the pills were prescription, at first, but the drug usage never stopped once it got started. Nor did my dad's drinking or the escalating arguments aggravated by mind-altering substances."

Cady hauled in a deep, fortifying breath. West's silent, solid presence at her side fed courage to her.

"Eventually," she continued, "it wasn't only pills Mom was taking. I'd find syringes around the house. I was too young to really know what the needles were all about, but I remember feeling this horrible sense of shame and dread. When I would find one, I would hide it, hoping my mom would be able to quit whatever she was doing if I could keep the syringes away from her. That was nonsense, of course—she just obtained more, along with the drugs—but that's how my child's mind worked."

West squeezed her arm. "Sounds like your child's mind was pretty sharp, actually. You were doing your best to protect your mother. It's a sad thing when a youngster is put into that position, and an all-too-common occurrence. What about your sister, Tracy? How did your mom do in caring for an infant?"

Cady gave him a tight-lipped look and shook her head. "By the time I was six years old, I was her de facto parent."

"Weren't you in school by then?"

"Sure, but we only lived a couple blocks from the school, and I'd race home every day, often to find Tracy in a dirty diaper and barely fed."

"What about your dad? Didn't he care that his children were being neglected?"

Cady shrugged. "I don't know if he knew, much less cared. He'd found another job by then. Construction. But he rarely came home after work. He went out drinking with the boys and might manage to stagger into the house well after Tracy and I were in bed. Then the arguments would start up. For some reason, Tracy would sleep through them. Probably the sound was normal to her and didn't rouse her. But I would lie awake, listening, with my head under the covers." A shiver coursed through her as her gaze focused on her feet slowly scissoring one step after the other.

A soft growl came from West. "I'm sorry you had to live through all that."

Cady's head jerked up. "The point is that I'm alive, and my sister isn't."

"How did that happen?" West's tone was tender.

"Fast-forward about a decade. I'm a teenager, and Tracy is ten. We've been through the wringer, over and over again, with my mom overdosing, going to the hospital and then being sent through inpatient treatment, only to return home and, soon after that, to the needle. My dad would promise to sober up if the courts would let him keep custody of his daughters, and he'd do well for a short while, but it would never last."

Cady shuddered and heaved a long sigh, ugly images crowding her head. "Soon after the final time Tracy and I were nearly removed from parental custody, my dad was taking my sister to the doctor for an ear infection when they were involved in a car accident. Turns out my dad was still a closet drinker. By this time, he could imbibe a lot and not show many external signs. His blood alcohol level was off the charts, the accident was his fault, my sister was killed, and two of the four people in the car he hit also died."

"Whoa!" West shook his head like a dog would shake off water. "That's a whole lot of blows for a young girl to absorb."

"It would be plenty even if that were the end of the story. My dad went to prison, of course, where he is to this day. I never go see him, only partly because he won't allow me on his visitor list. He's basically disowned me because I testified against him about his drinking habits during his trial."

"Ouch! That must have been hard."

"More than you know."

"What about your mother? Do you see her?"

Cady shook her head. "During the whole messy trial, my mom overdosed once more. She survived but she was never the same. She'll be in an institution for the rest of her life."

"And you went into the foster care system," West said.

"Yes, but only for a couple of years. My foster family was truly very nice. I'm not sure I was always nice to *them* with all the mess going on in my head, but growing up has made me appreciate them. I stay in touch with a card and letter at Christmastime."

West made a humming sound. "I hate to ask, but are you sure your dad is still in prison? Sounds like he has a grudge against you."

"Very sure. I check online every month. My last check was the day before the intruder attacked me in my bedroom, and my father was exactly where he should be. So, no, he's not out and about executing mayhem."

West pursed his lips and let out a huff. "Then, you're right. I don't see how any of this past history has bearing on the attempts on your life. Do you go see your mother?"

She bowed her head. "Since we were living in New Jersey at the time all this occurred, she was court-committed to the Twin Oaks Care Center in Phillipsburg. The state has legal custody of her as a vulnerable, indigent adult. My rights are limited, but I'm allowed visitation and to receive updates by telephone. I went to see her a couple of times, more out of duty than anything, but she didn't acknowledge my presence. I have no idea if she knew who I was. She responded more to her caregivers than she did to me. I call regularly to see how she's doing, but I haven't been back to see her since I married Griff." Her head lifted, and her gaze sought his. "Is it terrible of me that I never wanted to introduce him to my mother?"

West clucked his tongue. "Understandable. After hearing the story, I admire you even more as a strong and resilient person."

"You do?" Cady blinked up at him.

They stopped walking and faced each other.

"I do," West said, voice rumbly as if his throat were tight.

In response, Cady's throat constricted. "That's not the reaction I expected," she rasped.

"Why not? You're amazing to come through all that horror as a responsible adult with a healthy moral compass. Did your faith in God help you with that?"

"Yes...and no. My foster parents introduced me to Jesus and the Bible, but not much of it stuck until I met Griff. You know what a strong faith he had. But now Griff is gone, and I'm not sure where I stand with God anymore."

"He's right here with you." West's palm cupped her cheek. "And I'm here, too."

Cady's mouth went dry. What might it be like to feel those strong, broad lips on hers? What was the matter with her that she was considering this idea?

She whirled abruptly away, and a bee buzzed past her ear, accompanied by the blast of a firecracker. Cady lurched and gasped. West's body rammed into hers as he swept them behind a nearby garage and pressed her against the wall.

"What on earth?" she burst out, heart slamming against her ribs.

"We're being shot at," he snarled, as he yanked his gun from his holster.

The shot had come from somewhere behind them. West peered around the corner of the garage back along their route. No one was in sight, but a car engine revved and a dark blue sedan shot past the end of the alley with a screech of tires. Probably the shooter's vehicle carrying him or her way from the site of the attack. After that loud gunshot, the perp wouldn't want to stick around long enough for the cops—or his Triple Threat team—to respond. Cady wasn't wrong when she sensed being watched if the attacker's vehicle was lurking in the area so often that he or she was nearby to catch them in the open the one time they went out for a stroll. The current attack had an impromptu feel to it— an assault of opportunity.

A shout from the alley across the road, near Cady's house, captured his attention. Darius's compact, powerhouse figure darted into view through her backyard gate. At this distance, West couldn't make out the gun in his hand, but his crouched, hands-together posture betrayed that he had one at the ready.

West put out his hand and waved toward his partner. Darius scurried toward them in full hypervigilant mode, head swiveling this way and that. The man soon arrived at their position.

"Any sign of threat?" West asked.

"None."

"Of course." West grunted. "I think I saw the shooter getting away in a dark blue sedan. The angle was wrong to catch sight of a license plate."

Darius snorted. "Figures! This creep is getting on my last nerve."

"My last nerve is already frazzled." Cady stepped out from behind West.

She was pale and her lower lip trembled as she hugged herself. West's heart broke for her. They had to put a stop to these attempts on her life, which meant they had to catch the attacker. It would help immeasurably if they could figure out why Cady was a target. The why would surely lead to the who.

"Let's get you back to the house." West gripped her arm and drew her along as they retraced their steps with Darius, their hovering bodyguard, on full alert.

They stepped into Cady's house, and West stopped in the kitchen and looked at her. "Do you want us to pack you and Baby-bug up and take you to a hotel until we have all this sorted out?"

Her head went high, chin thrust forward. "I will not be driven from my home." She pronounced each word like it had an exclamation mark after it. "Why would the attacker be deterred by changing my location?"

"It might take the person a while to find you again," West said.

"Or not," she added. "Could you protect me better in a hotel environment?"

"Not really," West conceded.

"And more civilians could be exposed to danger," Darius added.

"Then it's decided." Cady's gaze flicked to Darius and back to West. "We stay right here and defend my life and home."

"Your home!" West rubbing his chin. "Could this house give someone a reason to want you dead? It's worth a lot of money."

Cady opened her mouth and then shut it again with a snap. She slowly shook her head. "I don't see how killing me would help anyone acquire the house. The property is entailed for four generations to the next living relative."

"In other words, it can't be sold outside the family unless there is no heir."

"Yes. My great-aunt drew up this fancy entail with the help of her wily lawyer."

"Reginald Platte?" West asked.

"The one and only. The bequest skipped over my mother because of her condition and left the home to me, specifically, and my off-spring after me. If I were gone before Olivia comes of age, the property would go into trust until then. Another option will be allowed only if the family line ends."

"What's the other option?"

"It will go to the county historical society to be used as a museum."

Darius scowled. "Maybe some schemer in the historical society is determined to snag this place for public posterity."

West rolled his eyes at his partner. "I'll take that thought as tongue-in-cheek."

"For sure." Darius chuckled. "Cady alone seems to be the target. Eliminating her and leaving Olivia wouldn't get them any closer to historical society possession."

West grinned. "Keep that brain in gear, buddy. I—" He halted his sentence with a hiss of indrawn breath and turned toward Cady. "You said your great-aunt's will skipped over your mother. That means the inheritance is coming through your mother's side, not your father's. Would your mom know anything about this house—like maybe about a hidden means of gaining access?"

Cady shrugged. "Sure, she grew up here,

along with her single mother and her mother's sister—my great-aunt. But my mom's mind is gone. How would she remember anything about this place when she doesn't recognize me, her own daughter?"

"I don't know, but we can't ignore the possibility, even if it's a slim one. We need to talk to your mother as soon as possible." He checked his watch. "It's late in the day now, and we'll have to deal with the police again about this latest attack. But we head out for New Jersey first thing in the morning."

Cady's face took on a greenish tint. "Lord—" her gaze flew upward "—You wouldn't make me go there again, would You?"

West couldn't feel any lower about what he had proposed, but this visit had to be made. He knew it in his bones.

SEVEN

The next morning, Cady shot a sidelong glance at West's strong profile where he sat behind the wheel of the Blazer as they whizzed down the freeway toward her mother's institution in New Jersey. This new day had dawned bright and cheery. Too bad her mood couldn't match. How did soldiers like her husband, West and his buddies handle being shot at as a potential daily fact of life in combat situations? She'd hardly slept last night for nightmares of bee-bullets buzzing past her ears, alternating with nightmares about being smothered. They hadn't been able to give the cops much to go on about the shooting incident when they arrived last evening to investigate. Finding the bullet that had almost clipped her in the alley would be nearly as impossible as zeroing in on a suspect from West's description of the dark blue sedan.

This morning, Brennan ran another sweep of the house and also checked her vehicle before she and West took off. He found no trace of any type of tracker or surveillance device. As they were leaving, Brennan returned to his scrutiny of the house sketches, and Darius went off to interview the watch committee member who put together the welcome baskets.

"Baby-bug doing all right?" West asked, breaking into her somber meditations.

Cady glanced over her shoulder and managed a smile toward her daughter. "Since the car seat is buckled in with its back toward me, I can only make out her profile, but her little hands are busy playing with her mobile. She's not fussing, so I assume she's content for the moment."

"That's as good as it gets right now." West chuckled. "I've been keeping watch on our six to make sure we're not being followed."

"Are we?" Cady's heart rate picked up speed.

"Not that I can tell. I'm hopeful this little excursion will remain entirely under the radar."

"You know I'm not happy about our trip."

"I do, but the fact that you're sitting beside me tells me you understand the necessity."

"I still think we should call the care center and let them know we're coming."

"Negative. I'm not giving our enemy the slightest chance of finding out what we're doing. It's not like we need to verify your mother is going to be there when we arrive."

"True enough." Cady settled back in her seat.

"Why don't you grab a nap before the little diva decides she's hungry again."

Cady needed no more urging to close her eyes. Aside from the weeks of night feedings interrupting her sleep, she'd felt stressed every waking moment since the attack in her bedroom. Trusting West's capable hands on the wheel of her vehicle, and in a sense, on her life, Cady allowed exhaustion to claim her.

High-pitched squeals and fussing roused her. She looked at her watch to discover over an hour had passed. They were still on the freeway, but a cityscape was closing in around them.

"This is Phillipsburg?" she asked.

West nodded and jerked his head toward the back seat. "I think she snoozed a while along with you, but apparently her stomach has awakened her. I'll stop at a convenience store gas station before we head to the Twin

Oaks to see your mother. I can fill the tank while you feed Ms. Ravenous."

"Sounds like a plan."

A half hour later, they were nearing their destination. Next to the road, the dark waves of the Delaware River winked and blinked at them under the sunlight, flowing with them toward a place Cady was reluctant to return to. Her stomach clenched as they drove within sight of the three-storey brick structure that housed her mother and numerous other patients of diverse ages who were unable to live safely on their own.

"Very institutional," West commented.

"Tell me about it." Cady frowned and picked at an imaginary bit of lint on her shirt. "The last time I was here I thought the place felt like exactly that. The living conditions are sanitary and the staff seems competent, but it's so very institutional with little privacy. The sheer volume of patients under state care makes single rooms out of the question. Most patients have at least one roommate, sometimes more."

"Yikes! I can only imagine the upheaval if roommates aren't compatible."

"I don't envy the staff." Cady shook her head. "I wish I could afford to take over

Mom's care and have her placed in a private facility."

"Considering her neglect of you and your sister, that's a very kindly sentiment."

"She's my mother, no matter what. She gave me life. Besides, doesn't the Bible command us to honor our parents? I don't think it specifies that they have to be worthy."

West chuckled. "Right on all counts. For someone going through a rocky period in her faith, you sure live it."

Warmth spread through Cady's insides. "I can't remember the last time I so appreciated a compliment."

She refrained from adding how much more special the words were because they came from him. Vocalizing that sentiment might give him the wrong idea about her affections—if it *was* the wrong idea. What, exactly, were her feelings for this man? Now was not the time to examine the question.

West parked the Blazer in the center's spacious lot.

"You won't be allowed to bring in your gun," she told him.

He nodded and tucked his weapon into the glove compartment, and then they both got out. She thanked him as he retrieved Livvy in her detachable car seat from the rear of the vehicle. Squaring her shoulders, Cady faced the imposing building and trod up the sidewalk beside West and his precious burden.

The sterile scent of the place was as she remembered it, as was the chunky front desk in the outdated reception area. Refusing to further indulge her reluctance in West's presence, she led the way to the desk.

The man doing paperwork behind it looked up at her approach. "May I help you?"

"Yes," she said, "I'm here to see my mother, May Johnson."

Something indefinable flickered behind the man's eyes, and he frowned as he consulted his computer. "I'm sorry," he said several heartbeats later. "Mrs. Johnson is unavailable."

"Unavailable! Is she unwell? Has she gone to the doctor?"

"Yes… I mean, no," the man stammered, turning pale. "Let me get the administrator." He darted through a door labeled Administration.

Cady locked gazes with West. "What on earth is going on? When I called last week, the nurse said Mom was fine. 'Status quo,' she said. They *are* supposed to notify me of any significant change in her health."

West shook his head. "I don't want to

alarm you, but if ever I've seen panic, that was it."

Cady gulped against a dry throat. Her mother had not been anywhere near cognizant for a long, long time, ever since she started doing drugs, and Cady still struggled mightily with feelings of resentment and anger toward the woman. Yet, now, with all sorts of dark imaginings flying through her mind, how was it possible that Cady found herself ill prepared for any worsening in her mother's condition? Judging by the receptionist's reaction to their request to see her, whatever was going on was serious. Was she about to lose her mom in the most final way possible?

A heaviness settled in West's core as Cady gnawed her lower lip, attention fixed on the door through which the receptionist had disappeared. His gaze scanned the area. Small sitting room to the right of the desk, furnished in shabby chic, and elevators to the right of that room, along with a doorway marked Stairs. The stairway door sported a heavy lock panel. A key card scanner hung on the wall next to it. A pair of workers in scrub uniforms entered an elevator. One of them waved her name badge over a spot on the wall inside the cab, presumably another key card scanner, and the elevator door slid shut. Security was moderately sophisticated here.

Or was it?

Next to the telephone at the abandoned front desk sat an employee key card. No second invitation needed. He snatched up the card, grabbed Cady's arm and guided her toward the elevator.

"What—" she began a startled inquiry.

"Trust me," he said, and she went silent.

His gut said not to wait until someone official stepped out to deal with them. Hopefully, it would turn out that his instinct was guiding him correctly.

At the press of a button, the elevator doors slid open, and he ushered Cady into the compartment. "What floor is your mother's room?"

"Third."

He pressed the button for floor three and waved his borrowed key card over the reader. The elevator doors glided shut and the car began to rise.

Cady's gaze lifted to meet his. "Thank you. Every moment waiting there at that desk, I wanted to dart off and do what we're doing now. But I don't know if I would have had the guts to break the rules without you leading the charge."

West offered her a small grin. "Remember that little detail if they call the cops on us. It was all my fault."

"Right!" She rolled her eyes. "And you dragged me into the elevator, kicking and screaming. I don't think so."

The elevator stopped and they stepped out onto threadbare beige carpet leading down a long, wide hallway. Doors at regular intervals to the left and right lined the hall. Some of the doors stood open and some were closed, but none of the residents appeared to be out and about. The hallway was interrupted in the middle by a circular area featuring a tall desk. The crown of someone's bent head showed over the top of the desk.

"That's the nurse's station." Cady pointed to the desk. "Let's scoot to my mother's room before the attendant notices us. It's number 303."

She darted forward to the second door on the left. West followed in her wake. Cady paused at the closed door with her hand on the knob and gasped.

"Look!" She pointed at two parallel name-plates affixed to the wall beside the door.

Both names were filled in, but neither of them was May Johnson.

Cady's face went fire-engine red. "Come on."

She waved him after her as she charged toward the nurse's station. The corners of West's lips tilted upward. So much for being nervous about breaking the rules. Whoever was on duty at the desk had better watch out.

"Where is my mother?" Cady practically skidded to a halt at the station.

The attendant's head jerked up. "Who?"

"May Johnson. Where is she? Her room was 303. Has she been moved?"

The young woman's gaze flicked from Cady to West and back again. Finally, she rose. "Where are your visitor's badges?"

"Focus!" Cady snapped. "You're responsible for my mother's whereabouts and well-being. Where is she?"

Olivia began to fuss and wiggle in her car seat. West shushed and bounced her. It spoke volumes about Cady's degree of upset that she paid no attention to her daughter's cries.

The attendant blinked toward the baby, then took a step backward. "Who did you say you were looking for?"

"May Johnson. She's been a resident here for a decade."

The woman spread her hands in front of her. "I've only been working here for a month, but I assure you, I have no knowledge of a patient by that name, either on this floor or anywhere in the building. Are you positive you're looking for her in the right facility? There are other care centers in Phillipsburg."

"I know where my mother has been staying. I—"

"There you are," a breathless female voice interrupted.

West looked around to find a stocky, brunette woman hustling up the hallway toward them. Something about her carriage telegraphed authority. The administrator? He pressed his lips into a thin line. Time to face the music, but if this woman couldn't produce Cady's mother, pronto, it might be the administrator who danced to the tune.

He took a step toward her, blocking her access to Cady. "According to the nameplates, May Johnson's bed has been given to another. According to the staff member at this desk, May Johnson is no longer in this facility. If she's been moved to another one, Cady should have been notified. In fact, if May was moved to another facility prior to this employee coming to work here, whoever Cady has been talking to these past few weeks in order to receive updates on her mother's condition has been lying to her. Where is May Johnson?" West pronounced each word of the final query like a gavel coming down on a bench.

All authority wilted from the woman before him, whose name tag did indeed indicate that she was the administrator. She staggered sideways until she met the wall, as if she required its support to remain upright. The woman pressed the heels of both hands over her eyes.

Cady inserted herself between West and the administrator and brought her face to within inches of the other woman's. "Where is my mother?"

The dark intensity of Cady's tone drew a cringe from the administrator, but she let her hands fall to her sides, gaze bleak.

"We don't know." The answer came out in a taut whisper.

Cady let out a small shriek and tottered backward against West. He wrapped one arm around her, gently deposited the infant seat on the carpet and yanked out his cell phone.

"This is getting reported to the police." He tapped in the three digits for emergency services, as he glared at the administrator. "You can explain to them why the disappearance of one of your patients hasn't been reported."

EIGHT

Seated on a settee in the first-floor reception area, Cady gazed dully at the drama unfolding before her. What did it matter that the administrator and several other staff members were being arrested and handcuffed before her very eyes? Her mother was missing—had been since the day after Livvy was born—and no one seemed to have a clue where May Johnson was or how to find her. The cops had spoken to her and West and were still all over the place, interviewing staff and even a few patients, but no one was giving her any answers.

Livvy mewled and stirred in Cady's arms, drawing her attention. Her daughter's sweet, innocent face spread balm through her heart. A short time ago, Cady had finished feeding the baby in a private office borrowed for the purpose, and now the infant's tiny, rosebud mouth continued to make suckling motions as she drifted off to sleep.

What a fool Cady had been! As soon as she was up to the trip following Olivia's birth, she should have brought the baby here and introduced May to her granddaughter. Whether or not May would have understood the child's identity, or even cared, was beside the point. At least then Cady would have discovered much sooner that her mother was missing. Worse, maybe her mother wouldn't have gone missing at all had Cady been more faithful about visiting these past years. How more frequent visits might have made a difference Cady wasn't sure, but the question didn't make a dent in the iron armor of her guilt. May Johnson had neglected her daughters, and the surviving daughter had reciprocated with neglect. Why hadn't Cady seen that truth sooner? All the excuses she had made to herself about why she didn't visit rang hollow in her heart.

"You can stop beating yourself up now." West's sturdy figure settled onto the cushion beside her.

"Is it that obvious?" She shot him a bleak glance.

"It would only be more obvious if you hung

a sign around your neck that said in big black letters, I'M A TERRIBLE DAUGHTER."

"I am."

"Not true, but it's a normal reaction."

Cady spurted a bitter chuckle. "That's the first time the word *normal* has been used regarding anything to do with our family dynamics."

"Hang in there." He squeezed her hand.

Cady squeezed back like a drowning woman clutching a life preserver. He didn't even wince, just steadily held both her hand and her gaze.

"Let me update you," he said. "I just finished talking with the lead investigator on scene, and he was refreshingly forthcoming."

"Go ahead." She released his hand.

"Apparently, this facility has a negligence lawsuit pending in regard to another patient."

"Why am I not surprised?"

"When your mother first went missing, the administrator and several staff members were confident that they would quickly find her wandering around somewhere, and they could get her back with no one the wiser. Losing track of a patient with the results of the negligence trial in the balance would have been disastrous for the facility's case. However, when over twenty-four hours had passed without May being found, the cover-up became more complicated. Staff members who would have noticed May's absence were let go and replaced, and, as we discovered, her bed was filled with someone else. As long as you stayed away, they were golden until the trial was over, and then they could call you with a fictitious tale of May's sudden death and immediate cremation."

"I would have been furious not to have been notified of her death prior to cremation."

"Yes, but as you said, she's a ward of the state. Would you have wanted to come here to view her dead body?"

Cady shuddered. "For closure, maybe. But maybe not."

"There you go. Your fury would probably have been short-lived, and the Twin Oaks Care Center would have come out smelling like a rose."

Cady frowned. "Only until my mother was found somewhere. She can't simply have evaporated into thin air."

"Of course not, but—"

"But what?"

West's gaze darkened and he broke eye contact.

"Westley Foster, don't you dare pull punches on me now. What aren't you telling me?"

West sighed and returned his gaze to hers. "You're right. The administrator believes your mother fell into the Delaware River and is halfway to the Atlantic by now."

Cady moaned, and Olivia let out a squawk. Cady loosened her tense hold on the baby, who settled back into sleep. "That doesn't mean her remains won't be found."

"No, it doesn't, but if she did drown—and I'm not sure that happened—any remains found now would be difficult, if not impossible, to identify. Her DNA is not on file, only her fingerprints, which would be unlikely to survive that long in the water. I know because I asked the cops."

"And since no one would think to connect the unidentified body with me," Cady said, "they wouldn't have any reason to ask for my DNA to see if they could get a familial match."

"Exactly."

"What a diabolical solution to this facility's problems. I hope they close the place down after this."

"I expect the kerfuffle will die away with a change in administration and some policy and procedure adjustments," West said, "but I wouldn't hold my breath for a shutdown. Where would all these people go?"

Cady shook her head. "Never mind. That was spite and frustration talking. What did you mean when you said you aren't convinced my mother fell into the river?"

West shifted in his seat and looked away.

"You're doing that I-don't-want-to-come-right-out-and-tell-her thing again."

"This could be tough to hear, Cady."

"Tougher than all the nonsense we've been going through?"

"You have a point." He offered a grim smile, then sobered. "What if your mother is behind the attacks on you?"

Cady gaped at him, then shook herself. "What part of 'my mother's mind is gone' didn't you understand?"

"But I overheard a staff member who was being arrested say to the cops that May exaggerated some of her mental incompetence. That she was sly and devious and consciously used her disabilities to her own advantage."

Cady's gut clenched. What West suggested couldn't be right, could it?

She shook her head. "The devious part to get her own way sounds like the mother I once knew. But it's a huge leap to go from selfish and sneaky to ruthless and homicidal."

West's sharp gaze never wavered. "But if

she's more competent than anyone knows, it's not out of the question that your mother is behind the attacks on you."

Oxygen vacated Cady's lungs. As she'd experienced too many times in her life before, her world imploded on her.

"But why?"

The devastated wail in Cady's tone ripped at West's heart. "Didn't you say May grew up in the house you inherited and that she was passed over for the inheritance?"

"But how would she know any of that? Who would have told her? I didn't. It was impossible to hold a telephone conversation with her. She didn't track well enough with what was being said. At least, she pretended not to."

"I'm sure you notified the Twin Oaks of your move and the reason for it. Someone must have said something about it to your mother."

Cady's shoulders slumped. "That makes good sense, until you get to the part about my mother escaping so she can kill me because she lost out on the inheritance. My mother was always a master manipulator to get whatever she wanted, but in the passive-aggressive sense. I never knew her to act with actual aggression. If Mom is involved, it's as a pawn."

"Of who? Your father?"

"I doubt it. He always hated my aunt's place. Called it 'The Mausoleum.'" Her amber gaze locked with his. "There is one positive aspect of this notion of yours, though."

"What's that?"

"If my mother is out there trying to kill me, it means she's alive and not at the bottom of the Delaware."

The corners of West's lips twitched and he failed in suppressing his smile.

"What are you grinning about?" She looked at him askance.

"You. You're amazing. As if I needed more proof of what a good daughter—what a good *person*—you are. Even after all she's done to hurt you, you'd rather have your mother alive, and possibly trying to kill you, than dead and gone. Let's get out of here. We have some other avenues to investigate."

West took the sleeping baby from her mother's arms and settled the little one into her car seat. Cady walked at his side out to the Blazer. Her expression was intense but guarded.

"What's going through that lively mind of

yours?" he asked as he buckled Olivia's seat into the SUV.

She shook her head and did her own buckle. "When I've got the jumbled confusion sorted out, I'll tell you."

"Fair enough."

As he started the vehicle, his cell ringtone started to play. He checked the screen. Brennan.

He tapped the icon to answer. "Sitrep."

"We've got a situation, all right." His buddy's tone was grim. "You know Darius went to interview Mitch Landes, the neighborhood watch member who made up those gift baskets. He didn't return home at a reasonable time, nor did he check in, so I went looking for him. Found him fifteen minutes ago at the hospital."

"The hospital!" The words burst from West's mouth.

Cady shot him a wide-eyed look. "Who's in the hospital?"

"Darius." West hit the speaker button so she could be in on the conversation.

"Apparently," Brennan went on, "he was the victim of a hit-and-run when he was crossing the street to our company vehicle after the interview."

West's stomach clenched. "If he's in the

hospital, he must be alive." *God, please let him be alive.*

"Barely," Brennan said. "He's still in surgery. And it gets worse."

"How can that be?"

"This Mitch guy he went to talk to was walking Darius to his vehicle and was hit, as well. He didn't make it."

Cady let out a sharp cry and slumped in her seat.

West's insides went hollow. "We'll be there as fast as we can."

Cady jutted her stubborn chin. "Darius *cannot* die. There have been too many losses in our lives already."

West laid a hand on her shoulder. "Praying is the best thing we could be doing while we drive."

She nodded but with a slight frown. West understood. She was conflicted about prayer because she'd been experiencing a crisis of faith since Griff was killed. Yet, her heart was right even if her head was confused, and no one could convince him otherwise. She'd figure it out. He was going to have faith enough for them both right now. He ended the call with Brennan and got the vehicle on the road.

"Lord," he began quietly, "You know all

about this situation. Keep watch over our brave friend, Darius. Guide the medical staff in all their decisions and procedures. We ask that You preserve his life and restore him to us whole. And, further, we cry out to You for answers and solutions in this dangerous situation when someone out there is after Cady and doesn't balk at hurting others who stand in their path."

Small hums of assent and murmured amens came from Cady as he spoke.

"Please watch over my mother," she broke in, her voice cracking, "wherever she is, and help us find her."

"Amen to that," West confirmed. *And let it not be her who is targeting Cady.*

They subsided into silent conversation with the Almighty and their own musings. The tires gobbled up the highway, but not nearly fast enough for West. Judging by the way Cady fidgeted in her seat, she was as anxious as he was. Brennan hadn't called back with an update like he would if Darius was safely out of surgery. No news could be bad news. West's stomach churned.

"I don't get it." Cady broke the taut silence when they were about ten miles away from their destination.

"What don't you get?"

"All of it, to tell you the truth. None of these attacks make sense. Who would want to hurt me this badly that others are getting hurt trying to stop them?"

Her rush of words stopped on a soft choke, and West reached over and gripped her hand. Entwining their fingers was starting to feel so natural his heart ached. He was falling hard for this woman, and the timing couldn't be worse.

She squeezed back, took a deep breath and fixed her gaze on him. "But what I'm wondering about right now is the hit-and-run. Why did this creep try to shoot me, but then not use the gun on Darius and the neighborhood watch member? A bullet is precise. A vehicle as a weapon seems—well, sloppy."

"It was effective—at least partly. One man is dead." West rolled his shoulders as if adjusting a weight. "But maybe you gave yourself the answer. Perhaps the killer isn't a good shot. He missed you, after all."

"He missed me, yes. Thank God for that."

Her words held deep emphasis. At least she was finding things to be thankful about.

He returned both of his hands to the wheel. They were navigating through suburban traffic now. Soon, they reached the hospital parking lot. He grabbed the car seat from the back and carried a now wide-awake Olivia into the building. Such a shame the little one was being carted in and out of one medical facility after another the past days instead of spending her time peacefully at home in her own familiar environment. Of course, that home had not proven to be a safe haven, and it wouldn't be until they got to the bottom of how someone was getting inside.

The receptionist at the front desk directed him and Cady to the surgical floor. They boarded the elevator and glided upward. Soon the door slid open, and Brennan stood directly in front of them with his phone to his ear and the other hand reaching toward the elevator button.

"There you are," Bren said, pocketing his phone. "I was just going to call you while I went down to the cafeteria to grab a cup of joe and a sandwich."

"Update?" West stepped out of the elevator with Cady at his side.

She was clenching her fists so hard her knuckles were white. Instinctively, he stepped closer to her. If Bren was about to pronounce the worst about Darius, her reaction could be extreme.

"Darius is out of surgery," Brennan said.

"The doc says the next twenty-four hours will be critical. We just have to wait."

Cady burst into sobs, and West had no hesitation about gathering her trembling body close against his chest.

NINE

"I'm so sorry." Cady broke away from West's arms. Being that near him felt both comforting to her soul and dangerous to her heart. "I didn't mean to lose it. Partly it's relief that Darius is hanging in there. Another part is grief that this happened at all." She scrubbed hot tears from her cheeks with the heels of her hands.

"Understandable." Brennan's voice came out a little rough, as if he, too, were controlling strong emotion.

"Can we see him?" West asked.

"Not yet," Brennan said. "He's in recovery, so I told the charge nurse I was popping down for a bite while I had the chance."

"Let's all go." West ushered them back into the elevator car.

Ten minutes later, they sat in a cafeteria booth. The guys had each bought a ham sandwich, and Cady had been talked into a salad that she was scarcely able to pick at for the knots in her stomach. West and Brennan must be keyed up, as well. They'd barely tasted their sandwiches. Mostly they sat nursing their beverages of choice—West and Brennan with straight black coffees and Cady with a nonfat, decaf latte. She glanced at her little daughter next to her. Any minute now, Livvy would demand to join the refreshment club, too, but for the moment she was blowing bubbles and waving her fists in front of her face.

"Uh-oh!" Across from Cady, West's head came up as he stared at something behind her.

Cady turned to look. Detective Rooney was closing in on them with the usual slightly sour set to his mouth. Her heart sank. Now what? Was this guy going to try and pin the hit-and-run on her in spite of the fact that she'd been out of town with West at the time?

"Ms. Long and Mr. Foster," he drawled out as he stopped in front of their table. "It's a pleasant surprise to find you here, too. I came to interview Mr. Abernathy, but now I can take care of business with all of you." The man pinned Brennan beneath a stern glare and pulled out his little notebook. "I understand you were not with Mr. Creed when he was struck by the vehicle."

"That is correct." Brennan took a sip of his coffee and offered no free information.

Cady hid a smile by turning her attention toward Livvy, who had begun to make small fussy noises, a prelude to outright crying.

"And you found out about the accident how?" Rooney pressed.

"First, it was no accident. Second, when my buddy didn't return home in a reasonable time period, I went looking for him. By the time I traced his route to the home of the man he'd gone to visit, the crime scene on the road had been processed and vacated, allowing traffic to pass once more. An upset neighbor who was out in his yard told me what happened, so I rushed to the hospital."

"What was Mr. Creed doing at the home of Mr.—ah—" Rooney consulted his notebook "—Mr. Landes?"

"He's the guy that packages up all the welcome baskets for the neighborhood watch, but I assume you know that."

Rooney's shoulders drew back. "Of course, we know that, but what I want to know is why Mr. Creed was attempting to do our job for us? I warned you about—"

West rose from his seat to his six-foot-two-inch height. "What I want to know is why your people weren't doing their job. Apparently, the killer figured Mr. Landes knew something incriminating and told Darius about it, or why run them both over? Had you or someone from the PD interviewed Landes yet?"

Rooney turned so red that Cady sucked in a breath. She began unbuckling her daughter from the infant seat.

"We interviewed him," Rooney snarled, "but he was adamant that it wasn't possible the basket delivered to Ms. Long was tampered with—not on his watch."

Cady rose and faced the detective with her hungry, whimpering child in her arms. "A likely story to give the police when he feared being held liable for someone's poisoning. Mr. Landes may have told Darius a different story."

Rooney scowled. "We won't be able to find out until Mr. Creed wakes up."

Cady smiled at the man. "I'm glad to hear you're thinking positive about Darius's recovery. Now, if you'll excuse me, my daughter wants to be fed."

"Just a moment." The detective held up a forestalling hand. "I received a call from the Phillipsburg PD. They say your mother disappeared from her care facility weeks ago and is extremely mentally unstable. They also said she grew up in the house where you live. It's possible in her mental state that she headed for home."

"How? She has very limited resources."

Rooney shrugged. "She might have caught a ride with someone out of Phillipsburg or cadged money for bus fare. We are to be on the lookout for anyone who matches her description—especially on the streets among the homeless."

"I appreciate any help finding her."

"We'll find her." The detective jerked a nod. "With you off the suspect list, I now have a new prime suspect." Rooney smirked, turned on his heels and tromped away.

Cady turned desperate eyes on West. "How did the Phillipsburg PD know about the situation with me and my house—and that my mother used to live there?"

Color flushed West's cheeks. "You can blame me. I told them the whole story while we were at the Twin Oaks. Did you not want them to have the full picture and understand the urgency of locating her?"

"What I didn't want is for my mother to be a murder suspect." Her tone was harsh, but Cady couldn't seem to help herself. "Don't you understand that she simply isn't mentally capable?"

"The staff at Twin Oaks seemed to think she's far more capable than she's let on."

"Deception from her, I can believe. Murder, no." She stomped away with her daughter toward the ladies' room.

She returned fifteen minutes later to a subdued atmosphere in their booth.

"Did you hear something about Darius?" She gazed from West to Brennan and back again.

"Nothing new." Brennan shook his head.

West cleared his throat. "We've decided that I should take you and Baby-bug home. There's nothing we can do here. Brennan can keep us posted."

Cady opened her mouth to protest, but snapped it shut. West spoke the truth. There *was* nothing they could do here—especially her and Livvy. If she were honest with herself, she had to admit exhaustion dragged at her with every step.

"All right." She nodded.

West and Brennan shared slightly open-mouthed looks.

"What? You were expecting an argument?"

"No, ma'am." West rose, a tiny smile playing around his firm mouth. "Let's be on our way."

Fifteen minutes later, West pulled into Cady's driveway, and her spirits lightened. She did love this old place, even though she'd lived here only a short time. West gallantly opened her door for her, then went around and retrieved Olivia.

"Time to get you out of that car seat for a while." Cady reached over and tickled the bottom of her daughter's chin as West ushered them up the stairs to the front door.

Why did his hand in the small of her back feel so right? Why did it feel so wrong, at the same time? She wasn't over Griff yet, that was why. Maybe if she could make some sense out of her husband's death, she'd be able to move on. *Please, God, help?* Like such a pitiful prayer was going to make a difference. Cady heaved a long, silent sigh while West unlocked and opened the door.

They stepped into the foyer, and something soft crunched beneath Cady's feet. She halted and the breath froze in her lungs. Someone had been in the house during their absence. Whoever it was had trashed the place. The tiered planter by the foyer window had been upended and dirt, along with the sorry remains of spider plants, had been strewed across the area under and around her feet. A framed photo of Griff and her on their honeymoon had enjoyed pride of place on the entry table, but the precious keepsake now lay faceup on the hardwood floor. A starburst of shattered glass obscured their smiling faces, as if someone had ground their heel on top of the picture.

A guttural moan tore from Cady's constricted throat.

West thrust the baby carrier into Cady's hands and swiped his pistol from his side holster. They could go into full retreat, leave the house and drive away as fast as possible, but that wouldn't bring Cady and Olivia any closer to the ultimate safety of discovering and stopping whoever was perpetrating these heinous acts. Besides, the killer had proven that he or she was able to attack anyone anywhere, anytime. West would be better able to protect his charges in the smaller environment of the home's interior—that is, if the intruder still lurked inside. Something about the deep stillness of the house suggested they were alone, but he couldn't be certain until he'd cleared every room.

"Call 9-1-1," he told Cady, "and stay directly behind me as we move from quadrant to quadrant. The safest place for you and Baby-bug right now is on my six."

Cady's whispered tones into her cell phone told him that she was complying with his instructions to the letter as they edged into the living room. Some of the furniture had been upended and pictures and knickknacks had been smashed, but no one lay in wait. They continued into the kitchen, which was untouched and vacant of other human life. West checked the door to the basement, but it was still locked from the outside, so the intruder couldn't be down there.

Then they proceeded to the dark-paneled study. West flicked on the light and scanned the area, his pistol matching the swivel of his gaze. No one. This room, too, appeared to have escaped the violence. Quickly and quietly, they checked out the rest of the house, upstairs and down. The intruder was gone, and the destruction was confined to the foyer and living room. They returned to the main living space. West righted the Pabst chair and motioned Cady to have a seat. She looked ready to collapse. The cops would just have to deal with the fact that he'd moved a chair.

Cady nodded and sank into it, settling the infant seat on the floor beside her. "Thank you," she murmured. "If you were not here with me, I don't know what I would have done."

"You're most welcome." His voice had gone a little rough. Her gratitude—or rather, the need for it—broke him up inside. "I'm sure you would have done exactly the right thing."

Cady shook her head. "I'm not certain of that at all. Look how I fared the night I was attacked in my bedroom. Supposedly, I did all the right things, but still—"

"You were clobbered on the head, and someone heavier than you tried to suffocate you. There was nothing better you could have done."

"And I almost died." Her thin whisper tore at West's heart.

He squatted down in front of her and captured her gaze. "Sometimes people do all the right things, but circumstances conspire against them. Thankfully, you called for help."

"And it arrived in time." The edges of Cady's mouth tilted slightly upward.

Her shining gaze undid West. A deep groan heaved from his chest and he covered his eyes with his hands. "We didn't arrive in time for Griff. We fought so hard to get to him, but—"

"Stop!" Her gentle fingers parted his hands from his face. "I know you and Darius and

Brennan. If Griffon could have been saved, you would have saved him."

West swallowed against a dry throat. "I can't tell you what the mission was, but I can tell you that a bunch of people are alive today who wouldn't be without your husband's bravery and sacrifice."

Cady tilted her head, expression turning tender. "And that's what being a soldier is all about. I know that in my head, but my heart is still working on it. Give me time."

"All you need."

Their faces were so close to each other that Cady's breath fanned his cheeks. Only a few inches separated his lips from hers, but he didn't dare close that gap. Her plea for time stood like a wall between them. Would that wall ever come down? West pulled away.

Cady's gaze roamed the room. "Do you notice something odd?" Her tone had gone hard.

West followed the trajectory of her gaze from item to item. "The destruction in the living room and foyer looks staged in a very specific way."

"Just what I was thinking. Some of the antique furniture may appear to have been thrown around, but it was moved very carefully. See?" She patted the wooden arms of her chair. "Not a scuff or a scratch. On the other hand, things that *I* added to the space, mostly knickknacks and pictures, were destroyed with venom. Correct me if I'm leaping to conclusions, but I think that tells us this person is obsessed with keeping the place exactly the way it was when my great-aunt Anita lived here."

"I'd say that's a spot-on deduction. Unfortunately, it also indicates that the individual is intimately familiar with the home and the way it was in years gone by."

Cady's head drooped. "I know my mother fits that description to a tee. I can understand her having a passion for this house, but I can't wrap my head around the idea that she has transformed from manipulative to murderous."

The wail of a police siren closed in and stopped outside. Soon they were joined by a pair of officers, but this time not the same two uniforms who had answered the call when Cady was attacked in her bedroom and when the bug was found. West tersely informed the pair of the situation, including the fact that he'd moved one chair from its upended condition. They shook their heads and performed the same search West and Cady had done and ended up rejoining them in the living room to report the same results.

"We'll get forensics in here to look for trace evidence and dust for prints," one officer said, holstering his weapon.

Cady rose. "If you'll excuse me, I'm going to take my daughter upstairs to her room and change her."

The officer nodded permission, and Cady carried Olivia from the room. If West was going to be honest with himself, she carried his heart, as well.

TEN

Upstairs in Livvy's bedroom, Cady cooed and chatted to her daughter while she changed the diaper. Livvy kicked and wiggled, showing no signs of wanting another nap. She was starting to stay awake for longer periods of time, which was fun but could be challenging when Cady had housework or laundry she needed to do.

Her upbeat manner with her daughter belied the churning tension of her thoughts. Another home invasion. At least this time, no one had been in the house to take the brunt of an attack. Whoever had broken in—no, check that, no signs of break-in—whoever had gotten inside by some mysterious means had expressed clear signs of rage toward her personally. The fury probably stemmed from the fact that she wasn't dead yet.

Could her mother be so jealous of Cady's inheritance of the family home that she'd become homicidal? Even if that were so, was her mother's damaged mind capable of conceiving and executing the savvy and diabolical plans that had not only nearly succeeded in killing Cady, but Darius and West, as well? The idea seemed far-fetched, but who else could be doing these things and for what reason?

Then there was the issue of the attraction she had begun to feel for West—an attraction that she'd had the impression he reciprocated. Obviously, that impression was nothing but wishful thinking on her part, because his words downstairs explained the matter fully. Guilt, not attraction, motivated him. She'd had no idea how deeply he, Darius and Brennan felt responsible for Griff's death. She didn't blame them for the loss of her husband. Not at all. Her response to West that if they could have saved him, they would have, was entirely genuine. But, apparently, they couldn't quite exonerate themselves for his death, and now West felt extraordinarily obligated to Griff's widow and daughter.

Cady ground her teeth together. Once this horrible business was resolved, and if she survived, it would be best if she distanced herself from West. They both needed to get on with their lives. Why did that decision sound exactly right to her head, but exactly wrong to her heart? Cady picked up her daughter and snuggled and kissed her. Her heart would just have to get over Westley Foster. She had this little one to fill her days and her affections.

Sounds of activity downstairs let her know that the crime scene techs had arrived and were processing any evidence. *Please, God, let there be some this time.* Surely, the perpetrator of these crimes would make a mistake at some point.

The front stairs let out telltale creaks and groans. Someone was heading in her direction. She turned and West appeared in the doorway. Her heart panged. Why did he have to look so good? Why did he have to *be* so good? It was going to be excruciating to push him away.

"Brennan just called," he said. "I told him what went on here, but that he should stay at the hospital with Darius. If that neighborhood watch guy told him something—"

"Our killer might want to finish him off," Cady finished his sentence.

"Bingo." West nodded. "But there is a little good news. Darius's vital signs have stabilized already, much to the doctor's surprise. He hasn't woken up, but they're upgrading his condition from critical to serious. Bren thinks they'll be moving him out of the intensive care unit sometime in the next few hours."

"That *is* good news." A smile bloomed on Cady's face.

"For sure!" The brightness faded from West's face. "Then there's the bad news. Bren finished examining those house plans from the lawyer's file, but they yielded no clues about a secret entry into the house. They didn't eliminate the possibility, either. The sketches are simply too bare-bones to provide that sort of detail."

Cady huffed. "I rekeyed the locks soon after I moved in, as well as updating the security system, so I don't see any other way for the killer to be gaining access to the house than by some secret entrance. So much for finding out about its location the easy way. That leaves us with whatever might be stored in the attic. Going through that stuff will be a big job, but I don't see any way around making the attempt."

"Agreed. I'll hang out downstairs until the crime scene people leave and then I'll clean up the mess."

"Thank you. Facing that devastation again wasn't something I was eager to tackle. I'll stay here and play with Livvy. Maybe by the time she goes down for a nap, we'll be ready to start in the attic together."

"Sounds like a plan."

His grin warmed Cady from top to toe. *Chill!* She scolded herself. Too bad she hadn't been willing to admit to herself that her feelings for West were growing beyond friendship until it was too late to nip them in the bud. Now she could add that area to the places in her heart that needed to heal.

A half hour later, Livvy finally wound down and started rubbing her eyes with her little fists. Cady nursed her, and she fell asleep. Her tiny, perfect features and the winsome contrast of dark lashes against plump, rosy cheeks sent a pang through Cady—part joy at such a gift in her life, part envy at the innocent relaxation. What she wouldn't give for a little of that right now!

Cady placed her daughter in her crib and went to find West. She met him coming up the steps.

"All tidied up down there," he said. "I hope you don't mind that I popped a frozen lasagna into the oven."

"Perfect."

He looked at his wristwatch. "That gives

us about an hour to start rummaging around up there." He pointed over their heads.

Cady turned and led the way to the attic stairs, which were opposite the locked and boarded up servants' stairwell. Opening the door released a waft of stale air. Cady sneezed, and West let out a muted cough.

"Into the trenches," he said.

Cady allowed herself a small chuckle. Humor, even the ironic sort, was in short supply around here.

West flicked a switch to turn on a bare light bulb overhead, and they trod up steep, creaky steps. Dirt-streaked, round windows at the front and back of the cavernous space let in enough fading daylight to illuminate a rabbit warren of stacked boxes and scuffed-up trunks thick with dust. Against a side wall, a jumble of larger items filled a set of ancient shelves. Here and there a piece of discarded furniture or a garment rack filled with faded, vintage clothing peeked out of the morass. Near the stairs, a couple of short stacks of medium-sized plastic storage containers didn't wear quite as much dust, clearly more recent additions to the clutter.

West let out a low whistle. "You weren't kidding when you said this would be a big job. I don't even know where to start."

"A part of me sees this as a treasure trove of history. If the circumstances were different, I might enjoy the exploration. But with time of the essence, I would suggest we turn on every hanging bulb and take a quick walk-through to see if we can spot any likely places where something like house plans might be stored—specifically an old desk or a trunk that dates back to the nineteenth century."

"Sounds logical. With your interest in vintage objects, you might make a good antiques dealer. There may be enough stuff up here to get you started."

"You know, that's one career I've never considered. I was a store clerk when I met Griffon. I'll have to give the idea some thought. Oh, and by the way—" she shot him a sidelong look "—smooth way to distract me from the current danger and help me focus on a good future."

"Thank you for seeing through my devious ploy, but I was serious, too."

"I know." She waded into the maze.

A half hour later, they met again at the top of the stairs.

"Anything?" Cady prompted.

West shrugged. "I ran across an old roll-top desk. It wasn't locked, but when I rolled back the lid, it was empty."

Cady flopped her arms against her sides. "I found a couple of ancient trunks, but one contained knickknacks and wall hangings, and the other was full of clothing items from the early twentieth century—a vintage clothing dealer's dream, because they were in good shape."

West frowned. "That means we have to start looking through every container up here. But first, we need to check on the lasagna and maybe throw together a salad to go with it."

Cady stepped forward and her knee bumped a stack of plastic totes. The stack toppled over and tubs skidded everywhere. One popped open, releasing a collection of holiday decorations. She groaned and bent toward the mess then froze, her gaze captured by the label scrawled on top of the container that had been on the bottom of the stack: Maylene's Things. The breath stalled in Cady's lungs.

"What is it?" West touched her shoulder.

Slowly, Cady straightened, pointing at the labeled tub. "My mother's full name is Maylene. That's her stuff."

Cady's heart galloped in her chest. Did she

have the audacity to rifle through items from her mother's early life that had been valued enough to store away? The act would feel like an invasion of privacy. Yet, what choice did she have? They needed answers about the dangerous things that were happening now, and the slightest lead could be golden.

Of course, the tub might contain ordinary items like school papers or awards or even special toys that might at least give Cady insight into the type of child her mother had been before hard knocks and drugs had transformed her adult life. Then again, her mom had always insinuated that her upbringing in this house had been far from conventional. It was possible that this benign-looking container could hold information that might explode her world once again. Could she bear one more awful revelation about her family?

West laid a serving-sized bowl of tossed salad in front of Cady at the kitchen table. She nodded in wordless acknowledgment. Maybe he should have insisted she open the container of her mother's things *before* they sat down to eat, but she'd said it could wait. West was getting mixed messages from her body language. Her pale face and subdued demeanor signaled that she dreaded the chore, while her continual darted glances toward the living room, where West had brought the container downstairs and deposited it, telegraphed that she was anxious to find out what was inside—for better or worse.

Should he pray that the contents proved to be innocent trinkets from a little girl's childhood, or that they would discover a clue to what was going on here today? The former might be easier on Cady's emotions, but the latter might help keep her alive.

Somehow, the two of them plodded through dinner. West forced himself to eat every bite, the way he had done when his squad was on a mission. One never knew when the next opportunity for a meal might come. Cady nibbled here and there, but mostly pushed her food around with her fork.

"Whatever is in that container," he said, "we'll get through this together."

Her head jerked up, and her gaze lasered into him. "Together? No, we can't!" Her body gave a small shudder and she lowered her gaze. "Sorry. Major overreaction. Yes, I'm beyond thankful for all Triple Threat Personal Protection Service is doing for me now, but when we get through this, we can't stay together." She peered up at him as if fearing her next words. "You deserve to pursue your career and have a life."

West wrinkled his brow. What was she getting at? "I *am* pursuing my career, and I *have* a life that I appreciate very much. Right now, it's centered on protecting you."

"And one day soon it will be protecting someone else. What I'm trying to say is that you and the guys don't have to be tied to me for the rest of your lives. Livvy and I are not your permanent responsibility."

West wiped his mouth on his napkin, then crushed the paper in his fist. "Are you returning to our prior conversation about us gladly giving you a hand here and there? I thought we'd settled that issue. You're not a duty or a responsibility. It's our honor to serve you and Baby-bug."

Cady sat up stiff and straight. "What I'm getting at is that you don't *owe* us anything. I told you. I don't hold you or Darius or Brennan responsible for Griff's death. You can move on."

Move on? West's chest went hollow. She was telling him, clear as a bell, to back off as soon as this case was over. Did she sense his romantic interest in her? Was this her way of telling him she couldn't return those feelings and providing him a graceful way to exit her life? If that's what she wanted, he would have no choice but to grant her wish. But walking away might prove more difficult than any mission he'd ever carried out.

Offering him a brittle smile, Cady rose from the table and started gathering up the plates and bowls and silverware. "Let me put these in the dishwasher."

"No, let me do it. You can start on that container."

Hands full of utensils, she shook her head. "You cleaned up the intruder's mess down here and made sure I ate something. The least I can do is tidy up the dishes."

For a few moments, West watched her work with quiet efficiency. His heart ached to be able to enjoy her graceful presence every day. Yet, if she was telling him she wanted him out of her life, why did she look so sad? West shook himself and stood up. What was he thinking? Her world didn't revolve around him. She had plenty to be sad about that had nothing to do with an imagined romance between them. He needed to keep his head in the game.

"I'm going to do a walk around the perimeter outside and then perform a room check inside."

"All right." She didn't turn to look at him.

Heavyhearted, he got his jacket from the foyer closet. The autumn evenings were becoming a bit crisp. A slight crunch under his shoe betrayed that he'd missed a spot of dirt from the upended planter. He'd have to see to that later. He returned to the kitchen in order to exit through the back door, but Cady had gone. A floorboard creak from the living room told him she was in there, probably preparing to dive into that blast from her mother's past.

As he reached for the doorknob, a small shriek arrested him. Turning, he raced into the living room, gun drawn. Cady stood in the middle of the area rug, her gaze darting around the room.

"Where is it?" Her stare settled on him.

"Where is what?"

"Olivia's baby book. Where did you put it?"

"It wasn't in here when I cleaned up." He holstered his pistol.

"But I left it on that side table." She pointed toward the table next to the Pabst chair.

"You're sure you didn't bring it upstairs with you at some point?"

Cady planted her hands on her hips and beefed up her stare to a glare. "I haven't had a spare second to write in it since the day you charged home prematurely from the hospital. It should have been right here. Does that monster have Livvy's baby book?" Her voice choked.

Without a second thought, West strode to her and drew her close. At least she didn't pull away. Her chest heaved with a soft sob.

"I can't bear the thought." Her voice was muffled by his shirt, but he understood every word and the emotion that prompted it.

In his mind's eye, he pictured the perp's fingers slithering over the glossy pages and a shudder ran through him. Then molten steel flowed up his backbone and hardened into something icy and powerful. He'd felt anger before, perhaps even rage from time to time, but this exceeded anything he'd ever experienced.

"Ouch!" Cady wriggled away from him. "You have python strength."

"Sorry." West let his arms drop. "I was imagining what it might be like to get my hands on this creep."

A cold smile stretched her lips. "You and me both."

West's ringtone sounded, and he checked the screen. "Brennan," he told Cady and answered the call. "Is Darius all right?"

"Still hanging in there," Bren said. "But

that's not why I called. I forgot to let you know that I finished linking all the security cameras, as well as motion sensors, around the outside perimeter of the house. You can access the feeds from my laptop in the study."

"Wow! You got a lot done today."

"That's what I get paid the big bucks for." The Kentuckian chuckled.

"Maybe someday that'll be true." West gave an answering laugh and ended the call. "I won't need to go outside to perform a perimeter check, after all. Bren installed a full security system that I can access from his laptop. I can bring it in here while you go through the container."

Cady shook her head. "Why don't we go in there. If I sit here, I'll be constantly thinking about that baby book."

"Off we go then." He hefted the container and they went into the study.

The walls of the large room were done in dark wood paneling alternating with equally dark bookshelves. The furnishings were genuine Gothic Revival, including the massive leather-top desk that occupied the center of the area rug.

"That's an anachronism if I've ever seen

one," West said as he put the container down in front of one of the high-backed armchairs.

"What is?" Cady settled into the chair.

"Brennan's laptop perched on that dinosaur of a desk."

Cady let out a soft titter. "You're not a fan of antiques?"

West bit back the quip that had leaped to his lips. He couldn't say things like, *I'm a fan of the woman who loves antiques.* He didn't have that right, and judging by their recent conversation in the kitchen, it didn't look like he ever would.

Cady opened the tote, and West sat down at the desk and opened Brennan's laptop. They knew each other's passwords, so he had no trouble accessing both the current video feed and the video history. He spent an engrossing half hour studying the recordings. Nothing but a stray cat entered the property. How had the intruder accessed the house if he or she was not captured on video approaching it? And, once again, the intruder had not set off the interior security system by entering through a door or a window. All of these means of access were securely locked and showed no signs that they had been tampered with. Even if the intruder had possessed a key—highly unlikely since

Cady's wise rekeying of the property after she moved in—the alarm system would have gone off within seconds if the code were not entered. Doubly unlikely that the intruder would know the code as well as possess a key. No, there *had* to be a secret entrance to this house, most likely with a tunnel leading to it, and they *had* to find it before more people died—one special person in particular.

West's gaze flew to Cady, whose attention was absorbed in a notebook she must have taken from the plastic container of her mother's things. Even though Maylene had been raised in this house and might know the home's secrets, how likely was it that anything in a tub full of child's memorabilia would prove helpful to their current situation? Not all that likely. Rifling through the contents was nothing but a detour to what they needed to be doing. They had to return to their search for house plans.

Cady let out a sharp gasp and her head suddenly jerked up. She met West's stare with eyes wide enough to display the whites around the irises. "My mother had a half sister who grew up with her in this house. One she never, ever mentioned to me in my whole life."

ELEVEN

Cady stared open-mouthed at her mother's diary notebook. The childish block letters expressed juvenile resentment, a storm in a teacup that sounded normal for siblings growing up in the same household. On a day several decades ago, her ten-year-old mother had written, *H. may be my half sister, and Mother makes us share a bedroom, but that doesn't mean she can get into my things.*

Why had Mom never mentioned this sibling, a person who would be Cady's aunt? Then again, Cady never talked about her own sister, Tracy. The memories were too painful. Had something happened with this sister in her mother's childhood? Perhaps the sister had passed away. Perhaps not. Either way, something dark must lie here in her mother's past for this half sister, H., to have been erased from the family history. At no time had Great-Aunt Anita mentioned this person, either, when Cady was little and they visited her in this house.

"Is a full name for this half sister noted anywhere in the diary?" West's voice came from behind Cady's chair where he was peering at the notebook over her shoulder.

"I don't know. I'm not done reading."

"Keep at it then. If this H. is still around, maybe she thinks *she* should have received the inheritance. It's a lead to follow, anyway. I take back thinking it would be a waste of time searching through this tub."

West returned his seat at the desk and Cady went back to perusing the diary in her hands. She finished that one and went through two more diary notebooks that had been stored in the container. H. featured regularly in her mother's childhood musings, but was always referred to by the initial, never the full name. Judging by the frequently resentful and sometimes angry tone her mother used when talking about her half sister, the relationship between the two had been rocky at best. But what had happened to make the break so final and complete that the other girl disappeared from family lore?

Cady clenched her jaw as she turned to the final page of the last notebook. *C'mon, Mom, give us a hint here.* Her gaze scanned the last entry and the blood iced over in her veins.

H. and I were fighting today, and she tried to smother me with my pillow. I fought her off and gave her a black eye. I got sent to my room without supper for the black eye because Mother thinks I'm making up the story about the pillow, but I'm not. H. is acting all innocent and surprised that I would claim something like that about a pillow fight. I won't let her win. The word *won't* was triple-underlined. *Tonight, I'm going to do something about it.*

Cady groaned. "Oh, Mother, what did you do?"

Was she wrong about her mother's lack of homicidal tendencies? The significance of smothering by pillow wasn't lost on Cady, though a nasty, juvenile pillow fight could be blown up into something more than it was in a young girl's imagination. But if it were true, did her mother respond to H.'s assault in kind? What had happened? They needed to find out. But how?

"What's up?" West's question broke in on the hamster wheel of her thoughts.

She read the entry to him.

"Wow!" As he sat back in the desk chair, the vintage furnishing let out a loud creak.

"We need to find out the story behind this. Maybe your great-aunt's lawyer would know something. Sounds like he's been working for the family for a long time."

"Mr. Platte? Of course! Genius idea."

"Then it's back to Wyncote as soon as we can get an appointment. Maybe we'll make it all the way to his office this time." West grimaced.

A squawk followed by a wail came through the baby monitor Cady had brought from the living room into the study.

"Guess who's up?" Cady rose. "She'll likely be awake for a while now, and I won't get to bed very soon. All of this upheaval has really messed with her schedule."

West stood, hefting Brennan's laptop. "I'll keep this with us whatever room we're in so that I can continually monitor the cameras. But other than that, I think we should take the rest of the evening to enjoy Baby-bug."

"That sounds really nice."

In a sense it truly did. In another sense, her heart ached. They would be acting like a real family—but it would be a facade. Once West had fulfilled his obligation to protect her, maybe he could put his guilt to rest. At that point, for her own sanity, she would have to establish healthy boundaries between them.

The rest of the evening passed peacefully. Mere minutes after Livvy went down for the night, Cady laid her weary head on her pillow and mentally said a small prayer. *God, I know I've been keeping my distance from You since Griffon passed, and I'm still confused and hurting. But West's faith seems as strong as ever, even though he lost a close buddy. I guess I can try to hang on to faith, too. If You're not mad at me and still want to hear from me, please help us figure out what is going on and put a stop to it before anyone else gets hurt.*

Seconds after her prayer ended, slumber claimed her.

An uncounted time later, an odd noise roused Cady. Her breath caught, and her ears strained. Thunder rumbled nearby, and the pitter-patter of raindrops against the windowpane reached her ears. No, the strange sound hadn't been weather-related.

Cady lifted her head and stared toward the wall opposite her where the fireplace was. Next to the floor near the hearth, a thin line of light glimmered. As she watched, frozen, the steady glow, like that of a flashlight, grew to outline a doorway in the wall and the dark silhouette of a head and shoulders began to peek out from behind it.

Her paralysis fled. Heart pounding, Cady sat bolt upright and snatched her pistol from the bedside table. Holding the gun in both hands, she pointed it toward the shadow person who was attempting to enter her room.

"Stop where you are!" she shouted. *Please, God, let West hear me.* "I have a gun!"

The person let out a muffled grunt and their head withdrew. The secret door closed and blackness engulfed her bedroom once more.

From the front stairs, a caterwaul of creaks, groans and thudding footsteps assured Cady that West was coming. He burst through her door with a gun and small flashlight leading the way.

"I'm all right," Cady called, lowering her pistol, "but someone was entering my room through a hidden panel on that far wall. They left as soon as I said I had a gun."

West flipped on the light and Cady pointed to the spot. Amazing that there was absolutely no sign of a doorway. The ornately paneled wall looked solid and whole. The fireplace opening gaped at her benignly as if wondering what the fuss was about.

"I wasn't dreaming." Her tone was more defensive than she liked.

"I believe you. We knew someone had to

be getting inside through a secret passage-way. Now we just need to figure out where on this wall it is and how to open it."

Cady glanced at the digital clock on her bedside table. Only 2:30 a.m... She'd barely been asleep for three hours. West was fully dressed and tidy, so he probably hadn't slept at all, faithfully keeping watch all night.

Cady climbed out of bed and slipped her robe on over her pajamas and slid slippers onto her bare feet. "Let's get to it, then. Now that we know where to look, we should be able to feel some sort of seam where the opening is."

Twenty minutes later, she lifted her hands in surrender. If discouragement were a crown, she'd be wearing it. They'd examined every inch of the dark trim on light wood walls, including the chair rail.

"My prediction was false. If there's a door seam here, it's not discernable to the touch, much less visible."

West stood back, scanning the wall with a frown. "The seam has to be behind some of that heavy trim. We may have to take apart your wall to find it. Whoever constructed the passageway was exceptionally clever. We've got to be *more* clever."

Cady tapped her upper lip with a forefinger. "Hmm. If we can't find the door seam, maybe we can locate the latch or button or whatever it is that trips it open. Somewhere in or around the fireplace would be the logical place to conceal something like that."

"All right." West knelt in front of the fireplace's empty grate. "Let me move this out of here, so we can search thoroughly. The latch is bound to be well hidden so I wouldn't be surprised if I have to stand up in the flue and get a little sooty to find it."

"Freeze!" Cady cried as he leaned into the fireplace and grasped the grate. "Did you hear that?"

West looked at her over his shoulder. "Hear what?"

"As soon as you started tugging on the grate, I heard a slight click."

"You mean the grate is the latch?"

"No." Cady stepped forward and touched his shoulder where it was pressing against a lotus flower carved into the woodwork. "It's this."

She nudged West out of the way and shoved the heel of her hand against the center of the flower. The carving depressed into the wall. A sizable panel next to the fireplace, expertly encased in trim that hid the door seam, swung outward as softly as a whisper.

A waft of cool air bathed Cady's face, delivering a sudden memory.

Those few days ago, just before the intruder had hit her over the head, a chill had flowed over her and she'd shivered. At the time, she'd marked the reaction down to fear, but her chill hadn't been born of an internal emotion—at least not entirely. It had been caused by the dank air from this dark passageway hidden in her home. A fresh shiver shook her.

West palmed his sidearm from its holster and rose swiftly, pressing Cady behind him. Flashlight and gun aimed into the opening, he stepped into the passage. No one lay in wait. A pent-up breath eased from his chest. The intruder was probably in full retreat, but he'd learned long ago not to make unverified assumptions about the enemy.

"This access point is all clear," he called back to Cady. "Too clear. Whoever's been using this route as their private entrance has housekeeping standards. I expected cobwebs and dirt, but the passage has been swept and dusted."

Cady snorted. "No doubt, the creeper didn't want to leave footprints in the dust in case the secret passage was exposed."

"A fair deduction."

She stepped up to the passage and peered into it. Her face was pale and her lips tremulous but judging by the set of her jaw and the gleam in her eyes, guts were gaining ascendancy over fear. She pointed deeper into the hidden hallway.

"There are stairs." She started to move toward them, but West halted her with a gentle grip on her arm.

"Not you. Me."

Cady planted her hands on her hips and stuck out her chin. "Not you. Us."

"Our killer may have set booby traps for anyone coming after them. Or they may be lying in wait anywhere along the way."

"Are you or are you not trained to perform dangerous reconnaissance missions?"

West flattened his lips. "But not in tandem with a civilian."

"You've never escorted civilians through risky territory?"

How was he supposed to answer that? If he admitted he'd done so, Cady won the argument. If he denied doing so, he'd be lying.

"What if Olivia wakes up?" he asked. Nice trump card, if he said so himself. West hid a smug smile behind an impassive expression.

Cady rolled her shoulders. "As late as she

went down for the night, she should sleep for more than an hour yet. But *I'm* not going to get another wink of sleep until we ensure the intruder isn't going to get in again. And, remember, during that first attack, I heard noises downstairs before they arrived in my bedroom. There is probably more than one hidden door. What if you're in there exploring and the killer pops out through another one and comes after me? No, thank you."

"You've got your gun."

"Fat lot of good it did me during the first attack. Even if I had the chance, I don't know if I could shoot anyone. That's your department. Like you said earlier, the safest place for me right now is square on your six."

West scowled at her. "Grab your gun and throw on some sneakers. Those flimsy slippers aren't enough protection for your feet in unknown territory. Hop to it! We're wasting time."

His full-on army sergeant snarl didn't dent her triumphant grin as she rushed away to comply with his demands. A guy might have to admit when he was licked, but he didn't have to like it.

She was back at the passage as quickly as he could have expected one of his trained squad members. In addition to the pistol, she had also brought a flashlight from her side table. At his approving nod, she blushed and West turned away before she could glimpse his heart in his eyes. This woman had come to mean the world to him. Now, it was up to him to protect that world—with his life, if necessary.

"Stay close," he said. "Train your beam around one side of me and straight ahead. That will provide steady illumination. I'm going to be playing my light over every inch of territory as we move forward. We can't afford to miss anything."

"Roger that," she responded, and West allowed himself a grin.

They moved to the head of the steep stairway that plunged downward.

"No stairs going up toward the attic," he observed aloud.

West cautiously led them down the narrow steps, noticing nothing that would indicate traps laid. Shortly, they arrived at a small landing where it didn't make sense for there to be one. It was too soon for them to have reached the next floor of the house.

"Could there be a door here?" Cady half whispered to him.

He traced his beam up and down the wall and found a latching mechanism.

"Move back," he warned, and she retreated several steps upward.

Hyperalert for any surprises, West depressed the latch and a narrow door swung open. He went through the opening, gun and flashlight first, then his head.

He let out a short chuckle. "The door leads onto the servants' stairs, but the stairwell is still locked and boarded up from both ends, not to mention missing several steps. And the space is full of undisturbed dust, so our intruder can't have ventured here. Let's keep going."

"Right." She came up behind him again, the warmth emanating from her a contrast to the dank chill that flowed toward them from somewhere in the deep darkness below.

After a sharp turn, they arrived at another, more spacious landing that seemed sensibly placed, as far as distance between floors was concerned. West played his light over the surrounding area. Again, no sign of a booby trap. There was, however, a latch like the one he'd tripped next to the servants' stairs, indicating that this was a hidden door panel, and one new anomaly—a rectangular cutout about the dimensions of a mail slot with a knob and a hinge slightly below his eye level. He tugged open the cutout and uncovered a pair of peepholes. He looked through them and found himself staring at Cady's Pabst chair. His insides went molten. Some life-form lower than pond scum could have been staring at Cady with evil intent for who knew how long—perhaps since the day she'd moved in. No wonder she'd sometimes felt like someone was watching her.

"What do you see?" Her tone was thin and pitched slightly higher than normal, but that was the only sign of her anxiety.

Lots of people would be hysterical with all that had been happening. Cady was holding it together remarkably well.

West turned toward her. "I see the living room from the vantage point of the fireplace wall. I'm assuming the door here is hidden similarly to the one upstairs."

Her brow furrowed. "I don't understand. Why didn't they step out and try to end me sooner if they had this kind of access anytime of the day or night?"

"Good question. I think we'll have to return to the assumption we made early on, right after the tea incident. This person was biding their time for you to drink the poison and die. The cause of death might easily have been missed and attributed to natural causes. When time passed and you didn't drink their poison, they went to plan B and attacked you in the night."

Cady shuddered visibly. "Had they succeeded, I suspect they would have tried to arrange the scene to make it look like a freak accident or something—anything—other than murder."

"But they didn't succeed, and then I drank the tea, and the poison was a secret no longer. Ever since then, the attempts have grown progressively more blatant and desperate."

"I don't like desperate," she said. "Desperate people do extreme things. But at least there's one bright spot."

"What's that?"

"Detective Rooney will have to take back those insinuations he made the first time he came here to investigate—that I imagined noises on the first floor."

"He'll have to eat a lot of his insinuations and wrong conclusions." West nodded toward the stairs that continued downward. "Let's keep going to the end of this thing."

One cautious step at a time, he eased them onward.

"Basement level, here we come," Cady murmured in his ear.

"Basement level, here we are," West confirmed as they came to the end of the stairs and reached an enclosed space the size of a small, narrow hallway that ended in a blank wall with no direct access into the actual basement, only this small compartment at basement level.

To one side of them gaped a ragged opening in the concrete foundation, just large enough for a human being to slip through sideways. The musty chill that permeated the passageway originated from the tunnel beyond. A steady *plink-plink-plink* sound carried faintly to West's ears. Water was dripping a little distance away, but it wasn't trickling into the house. No moisture was evident on the cement floor under their feet.

West played his beam through the hole. The light was swallowed in darkness before it could reach the end of wherever the tunnel led, but within the tunnel it illuminated shoring beams and evidence of human chiseling in the rocky spots from decades ago. Contemporary technology would result in much smoother, more even walls.

"This hole in the concrete between the house and the tunnel looks like it was made recently and inexpertly through an area in the foundation that appears to have been walled up at some point with inferior material."

"Another confirmation that our creeper has to be someone with intimate knowledge of the property," Cady said, peering into the opening.

"Certainly. Someone would have had to know the location of the tunnel and how to get into it, follow it to the house and patiently chisel out a new opening to the passageway."

Cady backed away from the opening. "Are we going in?" Her tone was the opposite of enthusiastic.

West shook his head. "We don't need to go any farther. In fact, it would be unwise. The tunnel shows every sign of being old and neglected. I'm not sure I would trust the shoring beams. A few of the ones I could see are cracked and sagging. This recently made hole is the point where we need to cut off access to the house." He waved toward the tunnel opening. "However, it's not going to be a quick and simple process. Bren and I will get in here tomorrow—" he glanced at his watch "—er, later this morning with brick and plaster."

"Our intruder would be an idiot to try to come back this way again tonight," Cady said. "And so far, they haven't struck me as stupid. Cunning, yes. Stupid, no." Cady turned and began walking the perimeter of the confined space.

West went back to assessing how much brick and plaster he and Bren might need.

"I wonder where this claustrophobic little hallway lets out into the basement," Cady said. "Ah, here's the latch."

West whirled, caution on his tongue, but he was too late. She depressed the latch and a distinctive click raised the hairs on the back of West's head.

"Freeze!" he cried out. "Don't move a muscle."

Her wide gaze darted toward him but she complied, standing stock-still with the latch pushed down under her slender fingers.

West swallowed against a dust-dry throat. None of the other latches had made a sound when depressed, but he'd heard that kind of terrifying *snick* before. A pressure switch. If Cady let up on the latch, some sort of IED—improvised explosive device—would blow them into eternity.

TWELVE

As West explained the situation, Cady's heart pounded in her throat. How could she have been so careless, messing with the latch without having West check it out first? Now that they had discovered the intruder's access point to the house, she'd allowed herself a false sense of security. A natural reaction. Perhaps their adversary had a background in psychology, because here, where she'd let her guard down, is where they had laid the booby trap.

"Hold still and let me find out where the explosive device has been planted." West knelt by her side and gazed closely at the depressed latch. He made a humming noise.

"What?" Her voice came out far sharper than she'd intended, but his seeming calm was getting on her last frayed nerve. Every molecule in her body wanted to scream and run, which was the very thing she could not do.

"Leading out from the latch are wires embedded in the wall under a thin layer of new plaster. Even *I* might have missed them before pressing the latch."

"Way to make me feel better about doing a dumb thing."

"Did I?"

"No."

"I didn't think so." More humming and then a cluck of his tongue. "Very clever."

"I don't like the sound of that."

"The device is embedded in the false wall between the basement and this hidden room. I'm going to have to scrape away the new plaster to get to it."

"With what?" Cady cautiously switched her weight from one foot to another without letting up on the pressure against the latch.

"A soldier never goes anywhere without his knife."

"Hurry! Please!"

"Hang in there. You're doing great."

More of that fake calm. Cady gritted her teeth. Scraping sounds continued for an eternity.

"Here you are, you lousy little critter," West intoned softly, clearly not talking to *her*.

"Are you addressing the bomb, or are you referring to the person who planted it?"

"Both."

"Can you disarm it?"

"Yep. Just did." West rose with a small cylinder in one hand and what looked like a battery pack from a toy in the other. "The cleverness was in the concealment. This IED is super simple. Disengaging the battery pack from the canister renders it harmless."

Cady remained frozen in place, staring at the deadly device. She could scarcely haul in a full breath.

"You can let go of the latch now," West prompted, his words and expression soft and tender.

With a cry, Cady released the latch and threw herself into his arms. He drew her in against his strong chest. His heart thrummed against her ear in double time. He hadn't been nearly as calm as he'd pretended. Sobs broke from her throat and she let the tears flow. His soft murmurs of assurance spread a warm balm through her. And was he showering kisses on the top of her head?

Cady lifted her face to his and the kisses fell on her lips. She responded in kind. When was the last time she'd felt so secure and at home? Before Griff died, of course.

Griff!

Gasping, Cady wrenched herself away from West and turned her back on him. Did he groan softly with the separation? Her insides echoed the groan, but she couldn't do romance. Not right now. Especially when her eager reaction to West might be nothing more than intense relief. And his? Well, he'd already made it clear he was in the grip of survivor's guilt over Griffon's death. No, it was better and wiser for them both if they kept their relationship to nothing more than friends.

Composing herself through sheer willpower, she turned toward West. "Livvy could be waking up for her feeding anytime. I need to return to her."

"Of course." West nodded, his face impassive. "I'll call the authorities to dispose of this IED. They're going to be very interested in this secret passageway, too. I doubt they'll volunteer to stop up the hole for us, though." He grimaced.

"Thank you…for everything. After I feed Livvy, she should go back to sleep. I'll try to grab a little more shut-eye in the rocker recliner in *her* room so the police can have free access to *my* room."

"Sounds like a plan." West nodded as he pulled out his cell phone.

Cady hurried up the steep stairway toward her chief treasure in this world, her daughter. If circumstances required her to give up this house to keep Livvy safe, she'd do it in a heartbeat.

Several hours later, Cady roused to find herself in her daughter's room. The silence in the house indicated that the authorities had come and gone. How could she have slept through the muted ruckus? The fact that she had done so was a clear indication of how exhausted she had been. Still was. *Refreshed* did not describe how she felt right now.

Time to be up and at it, nevertheless. Livvy was stirring in her crib and would be up for the morning soon. A quick shower would go a long way to fortifying herself for whatever was going to come at her today, though how it could be more nerve-wracking than last night's near-miss with the bomb, she couldn't imagine.

As soon as she was showered and dressed, Cady put in a call to Mr. Platte's office, and that sweet-voiced receptionist of his said they could stop in anytime after lunch. The man had no court scheduled so he would be in the office attending to paperwork.

Cady ended the call and went downstairs. She stepped into the kitchen with her daughter in her arms to find West seated at the table nursing a cup of coffee. He was wearing the same clothes as last night, so a shower and change had not yet been on his morning agenda. The responsibility he felt for her had to be wearing on him. After their kiss last night, would they be able to regain a natural camaraderie?

She gazed at him, searching for words that would come out casually. West didn't seem similarly tongue-tied. He greeted her with nonchalance, showing no sign that their kiss was in his thoughts. Her heart pinched. Did he regret kissing her last night? Did she? She probably should, but she didn't. She'd lock that moment away in her heart as a special memory to overlay the terror of the previous minute when he disarmed the IED.

"Have you heard an update on Darius?" she asked.

West nodded. "He's awake, and the doc says he's going to pull through."

"That's great news." A smile broke out on Cady's lips. "We should go visit him before we head for the lawyer's office."

"Let me grab a shower first. I'm feeling as ripe as the muskmelon I ate with my breakfast this morning."

Cady laughed as the humor untied much of the knot in her chest that she seemed to be carrying around permanently these days. "Sure thing, Mr. Melon."

West grinned and rose. At the sound of feet on the stairs behind her, Cady gasped and whirled. A thickly built man wearing a grit-streaked yellow coverall stepped out of the open basement door, followed by another younger man in similar garb. They were each carrying tools and large plastic tubs with metal handles. She gaped at them.

The first man glanced at her, then focused on West. "We're done down there. We drilled and inset bars across the opening and then applied concrete. The 'crete will set within twenty-four hours, but the bars will keep out any intruders until then."

"Thanks for the quick work on short notice." West nodded at the men in the coveralls, who headed toward the front door. Then he turned to Cady. "Sorry you were startled. I neglected to tell you how accommodating the cops turned out to be—Detective Rooney, especially. He got right on the horn to a contractor who owed him a favor... Well, as soon as he finished reaming me out for us traipsing through the tunnel and fudging up potential fingerprints by disarming that bomb myself."

Cady barked a laugh. "Did he think it would have been better if you'd let it explode?"

"With Rooney, who knows? But I think

hauling the contractor out of bed was as close as he'll ever come to apologizing for his wrong assumptions about you. Saves me and Brennan a messy job, too."

Cady inhaled a long breath and let it out slowly. "Wow! Knowing that tunnel is sealed lifts a great weight from me."

"Ditto," he said. "Why don't you grab some breakfast while I clean up."

As soon as West returned from his quick washup in the bathroom, and Cady finished a piece of toast and jelly, they were on the road.

"Did the cops explore that underground tunnel?" She glanced over at his strong, appealing profile and her wayward heart gave a little kick against her ribs. Inappropriate reaction. She squelched it.

"Nope," he said. "They agree with me that the shaft is getting ready to fall down around someone's head. It's not worth risking people's lives. They sent a K-9 in there and the dog nosed around for a while but came back without signaling human presence. Our creeper was long gone, and it would be pointless for them to return to the tunnel now that it's been discovered. For safety reasons, we may have to dig up the yard to expose the tunnel and fill it in before it collapses all of a sudden with someone standing on top of it. I wonder how far it goes. Probably to the edge of the property. Maybe under or around the utility shed?"

Cady shrugged and shook her head. "Could be farther out than that. When the home was first built, it sat on a sizable acreage that was gradually sold off as the family fortunes diminished, the cost of living increased and suburban sprawl gobbled up all the land it could get. The home is the last bastion of our family's heritage, which is one reason my great-aunt was so persnickety in her will about its ownership."

"Where do *you* think the tunnel ends up?"

She shrugged. "Maybe the family crypt that sits beneath the chapel in the local cemetery two blocks away."

West started to laugh but she shot him a dark look and he sobered. "You're serious. A Gothic house with a secret passage *and* a family crypt?"

She allowed a small smile to play across her lips. "Those scary historical romance novels need a basis in fact. Our family is a real-life illustration, complete with deep, dark secrets…apparently." She grimaced. "Maybe if H. died—for whatever reason— we will find her remains in the crypt with a nameplate and pertinent dates. We should go there, as well the lawyer's office."

West whistled low under this breath. "I guess we add to our to-do list." His glance over at her telegraphed a question. "Everything about this house is intensely personal to you, isn't it?"

She nodded. "Growing up, we moved around a lot. If we stayed anywhere more than eighteen months, that was a long time. But at least twice a year, sometimes more often, we would make the trek to Glenside. We might stay for a few weeks when Daddy was between jobs, or just for a holiday visit. My times there were the happiest of my childhood. Whoever has been creeping around doing violence is trying to tarnish those memories. I'm not going to let them."

Famous last words. She turned away from West's perceptive gaze and stared out the window at the passing boulevard. He was giving all he had to protect her. It wouldn't do to let him know how insecure she was about the outcome of this duel of wits with their devious and determined adversary.

West didn't need Cady to tell him how scared she was beneath that courageous front, though it might be healthy if she let her feelings out. Why did she believe she had to be brave all the time, even in front of close friends? Were friends all they could ever be? His heart throbbed. Their kiss had been, hands down, the most glorious thing that had ever happened to him. But the wonderful moment had passed all too quickly, and now they were back to square one in their relationship. Maybe not even that. It was as if she continually took one step toward him and then two steps back.

And what was the matter with him that he was wasting time thinking about their relationship right now? *Head in the game, buddy.* He gave his full concentration to driving. Sort of.

When West escorted Cady and Livvy into the hospital room, Darius was sitting up in bed. A cast encompassed his left arm and road rash decorated one side of his face.

West strode up to his friend and scowled down at him with arms crossed over his chest. "You look terrible, man."

Darius grinned with one side of his swollen mouth, clearly taking the gruff insult for the expression of affection that it was. "Better than you'd look if you'd gone toe to toe with the grille of a speeding vehicle."

Brennan rose from his seat on the opposite side of the bed, yawned and stretched his arms. "Babysitting this dude has been a bore and a half. Lazy lout sleeps all the time."

"That's me being productive by promoting my healing." Darius shot a mock scowl toward Bren.

All three of them, along with Cady, joined in a chuckle. Darius offered West his uninjured hand and West clasped its warm strength, silently thanking God for his friend's survival.

"Now, out of the way, dude." Darius waved West aside. "The real healing has arrived. Let me get a look at my honorary sister and niece." He motioned toward Cady and Babybug.

Smiling, Cady stepped up to the bed and settled Livvy in a supported sitting position on the covers beside Darius, who chuckled and tickled the baby's cheek. Letting out a tiny chortle, she waved at her honorary uncle's fingers and accidentally grabbed hold of one and hung on to it. If a face could melt into warm goo, Darius's did exactly that.

"What's the update?" Brennan interrupted the pleasantries.

West filled them in on Cady's and his adventures in the night. His short, terse treatment of the bomb incident drew angry mutters from this team, followed by murmurs of satisfaction that the intruder's access to the house was terminated.

"That's my report," West concluded. "What about you, Darius? Why do you think the killer went after you and the neighborhood watch guy?"

"Yes," Cady said. "Did the man who packed the baskets tell you something worth a hit-and-run over?"

"The cops asked me that, too, this morning," Darius responded.

"Detective Rooney?" Cady made a sour face.

"No, Detective Leticia Grace." Darius pronounced the name with a lilt, as if it deserved to be set to music.

"She seems like a decent human being." Brennan rolled his shoulders in a shrug.

"And easy on Darius's eyes, I presume?" West added, staring pointedly at his partner in the hospital bed. The man maintained a poker face.

"Is she single?" Cady asked.

Brennan chuckled. "Mr. Smooth, here, managed to finesse that information out of her with a little counter-interrogation, and yes, she is."

"Are you going to ask her out?" Cady persisted, a smile lighting her face.

Darius held up a forestalling hand. "Hold on, there. We've got to settle our present business first. But after that I might give it some serious thought." A tiny grin flashed across his face.

"Back to Cady's original question," West said. "What did Mitch Landes tell you that made trying to kill both of you a necessity?"

"I don't know for sure, though he did get pretty chatty when he found out we're both Philadelphia Eagles fans. We jawed football for a while, then he loosened up and answered my questions about the gift baskets."

"There must have been something critical in all that jabber," Bren put in. "And our enemy knew Landes told you as soon as the words came out of his mouth. The cops found a listening device in Landes's home like the one in Cady's. It had been stuck to the inside of his mail slot, which was next to the living room, so it could have been put there anytime when Landes was gone and the person wouldn't even have had to gain access to the house."

"Scary sneaky." Cady shuddered visibly.

West frowned, mentally seconding her assessment.

Baby-bug started to fuss mildly. Cady picked her up and put the baby to her shoulder, patting her small back.

Darius furrowed his brow. "The only thing that stands out to me is the dude bragging about himself for, as he put it, his 'exemplary citizenship that is so lacking in today's culture.'" Darius emphasized that final phrase with a one-handed quotation mark sign. "On the way to deliver Cady's gift basket, he said he stopped to help a middle-aged woman change her flat tire. I told that to Detective Grace, and she admitted Landes hadn't shared that tidbit in their original interview with him. The flat-tire woman could have accessed the basket while our guy was busy helping her out."

"Did Mr. Landes offer a description of the woman?" Cady's voice emerged rather breathless and her face took on a pinched look.

West stepped closer to her. *Please, God, for Cady's sake, let the description* not *match her mother.*

Darius nodded. "She was about five feet four inches tall, heavyset, had short, light brown hair with sprinkles of gray and 'cat eyes,' his words not mine."

Next to West, Cady let out a sharp gasp.

He swiveled, barely in time to support her as her knees buckled. He helped her into a nearby chair.

Cady's gaze riveted on him as she sat clutching her daughter like a lifeline. Her lower lip trembled, and she was as pale and shaky as that day he'd charged into her bedroom to save her from the intruder.

"Cat Eyes," she whispered hoarsely. "That was my mother's nickname growing up, because her eyes are amber. Just like mine. My mother is a murderer. She's trying to kill me!"

That final sentence emerged in a forlorn wail that ripped sharp claws through West's heart.

THIRTEEN

"We absolutely *are* going to go talk to Mr. Platte about this mysterious H.," Cady told West firmly as they walked out to her Blazer from the hospital. He'd suggested maybe the visit wasn't necessary because now they were almost positive about the identity of the person who was after her. "I need to know if my mother was homicidal in her youth or if her long-term drug abuse morphed her into a cunning and ruthless killer. I can still scarcely believe the damaged person I knew in the care facility has managed to carry out all this mayhem, but there seems to be little doubt left."

"Finding her is the priority," West said. "Triple Threat doesn't have any manpower to spare to look for her. With Brennan on his way to his own place to catch a little shut-eye and with Darius out of commission for some time, that leaves me to stick by your side. We'll have to let the police keep looking for your mother. They have the citywide resources to do the best job of tracking her down, anyway."

"I *do* want them to find her, but I *don't* want them to hurt her."

"I can understand that."

"We have time to drop by the police station before we get lunch and then head for the lawyer's office. I want to communicate my feelings clearly to Detectives Grace and Rooney."

"And we should share with them your thought about the tunnel leading to your family crypt. They will probably want to check it out."

"All right, but please don't mention my mother's journals or their contents to the police," she said as she buckled her seat belt. "At least not until we know for sure that what happened to H. would be of any interest to them."

West went still with his hand on the key in the ignition, and his gaze lasered into her. "I'm not positive we shouldn't tell them everything."

"Please," she repeated. "It's my mother. She's in enough trouble. I can't bring myself to add to it unless we find justification."

"All right." His expression softened. "You're the boss." He turned his head away and started the vehicle.

As they drove out of the parking lot, Cady looked over her shoulder at Livvy. With the car seat's back toward her, she could make out only her daughter's profile, but Livvy's little eyelids seemed to be getting heavy. Not surprising, since she'd been fed and changed before they left the hospital, and it was about time for her morning nap.

Cady suppressed a yawn. If only she could join her daughter in slumber land. She hadn't enjoyed an easy night's rest since the wee-hour attack on her in her bedroom. And West had had even less sleep, not to mention he was in recovery from poisoning. She glanced over at him, but if he was experiencing exhaustion, it didn't show on his face.

"Thank you," she said softly.

He glanced at her, then returned his gaze to the road. "Just doing my job, ma'am." He accompanied the words with a sidelong smile.

A tension she hadn't realized was present loosened its grip around her lungs. The mild teasing assured her that, despite not agreeing with her about telling everything to the cops, he wasn't angry with her.

"You'll get a wonderful recommendation from me to put on your website if you want it." She infused a lighthearted tone into her banter.

"Testimonials from grateful clients are always welcome." He shot her a grin, then sobered. "But only after the client is delivered safely on the other side of whatever caused the need for our services. We're not quite there yet."

"That will happen as soon as my mother's in custody."

"Can't be long now. I mean, where could she be that she could stay in hiding indefinitely?"

A short time later, Detective Rooney asked Cady the same question as she sat with Detective Grace and West around Rooney's battered desk at the precinct.

"The tunnel?" Cady made the tentative thought a question rather than a statement. "At least up until we exposed its location. Now that the tunnel's been discovered, I don't know where she might go." She stretched out her palms in a helpless gesture.

Rooney grunted his skepticism. "If food, water and sanitation were the only problems with the tunnel hideout scenario, I'd say maybe she's been holed up in there until she had to flee last night. But setting up and powering the tech equipment for all the surveillance she's been doing would be difficult for anybody in a primitive shaft over a century old, much less someone who's been institutionalized for years."

"My mother *was* computer-savvy and very smart right up until that last near-fatal overdose."

"Good to know." Rooney started making a note on the pad in front of him.

Cady caught her tongue between her teeth and barely restrained herself from biting down. What was the matter with her that she was bolstering the case against her mother in order to defend the woman's intellect? Cady had testified against one parent in a criminal trial, and now it looked like she was going to be stuck in the same position with the other parent.

Her family was such a mess. Another reason West needed to walk away from her once the danger had passed. Who needed the baggage she came with? Griffon had been her perfect mate because he understood baggage and came with plenty of his own. West, on the other hand, had won a little envy from Griff because of his wholesome, happy-family upbringing.

"We *are* following up on the technology angle," put in Detective Grace. "It's likely she stole the equipment because, supposedly, she left the care facility with only the clothes on her back."

"Since then," West said, "she's had to steal a vehicle, obtain a gun and build a rudimentary bomb. A very resourceful person."

And ruthless and determined. Cady kept those self-evident thoughts to herself.

"When you find her," Cady said with emphasis, "please remember that she's damaged and quite likely not responsible for her actions."

"Rest assured," said Rooney, "we will handle the situation appropriately. Trust us, Mrs. Long."

Cady didn't respond. If her mother was the culprit behind all this terror, she couldn't simply trust the woman's fate to people who didn't care about her. She and West had to find her mom *before* the police did. She trusted him absolutely to go the extra mile to protect both her and her mother, whatever it took.

Carrying her daughter, Cady followed West out of the precinct toward the Blazer, which was parked only a short distance from the station. West's body language said he was in hypervigilance mode, but how likely was it that her mother would try anything this close to the cop shop? Then again, Mom *was* mentally unstable.

"What's that?" Cady pointed toward a sheet of paper flapping in the breeze, caught on the windshield of her vehicle.

"Stop!" West motioned for a halt with a raised hand.

Cady's heart double-timed as he performed a long, careful, 180-degree turn, gaze scanning everything everywhere—people, buildings, vehicles.

"Follow me, and stay close," he ordered with scarcely a glance in her direction. His attention was fully occupied with their surroundings. "The paper could be some useless advertisement, but we're not taking chances."

They advanced slowly toward the Blazer. If Cady crept any nearer to the solid shield of his body, she'd be treading on his boots. The crisp and refreshing autumn atmosphere suddenly felt close and heavy.

She glanced down at her daughter still sleeping in her car seat. What if some sort of attack happened right here and right now? Olivia would be caught in the middle of it.

"I won't let anything happen to you, sweetie." Her tone was low and fierce.

"Hang on to that attitude," West said, matching her tone. "Here we are." They halted beside the Blazer.

He pulled a pair of light gloves from the pocket of his jacket and tugged them on, then snatched the piece of paper from the windshield wiper. Cady held her breath as he examined it. Benign or threatening? His low growl conveyed the latter. Hot tingles shot through her from the top of her head to the soles of her feet.

West turned, holding the paper up before her face.

You can't win, Cady-girl. They'll never find me.

Even if her mother hadn't used the personal nickname, she would have known the handwriting. Not the childish scrawl of the diaries, but a mature, angular script that had featured on her frequent late-to-school notes when she was a child.

"My mother was here." Cady breathed out, staring into West's grim face. "Only twenty yards from the police station. They really aren't going to catch her."

FOURTEEN

An hour later, Cady stared down into her plate of food in the small restaurant where they'd stopped to eat lunch. Normally, chicken fettuccine was one of Cady's favorite meals, but at this moment, every bite was like choking down sawdust.

Across from her, West laid down his fork beside his clean plate. "Rooney looked ready to chew nails and spit out tacks when he read the note. If I live to be a hundred, I'll never forget the expression on his face when we returned to the police station and handed him that paper."

Cady scrunched her face at him. "I'll be happy just to live to my next birthday."

West sat back sharply. "Morbid much?"

Cady's face warmed. "I'm sorry. That was a stupid remark, and I didn't mean it. It's just—"

"No, it's okay. You have every right to be stressed."

"Yes, but not to take it out on you. I sounded like I don't trust your protection."

"Do you?"

"Totally." She met his somber gaze. "I can't think of anyone else I'd trust more with my life."

"Except God?"

Cady dropped her gaze. How was her trust doing in the God department? It had suffered a nearly fatal blow with Griffon's death, but it wasn't gone—not entirely.

Slowly, she nodded. "I'm getting there, and you're helping."

West beamed at her. "One of the nicest things anyone's ever said to me."

"Don't let it go to your head." She smirked at him.

"No worries. I won't. Now clean that plate." He tilted his empty dish toward her. "We all need to keep up our strength."

"Aye, aye, Sarge!"

West made a sour face. "That's navy meets army. Ain't gonna happen, sweetheart."

The final word hung pregnant between them. Cady bent her head over her plate and began shoveling pasta into her mouth. Surely it wasn't his jesting endearment that suddenly put the flavor back in the food? If it was, her heart was in big trouble.

Once Cady joined West in the clean-plate club, changing and feeding Livvy occupied an additional half hour, but finally they got on the road toward the lawyer's office. West again took the wheel. His brow was furrowed and his gaze intense, darting between the highway and the rearview mirrors.

"You think we're being followed?" Cady asked.

"How else did your mother locate us at the police station? I'm more than furious with myself that I didn't spot the tail, and I can't see one now."

"What if there's another way for her to keep tabs on us?"

"You mean like a tracking device? Not on this vehicle. Bren swept the Blazer when he did the house yesterday and came up clean. But I forgot to mention he also installed an anti-tracking device in here, so anything subsequently installed, including anything on our persons or within our personal effects, would be blocked once we got into the vehicle."

"Efficiency is Brennan's middle name."

"Don't tell him that. He might start to think he's worth twice as much as he's being paid."

"Which, if you guys have your way for this job, is exactly nothing."

"I'm glad you see my point, and we *will* have it our way."

A giggle spurted from Cady's lips. "Is that what you call humor in the trenches? You may be the only person on this planet who could make me laugh right now."

They came up on Mr. Platte's office building and, thankfully, one of the spaces in the office lot was empty. West pulled into it.

"Wait just a moment." He got out, head swiveling this way and that. "Okay, let's go inside. No bicycles in sight."

As she emerged from the vehicle, Cady shuddered at the reference to the biker snatching Livvy in her stroller.

"Now that," she said, "was not funny."

"You're right." West collected Livvy out of the back seat. "Nothing about that scenario amused me one bit."

They stepped through the front door and Cady inhaled a long breath of the faintly eucalyptus-scented atmosphere in the reception area. She needed to be calm for this interview, especially if she learned more unwelcome, and potentially tragic, information about her mother.

Jasmine, the twentysomething receptionist, welcomed them and escorted them down a hallway. They continued past the glassed-in office of the paralegal, Maude Hankins, who Cady had chatted with briefly when she came to the office about the will. The woman's salt-and-pepper head was bent over work at her desk and she didn't spare them a glance. The receptionist's knock on the door at the end of the hall was answered by a gravelly voiced invitation to come in. Their escort opened the door and Cady stepped inside with West, carrying Livvy, close on her six.

The balding lawyer, his seventy-plus years evident in a face etched with lines and wrinkles, rose and held out his hand. "Mrs. Long, good to see you again."

Cady said hello and clasped the man's paper-dry palm, then introduced West. Another greeting and handshake were exchanged.

The elderly lawyer peered down at the baby in the car seat and smiled, softening the stern set of his countenance. "I see you brought my tiniest client with you." He lifted his gaze. "Welcome. Please have a seat." The man waved at a pair of padded guest chairs in front of his desk, then settled into his own chair and eyed them expectantly. "What can I do for you today?"

Cady bit her lower lip. How did she begin to ask about intimate family details? Where did she even start?

"We've been sorting through Cady's attic," West said, "and we found a set of diaries from her mother's childhood that mention a half sister with the first initial *H*, but not a full name. Cady is understandably curious about a relative she's never met. Do you know anything about this 'H'?"

West's nonchalant approach would do nicely. She shot him a grateful look and he answered with a small nod.

Mr. Platte pursed his lips. "Hmm. I imagine the diary is referring to Hannah. Sad story."

Cady's insides clenched. "What was sad?"

The lawyer leaned back in this desk chair and folded his hands over his slight paunch. "Hannah was born to your grandmother out of wedlock a year before she married your grandfather and two years before your mother was born. Then your grandfather passed when your mother was only three years old, and the little family went to live with your great-aunt. From Anita, I understand the pair of youngsters were a mighty handful." Platte chuckled. "Hannah in particular. Such a shame we never got to know if she would have straightened out and become a productive adult. She passed from this life at the age of twelve."

"What happened?" Cady leaned forward.

West reached over and enfolded her hand in his own. She tightened her fingers around his palm.

"Meningitis," Platte said.

A pent-up breath blew from Cady's lungs. Natural causes, then. Nothing related to her mother and the childhood feud between half siblings.

"I was attending a conference in Chicago when it happened," Platte went on. "When I returned, I found out I'd missed the funeral and everything. But that sort of illness can strike suddenly and kill quickly, and there had been a rash of it going around at the time. The little girl died in the night in her bed. So sad." Platte shook his head. "Even sadder, it happened only a month after your grandmother passed, leaving May and Hannah orphans. Anita, of course, stepped in and finished raising May. She did her best, but perhaps the derailing of your mother's life could be laid at the door of all the tragedy in her youth—loss of father, mother and sister. As a child, May was so bright and promising, but—" The lawyer left the sentence unfinished and gave his head another shake.

Cady cleared her throat of a lump that had suddenly developed. She and her mother had lots of loss in common. "Was Hannah buried in the family crypt?"

Platte blinked owlish eyes at her. "Why, I imagine so. I never asked. Nor have I had the opportunity to notice. As you know, I was an honorary pallbearer at Anita's funeral, but at my age I did not venture down those steep stairs into the crypt."

"I didn't go down for the interment, either," Cady said.

Platte emitted a chuckle that sounded a bit like fall leaves rustling in the wind. "Understandable. You were quite advanced in your pregnancy. If you want to know the answer to your question, I guess you will have to look for yourselves."

"We'll do that," West said. "Pay our respects."

Cady locked gazes with him and his hand squeezed hers gently. That touch offered the only warmth amidst the chill that was creeping over the rest of her.

At least, now they knew Hannah was indeed dead, but the only assurance Platte had offered them as to the cause was hearsay from his client, Cady's great-aunt. Had there been some sort of cover-up to protect the surviving child, Cady's mother? Or were the horrific events of the past few days turning her into a conspiracy theorist? Better that, than to be right in her awful suspicions.

As they drove away from the lawyer's office, West offered an open ear as Cady shared her theory with him, but he would need more evidence in order to be convinced.

"Until we have any proof otherwise," he answered, "we should take Mr. Platte's version of events at face value. We could go to the courthouse and find Hannah's death certificate."

"That's the kicker." Cady turned bleak eyes on him. "Locating a death certificate could mean nothing. One of my great-aunt's friends—sort of a long-term beau—was a doctor. I remember him being putty in her hands. Whatever she said, his answer was always, 'Whatever you say, my dear Anita.'"

"Colluding in covering up a murder is a pretty hefty accusation to lay at a physician's door."

"It's a hefty accusation to lay at anyone's door, and I'm not saying he would have consciously colluded. But if my great-aunt insisted meningitis was the cause of the sudden death, especially since the disease was going around at the time, he could have caved without a second thought."

"Wouldn't there have been an autopsy?"

"Not necessarily, if the family didn't want one and a doctor certified the cause."

"You make a good case, but I hope you're wrong."

"You have no idea how happy it would make me to be wrong. But first I want to check out the family crypt to make sure that's where she's buried. The name plaque would supply a date of death that would come in handy when asking for a copy of a death certificate."

"What if your mother is hanging out down there? She's a dangerous woman."

"I know, but *you're* with me."

He shook his head. "I'm not sure—"

"Please." The wealth of feeling in her amber gaze tied his heart in knots. "Chances are that she isn't there. At least not anymore. We know she was out and about this afternoon leaving a note on my windshield."

West heaved a long sigh.

"Thank you." Cady reached over and squeezed his hand.

He lifted a corner of his mouth in a half smile. One would think he'd handed her the moon instead of caving to a potentially risky request.

"Here's the deal," he told her. "If we find

any sign that she's in there, we're going to revisit this conversation and, depending on what circumstances we discover, make a wise choice as to whether or not to call in the authorities."

"I can live with that." Cady nodded. "We can at least check for Hannah's burial plaque and look around for any evidence that the tunnel from my house reaches that far. No harm done."

West glanced at the clock on the dashboard— 2:10 p.m. "How's Baby-bug doing?"

Cady swiveled her head toward the back seat. "Just cashed in on her afternoon nap."

"Then she won't need to be fed until she wakes up. Let's drop her off with Bren while we go traipsing around the graveyard. If he's not up by now, he needs to be."

When they arrived at his apartment, Brennan was, indeed, awake and tickled to look after his honorary niece for an hour or so.

"When we get back," West told his partner, "we'll all go to the hospital and visit Darius."

"Let's do it," Brennan said, offering his fist.

West bumped it with his own and ushered Cady toward the door.

"Be careful out there," Brennan called after them.

West looked over his shoulder at him. "You know it."

The drive to the cemetery was short and quiet with Cady brooding beside him. For her sake—no, for all their sakes—her mother needed to be apprehended soon. The woman was a menace to society. The personnel at the center who lost track of her had a lot to answer for.

Yet once the danger was past, what did the future hold for Cady and him? He and the guys had offered to help her with renovations and upkeep on the house, but it was going to be torture hanging around her as nothing more than an arm's-length friend. West shoved the unproductive thoughts away. He needed all his focus right now to ensure that Cady *had* a future—even if it was without him by her side.

"Here we are, then," he said as he turned the vehicle onto the cemetery grounds. "Direct me how to get as close as possible to our destination."

Cady obliged, taking them through winding paved routes almost to the far end of the cemetery.

"There," she said, pointing to a compact but stately chapel building made of weathered white stone.

Stained-glass windows, mainly in dark blues and vivid greens, lined the sides of the main structure. A tall white cross stood on top of what appeared to be a boarded-up bell tower. West parked the Blazer under the shade of an immense old oak tree nearby.

"According to Great-Aunt Anita," Cady said, gaze riveted on the building, "this building is far older than the Frank Heyling Furness house I inherited. The first of my ancestors to immigrate to the United States in the early 1700s came over from England with a significant fortune and the stones and boards and furnishings of this chapel that they'd had dismantled and shipped over from their British estate. In keeping with ancestral tradition, a crypt was dug under the building for family remains, and the chapel hosted an active community congregation until the middle of the nineteenth century when the county bought this whole acreage as a cemetery. Part of the deal, however, was that our family retain perpetual rights to the chapel and the crypt beneath."

"You have a fascinating heritage," West said.

"Fascinating? I hadn't thought of it that way. Tragedy seems to have dogged our steps for many generations."

"How about we work toward bringing that legacy to an end?"

Cady's head swiveled his direction. Her eyes were wide and luminous. "I'd like that very much." Color suddenly flushed her cheeks, and she quickly turned away and got out of the vehicle.

What was that reaction all about? West emerged from the vehicle and trotted to catch up with her as she marched toward the chapel, determination in her stride.

"Whoa!" he called out. "Stick with your bodyguard. Remember?"

She slowed down and he reached her a few feet shy of the chapel's two front steps.

"Sorry." She offered him a sidelong look. "I just want to get this visit over with. The place has always given me the creeps."

"I think the chapel is charming." He scanned the building up and down.

"Structurally? Certainly. I might appreciate the church more if Great-Aunt Anita hadn't always talked like our ancestors were alive down there under our feet. That kind of talk gives nightmares to a little girl."

"Sounds like your great-aunt was quite a unique character."

"I loved her, and she loved me, but 'unique character' pretty much sums her up."

"Where's the key?" West gestured toward the padlock hanging from a heavy chain looped through the handles of the double doors.

"It's on the Blazer key chain along with the house keys."

"Platte gave it to you?"

"The one and only. He kept one and gave me one at the will reading. I didn't bother having the locks changed on this building like I did the house."

"Your mother wouldn't have a key?"

"No."

West snorted. "Then that's another thing she would have had to steal, either from Platte's office or your purse, and since you have your key, I wonder if the lawyer still has his."

"Let me make a quick phone call and find out."

West waited patiently while she talked with the receptionist.

"Mr. Platte's key is right where it's supposed to be," she said as soon as she ended the call. "Maybe that's a good sign that I'm wrong about the tunnel, and she was never here."

"Or maybe she managed to get her hands on one of the two keys, had a copy made and returned it."

Cady shook her head. "My mom may know her way around a computer, but she has no breaking-and-entering skills. She would have had to break into somewhere to get her hands on a key *before* she would have been able to access the tunnel. That scenario is quite a stretch."

"All right, then, assuming she didn't have the skills to sneak into a home or office and acquire a key, if the tunnel access is here, she would have had to break into the chapel in some other way. Neither the chain nor the padlock shows any signs of tampering. Let's walk around the building and see if there are any windows broken or other points of unauthorized access."

A cautious circuit revealed nothing broken or even mildly suspicious. The rear entrance at the base of the bell tower was boarded up and didn't budge when West tugged at it.

"So far so good," West said. "It's possible she was never here."

"I don't know whether to be happy or disappointed about that. We still don't know how to locate her."

They trod up the steps and he pulled the Blazer key chain from his pocket.

"It's this one." Cady pointed to one of the keys.

He undid the lock and opened one of the doors.

"Just to be on the safe side," he said as he drew his gun and stepped over the threshold, motioning Cady to wait on the stoop.

Odors of dust and old woodwork greeted him in the gloom, as well as a mild chill that inhabited closed-up old structures most of the year in this northern climate. The small amount of sunlight that came through the door behind him and filtered through the stained-glass windows outlined dark shapes that he assumed were pews, but the far end of the building was swallowed in blackness. However, no sense of human presence disturbed the peace and quiet.

"The light switch is on the wall to your left," she told him.

He flipped the switch, and a surprising amount of contemporary lighting brightened the space. Yes, those shapes he'd seen were pews. Antiques from the look of them, as was the thick pulpit, dark with age, which stood on the chancel up front. Behind the pulpit, a masterpiece of a carved wooden cross spanned nearly the entire back wall.

"I'm not an antiques aficionado, but this place has a tranquil vibe. Not creepy at all."

Cady came up beside him rubbing her arms

and gazing around the space as if seeing it for the first time. "I can see what you mean. It's a bit of a time capsule. When I was here for my great-aunt's funeral, I hadn't been in the place since childhood and I wasn't thinking about aesthetics. Now, I'm trying to put on fresh eyes. Those stained-glass windows are beautiful...and that cross!"

"Where is the entrance to the crypt?"

She made a face at him. "Way to burst a girl's art appreciation bubble. But I suppose that's what we came for."

West followed her up the aisle to the front of the church. The old hardwood floors had to still be in great shape because they made no creaks or groans. Their movement was nearly soundless. No footprints but their own showed in the thin layer of dust on the floor. Another good sign that this place had not recently served as a killer's hangout. Nevertheless, he wasn't ready to holster his pistol yet.

As they got closer to the chancel, it became clear that what had appeared to be the rear wall where the cross hung wasn't truly the end of the building. A walled-in space jutted out with a door on one side.

Cady motioned toward the door that stood before them. "I'm not working any latches without you checking them out first."

"Quick study." West examined the knob and the door's framework. "I think we're good to go. No booby traps."

"Then let's brave the depths."

The hinges creaked slightly as the door gave way to West's shove. A short concrete threshold introduced a set of cement stairs that were every bit as steep as the wooden ones in the hidden passageway at Cady's house.

"I see what Platte meant. Not a safe descent for the pregnant or the elderly." He frowned at the stairwell. "You might be right about this being the outlet for the tunnel. The stairs are dust-free. They've been swept recently."

Cady shrugged. "I'm not sure the cleanliness means anything. The entire crypt would have been polished up before my great-aunt's funeral. Mr. Platte's office would have seen to that. Dust accumulates at glacial speed inside a stone-enclosed space."

"Point taken." West nodded. "But we still can't be certain. Zip up your jacket. One thing's for sure, it's going to be chillier down there than up here. Let me lead the way."

With a flip of the light switch, he started down the stairs and Cady's footsteps followed. In fact, the crypt seemed to be larger than the footprint of the building above. Marble pillars set at regular intervals supported the chapel structure and allowed for the large open space below. They reached the pale marble floor and West slowly performed a complete turn, scanning the area.

"Impressive!" He let out a low whistle that echoed slightly in the stone cavity. He lowered his gun to his side. "No sign that it's been used as a criminal techno-lair."

Vaults lined every surrounding wall, many of them with name and date plates attached, but a fair number of them remained unlabeled.

"Plenty of room for new occupants," Cady said.

"Not a bad final resting place, though," West responded.

"I'm glad you feel that way," a throaty female voice purred from a spot behind them on the steps. "Because, very soon, it's going to be the final resting place for you both."

FIFTEEN

Tiny spider legs danced down Cady's spine. She knew that voice.

"I have an M18 military-issue pistol pointed at your backs," the woman continued in a deadly smooth tone. "Please turn around very slowly."

Cady's gaze darted toward West. His entire posture had transformed from at-ease to at-the-ready. He offered her a nearly imperceptible nod, and Cady complied with the demand in tandem with him. The woman hadn't been bluffing about the gun. The muzzle of the gun riveted her gaze and stole her breath.

"Drop the firearm, soldier," the woman snapped. "Then kick it away, and both of you get your hands in the air."

West let out an audible huff. Tension radiated from him, but he slowly lowered his gun to the floor and shoved it away from him with a nudge of his toe. Slowly, he lifted his hands to shoulder height.

Cady mirrored his posture. She tore her attention from the gun barrel and allowed her gaze to travel up the woman's thick body to her face.

"You're not my mother," Cady pronounced breathlessly.

She'd known that truth as soon as she heard this woman's voice, but now sight confirmed sound. Sure, the woman fit the description Mitch Landes had given Darius, which roughly corresponded with her mother's height and build, but this woman's "cat eyes" were green, not amber.

In her peripheral vision, she registered West's head turning sharply toward her. "Who is she, then?"

"Maude Hankins, the paralegal from Mr. Platte's office."

"AKA Hannah, the family reject." The woman let out a sour chuckle. "But that was a long time ago."

"Hannah?" Cady burst out. "But you're supposed to be dead."

"I was *supposed* to die, but in typical rebellious fashion, I refused to cooperate. That was Aunt Anita's favorite label for me— rebellious."

"Talk straight," West said. "You're not making sense."

Hannah finished descending the stairs, the pistol never wavering in its focus on them. "How would you feel as a little girl to wake up in an institution from a year-long coma brought on by bacterial meningitis and find out that what family remained to you had disowned you and left you in the care of the state?"

"But how could my great-aunt do such a thing?" Cady said.

"Easy enough to accomplish when I was technically an orphan. The official guardianship for May and I had not yet gone through after our mother's death. Auntie-dearest could still refuse legal custody of me, and she did."

"But why pretend you were dead? They had a funeral for you."

"The better to save face in the community." The woman's eyes flashed fire. "My aunt would not have wanted people to know she'd abandoned a sick child. At the funeral service, I'm sure my aunt's grief was very touching, though I doubt May shed a tear. She always was a cold one, and greedy, too. Now she had our house all to herself."

"This has always been about the house, hasn't it?" West spoke up.

"That house should rightfully be mine, and now I'm going to claim it."

If Cady had ever seen raw, ugly avarice, she was seeing it now. She swallowed against the sandpaper in her throat. "Where have you been all these years? Why didn't you come forward sooner? This seems like such an unnecessary way to get what you want. Killing me won't get you the house."

"There's where you're dead wrong—pun intended." The woman showed her teeth in a wolfish grin. "As your infant's only living relative, I shall graciously step forward and accept guardianship of precious Olivia. The house comes with her. It's a package deal."

Bile erupted on the back of Cady's tongue and blackness edged her vision. This creature *could not* be allowed to gain custody of her daughter.

"Don't!" West's bark froze Cady in the process of gathering herself to leap at Hannah. "At this range, she can't miss you this time."

Hannah's face reddened. "I won't miss a big lug like you, either. Best you remember that. Now ditch your cell phones, both of you."

Cady shrugged. "I left mine in the Blazer in my purse."

"Yes, I see you'd have nowhere to carry it when you're wearing leggings and a pocketless shirt. But you, soldier-man, ditch your cell and then turn around with your back to me."

West tugged his cell from his belt and dropped it to the floor.

As he turned, Cady desperately sought his gaze. She received a wink as her reward. Did the gesture mean West had a plan? *Please, God, let it be so!* Or was he offering empty hope to keep her as calm as possible? Maybe a little of both?

"Directly in front of you and at about thigh-height," their tormenter went on, "whose nameplate do you see?"

"It appears to be your supposed resting place," West answered, his tone tight and even—too even.

Yes, West was definitely planning something. And whether his plan worked or not, he *would* defend her to the death. Of that, she had no doubt.

"Very good," said Hannah. "The seal on the door is broken, as you will see if you look closely. Open it and pull out the casket on its supporting tray."

A sharp click was followed by the soft rumble of small wheels. Cady gritted her teeth and shifted from one foot to another then back again, keeping her weight on the balls of her feet. When West made his move, she needed to be ready to go into action.

"Lift the lid," Hannah prompted.

A long creak grated in Cady's ears. West's deep gasp sent a shiver through her. She'd never heard that level of shock come out of him.

"Cady," his voice rasped, "if this is who I think it is, then you need to have a look."

"By all means, look." Hannah made a slight gesture with her gun.

Cady formed fists with her hands against the compulsion to smack the smugness from her evil aunt's face. Slowly, she swiveled around and stared into the open casket. Her jaw dropped, but no sound came out of her mouth. Pulse throbbing in her ears, her extremities went numb. Then, as if a cork had been popped, a scream erupted from her throat.

"Mother!"

"Cady, she's alive." West grasped Cady's shoulders. He should have prepared her better for what she was about to see, but he'd been so stunned himself.

The scream faded away and her eyes regained their focus.

"She's not d-dead?" Her voice quavered.

"No." West shook his head. "Drugged, I think." He faced Hannah with raised eyebrows, and the woman jerked a confirming nod.

Wordlessly, Cady reached out and put a hand in front of May's face. "I feel her breath. You're right, she *is* alive."

"For now." That self-satisfied purr had returned to Hannah's voice. "Someone needs to take the blame for your deaths and all the other terrible things that have been going on. I think I've done an excellent job so far in setting up that scenario. Now, we can proceed to the final act in this little tragedy."

Bright red suffused Cady's face, and she whirled toward the woman who held them at gunpoint. "You kidnapped my mother from her care facility."

"Don't get wild now," Hannah said. "No kidnapping was necessary. Only a little spying on the overworked and underpaid staff to discover the code to open the rear gate to the fenced-in outdoor recreation area."

West could readily believe that version of

events. It had been all too easy for him to acquire a key card to operate the supposedly secure elevator at the Twin Oaks.

"You're very good at spying," he said, assessing the distance between him and that M18.

He shuffled a small step forward, attempting to close the gap. His only chance to reach their captor before she shot him was to create a distraction so the weapon might waver away from him.

Hannah grinned. "Glad you noticed. Once I had the code, I was able to slip onto the property unobserved one day while May was outside. She was so glad to find out her sister was still alive that she came with me willingly."

Cady's eyes narrowed. "I doubt that. I found several of my mother's journals. You two fought like cats and dogs. There was genuine animosity. You even tried to smother her with a pillow, just like you tried to smother me."

Hannah clicked her tongue. "Ancient history. Let's let bygones be bygones, shall we?"

"One thing, though." West eased himself another few inches in the woman's direction.

"What is it now?" she snapped.

"Why have you suddenly shown up after all these decades?"

"I'm wondering the same thing," Cady said.

"I don't owe either of you an answer." Hannah's eyes narrowed to hard slits. "But I'll give you the short version. My husband passed away two years ago after a long illness that devastated our finances."

"I'm so sorry." Cady's voice bled sympathy in spite of her anger. "I know what it's like to lose someone you love."

The woman snorted. "I didn't say I loved him, but I loved our lifestyle and—poof—it was all gone. We lost the house and everything. He finally passed—or rather, I helped him pass so I could collect a little life insurance to get me started again. Then I decided, why settle for a meager sum and struggle to make rent in a dumpy little apartment in my middle age? Why not go take what should be mine from my not-so-loving family? So, I accepted the paralegal job with that living anachronism, Platte, under my middle name, Maude, and married name, Hankins, so no one would connect me with our family. Then I started working my plan, and here we are."

"Yes, here we are," West said, shuffling marginally forward, "but how could you know that your aunt Anita would die soon and create the opportunity for you?"

"One thing you should know about me." Hannah's expression morphed into a slimy smirk. "I create my own opportunities."

Cady gasped. "*You* killed my great-aunt? But how? The doctor said her bad heart finally gave out."

"Sure. With a little help from me, slipping into the house through the passage and substituting her meds for a placebo. Then it was only a matter of time—a short time, as it turned out."

"That's—that's—" Cady seemed to struggle to find a word strong enough.

"Despicable," West finished for her.

"What you think of me is immaterial." Hannah lifted her chin. "Now, enough chitchat. Soldier-man, kindly take May in your arms, and Cady-dear, help out your auntie by pressing the lotus flower in the fresco to your immediate right."

The hairs on the back of West's neck stood to attention. He needed to make his move while his arms were not burdened with the limp form of Cady's mother. The cell phone he'd been forced to drop lay close to his feet. What if it could provide the distraction he needed? Whatever he did would be a long shot, but it might be their only shot.

Quick as a blink, he kicked out his foot and sent the cell phone skittering across the floor. The noise was sharp and loud in the marble-enclosed space. Hannah jerked, and her head and her gun started to follow the direction of the sound. West leaped toward her stocky figure.

With a shriek, Hannah corrected her reflexive turn. A gunshot echoed through the chamber. White heat struck West's head and blackness swallowed him whole.

SIXTEEN

"West!" Cady melted to the floor beside his prone body.

Blood poured from a gash in the side of his head. Without a second thought, she shrugged out of her jacket and pressed it to the wound with one hand. She laid the other hand on his chest, searching for a heartbeat. It was there, strong and even.

"Thank you, God," she breathed out.

"What a bother!" Hannah snarled. "Now you'll have to drag both this lug and your mother into the chamber by yourself."

The woman sidled over to the wall and pressed the lotus flower. A section of the wall swung open, and the dank chill of the tunnel added to the cold of the stone crypt. Cady shivered but did not leave off applying pressure to West's head. The bullet had only grazed him, but it had packed a mighty punch.

West groaned and his eyes opened, but they remained unfocused. He blinked and his brow furrowed.

"What kind of truck hit me?" he croaked out.

Hannah patted her pistol. "The full metal jacket ammo in this SIG Sauer should make a man feel like a semi sideswiped him."

Cady glared at her aunt.

"Don't mess with me, young lady. I spent four long years in the military. Enlisted when I was eighteen. It was either that or go to prison. Thankfully, my early indiscretions while in foster care are now a sealed record. I wouldn't want any taint from the past to stand between me and obtaining custody of little Olivia."

A growl left Cady's throat. Her muscles tensed for a leap.

"Ah-ah-ah!" Hannah admonished, waggling the pistol. "Just get Mr. Hero into the tunnel, then come back for May."

Ducking her head, Cady put an arm under West's shoulders and helped him to a sitting position. It wouldn't do to let their captor see reflected in her eyes the fierce determination in her heart. One way or another, even if it cost her life, she *would* stop this woman from ever touching Livvy.

Half crawling, half staggering together, she managed to guide West into the tunnel.

"Keep going," Hannah called after them, urging them on until they were a good twenty feet into the passage, and the light from the crypt was surrendering to the darkness of the tunnel. "That's far enough."

Cady let West sink to the chill, damp floor with his back to the side of the tunnel. His deep groan echoed an ominous moan from the wooden support structure around them. Parts of this passage had been burrowed through rock, but other parts were nothing more than dirt and clay shored up by the failing strength of ancient wooden beams.

"Get back out here and help your mother." Hannah's tone was a snarl. "She's waking up."

"I'll be right back," she told West. "Keep holding this jacket to your wound. We need to get the bleeding to stop." She barely made out his bleary gaze in the gloom.

He grabbed her wrist. "Don't lose heart. We're going to get out of this…somehow."

She touched his cheek softly with the tips of her fingers, then disengaged herself without a word. Returning to the crypt, she found her mother stirring in the coffin where her half sister had placed her.

She whirled on her aunt, who was maintaining a wise distance from Cady. "Has she been kept in here the entire time she's been missing?"

"Hardly." Hannah snorted. "She's been leading the pampered life in a cozy little cell in the basement of my home. I only brought her here last night when you cut off my access to *my* house. I figured since you're a bright girl, you were likely to deduce that the crypt might lie at the end of tunnel and would come here to investigate. I made my plans accordingly, and you walked right into them."

"But how have you been getting in and out of the crypt? Sure, I see now how easy it would have been for you, working in Mr. Platte's office, to get your hands on the front door key and have it copied. But the dust in the chapel was undisturbed by any footprints."

The woman shrugged. "I have my ways—because I'm smart. Those nails in the rear entrance's boards are all loose, but you have to trip a mechanism at the base of the door to get it to open up."

Cady's stomach turned as she stared at her aunt Hannah and thought of all the woman had done. How was it possible that she was related to this terrible human being?

A groan from the casket drew her attention toward her mother. The woman's eyes fluttered open.

"Wha—? Where?" May croaked, then blinked and focused in that vague fashion that had been her mother's look since the overdose. "Cady-girl?"

Cady's heart thrilled at the recognition. Her mother hadn't even acknowledged her presence the last time she'd visited the Twin Oaks. Bad on her that it had been years ago. Cady had left the place thoroughly discouraged that day and then got distracted by her taste of happiness with Griffon. She hadn't wanted anything to disturb the idyll of love and belonging that had proven all too short.

Her mother lifted an arm and touched her cheek as if she'd decided to care about her daughter again. "I—I've been writing notes to you. *She* made me do it at first, but then I realized I wanted to talk to you. It's been so long. In that place they put me—" she blinked watery eyes "—I didn't want you to see me there, so when you came to visit, I pretended not to know you so you would go away."

Cady's breath caught. Her mother had always known her, but some convoluted sense of shame at being placed under care had caused her to pretend otherwise.

She leaned closer to her mother. "Did you write a note that said we weren't going to catch you?"

"Catch me? No. I wasn't running away. I wanted to go to you, but *she* wouldn't let me." The childish tones were typical of her brain damage, but clearly glimmers of intelligence remained.

Hannah let out a brief chuckle. "I only needed samples of her handwriting to practice with in case I ever had the opportunity to write something to taunt you. Today, I had reason to go to the Glenside police station on legal business, and who do I glimpse there but May's little daughter and her white knight? Leaving the note on your windshield was a genius touch of opportunity."

As if she were moving through water, Cady's mother struggled to sit up. No doubt the residual effects of whatever drug she'd been given. Cady reached in and helped her mother leave the casket. The woman looked back at what she'd been lying inside and gave a small shriek.

"You!" Cady's mother stiffened and glared at Hannah. "You've always been spiteful.

Mean. When I was little, you hurt me. You hit me. You tried to kill me. Not once, but lots. Mommy didn't believe me, but Auntie did. *That's* why she gave you away."

"And I believe every word Mom just said." Cady took her stand beside her mother.

Hannah rolled her eyes. "Just get into the tunnel. You can do a little mother-daughter bonding while you're waiting for the end to come. You never know quite when the shoring in that passage will collapse. Don't worry, it'll happen soon. I plan to help it along."

With an arm around her mother's shoulder, Cady steadied the older woman, prematurely stooped in her posture, and guided her toward the tunnel opening.

Her mother looked at her and smiled. "*She* showed me the baby book. I'm a grandma."

Cady glared over her mother's shoulder at her evil aunt. "You took Olivia's baby book. Where is it? I want it back."

"Nonsense. You won't be needing it where you're going. Keep moving!"

Near the tunnel entrance, Cady's mother balked. Eyes wide, she turned toward her half sister.

"*This* is the passage we were told about when we were children. You found it. Remember how we used to hunt through the house for a secret door into it?"

Hannah snorted, stepping closer to them. "*I* found all the doors when we were kids and never told you. I've always been the clever one. Here is your chance to go exploring." She took one hand off her gun and made a shooing motion with it toward the gaping darkness of the tunnel.

Only the slightest increase of tension in her mother's back muscles warned Cady of May's plans. In a smooth motion that Cady would never have believed possible of her damaged mother, the woman shoved Cady with both arms toward the meager protection of the tunnel, then whirled and launched herself at her half sister.

With a cry, Cady stumbled backward into the passage, windmilling with her arms. The backs of her legs from the knees down struck a hard object. She lost the battle for balance and sprawled with a thump onto the hard-packed earth.

Sounds of a violent struggle reached her ears as she fought to draw oxygen into her lungs. A gunshot sounded, then another, and then the tunnel door suddenly whooshed shut, sealing her in darkness.

* * *

"Cady!"

West's ribs ached where she'd slammed into him as he was crawling toward the tunnel entrance. He didn't yet trust himself to stand up on his own steam. Was she all right? She'd hit the ground with a mighty thud. He groped in his belt for his utility light and clicked it on. The beam illuminated her still form. She was lying on her back.

He crawled to her and peered into her face. At least she was conscious, gazing up at him with a pained expression. Had a bullet struck her? Suddenly, her chest heaved, and she drew in a deep, rasping breath.

"Are you hit?" He began scanning her with the flashlight for any sign of blood.

"I'm not shot, West." She wheezed a breath. "But someone out there might be." Her gaze flew toward the tunnel exit. "Mom!" she cried out. "Are you all right?"

She fell silent and West went still, straining his ears for any sound from outside the tunnel. Ringing silence answered.

"Let's get out of here," he said. "There's got to be a latch on this side of the door."

"If it's not booby-trapped." She struggled into a sitting position. "Are you still bleeding?"

"I don't think so, but a mariachi band is

playing up a storm in my head." Summoning his strength, West propped his back against the wall and worked himself upward into a standing position. "Here I go."

He stepped away from the wall and staggered. Cady grabbed his arm and led him to the secret entrance door.

"Okay, I've got my feet under me now," he told her. "You can let go."

She complied as he trailed the thin beam of his small flashlight over the expanse of the door blocking their freedom.

"Here it is." He leaned close and examined every inch of the mechanism. "There's no bomb attached."

"Let's go, then!" Cady's breath was hot on his neck.

She must be ready to jump out of her skin, wondering what happened to her mother. West depressed the switch. Nothing happened. He pressed harder. Nothing. He released the latch and it popped off its anchors and fell to the floor.

A long groan escaped his throat. "The door hasn't been booby-trapped. It's been sabotaged. It won't open from this side."

"No, no, no! I have to find out what happened to my mother." Cady barged in front of him and began pounding with her fists on the door. "Let us out of here!"

West gripped her arm. "Take it easy. We'll get out, but this isn't the way."

With a sob, she turned and buried her face in his chest. He welcomed her. Nothing felt more right than Cady in the circle of his arms. If only he could help her understand that he cared for her as much more than a friend. But no amount of "if only" could help her love him back if she didn't. Or couldn't. She'd loved Griff with all her heart. Maybe it was a once-in-a-lifetime love. That's the way it happened with some people. If only Cady wasn't that once-in-a-lifetime for *him*.

Almost immediately, she lifted her head and backed away. He let her go, as he knew he must.

She shivered and hugged herself. "Sorry about that. We need to get out of here. I have to check on my mother."

"Of course. No need to apologize. Here," he said, slipping out of his jacket. "Yours is covered in blood. Put mine on."

"No, I—"

"No argument."

She accepted the garment and shrugged into it. The jacket swallowed her whole. He helped her roll up the sleeves so her hands were free.

"What was that you said about another way out?"

"It's an assumption." West began walking deeper into the tunnel, playing his flashlight beam ahead of him. They didn't need more nasty surprises. "I'm hoping the builders of the tunnel used common sense and provided more than one exit to the passage. I can't picture a tunnel going straight 1300 feet—that's about two city blocks—with no other exits than one end or the other. We have to find an alternate exit. I have one clue."

"What's that?" Her voice came from close on his heels.

"When we were at the house standing at the tunnel entrance, I kept hearing water dripping. Where was it coming from, if not seeping in from the outside somewhere?"

"Of course! It was raining that night, and the water needed some open channel to get into the tunnel. You're a genius."

"Hold the praise. We haven't found the exit yet. If it is an exit and not some fluke of a fissure in the earth."

"We'd better locate it in a hurry because my evil aunt said she was going to collapse the tunnel on top of us."

West stepped up his pace, despite the stab of pain in his head with every footfall. The tarry creosote smell from the cured wooden beams crowded his nostrils. He estimated they'd traveled about a block when the packed earth under their feet started to become soggy and then downright muddy. Their shoes made squishy, sucking noises as they walked.

"I wonder why Hannah didn't track mud into the passageway at the house," Cady mused aloud. "That would have been hard to sweep away."

"She's a planner." West glanced back at her over his shoulder. "I assume she wore galoshes for the trek up the tunnel and then took them off before she went into the house."

"Galoshes would be nice right now. My feet are freezing."

"Stop right here." West halted and Cady bumped up against him. "Look." He pointed his flashlight beam upward, illuminating a chunk missing from the ceiling of the tunnel. The gap surrounded a sizable pipe.

"A drain pipe?"

"If I'm not mistaken, that's a city sewer line. Over time, rain seepage around the pipe from above eroded the top of the passage and it fell in, exposing the pipe. Now, every time it rains, the drippage gets into the tunnel. I'm amazed that the secret passage wasn't exposed when they originally laid the pipe. They would only have to had to dig a foot or two deeper."

"How does that help us?"

"It might not." West frowned and met her expectant gaze. Her patent trust spread warmth through him, despite his gooseflesh from the chill of the tunnel. "Then again, it might." He offered a small smile. "I wouldn't be surprised if the whole section of earth above us is weakened by the gaping hole below. A little determined digging could open an escape route if it doesn't drop the tunnel on top of us. So, it's going to be risky."

"So is doing nothing." She flopped her arms against her sides. "But digging with what?"

"What did I tell you before about a soldier never being without his knife?"

"How are you going to reach way up there to chop out the earth?"

"I'm not. You are. I'll get down on my hands and knees, and you'll have to stand on my back. It's going to be a dirty job."

"What do I care about a little mud and muck?" Her chin jutted. "I need to find my mother, and I need to get back to Olivia. She's got to be starving by now."

"That means we can count on Brennan to be looking for us, which can only be a good thing."

"What are we waiting for? Let's get started."

West handed her the knife and the flashlight, then got down on his hands and knees. The cold mud sucked him in to above his wrists and around his knees. It wouldn't be long before his hands went numb.

"Step up on my back. Your head should be nearly level with the pipe, and you can use it to steady yourself. Then start chopping at that loose earth above it."

Her weight pressed down on him. Thankfully, she was wearing flats, not heels. Chopping noises, accompanied by grunts of effort, reached his ears. Mud and dirt began raining down on him.

"The soil is coming loose pretty easily." She puffed. "But it keeps falling in my eyes."

"I'm not surprised. It's raising the dirt level around me but keep going. I'll let you know if I'm about to be buried.

"Stop," he called a few minutes later.

She climbed down off his back and he stood up, brushing clods from his body. With fingers stinging from the cold, he took the flashlight from her and directed it toward the hole she was digging above them.

"Impressive. You've made several feet of progress."

"Yes, but the soil is becoming firmer, and I don't know how much farther we need to go to get to the top. I'm already at the end of my reach."

"Time for you to sit on my shoulders."

He knelt down and she climbed on. Slowly, he rose, clinging onto her lower legs to help her balance. Clods of dirt and small roots began raining down on him again. Then the roots began to get bigger, accompanied by the odor of loamy topsoil. Suddenly, the chunks of earth contained bits of grass.

"I see the sky!" Cady burst out. "It's just a small opening, but—"

Her words were swallowed by a deep boom, like that of a detonating IED. The sound came from a location only a short way up the tunnel. An ominous rumbling began, and the earth shook beneath West's feet. He struggled to maintain his balance.

"The tunnel is collapsing!" he shouted. "Get out now!"

He put his hands underneath her and shoved her upward. More dirt and grass poured down on him, and then she left his grip. With a crack and a groan, the tunnel beam nearest him deserted its post and plummeted to the ground mere inches from his head. Great gobs of earth began crowding around him. He leaped upward, grabbed the sewer pipe with both hands and performed a pull-up. The imploding tunnel sucked at him, but he levered himself to a squat on top of the damp pipe.

Fresh air and sunlight beckoned through the narrow hole above him. But as he attempted to stand, his feet scrambled for purchase on the slippery copper.

An arm reached down through the hole. Not Cady's. Too hairy and masculine. He grasped the offered hand, steadied himself and surged upward. His shoulders broke new soil as he sprawled out onto the firm, welcoming lawn of Cady's backyard mere feet from the utility shed.

A familiar face grinned down at his prone body.

"Hello, again, Mr. Foster," said Detective Rooney. "I gotta say, this has been the most unusual case I've ever worked."

SEVENTEEN

Seated in Olivia's nursery, Cady kissed the top of her baby's downy head, giving silent thanks to God for the privilege of feeding her precious child once again. Cady was still a mass of dirt and mud, but Olivia didn't care about her mother's attire and cleanliness as long as dinner was served. Brennan had brought her right over as soon as West called him to say they were all right. Thankfully, the Triple Threat team possessed an emergency car seat for their honorary niece.

When Cady and West didn't return to Brennan's place in a timely manner, he had called Detective Grace to have the police start looking for them, beginning with the chapel and crypt. They'd found Cady's mother in the crypt badly wounded and called an ambulance to take her to the hospital, but their nemesis, Hannah, was missing. When Cady and West had not been found there, Rooney had gone to Cady's house, which was how he had been present to give West a hand, literally, in escaping that death-trap tunnel.

The murmur of voices carried to her from downstairs. That would be West continuing to bring Detective Rooney up to speed on all that had happened. Detective Grace was still at the scene of the crime at the cemetery.

Olivia's eyes drifted closed. Cady rose and placed her daughter in the crib. The little girl let out a contented sigh. Cady would do the same as soon as she had a shower. A half hour later, she came downstairs, hair still wet, to find West and Brennan sitting at the kitchen table, but no Rooney.

"The detective didn't want my statement?" she asked.

"His partner called him," Brennan said, "and he took off like his feet were on fire."

"I'm sure he'll expect a detailed statement later," West added.

Cady did a double take at him and sucked in her lips to hold back a laugh.

"What?" He spread his grimy arms and grinned at her, teeth gleaming white in a mud-streaked face. "Not tidy enough for you?"

"Did *I* look like that?"

"Oh, yeah" and "You know it" came out in sync from the men.

Cady shook her head. "The only clean part of you is that white bandage around your head. You really need to let a doctor examine your wound."

"No need," West said. "Bren is a pretty fair medic. How do you think we managed on the battlefield? Not very often we had a doctor in our back pocket."

Brennan nodded. "I got the med kit out of our company truck, disinfected the wound and threw in a few stitches where needed. Other than that, all symptoms of concussion have subsided. I can vouch that Sergeant Westley Foster has a very hard head."

The men exchanged grins, but Cady frowned.

"If macho time is over, then I need to insist that an actual doctor examine you, West. You guys didn't let me get by without professional attention when I had a little head bump."

"She makes a persuasive case," West said to Brennan.

"I'll take you," Cady said. "I need to go to the hospital and find out how my mother is doing, anyway. Brennan, can you stay with Olivia? She's fed and changed and should sleep for a while."

The Kentuckian smiled. "I'm your willing

nursery grunt. I hope she wakes up before you get back so we can have a little bonding time."

West rose. "I wouldn't let you go to the hospital alone, anyway. Hannah's out there somewhere. You won't be safe until she's caught."

"Surely she's running as fast and far away from here as possible."

"We can't assume that. Not with this woman. She's obsessed."

"I agree," Brennan said. "We're not ready to sign off on this job yet."

"All right." Cady lifted her hands in surrender.

"But," West said, "I'm going to make a quick pit stop at my house for a shower and change of clothes. *Then* we go to the hospital."

Cady groaned. "Fine, but make it quick."

"You have no idea how fast a soldier can shower."

"Even one as grimy as you?"

"*Especially* one as grimy as me. Let's go." West led the way out to the Triple Threat truck, because her Blazer was still at the cemetery.

Inside twenty minutes he was clean, and they were almost to the hospital.

"We've had way too many visits to this place," Cady said as the massive building came in view. "There's such a great sadness in my heart for all the devastation that's been wrought."

"You're a tender soul in spite of all that you've been through. I admire that."

"But my family—"

"Your family is not *you*. The way I see it, you have the start of a perfectly wonderful family with Olivia. Your future is a blank page that beckons you to write whatever you want on it."

"Wow!" She gazed over at him. As it had been doing lately, that strong, unique profile sent a zing through her heart. She quickly looked away. "That's amazingly poetic."

"What? You don't think an ex-soldier can have any poetry in him?"

"I didn't mean that at all. I meant I hadn't considered my life from that perspective, and it took me by surprise. You constantly challenge and inspire me when I default into Eeyore mode. You're good for me."

"I am, aren't I." The solemnity of his words seemed like a container for so much left unsaid.

Cady studied him as he guided the vehicle into a parking spot. She would probe him for his deeper meaning if she didn't so badly need to get inside the hospital and find out what was happening with her mother.

They got out and headed for the emergency entrance. An ambulance idled near the door with a pair of EMTs chatting on the sidewalk next to it.

"—never seen anything like it," one said as they drew near.

The other grimaced and shook his head. "To die in an underground crypt. The world just got weirder."

Cady's heart leaped into her throat and she sprinted up to them. They cast astonished eyes on her.

"Who? Who died in the crypt?" She gripped one of them by his scrubs shirt.

The man raised his arms and tried to back away, but Cady's grip was unbreakable.

"Tell me!" She shook him.

"Take it easy." West's gentle tones came from behind her.

His hands reached around and helped her disengage from the hapless emergency medical technician. Both EMTs were gazing at her like she'd lost her mind.

"I'm so sorry," she said, clapping her

hands to her cheeks. "But I have to know. My mother was shot in our family crypt less than two hours ago. Is she— Is she—"

"Dead?" One of them finished her sentence for her.

"No," said the other one. "We brought the GSW in an hour ago. She was in bad shape, but alive when we delivered her."

"GSW?"

"Gunshot wound," West said.

"Then who did you just bring in?"

"A Jane Doe covered in muck. They're going to have to give her a bath to get a look at her and start the ID process."

The other EMT shook his head. "Yeah, well, I think the cops have an inkling of who she is, but they weren't saying just yet."

Cady's breathing came in short gasps. She whirled toward West. She had more than an inkling. "We have to check this out."

"I agree." West's warm, strong hand closed around hers.

She gripped it like a lifeline.

He looked toward the EMTs. "Which way is the morgue?"

How could one dainty hand in his turn this grim walk down hospital corridors into a stroll in the park? He was so far gone on this woman. The road signs in his life might just as well read Heartache Ahead. He loved her too much not to give her all the space in the world to find happiness. If their suspicions about the identity of the dead woman were correct, then the time to pull back from Cady lay dead ahead.

No pun intended. The words trailed through his mind as he caught sight of a plaque pointing them in the direction of the morgue. They were getting close to finding a crucial answer.

A pair of double doors sprang open ahead of them and Detective Rooney walked into the hall. At the sight of them, his expression registered surprise and then returned to its usual flatness.

"News travels fast," he said. "I was about to call you."

"We were here to check on Cady's mother," West said.

His quick glance at Cady showed her face ice-pale and a muscle visibly twitching in her jaw. Who could blame her for grinding her teeth?

"How is your mom?" Rooney asked.

"We don't know yet," Cady spoke up. "We

heard about the Jane Doe from the crypt. Is it her—my aunt?"

Rooney's gaze rested solemnly on Cady. "Would you like to see?" The tone was gentle and inviting, not pushy.

"Please," she said. "It would give me peace of mind."

"I thought as much."

West's eyebrows climbed toward his scalp. Who would have thought Rooney could possess an ounce of sensitivity? But who was he to think badly any longer of a guy who had saved his life?

The man led them through the double doors into a cool, dimly lit room where several parallel gurneys held silent and shrouded occupants. He took them to the nearest gurney.

"Are you ready?" His gaze was on Cady.

She nodded and he tugged back the sheet. The woman's face was still grimy, but West had no trouble recognizing Hannah. Beside him, Cady let out a tiny cry and leaned into him. He put an arm around her shoulders.

"It's her," she breathed out softly.

"It's over," West said.

"For you it is." Rooney's gruff tones had resurrected. He made a sour face. "For me, it's on to the next case."

"What happened?" Cady said. "By the looks of things, she got caught in the tunnel collapse."

Rooney shrugged beefy shoulders. "When we found your mother on the floor of the crypt, she regained consciousness long enough to tell us how to open the secret door. We found this one—" he swept a hand over the body on the gurney "—only a short way inside. One hand was still clutching a remote control. We assume she used it to trigger the destruction of the tunnel."

"Couldn't she have done that from outside the passage?"

"Again, this is conjecture based on logic, but we assume the bomb didn't go off like she intended. Maybe the range wasn't right, so she went inside the passage to get closer to it. Then suddenly—*kaboom!*—and she didn't make it out in time."

Cady reached out and touched the woman's cheek, then jerked her fingers back. "So cold already. I'm going to work on forgiving her." She looked up at West with pleading eyes. "You'll help me, right?"

West's mouth went dry. How could he bear to hang around Cady long enough to help her with spiritual issues when his heart was already in shreds over her?

A sudden chuckle from Rooney pulled his attention away from Cady. The man was heading out of the room. Arm still around her shoulders, West drew Cady toward the double doors after him.

"Let's go check on your mother," he said.

"And Darius, too," Cady added.

On the surgical floor, they were directed to a sitting room to await the outcome of May's surgery. Barely had they stepped into the waiting area when a woman in full scrubs arrived.

"Is anyone here for May Johnson?"

Cady rushed forward and West followed.

"Me," Cady said. "I'm her daughter."

"Come with me." The surgeon led them into a small anteroom and closed the door.

West was practically holding his breath while Cady wrung her hands.

The doctor turned toward them and smiled. "Good news. We were able to repair the internal damage, and with blood transfusions, antibiotics and proper bed rest, I expect she'll make a full recovery."

Cady squealed and flung her arms around West. He wrapped her close, inhaling the fresh scent of her shampoo. *Thank you, Jesus.* His happiness for Cady couldn't have been greater if it was his own mother who'd received the positive prognosis.

The doctor opened the door, then turned and smiled at them again. "You and your husband look like you could use some rest. We'll take good care of Mrs. Johnson while you take care of yourselves." She withdrew and closed the door.

West loosened his hold on Cady and she drew back, looking up at him.

"Husband?" she whispered.

West's heart squeezed in on itself. At least she wasn't pooh-poohing the idea as nonsense. He turned away, walked over to the window and gazed down onto the hospital lawn.

"I have a confession to make," he told her.

"What is it?" Her voice came from directly on his six. He hadn't heard her walk up behind him over the pounding of his own pulse in his ears. "I've sensed you've been holding something back from me. Don't you know you can tell me anything?"

West turned around and gazed down into her sweet, beautiful upturned face. "What I'm about to tell you comes with absolutely no expectations. I just need to say it. Then we never need to talk about it again." He swallowed deeply. "I'm in love with you, Cady Long. God, help me, because I can't seem to help myself."

For an eternity, she gaped up at him.

"Say something...anything," he prompted.

"You love me?" Her words vibrated with an intensity that quivered in his bones.

"Is that so hard to believe?"

"Yes." A smile burst over her features. "I thought someone like Griffon—you know, with a hard-knock past—was the only kind of guy who could love me."

West gripped her shoulders. "You're the sort of woman most men dream of loving—kind, honest, faithful, trustworthy, and let's not forget, courageous in the face of all kinds of fear and danger. You're beautiful, inside and out."

Tears welled up in Cady's eyes and trickled down her cheeks. "I have something to say to you, Westley Foster. I—I think I love you back. At least I'm heading pell-mell in that direction."

"Do you mean it?" He dipped his face close to hers.

"With every molecule of my being. Besides possessing the priceless gift of helping me laugh, you're my handsome, intelligent,

resourceful and brave personal protector."
She flung her arms around his neck.

How could he even begin to describe his
feelings as his lips claimed hers? Wonder?
Joy? Jubilation? Yes, all the above and much,
much more.

EPILOGUE

Eighteen Months Later

Hand in hand, Cady and West stood on the sidewalk gazing at the Frank Heyling Furness home she had inherited. Contractors were going in and out of the front door with renovation materials, and painters were busy on the outside trim.

Cady looked up at her husband-to-be and smiled. "I'm glad we let the property revert to the county historical society as a future museum. The place was really too much of a handful to be a private home anymore. This way, many people will be able to enjoy its grandeur and history. I think Great-Aunt Anita would be happy about that."

"We can bring Baby-bug here for a tour when she gets a little older and can appreciate it," West said.

Cady looked down at the stroller by their

knees where a nearly two-year-old Livvy was observing with bright eyes a pair of butterflies flitting nearby.

"And any other children we might have," she added to West's thought.

"Yes, we'll bring them all. The more the merrier." West laughed and drew her hand to his lips.

Cady thrilled to his warm kiss. How did she deserve to be so blessed? The answer was simple: she didn't deserve it. No one *earned* true love like this. It was a gift of grace, pure and simple. She was coming more and more to understand that truth, both in her relationship with God and with West. He'd been right. Their future was a blank page, and with the Lord's help, they were filling that page day by day with both weathered challenges and happy times.

Together, they'd bought a lovely Victorian home not far from here that they were in the process of renovating themselves. And Cady was indulging her penchant for antiques in its furnishings. Besides being a full-time mom, she was also going to school to become a psychologist. It was a good career choice for her, considering her mother was now under her personal care. Though May would always display childish behaviors, time had evidently wrought enough healing in her mother's psyche that she had been deemed sufficiently well-adjusted to live under supervision outside of an institution. Cady and West were building her a small suite of her own within their house.

West's business had taken off. Triple Threat Personal Protection Service had more clients than it could handle, and as a result, West had hired more personnel and was traveling less and less while he handled the logistics from the office. This situation suited Cady more than fine, seeing that tomorrow afternoon she would once again change her surname when she and West said "I do" in an intimate ceremony at the small, welcoming local church they'd begun attending.

Cady would always love and remember Griffon, treasuring the time they'd had together. She and West were committed to bringing Livvy up to know all about her biological father and to revere him. But West would be the one who would raise her. They were truly starting a new family legacy, one that would be healthy and strong and grounded in the Lord.

West tugged on her hand, drawing Cady out of her reverie. They continued on their walk together, enjoying the spring greenery, colorful blooms, and the pleasant floral scents the warm breeze carried to them.

Cady looked up at him and as always, that strong profile lent her heart an extra kabump. "You are going to be a great father."

"How do you think I'm going to do in the husband department?" He sent her a mischievous grin.

She canted her head with a small smirk. "Hmm. I'm sure I'll be letting you know."

West tilted back his head and bellowed a laugh. "I'm sure you will."

"But I know one thing." She leaned into him. "I can hardly wait to find out."

* * * * *

Dear Reader,

It was my pleasure to finally usher Cady and West into their happily-ever-after. I hope you enjoyed the journey, and I also hope that certain aspects of the story ministered blessing or insight to your hearts.

Families can be complicated—not always as complicated as Cady's, but certainly with their challenges. Nevertheless, God's plan for human life has always revolved around the mutual love, belonging and safety intended to be found in family groups. In fact, the family is so foundational that Scripture uses the family analogy to describe our relationship with all others who claim the name of Christ. No wonder the institution of the family has been under perpetual attack up to this present time! Even when it looked like Cady had lost all her family relationships through one tragedy or another, God called others into relationship with her to fill those roles. We can count on God to do the same for us, starting with Himself as our heavenly Father.

West took his role of protector and defender of Cady and Olivia as a sacred trust delivered to him by God. Such courage and faithfulness do credit to the military credo and, even more significantly, honors the name of Christ. In a sense, all Christians are called to display such courage and faithfulness in ensuring justice and provision for the widow and the fatherless, i.e. all the defenseless. In so doing, we serve our fellow human beings, particularly those of the household of faith, and we glorify God.

I enjoy interacting with my readers. You can visit me at www.jillelizabethnelson.com or stop by my Facebook page at www.Facebook.com/JillElizabethNelson/Author. I'd love to "see" you there.

Blessings,
Jill Elizabeth Nelson

ReaderService.com has a new look!

We have refreshed our website and
we want to share our new look with you.
Head over to ReaderService.com
and check it out!

On ReaderService.com, you can:

- Try 2 free books from any series
- Access risk-free special offers
- View your account history & manage payments
- Browse the latest Bonus Bucks catalog

Don't miss out!

If you want to stay up-to-date on the latest at the Reader Service and enjoy more Harlequin content, make sure you've signed up for our monthly News & Notes email newsletter. Sign up online at ReaderService.com.

RS19

"Are you annoyed with me?"

Marc asked with beguiling innocence.

He couldn't be serious, Diana decided. Nobody was that dense. "You order me around, treat me like a child, fling around empty endearments, and you wonder if I'm annoyed? Take a good guess, *mon grand general*."

He grinned at her. "Turn on the broiler and get me the cheese and butter."

He was teasing her, of course. At least he had a sense of humor, however irritating it might be. "All right, but you'll be lucky if they don't wind up on your exalted head."

"Do you lose your temper this way with your clients, too, or just with me?"

"Monsieur Rochard, even the worst of my clients isn't as aggravating as you are."

"At least you're not indifferent to me. The endearments are completely sincere, by the way. I'm crazy about you. Come taste this. You'll feel much better...."

Dear Reader,

The Silhouette **Special Edition** selection has seldom been more satisfying than it is this month. For starters, beloved **Nora Roberts** delivers her long-awaited fourth volume of THE O'HURLEYS! *Without a Trace* joins its "sister" books, the first three O'Hurley stories, all now reissued with a distinctive new cover look. Award-winning novelist **Cheryl Reavis** also graces the Silhouette **Special Edition** list with a gritty, witty look into the ironclad heart of one of romance's most memorable heroes as he reluctantly pursues *Patrick Gallagher's Widow*. Another award-winner, **Mary Kirk**, returns with a unique twist on a universal theme drawn from the very furthest reaches of human experience in *Miracles*, while ever-popular **Debbie Macomber** brings her endearing characteristic touch to a wonderfully infuriating traditional male in *The Cowboy's Lady*. Well-known historical and contemporary writer **Victoria Pade** pulls out all the stops (including the f-stop) to get your heart *Out on a Limb*, and stylish, sophisticated **Brooke Hastings** gives new meaning to continental charm in an unforgettable *Seduction*. I hope you'll agree that, this month, these six stellar Silhouette authors bring new meaning to the words **Special Edition!**

Our best wishes,

Leslie Kazanjian
Senior Editor

BROOKE HASTINGS
Seduction

Silhouette Special Edition

Published by Silhouette Books New York

America's Publisher of Contemporary Romance

For the people who helped me with this book:
Judy Myers, Bianca and Bruce Raines,
Alan Raines and David Kaplan,
and Sandra Cope and Dr. N. Vijayan.
Thanks to you all.

SILHOUETTE BOOKS
300 East 42nd St., New York, N.Y. 10017

ISBN: 0-373-09630-5

First Silhouette Books printing October 1990

Printed in the U.S.A.

BROOKE HASTINGS

is a transplanted Easterner who now lives in California with her husband and two children. A full-time writer, she won the Romance Writers of America's Golden Medallion Award for her Silhouette Romance, *Winner Take All*. Brooke especially enjoys doing the background research for her books and finds it a real challenge to come up with new plot twists and unique characters for her stories.

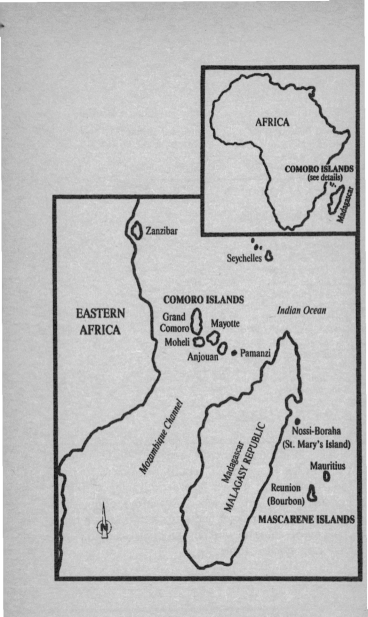

Chapter One

Diana Van Slyke was glad Gertrude Klostermann was dead. It wasn't a nice thought, but then, Mrs. Klostermann hadn't been a nice woman. As a child, Diana had watched helplessly as her father sold Mrs. Klostermann some of the family's most precious heirlooms; as an adult, she'd repeatedly tried to buy them back. The old witch had toyed with her for eight long years, saying yes and then changing her mind, enjoying the game almost as much as she'd enjoyed acquiring a fabulous collection of art and antiques.

Her will hadn't been a surprise, not to Diana, who might have been Gertrude's favorite victim but certainly wasn't the sole one. After promising paintings and furniture to the most prestigious museums in New York, she'd left them exactly nothing. Instead, everything would be sold at auction, with the proceeds going to her closest relation, a great-nephew in Germany named Dieter Schmidt. Diana could imagine the pleasure it must have given her to picture museum curators, antique dealers and wealthy collectors fighting like piranhas over each and every item that came under the hammer.

She'd named Conable's as the consignee, no doubt because no auctioneer in New York could separate bidders from their money as adroitly as the company's president, Nelson Conable, Jr. Diana arrived at the firm's Madison Avenue auction house about an hour before the seven-thirty sale. The galleries were already packed with well-dressed people taking last-minute looks at the merchandise to be sold off. She made small talk with Nelson for a minute, then registered for a paddle number and made her way through the north exhibition hall to the gallery at the far end.

It held antiques from the seventeenth and eighteenth centuries, most of them crafted in America but a few imported by wealthy colonists before the Revolution. The pieces here were worth considerably less than the exquisite European furniture displayed elsewhere, and Diana hoped that would work in her favor. If she were lucky, the bidders would hold back, waiting for the most exclusive merchandise to go on the block before loosening their purse strings; if not, they would succumb to a mounting frenzy of competitiveness and bid record amounts on absolutely everything. Knowing Nelson's skill with the hammer, she was afraid it would be the second.

She gazed at the pieces that once had belonged to her family. There was an oval gateleg table and eight walnut banister armchairs; a massive, Dutch-style secretary, an ancient oak chest and a Queen Anne-style painted chinoiserie highboy; a looking glass and set of chairs in the Chippendale style, a damask-covered settee and a mahogany sideboard inlaid with marquetry of tulipwood; and finally, a large, boldly patterned carpet imported from Turkey.

She walked to the chinoiserie highboy and pulled open a drawer. This graceful chest, with its slender cabriole legs and rich gilding, was her favorite piece. She hadn't seen it in over fifteen years, since she'd been a girl of sixteen, but she remembered every detail.

The bottom-center drawer was a little tight, and the carved design at the base had a sprinkling of tiny, almost invisible nicks. During her childhood, her mother had told her fanciful stories about the golden pagodas, dragons and flowers that adorned its dark, lustrous surface. Her throat tightened. Her mother had died when she was nine, but the treasures in this room still linked them together.

She caressed the wood as if it were an old and dear friend. She'd sacrificed a great deal for the money that would enable her to buy back this chest and the other family heirlooms in this room—her dreams of a career as a scholar, any semblance of a normal life, even the marriage she'd once been naive enough to believe was happy. She didn't doubt for a moment that it would be worth it. She couldn't. It would have been too painful.

As she turned away, she noticed a tall man with dark curly hair examining the Dutch-style secretary as if he definitely meant to buy it. He felt inside pigeonholes and tested drawers. He peered at hardware and ran his fingers over decorative molding. Afterward, apparently satisfied, he strolled to the mahogany sideboard and inspected it just as thoroughly. It was in virtually flawless condition and would probably fetch more than any other antique in the room.

She figured it was just a coincidence that he was interested in two different items from the Van Slyke collection, but then he consulted his catalog and walked straight to the damask-covered settee, and she began to fear that it wasn't. Wanting to size up the competition, she moved a little closer.

Her first impression was one of wealth, composure and confidence. He wasn't a Wall Street type; his hair was too long, the style too casual. He wasn't an effete socialite, either. His strong, angular features were too rugged-looking. His suit was European in cut, a nubby gray-and-black silk weave with pleated, slightly baggy trousers and a loosely constructed double-breasted jacket. He'd added a white shirt, patterned tie and tasseled loafers.

The outfit was dashing and expensive, but in Diana's opinion only a few categories of men could wear such clothes without looking effeminate or silly. Great-looking hunks in their teens or early twenties, but this man looked about thirty. And sophisticated Europeans. There was nothing effeminate or silly about him. He radiated an erotic virility that even Diana noticed, and she was usually oblivious to such things.

He was probably a foreigner, then, but it was unusual for Europeans to collect American antiques. She stared at him. She had the oddest feeling that he was Gertrude Klostermann's great-nephew, Dieter Schmidt. Just because the old witch had been dead for four months, that didn't mean she'd stopped making Diana's life miserable. Maybe she'd left him instructions to bid on the very pieces Diana wanted, but if so, he damn well wasn't going to get them.

She walked over to him, smiling at him as he sensed her presence and turned around. Not a trace of resentment or competitiveness showed on her face. Van Slykes never displayed such vulgar emotions in public. It would have been unthinkably common.

"Good evening," she said to him in German. "I'm Diana Van Slyke." She knew he would recognize the name Van Slyke from the provenances listed in the catalog. The phrase *From the mansion on Van Slyke's Island* appeared after the description of each item her family had once owned.

He looked startled at first—almost stunned—but quickly composed himself. His eyes were a light, icy blue. Very Teutonic, she thought.

She offered her hand, but instead of shaking it, he brought it to his lips. He was strikingly handsome, but she heard no bells peal as he brushed a kiss across the back of her hand, felt no rush of warmth. Ever since her divorce, the only invitations she'd received—or cared to—had been strictly business.

"I never would have guessed that," he said with a smile. "From what I was told about you, I assumed you were older. More intimidating. And far less beautiful and charming."

He made a brief but obvious inspection. She was wearing a black-and-white silk sheath and pearl jewelry, a softer outfit than her usual business suits but hardly a sensual or revealing one. As usual, she'd coiled her curly red hair into a bun at the nape of her neck and applied only a little makeup, just enough to cover her freckles, darken her brows and outline her lips. Among the stunning and glamorous women of New York, she was nothing special. Not thin or elegant enough—pretty perhaps, but certainly not beautiful.

It didn't occur to her to wonder what this stranger thought of her; she was too curious about who he was. Far from sounding foreign, he'd had no detectable accent at all. And he'd looked at her so strangely at first. Why? What had he been told about her, and why would he have discussed her with anyone in the first place?

"I'm sorry," she said. "I thought you were Dieter Schmidt—Mrs. Klostermann's great-nephew."

He looked amused. "And why would you think that?"

"It was a hunch. The way you're dressed . . . I thought you were European."

"I am. French."

Although he looked the part, she was more bewildered than ever. "You don't sound French. You sound American."

"Thank you." He paused. "I think." He pointed to the mahogany sideboard. "That's my favorite piece—that and the chinoiserie chest. I'm going to buy both of them."

Buy, she repeated to herself. Not *bid on*. He'd spoken pleasantly enough, but as far as Diana was concerned, he'd thrown down a figurative gauntlet. Again, nothing of her feelings showed on her face. Not only would it have been uncultured to contradict him; there were better ways than arguing to get what one wanted.

"You've got excellent taste," she said. "They're the two best pieces in the room. They won't come cheap."

He nodded matter-of-factly. "Yes. Close to twice what's listed in the catalog, perhaps."

Obviously he had deep pockets. She'd hoped he wouldn't. She didn't want him bidding her up. "Are you a dealer, then, Mr . . . ? I'm sorry. I don't believe you told me your name."

"You're right. I didn't." He gazed at her for several seconds longer, making her wonder if there were remnants of dinner on her face. "I'm not a dealer. I'm not even a collector. I moved to New York about two weeks ago, into a town house in the East Sixties. I'm in the process of furnishing it. When I heard that some pieces from Van Slyke's Island were going to be auctioned off, I decided to take a look. And now that I've looked . . ."

"You've decided to buy." If he'd just purchased a town house on the East Side, his pockets were as deep as the Cayman Trench. "Is there any special reason for your interest?"

"In Van Slyke's Island?" He smiled again. "Of course there is. I hope you won't be insulted if I suggest that we come to a private arrangement. If you don't bid against me on the sideboard and chest, I won't bid against you on the other Van Slyke pieces."

He was nothing if not mysterious. Under other circumstances Diana might have been intrigued, but she had the sense that he was withholding information simply to frustrate her, and that annoyed her.

It would have been both rude and foolish to let it show, though, so she started to explain why these pieces were so important to her. "You said you'd spoken to people about me. If you have—"

"Not people. One person. An old family friend. If my information was wrong, it's because most of what she knows comes from the newspapers and TV."

"And what does your friend think she knows?"

"That you're an investment banker who's put together a string of major deals. She says they call you Princess Di on the Street." He meant Wall Street. "You're also the president of the Van Slyke's Island Foundation, which you established in order to restore the old mansion on the island. You plan to turn it into a museum eventually. You have no use for the New York social scene but show up at fund-raisers every now and then, when the charity is one your family supports."

All of that was common knowledge. There had even been an article in *National Geographic* the previous March mentioning Van Slyke's Island, Diana's work there and the family's connection to a French pirate who'd married one of Diana's ancestors. He'd died at sea in 1698, supposedly leaving a secret fortune behind. Crackpots who wanted to search for buried treasure had been plaguing her ever since.

"Your friend's information was accurate," she said. "About Van Slyke's Island—"

"There was one thing more. She said your escort is always your father." He moved closer, his eyes warm with admiration.

She took a confused step backward. She wasn't used to men staring at her that way. It was her talent for business that usually interested them, not her looks.

"A tragic waste, if I may say so," he added. "You have the most beautiful eyes I've ever seen—as green and clear as the waters of an alpine lake I used to visit as a child."

Enlightenment dawned. She'd spent a summer in Paris during her student days, and more than one Frenchman had talked to her that way. Steamy stares and extravagant compliments came as naturally to them as eating and sleeping. A five-minute acquaintance was more than long enough for them to swing into action. It meant nothing.

"I wear tinted contact lenses," she said crisply, then returned to her original subject. "If you know about the foundation, then you should understand why I want these pieces. They're a part of history. They belong on Van Slyke's Island where the public can learn from them and enjoy them. The museums represented here tonight agree with me. They won't bid against me. Neither will the dealers, because they know they can't outspend me and still make a profit. I hope you'll be generous enough to follow their lead."

It was as though he'd stopped listening after the first sentence. "Tinted contact lenses, eh? I'll look forward to seeing the real color of your eyes, *chérie*. Of course, I'm looking forward to many other things, as well. Dinner tomorrow night, for one."

The man was part wolf, part chauvinist. Diana took a deep breath and adopted the gently reproving tone she used with difficult clients. "You astonish me, *monsieur*! You insist on bidding against me, you refuse to tell me your name, and you won't explain why you're interested in my furniture, and yet you want me to go out to dinner with you. Surely you don't expect me to accept!"

"Go out to dinner?" he repeated. "I must have missed something. I don't recall inviting you out."

"But you just said—" Blushing, she cut herself off. He was right. He hadn't asked her out to dinner. He'd simply said he was looking forward to it. He couldn't have been any quicker if he'd anticipated her refusal and planned his response in advance.

Score one point for him, she thought irritably. She tried again. "Getting back to Van Slyke's Island—"

"Why should we talk about Van Slyke's Island when we can discuss Diana Van Slyke?" His voice was soft, seductive. "Such beautiful red hair. Did I mention that I have a weakness for women with red hair and freckles?"

Enough was enough. She smiled sweetly and spoke to him as if he were a slow-witted child. "Did I mention that I *don't* have a weakness for men who treat me as a sex object? Who imply that I shouldn't clutter my poor little head with things like history and philanthropy?"

"A sex object?" He looked astonished. "If that's how I've treated you, I apologize, but I don't think it's an insult to state the truth. You're very beautiful, Diana. Very alluring."

If she'd been either of those things, men would have been beating down her door, and they definitely weren't. She didn't reply.

"As for the size of your head," he continued, "obviously you're very intelligent. Not intimidating, I'm glad to say, but definitely formidable. I'm sure your island is very important to you, but I'm still going to buy those two pieces. Why should we quarrel over what can't be changed?"

"But it can be," Diana insisted. "You simply refuse to."

He conceded the point. "Very well. I refuse to."

"Why?"

"That's a question I have every intention of answering." He grinned at her. "Eventually."

Before she could ask when that happy day would arrive, an announcement came over the public-address system that the auction was about to begin. The Frenchman took her arm in a proprietary grip and led her out of the gallery, treating her like a child who was too simple or helpless to make her way on her own. She was far too polite to wrench herself free, so she had no choice but to endure it. In any event, his hand wasn't clammy or soft, but warm and strong. She didn't respond to his touch, but it didn't offend her, either.

He did, though, with his evasiveness, stubbornness and cool male superiority. As they walked through the center gallery, she said, "I'll pay as much as I need to, but I'm going to buy the Van Slyke heirlooms. I promise you, I want them much more than you do. They mean a great deal to me."

"And to me, too, *chérie*. This is your last chance to negotiate. According to the catalog, the chest and sideboard will be the last two Van Slyke pieces to be auctioned off. Let me have them, or you'll pay dearly for the others."

She could hardly believe what she'd heard. He had no legitimate reason to want those items, no emotional or historical ties to them. "You mean you'd deliberately bid me up on pieces you don't really want just to punish me for daring to oppose you?"

"Melodramatically put, but you leave me little choice. From what my friend told me, your funds are limited." They entered the salesroom. "If you spend too much on the earlier, less valuable pieces, you'll have to drop out of the bidding on the chest and sideboard."

He had her over a barrel and both of them knew it. Van Slyke's Island was a bottomless pit that swallowed up money. It wasn't just a matter of buying back the heirlooms her father had so cavalierly sold off; the house and grounds needed extensive repairs and restoration, as well, and it was costing a small fortune. She had workers out there five days a week, and they had to be paid each Friday.

She was so frustrated and exasperated that she forgot about being polite and yanked away her arm. Those who knew her would have been astonished. She never lost her temper, not even with the most obnoxious executives in America. Of course her emotions were much more deeply involved in Van Slyke's Island than they were in mergers and acquisitions. "It would serve you right if I stopped bidding and stuck you with something you hate," she snapped.

He remained completely unfazed. "I like all the Van Slyke pieces. I'm tempted to buy more than two, but I wouldn't want to anger you past the point of redemption." His eyes were twinkling. "If you stick me with something I don't plan to keep, I promise I won't resell it to you for more than ten percent above what I paid for it."

Aggravated or not, she didn't miss his teasing tone. He seemed to be playing some obscure game too complicated for a mere female to fathom. Who in the world was he, anyway? What did he really want? At a loss for words, she didn't have the wit to object when he followed her to a seat near the front center and sat down beside her.

She opened her catalog and tried to study it, but she couldn't help watching the Frenchman out of the corner of her eye. He'd shifted sideways in his chair and was regarding her with open amusement.

It was hopeless. Snapping the catalog shut, she took out her bidding paddle. Once and for all, she intended to find out what she was up against. "Please give me a straight answer. Are you really going to bid me up?"

"Are you going to let me have the chest and sideboard?"

"No," she said. Not if she could help it.

"Then yes," he replied. "I'm sorry, but you've brought it on yourself, you know."

Brought it on herself, hell! Wanting to kick him, she confined herself to hissing an insult. In French, because English would have been understood by the people around them and might have attracted stares. "*Voleur!*" Thief!

He burst out laughing. "Not really, although I'm pleased you speak some French. I'll only force you high enough to put a meaningful dent in your bank account. You'll have forgiven me by tomorrow night. I promise."

She didn't dignify that with a response. If she managed to buy the things she wanted, she'd never have to see him again. And if she didn't, it would be months before she could meet him to talk business. Although everyone had his price, she doubted she'd be able to afford this Frenchman's until she'd closed the Parkman-Fielding deal.

As people settled into their seats, Nelson Conable strode to the podium and grasped the gavel. Everyone quieted down. After a few seconds, he brought the gavel down hard. "Ladies and gentlemen, I'm honored to present the collection of the late Mrs. Herbert Klostermann, a woman of truly exceptional taste." He permitted himself a small smile. "But no less so, I'm sure, than everyone here tonight." As the audience chuckled, the curtain behind him rose and a beautifully embroidered sampler appeared on the revolving stage. "The first lot of the evening is a sampler of the family tree of the Revolutionary War hero Edward Holt of Boston, embroidered by his granddaughter Susannah in 1803. I'm opening the bidding at ten thousand dollars."

A woman Diana recognized as a collector raised her hand. "Thank you to the woman on my left," Nelson said. "Do I hear eleven? Eleven from the gentleman in front. Twelve from the phone on my right. Thirteen from the far-right corner. Fourteen from the gentleman in front." He paused and smiled. "Thank you for getting into the spirit of things so quickly, ladies and gentlemen."

The audience laughed, and the bidding continued. When it was over, the collector on Diana's right had bought the sampler for twenty-six thousand dollars. Nelson noted the price and paddle number in his auctioneer's book as the stage rotated and the next lot came into view, a silver teapot by Paul Revere.

Diana would have loved to buy it, but she was saving her money for heirlooms from the Van Slyke mansion. There were dozens of pieces still in other hands—everything from porcelains to lighting fixtures, from a ship's figurehead to a harpsichord. Even with the financial help of her family and friends, the task often seemed overwhelming.

The first lot from the Van Slyke mansion appeared on the stage a short time later—the eight walnut armchairs, sold as a set and estimated at eighty to ninety thousand dollars. Diana knew they'd go for more, probably for well over one hundred. Nelson had worked the crowd like a master puppeteer, making them feel it would be an embarrassing personal defeat to leave this auction without at least one item from Gertrude Klostermann's magnificent collection.

The bidding opened at forty and quickly climbed to seventy. Diana's first bid was fifty, her second seventy-five. When the Frenchman remained silent, she began to hope he hadn't been serious about bidding her up.

He had, though. He entered the fray at eighty, then offered one-oh-five to her one hundred. The last bid from anyone other than the two of them was one twenty. Diana said one twenty-five; the Frenchman said one thirty. She gave him a look even colder than Mont Blanc and indicated to Nelson Conable that she wanted to bid one thirty-one—to test her opponent's resolve. He countered with one thirty-five. The bid rose by increments of a thousand after that, until Diana offered one forty and the Frenchman simply sat there.

Nelson smiled. "Is the battle over, sir?" There was an appreciative titter from the audience. The Frenchman made a gesture of surrender. "I see that it is. Do I hear more from anyone? No? Then going once! Going twice!" His eyes scanned the room. "Sold to Ms. Van Slyke. Thank you, ma'am." He brought down his gavel and entered the sale in his book.

Diana looked at the Frenchman. The miserable *voleur* had cost her an extra fifteen grand but looked as innocent as a choirboy. Forcing her temper under control, she said evenly, "You've made your point. I hope you won't feel compelled to continue."

"That depends," he replied. "Will you let me have the chest and sideboard?"

"You already know the answer to that."

He smiled. "I thought it might have changed."

"It hasn't." She lifted her chin and turned away, openly and deliberately snubbing him.

"Lot number six," Nelson announced as the stage slowly revolved, "also from the old Van Slyke mansion, a walnut gateleg table. Will someone start me off with fifteen thousand dollars? Thank you to the gentleman on my right."

Again the bids went up rapidly, the Frenchman joining in at thirty-five. When the pattern from the previous sale repeated itself—everyone dropping out except Diana and the Frenchman—Nelson cocked up an eyebrow and drawled, "What, again? Perhaps we should separate the two of you. Otherwise there might be bloodshed before the evening is out." The audience howled with laughter. Even Diana smiled.

"Do I hear fifty?" Nelson asked, looking at Diana. She nodded. "Thank you, Ms. Van Slyke. Sir? Will you make it fifty-five? Thank you. Anyone else?"

This time the Frenchman bid her up to seventy thousand dollars, fifteen or twenty more than she'd anticipated paying. She wasn't smiling anymore. She would run out of money at this rate.

"Had enough?" he asked pleasantly.

She didn't reply, sitting stonily as the stage revolved and a musical clock came into view. She tensed when the Dutch-style secretary went on the block a few lots later. Would he continue or let up?

It was the first. To the audience's delight, he topped Diana's bid three straight times. Even Nelson's wry comments couldn't get a smile out of her after that.

It continued with each and every piece, the Frenchman bidding her up an extra fifteen here, an extra twenty there. He always let her win, but as he'd promised, he made her pay dearly for the privilege. To add insult to injury, after each sale he cheerfully asked whether she was ready to give up yet.

She didn't even look at him, much less answer. She was fiercely devoted to Van Slyke's Island and had waited years to buy these pieces back. Now some stranger was trying to steal what was rightfully hers, and she was furious with him for it. Never mind bloodshed. She wanted to strangle him.

But she was also an investment banker who'd played hardball with some of the biggest boys in town, and in some small corner of her mind she felt a grudging admiration for his tactics. He wanted certain pieces badly and she was in his way. Maybe he couldn't afford a bidding war after shelling out a fortune for the town house and maybe he was just frugal, but his strategy was flawless.

By the time the chinoiserie chest went on the block, he'd cost her more than a hundred thousand dollars. Her budget was in shreds and her self-control was hanging by a tattered thread. She loved that chest. She was determined to have it even if she had to raid her personal retirement account to cover the cost. The fact that he was apparently equally determined didn't sway her a bit.

As usual, both of them sat out the early bidding. She finally looked at him, knowing it was pointless to talk to him but unable to help herself. This wasn't some cold business deal. This was her life's work, her tribute to her mother's memory.

"I want that chest," she hissed. "If you have any decency at all, you'll let me have it. It belongs in my museum, not in your damned town house."

He smiled. "In that case, *chérie*, I suppose I'll have to sell it to you eventually."

Right, she thought. *In twenty years at an exorbitant price.* She was so tense that her hands were shaking. She barely recognized herself. She was never this wildly emotional—not since the night she'd come home unexpectedly and found her husband and her cousin in bed together.

She turned her attention to Nelson, nodding when he asked for a bid of seventy. When the Frenchman bid eighty, a buzz of excitement filled the air. The battle had recommenced, and everyone in the room was enjoying it immensely.

Nelson's eyes jumped between Diana and her adversary like those of a man watching a tennis match. Eighty-five...ninety...ninety-five...one hundred... Her throat tightened and her head began to throb. She bid one-oh-five; he bid one ten.

"I have one hundred ten from the gentleman in the center," Nelson said. "Do I hear one fifteen?"

Diana looked at the Frenchman. She wanted to be icily intimidating, but to her horror, her eyes filled with tears. He frowned and looked down, and she hastily turned away. She didn't know what to make of his reaction. Was it guilt? Disgust?

She nodded at Nelson. That was it. She couldn't go any higher—not and keep meeting her payroll. "I have one hundred fifteen thousand dollars," Nelson said. "Do I hear more?" He raised his gavel and waited.

Diana steeled herself to lose, but the Frenchman didn't bid. She was bewildered. Surely he could have afforded to. Had it all been a sadistic game, then?

"Going once!" Nelson announced. "Going twice! Gone! Once again, sold to Ms. Van Slyke."

Diana was holding her paddle in a death grip now. She relaxed her hand and closed her eyes, fighting to calm her nerves. Another few lots and the sideboard would come under the hammer. She had to think. Maybe she could get an advance on her next bonus, or even a bank loan. But if the Frenchman bid her into the stratosphere again...

"Diana." She felt his hand on her shoulder and flinched, her eyes flying open in surprise. "Your reputation on Wall Street... I thought you were much tougher. I'm sorry I upset you so much. I didn't intend to."

So he'd given her the chest out of pity. She hated the idea—hated women who used tears to manipulate men and men who were stupid enough to fall for it. Women like her cousin Tracy, with her trembling lips and whispery voice. Men like her ex-husband John, who thought he was Tracy's big, strong protector.

She squared her shoulders and met the Frenchman's eyes. "I suppose I should have cried sooner," she said.

"No. I wouldn't have believed it. Not from you." He ran his finger down her cheek, then dropped his hand. "You've got too much spirit. You had to run out of money before you weakened. And even then, it took the fight out of you for only a minute." He smiled at her. "You see? You're recovering already. In fact, I'll bet you're hatching some scheme to finance that sideboard."

Her anger began to dissipate, probably because he was a worthy opponent and she was flattered by his compliments. Unlike all that nonsense about her looks, they'd actually made sense. Besides, she was amazed by how well he'd read her. "You're right. After all, it's what I do for a living—arrange for people to buy the things they want."

"Multimillion-dollar companies, you mean."

"Yes."

"I'm sure you're good at your work, *chérie*, but you're being irrational about the sideboard. Take my advice and let me have it. Sooner or later, you'll probably be able to talk me into selling it, and the less I pay, the less I'll charge you."

"It's that 'probably' that bothers me," she said.

He laughed. "Then it seems we're in for another battle, but this time, I promise you you'll lose."

"We'll see," she said. The Parkman-Fielding deal was the biggest of her career. It would earn her a huge bonus. She'd never spent money she didn't have before, but in this case, it seemed to be necessary.

Four lots later, the stage revolved and the sideboard swung into view. Nelson opened the bidding at sixty thousand dollars. The Frenchman raised his hand at eighty, and Diana bid eighty-five. Nelson smiled. "Ladies and gentlemen, it seems to be show time again. Do I hear ninety? Thank you, sir."

Nelson looked at Diana, who nodded. The bidding continued at a rapid-fire pace—one hundred . . . one-oh-five . . . one ten . . . one fifteen . . . Everyone else had dropped out by then, and even Diana was having second thoughts. One fifteen would have been rich for her blood even if she'd had a healthy bank balance, and she didn't. She hesitated after the Frenchman bid one twenty, telling herself she could survive without this one piece, but its rare beauty and her own competitiveness got the better of her. She raised him by five thousand dollars.

He immediately bid one thirty. Diana offered one forty; he countered with one forty-five. She went to one fifty; he answered with one fifty-five.

Her common sense reasserted itself at that point. One sixty was just too high, especially when she didn't have the money. Besides, an amount like that would buy a great many heirlooms still in the hands of other collectors. She thought about turning the tables on him and deliberately bidding him up, but she didn't trust him. He might have dropped out of the battle the way he had with the chest and left her holding the bill.

"I have one hundred fifty-five thousand dollars," Nelson said. "Do I hear one sixty? Ms. Van Slyke, don't tell me you're finally going to let the gentleman win one!" Diana smiled and shrugged in defeat as the audience laughed. "Fair warning, then. Going once! Going twice!" He paused. "Sold to the gentleman holding paddle number ninety-two."

There was a burst of applause from the crowd as the hammer came down. Then the Frenchman leaned over and murmured in Diana's ear, "Any time you want to negotiate with me to buy it, I'm open to an offer."

She could tell he wasn't serious. He was simply teasing her, permitting himself to savor his victory. "And how do I contact you? I don't even know your name."

"All in good time," he said.

Arguing would have been pointless. "Far be it from me to interfere with the pleasure being anonymous seems to give you," she replied, "but perhaps you'll tell me just one thing. What has all the mystery gained you?"

He hesitated, as if he was debating whether to give her an honest answer. Finally he smiled and said, "Why, your attention, of course, *Mademoiselle* Van Slyke."

Chapter Two

Un coup de foudre, the French called it. A thunderbolt. Overwhelming, impassioned love at first sight. As a sophisticated Frenchman with fifteen years of experience in matters of the heart, Marc Rochard had been struck by this delightful and excruciating phenomenon before. But never, he thought as he entered his town house, with the intensity of tonight.

One look at Diana Van Slyke and he'd been lost. She was the most adorable creature he'd ever seen. Small and shapely, soft and ripe—she was miles removed from the bony American women in this wealthy East Side neighborhood, who'd seemingly starved themselves so completely that there was nothing left for a man to caress. Much to his delight, she had none of the brittle, painted sophistication that he'd seen so often on the streets of New York during his two weeks here. With her milky skin, expressive mouth and flashing eyes, she was as fresh as she was voluptuous.

Besides, as he'd told her, he had a weakness for red hair, especially that fiery shade of it, and found freckles absolutely enchanting. As for her eyes, while he was partial to green, he wouldn't mind if they were some other shade. It was what they'd revealed that had stopped him in his tracks.

It was obvious that she worked very hard to control her emotions. Given her triumphs on Wall Street, she no doubt succeeded most of the time, but she hadn't tonight. Annoyance, exasperation, outrage—he'd seen them all in her eyes, and been captivated. He liked women with passionate natures. And then, as if the thunderbolt hadn't been violent enough to begin with, those eyes had filled with tears and he'd melted completely. She had a gentleness and fragility that, for some reason, she struggled fiercely to conceal. At that moment, he'd gone from wanting her to feeling he positively had to have her.

In a perfect world she would have fallen into his arms, but he'd seen almost at once that he'd have his work cut out for him. In truth, he'd been amazed. As a Frenchman, he was as practical as he was romantic, and he knew without conceit that he was a highly desirable lover—young and handsome, wealthy and well-connected, accomplished in the delightful art of pleasing a woman in bed. Most women he met looked at him a second time, and then a third and fourth, and hoped fervently that he would look back. But to his chagrin, Diana Van Slyke had treated him like a eunuch. Indeed, if it hadn't been for his interest in the Van Slyke heirlooms, she never would have noticed he was alive.

He hadn't taken it personally, though. According to his friend Tina D'Angelo, Diana had divorced her husband two years before and hadn't been linked romantically with anyone since. Since she was a figure of considerable public curiosity, whose activities were monitored by the local media, he assumed she didn't date. He didn't bother asking himself why. It was of no importance. All that mattered was changing her mind.

From that point of view, tonight had gone well. She definitely knew he was alive now, if only because he was a thorn in her lovely side. To his regret, he'd had little choice but to make himself into her adversary, because she would have brushed him aside like a speck of dust otherwise and forgotten he even existed.

She was very successful, Tina had told him, very independent. A man had to demonstrate his greater strength before such a woman would take him seriously. But, *mon Dieu*, the effort it had required! She was so willful, so single-minded! She wouldn't be easily tamed, that much was certain.

It was all the fault of her job, of course. She'd needed a great deal of money for her island, and Wall Street had been the one place she could earn it. Marc knew she'd merely done what was necessary, but that didn't mean he approved. It was a shame, really, completely unnatural. No woman that young and lovely should have to work at something so taxing and complicated as investment banking.

It pained him to think of the long hours she put in and the trying men she had to deal with. He was determined to take her away from all that—to protect her, spoil her and pleasure her. She might resist at first, but the proper mixture of gentleness and strength would win her over. It was simply a matter of teaching her what was best for her.

He closed and locked the door. It was very late and the house was silent, but Tina had left a lamp on for him. He winced, almost wishing she hadn't. The decor in the foyer was an insult to the refined eye. It looked like Hollywood's version of a French bordello, full of ornate knick-knacks, fussy accessories and gilded baroque furniture of dubious quality. Everything was done up in some shade of red, except of course when it was gold, platinum or black.

Unfortunately Tina loved it. Like his grandmother, who'd left him this house in her will and was responsible for the appalling decor, Tina had a good heart but no taste. He didn't want to hurt her feelings by throwing everything into the street, so he was redecorating slowly. He hoped his true opinion would be less obvious that way.

As usual, he ignored the elevator and took the stairs. The master suite was on the third floor, along with Tina's bedroom and sitting room. Her door was ajar and a light was on, so he went inside. He wasn't surprised to find her up. Tremendously energetic, she considered sleep a waste of time.

She was sitting on a red velvet love seat, looking through a coffee-table book entitled *The History of the Metropolitan Opera*. He'd come across it in a bookstore that morning and bought it for her. A graduate of Juilliard, she loved music of all sorts and played several different instruments extremely well. While she hadn't been brilliant enough for the concert hall, she was in great demand as a rehearsal pianist for Broadway musicals and one-man shows.

"Hi, sweetie." She riffled the book's pages. "God, this brings back memories. I saw some of these productions when I was a kid. Music was my father's one extravagance. He was always taking us to the opera and symphony."

Marc sat down in a wing chair. He was well acquainted with Tina's history. She and his mother had been friends for sixty years.

"I'm glad you're enjoying the book," he said. "How was *La Bohème*?" She'd gone to the City Opera that night.

"I've seen better and I've seen worse, but I won't bore you with the details." She knew he was no opera buff. "Tell me about the auction. Did you see Diana Van Slyke?"

"Saw her, spoke to her and sat next to her." He smiled. "You might have told me how beautiful she is. It would have made it easier not to stare when I first met her."

"Beautiful? Diana Van Slyke?" Tina shrugged. "I guess the pictures I've seen have been lousy. So the two of you really hit it off, huh?"

"Not exactly. I fell violently in love. She didn't."

"Right, sweetie. You Frenchmen are always doing that, aren't you?" She pursed her lips. "Let's see now. There was the neighbor's daughter when you were sixteen, Lady Something-or-other when you were at school in Paris, that actress from *La Comédie Française*—"

He cut her off with an imperious wave of his hand. "They chased me, not the other way around. Besides, a man has to... What's that American expression? Oh, yes. He has to sow a few wild oats before he settles down. It makes him a better husband—faithful, knowledgeable about women, a skillful lover..."

He didn't finish the list because Tina was laughing too hard to hear him. He loved her dearly, so he didn't mind it when she treated him like a callow boy who knew nothing about life. "Go ahead and laugh," he said. "I'll remind you of it on my wedding day."

She finally contained herself. "Your wedding day? My, my this *is* serious. You've never mentioned marriage before. But to Diana Van Slyke? Really, honey, of all the women to fall for..." She shook her head. "You poor thing."

He took umbrage at that. "Why am I a poor thing? Are you implying that there's something wrong with her?"

"There's nothing wrong with either of you, but the combination..." She leaned forward a little. "Diana is bright and successful. She's used to running her own life exactly the way she wants to. Don't try to tell me that a liberated woman is your idea of a good wife. I guess you think you'll be able to charm her into doing whatever you want, but—"

"Of course I don't. I'm not stupid. A few hours was long enough for me to see how stubborn she is. She would only dig in her heels and refuse."

Tina raised her eyebrows. "Oh? Then you've decided it's pointless to try to change her?"

"I didn't say that. I'll spoil her completely. Overwhelm her with passion and devotion. What woman in her right mind would choose to work eighteen hours a day when she can be taken care of by a husband who adores her? She won't be bored. She'll have our children to look after."

"Your children. I see." Tina closed her book and set it aside. "Listen, sweetie, you're a charming boy and I know the girls at home are crazy about you, but take it from me. Even if she falls head over heels in love with you, Diana Van Slyke will never put up with your prehistoric attitudes. Do yourself a favor. Marry someone French."

"What prehistoric attitudes?" he asked with a frown. "I have no idea what you're talking about."

"You really don't, do you? I've always known that your father has opinions out of the Dark Ages, but you do have a mother, Marc. Didn't Tiffany teach you anything about women?"

"Raised my intolerably chauvinistic consciousness, you mean?" He laughed. "Of course she did. Unlike my father, I don't believe that women are weak, impulsive creatures who are inferior to men. I don't see them as temptresses who'll try to lure me to my ruin the way Eve lured Adam. I've never even cared whether my wife was a virgin."

"A good thing, too, since Diana's been married."

Marc preferred not to think about her ex-husband. The man was obviously a fool; he'd once had the right to make love to a perfectly enchanting creature and let it slip through his fingers. Without a doubt, the divorce must have been this villain's fault. A gentle, virtuous woman such as Diana couldn't possibly have been responsible.

"Then she'll appreciate me all the more by comparison," he said. "As for what else my mother taught me . . . I know what a good marriage is. I've seen what makes a woman truly content. *Maman* has been supremely happy all these years. She's devoted herself to being a wife and mother and never felt there was any lack in her life. Quite the opposite."

"Because she entertains constantly, presides over the seemingly endless restoration of your house and grounds and keeps the books for the business."

The family owned a pair of vineyards in the Bordeaux region of France, near the village of St. Emilion. "Naturally she helps my father with his work and takes an interest in his estate. It's part of being Madame Rochard."

"So it's all right for a woman to work, as long as—" Tina stopped and shook her head. "Never mind. I'll leave it to Diana to drag you into the twentieth century. She'll have her work cut out for her, too."

Although Marc was too polite to say so, he considered Tina's attitude to be the result of her unfortunate past. After all, she'd wasted thirty years of her life on a married lover. She'd never known the joys of having a man look after her or experienced the pleasures of being a wife and mother. Independence had been an unhappy necessity that, being human, she'd turned into a virtue. Now she considered it best for every woman in the world, but it wasn't best for Diana.

He didn't want to argue, though, so he smiled and said, "In that case, I'll look forward to being reformed. There's just one problem. I doubt she'll agree to go out with me."

"Why not? If she liked you enough to sit with you—"

"I didn't give her a choice. It was—business, I suppose you could say. When it comes to anything more . . ." He frowned. "Frankly, she doesn't even realize that she's a woman and I'm a man. That's the first thing I'll have to change."

Tina looked at him as if he'd lost his mind. "Marc, sweetie, being female, I happen to know a little about women, especially American ones. They want a man who respects them—who listens to what they have to say. Take my advice and make friends with her before you make a pass."

In Marc's experience, a woman became more tractable once she was sleeping with a man who pleased her in bed, but he didn't say so. It only would have gotten him accused of being a chauvinist again. Besides, he understood that the situation called for patience and finesse. "Naturally I'll do that. I want to know everything about her. I thought I'd start by getting myself invited to her apartment for dinner tomorrow night. You mentioned that she lives with her father and spinster aunt. Do you have any idea where?"

"The apartment's on Central Park South. It said so in an article I just read. Her father gave a party there to celebrate the hundredth anniversary of that historical journal he edits—*The Manhattan Island Quarterly*." She reached for a phone book. "Maybe I can find an address."

After several minutes of squinting at tiny print, she put the book aside. "Their home number isn't listed, but there's a *Manhattan Island Quarterly* at an address uptown. It's probably near Columbia University. Her father teaches history there."

Marc had looked forward to seeing the expression on Diana's face when he showed up at her apartment for dinner, but obviously it wasn't to be. "Thanks for your help, *chérie*. I don't suppose he'd be working on a Sunday, but perhaps I can arrange something for later in the week."

He kissed Tina good night, then walked across the hall. If the foyer resembled a bordello, his bedroom reminded him of a prosperous madam's sanctum sanctorum. It was intensely feminine, with spindly furniture that looked as if it would collapse under a man's weight and an aggressively florid decor. There were flowers everywhere—on the carpets, the drapes, the upholstery, the canopy over the bed and even the pictures on the walls. Big, bold flowers, in the inevitable red, gold and black.

He grimaced, wondering how his grandfather had stood the place. Earlier that week, he'd purchased a pair of Oriental carpets and a four-poster bed, but they wouldn't be delivered until Wednesday. He stripped off his clothes, thinking that Wednesday couldn't come soon enough.

He slept till nine the next morning, walking groggily into the kitchen to find Tina in the adjacent breakfast nook, sipping coffee as she read the Sunday paper. The kitchen was the one room in the house that didn't offend him. It was black-and-white, and very spare. Otherwise he would have redone it immediately. One couldn't cook in an environment that gave one indigestion.

"Good morning," he said. "Are you hungry?"

"Don't ask me that," she groaned. "You know I'll say yes. And then you'll feed me something rich and fattening—"

"Umm. A *gratin*, I thought. Some Gruyère, grated potatoes, ham and eggs—"

"Don't go on. Please. I've put on five pounds since you moved here."

"And you look all the more charming for it. You were too thin before."

"I was just right. *You* may think that Renoir's women are the absolute ideal, but I don't." She set down her cup. "Gruyère? Ham and eggs? What else is in it?"

"Some onion, a little garlic, some chives and chervil, a dash of salt and pepper, a *soupçon* of cream—"

"Oh, God. Not cream."

"Only a few tablespoons. It will take an hour or so to prepare, so why don't you think of it as brunch?"

"If I say no, you'll make it anyway, won't you? And then I'll smell it and I won't be able to resist."

"True." He gathered together the things he would need. The kitchen had been a culinary wasteland when he'd first arrived, so he'd made a trip to the housewares department at Bloomingdale's and excursions to some of the finest food shops in New York. "If it would make you feel better, I'll cook you some fish for dinner."

"I'd have to eat fish for at least a week to make up for the cholesterol in this one meal, but it's worth a try. And Marc..."

"Hmm?" He peeled and sliced an onion and fed it into the Cuisinart.

"Remember what I told you about making friends with Diana before you try to seduce her? Forget it. Just feed her. If she has any sense at all, she'll fall in love with you after the first bite."

"I'll do that," he said. It was the first sensible piece of advice Tina had given him.

Later, after they'd eaten and cleaned up, he phoned the *Manhattan Island Quarterly*. Scholars worked odd hours, after all. But the call was answered by a machine, the tape informing him that someone would be in the office at ten the next morning. He would have to wait.

He spent the afternoon exploring the city. It wasn't a matter of pleasure—New York was far too large and crowded for his taste—but of business. All his life he'd wanted to own and run a restaurant. He'd recently decided to locate it in Manhattan and was looking for just the right spot.

In truth, he would have preferred his native St. Emilion or even Paris, but that was impossible right now. If he'd stayed in France, his father would have given him no peace. A deeply traditional Frenchman, Louis Rochard expected Marc to succeed him as the head of the family business. Indeed, as an only son, Marc had been trained for the job since birth.

Until recently he'd dutifully gone along, but then his grandmother had died, and the terms of her will had changed everything. He'd inherited her town house and a great deal more, and he'd decided to move to New York. He didn't plan to stay forever, just until his father had accepted the fact that he wasn't going to take over the winery. Then he would turn his restaurant in New York over to a manager and open a place in St. Emilion.

In the meantime his first order of business was to size up the competition. Each day, he'd gone out to lunch and sometimes dinner, taking a cool, critical look at the things each restaurant did well and poorly. He was only partially finished, but he already had pages of notes and ideas.

He hadn't expected a woman to distract him from the task at hand, but she had, and that was that. A man couldn't ignore a *coup de foudre*, not if he had the hot Rochard blood flowing through his veins.

Marc called *The Manhattan Island Quarterly* at ten the next morning and was told that Dr. Van Slyke would be in at noon. As Tina had guessed, the office was near Columbia, in a narrow old building of pedestrian design. As he checked the directory in the outer lobby, someone dashed inside and hurriedly unlocked the door. Marc followed, taking the stairs to the fourth floor.

The offices of *The Manhattan Island Quarterly* were to his right. The main door was closed but not locked, so he let himself inside. The first room in the suite contained a young woman with limp brown hair and glasses, probably a student. She was typing and didn't notice him, so he murmured a discreet "Good afternoon" to get her attention.

"Oh!" She started and looked up, then stared raptly. "Ohh...Um, hi. I'm sorry. I didn't realize anyone had come up."

He smiled warmly, enjoying a feminine reaction he'd come to take as his due. "I was looking for Professor Van Slyke."

"He's, uh... That is, his office is at the end of the hall. The door's open. You can go right in."

"He's—approachable, then?"

"Well, not really. He's very nice, but he's in his own world a lot of the time." She paused. "Is there anything I can help you with? I mean, if I knew why you'd come..."

"Professor Van Slyke and I are distant cousins," he explained. Very distant cousins, since their mutual ancestors, Philippe Rochard and Anna Van Slyke, had married over three centuries before, but cousins nonetheless. "I wanted to meet him."

"Oh. He'll like that, I think. Go on ahead, then."

Marc thanked her and made his way to Van Slyke's office. It was the picture of academic disarray. The bookcases were filled to overflowing, and the desk and even the floor were stacked with manuscripts and folders. Van Slyke himself, who was dressed in a V-necked brown cardigan over a checked shirt, was peering at a professional journal through a pair of half glasses. He had a fine head of graying brown hair and pleasing but ascetic-looking features.

Marc stopped by his desk. "Excuse me, Professor Van Slyke. Might I have a few minutes of your time?"

Van Slyke grunted but didn't look up.

"My name is Marc Rochard. I'm—"

"Rochard, eh?" He set down his journal and inspected Marc over the top of his glasses. "Spell that."

"R-O-C-H-A-R-D. I'm a descendant of Philippe Rochard and Anna—"

"That's impossible. Their only son died when he was sixteen and left no issue. Good day, sir." He stuck his nose back in his journal, ignoring Marc completely.

Marc continued as if he'd never spoken. "—and Anna Van Slyke. It's true that their son, Pierre, died along with Philippe at sea in November of 1698, but Pierre had married by then. His wife was the daughter of another pirate. Her name was Simone Saint-Denis. She gave birth to a son the following February. Three months after that, in May of 1699, the Royal Navy arrived in Madagascar to—"

"Eliminate the pirates there in order to protect English trade in the area. I'm aware of the facts, sir. I *am* an historian." He frowned at the briefcase Marc was carrying. "What have you got in there? Some sort of documentation?"

"Yes." Marc removed a Bible and two diaries and set them on Van Slyke's desk. "Simone and her son moved back to France along with her father, who bought a vineyard near St. Emilion and founded a winery, Château du Ciel. It's been in my family ever since. My father is the current owner."

"Château du Ciel, eh?" Obviously Van Slyke had heard of it, which meant he was something of a wine buff. The family's wines weren't famous, merely superb. "An interesting story. Why don't you sound French?"

"Because my mother was an American. Perhaps you've heard of my grandfather, Sam Parisi. 'The New Jersey auto-parts king,' they called him."

"Can't say that I have. Never taken much interest in business." Van Slyke opened the Bible. Marriages, births and deaths were recorded in front. "Let's have a look."

"Everything's in French, of course, so—"

"In French? How extraordinary!" He began thumbing the pages. "I was expecting Dutch or Spanish."

Marc felt a little foolish for stating the obvious. Besides, Van Slyke probably read French almost as well as he did. He knew the appropriate entries by heart: "Married, 3 February, 1698, Simone Thérèse Saint-Denis, daughter of Louis and Marie Saint-Denis, to Pierre Rochard, son of Philippe and Anna Rochard, by Father Jean Marquette, on Bourbon Island." Then, directly below, "Died, November 1698, in a storm while rounding the Cape, Pierre Rochard, 1682-1698." And finally, below that, "Born, 17 February 1699, on Madagascar, to Simone Rochard and the late Pierre Rochard, a son, Pierre-Luc."

"Fascinating," Van Slyke murmured. "And the other two volumes?"

"Diaries kept by Simone and her son Pierre-Luc. She was only barely literate, so there are frequent misspellings. The language is often archaic—" He saw the sardonic look on Van Slyke's face and thought the better of offering to translate. "—but I'm sure you'll be able to manage quite easily."

"I thank you for that vote of confidence, Mr. Rochard. These documents—where did you get them?"

"From our château in France." Marc explained that he'd read the article in *National Geographic* about the Madagascar pirates with special interest because of the family lore about a pirate having founded Château du Ciel. Seeing the name Philippe Rochard in the text, he'd wondered if the man was a distant ancestor. He'd searched through the old chests in the attic where family records were kept, and discovered the Bible and diaries. It might have been a hundred years, even two, since anyone had looked at them.

"Your daughter's name was mentioned in the *Geographic*, of course, so I wrote to her care of Van Slyke's Island," he finished. "The letter is self-explanatory, I think."

He handed the professor a copy. It explained that, after studying the article in *National Geographic*, he'd realized that he and Diana were descended from the same couple,

Philippe Rochard and Anna Van Slyke. He had a number of interesting documents in his possession, he'd added, including a map of a treasure cache buried by Philippe on a small, unnamed island, he assumed somewhere near Madagascar. Perhaps it was the treasure mentioned in the article. In any event, he hoped to meet her when he came to New York in late August.

Van Slyke read the letter, then chuckled. "Buried treasure! Thanks to that damn article, she's heard from fruitcakes all over America and Europe. All of 'em want to search for it. This map you mentioned . . . Do you have it with you?"

Mark nodded and showed it to him. "Obscure, isn't it?" Van Slyke murmured. "Ah, well, they always are. Don't suppose Diana answered you."

"No. In return, I got this." He handed Van Slyke the response, which was from an attorney named John Redmon. Redmon had thanked him for his interest in Van Slyke's Island and told him how he could contribute to Diana's work there. The letter had offended Marc deeply, especially Diana's rudeness in failing to answer him personally. Now, of course, he understood the reason for the snub.

"The standard form letter to crackpots," Van Slyke informed him. "How did you find your way to me?"

"A friend of mine mentioned that you were Diana's father, and a prominent historian. I thought you might be interested in the Bible and diaries."

"Your friend was right. I don't have time to look at them right now, but if I might keep them . . . ?" He didn't wait for an answer, but put the volumes aside. "How can I contact you to return everything?"

"Actually, I was hoping to meet my other Van Slyke relations as soon as possible. Perhaps you would be my guests at dinner this week."

"Dinner. I should have thought of it." He rummaged around in his desk, finally unearthing a business card. Scrawling something on it, he said, "It's my sister's birthday. The whole family will be over tonight. Here's our address and phone number. We'll see you at seven. I hope you like bicarbonate of soda."

Marc took the card. Van Slyke lived about ten blocks from his town house. "Bicarbonate of soda?" he repeated. "What do you mean?"

"The cook's with her sick mother. My sister burns everything, but she still insists on cooking. Tried to talk her into going out or getting something delivered, but she wouldn't hear of it. Says it's not proper."

Sometimes, Marc thought, the gods truly smiled upon a man. "I trained as a chef. Perhaps you'll do me the honor of letting me prepare and serve the meal."

He expected at least a token refusal, but Van Slyke jumped at the offer. "Damn right I will. I'd ask if you were any good, but it doesn't matter. Anyone's better than my sister. There'll be ten of us. I'll call her and tell her to expect you. Bring whatever you need. There's not much food in the apartment."

"I'll do that." They shook hands. "It's been a pleasure, Dr. Van Slyke. I'll look forward to tonight."

"It's William." Van Slyke picked up the journal he'd been reading. "Now where was I?"

He buried his nose in his work, in his own world again. Marc gathered up his map and letters and strolled out of the office. He could hardly wait to see Diana again. He was going to cook her a meal that would make her swoon at his feet in ecstasy. And afterward . . . He smiled to himself. Afterward was going to be delightful.

Chapter Three

Diana walked tiredly into her apartment. She'd had a long day and was preoccupied by the latest glitch in the Parkman-Fielding merger. She only hoped she could get things back on track when she phoned Fielding that night. As much as she loved to eat, she normally wouldn't have noticed the smell of food, but the aroma in the foyer stopped her cold.

In all the years she'd been coming to this apartment—as a child to see her grandparents, as a bride to visit her father and aunt, as a divorced career woman arriving home from work—never, but never, had it smelled this wonderful. She inhaled deeply. She didn't know how her father had done it, but somehow he'd convinced his sister Nelly to hire a caterer for tonight's party.

She could have hugged him for that. Family celebrations gave her stomachaches to begin with and Nelly's cooking would have made it that much worse. Still, family was family. The ties created by blood were more important than one's personal heartaches and resentments. She prided herself on how well she always behaved.

She squared her shoulders and continued down to the living room. As usual, she was the last to arrive. Nobody worked as hard as she did, but then, nobody made as much money. Not even her ex-husband John, who'd just become the youngest partner in the history of his law firm.

He and Tracy were snuggled together on one of the twin couches that flanked the fireplace. They'd been married for two years now, but Diana still found it painful to see them together. Since she was forced to do so constantly, the wound never had a chance to heal. Her heart didn't so much ache as fester, like an open, infected sore.

Not a trace of it showed on her face. She said a cheerful hello and walked over to Nelly, who was sitting across from John and Tracy on the other couch. An assortment of brightly wrapped packages was stacked on the table in front of her.

"Happy birthday, Aunt Nelly." She gave her aunt a kiss, then stepped back to admire her dress. "I see you've gone shopping. I love your new dress."

Nelly smoothed the fabric, a soft wool jersey in a warm shade of brown. "It's my birthday present to myself—an Oscar de la Renta. Cost me a fortune, but you're only sixty-five once. Or not at all, come to think of it, which is all the more reason to splurge."

Nelly was wraith-thin. Diana's father, who was sitting on Nelly's right, claimed it was from eating her own cooking too much of the time. "If I were a few sizes smaller, I'd beg to borrow it," Diana said.

She took a package out of her purse and set it on the table. It was easy to buy Nelly presents. Her numerous collections—everything from salt-and-pepper sets to telephones—filled every niche of the apartment.

"It wouldn't suit you," Nelly replied. "You're too young for it. Really, Diana, that gray suit... Why on earth do you wear such gloomy colors and boring—'' She cut herself off, looking to her left. Diana was relieved something had distracted her. As difficult as it was to endure her criticism in silence, it was pointless to keep explaining that a woman in a man's world had to dress conservatively.

Her aunt broke into a smile. ''Marc, dear! It's about time you left the kitchen, although everything does smell wonderful. Come meet the rest of the family.''

Diana turned around. She expected to see some fawning society caterer in the doorway, but found herself staring straight into the striking blue eyes of the Frenchman from the Klostermann auction. Once again, he was dressed in expensive Italian clothing, but he'd removed his jacket and rolled up his shirtsleeves. She was totally befuddled. He couldn't be a caterer. He was too self-assured, too wealthy.

He was looking at her with the same mixture of amusement and superiority as at the auction. Seeing him again, the events of that evening came flooding back.

This French thief—this *voleur*—had cost her at least a hundred and fifty grand. He'd made off with a sideboard that belonged on Van Slyke's Island, refusing even to tell her who he was. And then to top it all off, when she'd asked him what he was after, he'd made some ridiculously cryptic reply about wanting her attention.

Quite naturally she'd asked for an explanation, but he'd smiled mysteriously and refused to give her one. Out of patience with him, she'd ignored him for the rest of the evening. Totally unfazed, he'd insisted on seeing her home. If he hadn't been so cool and shrewd, she would have assumed he was mentally unbalanced.

It had been late, by then, and she'd been tired—too tired to attend the post-auction reception. She'd drawn herself to her full height, five and a half feet in heels, and told him very firmly that she would see *herself* home, and by some miracle, he hadn't argued.

She'd known he'd eventually get in touch, though. Once she'd thought it over, she'd realized that he wouldn't have bothered to prove how tough he was unless he'd wanted something further—an exorbitant price for the sideboard, perhaps, or a generous offer on other Van Slyke pieces he'd somehow acquired. But to see him here in her home, on far friendlier terms with her aunt than a mere cook would be, less than forty-eight hours later, and at a celebration that should rightly have been limited to her family... She didn't know what to make of it.

"Marc, this is my niece Diana," Nelly said, still beaming. "She's the guardian of the family's past, so I know you two will have a great deal to talk about. Diana dear, this is Marc Rochard, a distant cousin from France who suddenly appeared this afternoon and offered to make us dinner. His background is absolutely fascinating, but I'll let him supply the details."

Diana stiffened as he strolled to her side, silently cursing that damned *National Geographic* article. Relatives had been materializing out of thin air ever since, and every last one of them wanted to search for buried treasure. This one did, too, she assumed, but at least the others had simply written, not shown up on her doorstep.

She didn't buy a word of it, but she wasn't surprised Nelly had. Her aunt was hopelessly romantic when it came to the family's past. "Really!" she said. "How extraordinary."

"Yes. Really." He took her hand and brought it to his lips. It wasn't the perfunctory kiss of Saturday night, but a lingering caress. Even more vexing, he was gazing at her as if they were the only two people in the world. Blushing, she took back her hand and backed away.

"I was hoping to see you yesterday," he added softly. "Two days was far too long, *chérie*."

"You mean you two know each other?" Nelly looked at Diana's father accusingly. The two of them squabbled constantly. "You didn't mention that when you told me to expect him, Billy. Really, sometimes I think your head is so full of dried-up old books that the simplest—"

"Complain to him, not to me," her father interrupted. "I couldn't tell you what I didn't know."

"Didn't know, my foot," Nelly retorted. "It goes in one ear and out the other with you, that's all."

"That depends on who's talking and what they have to say," William shot back. "Rochard was worth listening to."

Diana could hardly believe her ears. Her father was as skeptical as Nelly was naive, yet this Marc Rochard—if that was really his name—had met him before tonight and convinced him he was a long-lost cousin. But when and how?

"I'm sure Daddy's telling the truth," she said to Nelly. "Mr. Rochard is a very mysterious man. I can vouch for that personally."

Nelly looked deflated. "Oh. Well, then, I'll look forward to hearing the details. Why don't you introduce him to the rest of the family, dear? You seem to know him so much better than I do."

"I'm beginning to think it would be redundant," Diana replied. "One way or another, he seems to know all of us already."

Marc took her arm and turned her away from the couch, toward a row of chairs opposite the fireplace. Four more members of the family were seated there. "Actually, I don't," he said, "but I would very much like to."

Her Aunt Babe frowned at him. "You look very familiar, Marc. Don't you think so, Henry?"

Her uncle shrugged. "Never saw him before in my life."

"Then I must have been on my own at the time." Babe studied him for a few seconds longer. "I'm sure I've seen you somewhere before. It will come to me eventually."

Diana didn't doubt it. Babe had traveled widely and knew people all over the world. "This is my aunt, Barbara Van Slyke," she said. "Everyone calls her Babe. She's a decorator—a real decorator, not one of those socialites who do nothing but shop and go to parties but call themselves decorators because it's fashionable to have a job."

Visibly amused, Marc took Babe's hand and brushed a kiss across the back. "It's a pleasure, *madame*. Perhaps you would give me your card. I need a good decorator more than you can possibly imagine."

"He's furnishing a town house on the East Side," Diana explained. Then, unable to resist, she added, "All the same, Mr. Rochard, I'm surprised you feel you need a decorator. You seemed to have such definite tastes the other night."

He grinned at her. "Very definite. Didn't I tell you I had a weakness for redheads?" He paused. "But I suppose you were speaking of furniture."

"You're right. I was. We met at the Klostermann auction, Aunt Babe. He bought my sideboard."

Babe was openly amazed. "You let him outbid you?"

"I had no choice. He bid me up so high on everything else that I ran out of money."

"And you're still speaking to him?"

"Again, only because I have no choice. After all, he's apparently family." Diana proceeded to her uncle. "This is my uncle, Henry Van Slyke. He's the president of the family firm, A. W. Van Slyke Publishers. Uncle Henry, Aunt Babe . . . I would tell you more about Mr. Rochard if I could, but he was rather vague the other night about who he is and what he does for a living."

"Actually, I'm between jobs," Marc said.

"As a chef, you mean?" Babe asked. A Van Slyke only by marriage, she didn't have the family aversion to pursuing a subject in the face of deliberate evasiveness.

"Not exactly," he said.

"Then you should be. Dinner smells delicious. Don't you think so, Diana?"

"Speaking of dinner..." Marc checked his watch. "The duck will be ready in forty-five minutes. Introduce me to the rest of your family, Diana, and then we'll eat."

Diana nodded and continued down the row of chairs. "This is my cousin Marisa, Babe and Henry's daughter, and her husband Graham Morrison. Risa is an editor at Van Slyke Publishers and Graham is a veterinarian with the Bronx Zoo. He specializes in primates."

Diana waited until they'd exchanged hellos, then asked Risa how she was feeling. She was pregnant with twins and tired easily. They usually had lunch once a week, but due to the Parkman-Fielding merger, Diana hadn't had time. She felt a little guilty about that.

"Fine," Risa said. "I just wish I weren't so huge."

"At least it won't be too much longer."

"Umm. The doctor says they might be early. He's going on vacation in the middle of next month, so I hope they'll wait until after the twentieth."

Diana's eyes twinkled. "In a pinch, Graham can always deliver them. After all, it wouldn't be the first time he's brought babies into the world. Isn't that right, Graham?"

"Absolutely. I keep telling her there's no difference between humans and chimps—"

"You've been spending too much time at the zoo," Risa grumbled.

"But think of all the parenting experience I get."

Diana laughed. She liked Graham a lot. He was bright and funny, sweet but strong, and split the housework with Risa fifty-fifty. "Right," she said. "I'll bet you can peel a banana in two seconds flat."

Still smiling, she led Marc over to the couch. Tracy was kneading John's thigh while John fiddled with Tracy's hair. Her stomach began to churn, but she tried not to let it show. "Marc, this is my cousin Tracy, Risa's sister, and her husband John Redmon. John is an attorney. He specializes in corporate law."

And Tracy specialized in shopping, lunching and charity work. Now twenty-five, she was exactly what John had wanted, a full-time wife, seemingly sweet and submissive, who bolstered his fragile ego and catered to his every whim. Diana tried not to resent their obvious happiness, but it was impossible. Two people she'd loved and trusted had knifed her in the back, and she doubted she'd ever get over it.

Marc kissed Tracy's hand, and then, seemingly oblivious to her beauty, turned his attention to John. "In a way, we've met," he said. "I received a letter from you about a month ago."

"A Van Slyke Foundation form letter," William explained to John. "The one you send to crackpots who want to look for buried treasure. Marc read the article in the *Geographic* and wrote to Diana. Mentioned that he had a treasure map. Obviously she took him for a nut case."

Diana regretted she'd sent a form reply to a letter that had deserved a personal answer, but not enough to apologize. Rochard had played too many games and cost her too much money. Besides, if he had information of genuine historical interest, he should have said so the other night.

"I'm afraid I've been too busy at work to do anything more than glance through the mail and stick on Post-it notes telling John how to answer it," she said. "Ever since that article, it's been coming in in droves. And whenever I see the word 'treasure' in a letter..."

"You assume it was written by a madman and tell your lawyer to send a stock reply." The indulgent smile was back on Marc's face. "That's perfectly understandable, *chérie*. I forgive you for your deplorable lack of manners."

"That's very generous of you," Diana said through clenched teeth. She hadn't forgiven the things *he'd* done, not by a long shot, and dearly wished she could tell him so.

Her life, she decided, was out of control. She attended family parties and smiled at Tracy and John because it would have caused awkwardness and unpleasantness if she hadn't. She continued using John as the foundation's attorney because replacing him would have led to tension and hard feelings. She was polite to the likes of Marc Rochard because Nelly and William had taken a liking to him and would have been appalled if she'd been rude. Someone should give her a medal for being the world's best sport.

Marc took her arm and started toward the door. "I believe I detected a note if irritability in that answer. Low blood sugar, obviously. You need to be fed."

"Far be it from me to argue." Diana waited until they were out of earshot, then added, "Just out of curiosity, Mr. Rochard, do you treat all women this way or is it just me?"

He frowned. "What way?"

"Like children who don't know their own minds."

He hesitated, then replied, "I admit I enjoy teasing you. You're so determined to be proper that it's hard to resist. I also enjoy looking after you. I'm a man and you're a woman, so it's only natural that I should protect you. If I've inadvertently offended you, I'm sorry."

He looked so solemn that she didn't doubt his sincerity. She just wondered how any contemporary male could be so backward. She'd worked with some difficult men in her time, but none of them had been as chauvinistic as he was.

Then again, he was French. Not only did Frenchmen flatter and flirt outrageously; they looked upon women as simple, rather fragile creatures who needed their guidance and protection. It drove her crazy, but it wasn't his fault. He was a victim of his upbringing.

Everyone sat down, Nelly at one end of the table and William at the other. Marc and Diana were next to each other beside the Morrisons and the Van Slykes and the Redmons were across from them. Diana began to relax as Marc lit the candles and dimmed the lights. Judging by the aroma, dinner was going to be superb.

Then Tracy smiled triumphantly and said, "Before we start eating, I have an announcement to make. The twins are going to have a cousin about five months from now. John and I are expecting."

For a strained second or two, the room was deadly quiet. Everyone knew that Diana had wanted a child. It had been John who'd insisted on waiting—waiting until he'd finished law school, waiting until they'd bought an apartment, waiting until he was a partner in his firm. The promotion had come a week ago. The pregnancy had started four months ago. For Tracy, he'd been willing to go ahead.

Diana felt empty inside. Tracy was everything she wasn't—tall and slender, young and beautiful, sexy and exciting. Diana's only advantages were integrity and a fat paycheck, and John had stopped valuing those things when he'd stopped needing her to support him.

She pushed aside the hurt as she had so often in the past and did what everyone expected her to. She smoothed over an awkward situation. "That's wonderful news, Tracy. Congratulations, John. It's nice when cousins are close in age, don't you think?"

"That's true," Risa said. "Look at Diana and me, Tracy. We're each other's best friends."

Diana gave Risa a grateful look. Even a bulldozer like Tracy would know she'd been put in her place. "I suppose so," Tracy said, "but still, that isn't the same as being sisters, is it?"

"That's true," Risa said. "You love your sister no matter what she does. You hold your cousin to a higher standard."

Tracy stiffened and paled, but Nelly rushed to put things right with congratulations and questions. Brightening, Tracy chattered about her plans to turn the study into a nursery and her desire for a large family. Diana smiled numbly, barely listening, thinking she'd made a mess of her life.

Then a pair of warm male hands settled themselves on her shoulders and she jerked around. For once, she didn't mind Marc's touching her. The human contact was comforting.

"Help me with the soup," he said.

"Sure." Glad to escape, she let him help her up.

The kitchen was on the other side of a pair of swinging shutter doors. Marc took a large pot and several plastic containers out of the refrigerator and set them on the counter. The empty soup bowls were stacked nearby.

"Cold soup?" she asked.

"It was a hot day." He uncovered the pot, dipped in a spoon and held it up to her lips. "Here. Taste it."

She did so, then sighed with pleasure. It was sheer heaven, like drinking fresh asparagus. "That's wonderful. Did you make it yourself?"

He looked insulted. "Of course I did. The bread, too, but I had it in the freezer. Do you think you can buy food this good at a take-out counter?"

"No. I guess I'm just surprised you're a chef. You don't look like one."

He tasted the soup using the same spoon as she had. "It needs more cream. Why not? What do I look like?"

"The truth? Given the clothing you wear—expensive, stylish, European—a French playboy." She studied him for a moment longer, taking in the lean muscularity of his frame and the strength of his features. "Or maybe you're actually a con man. You have a hard edge to you. I mean, that business about having a treasure map... Do you really expect me to believe that?''

"The map exists," he said, "and I'll have you know that I'm a model citizen. I've always worked hard for a living."

Diana wasn't about to let such a clear opportunity pass untapped. "Doing what, exactly?"

A slow smile spread over his face. "If you want me to tell you, you'll have to trade me some information."

"Such as?"

"Such as..." He folded his arms across his chest. "Why were you so upset about your cousin being pregnant?"

"I wasn't—"

"You were, Diana. Why?"

He'd seen a great deal more than she'd meant to reveal. "It's personal," she said.

"Obviously, *chérie*. So?"

"So I don't want to talk about it."

He stirred some cream into the soup and tasted it again, then ladled some into a bowl. "Fair enough. We'll discuss it some other time." He pointed to a plastic container. "Open that up and sprinkle a few asparagus tips on top of each portion."

Diana began to help, frustrated by his refusal to talk. Then again, negotiations were a way of life to her, and she was very good at them. If Marc Rochard was what he claimed to be, someone would tell him about her past eventually, but there was no guarantee that he would ever return the favor. He was very closemouthed.

Finally she said, "What you want to know is worth a lot more than what I want to know. I should get another question."

"Such as?"

"Such as... Why did you bid me up at the auction? Why did you want the sideboard so much?"

"That's two questions, but you're too beautiful to refuse." He walked to the refrigerator and took out some wine. "You go first."

"Oh, no, you don't. I don't trust you—not after what you did to me Saturday night. *You* go first."

"On the contrary, I told you exactly what my intentions were and followed them to the letter." He set down the wine and took out a corkscrew. "Except for letting you have the chinoiserie chest, of course, and that was only because I couldn't bear to see you cry. If I tell you I'm going to do something, I will. Don't ever doubt that."

Diana thought back to everything he'd ever said. Amazingly enough, he was almost right. "That isn't quite true. You promised I would forgive you—by last night, you said. I haven't. I still think you were a skunk to cost me so much money."

"But you'll change your mind. I made a slight miscalculation, that's all. It took me a little longer to get myself invited to your home than I'd planned on. Didn't I tell you I was looking forward to dinner?"

He certainly had, and now she knew what he'd meant. "I suppose you've been relishing the prospect for days—the shock in my eyes when I walked in and saw you."

"True, but I was looking forward to simply being with you far more. The soup is getting warm, Diana. Stop stalling and answer my question."

She hesitated. She found it hard to talk about John, but something about Marc Rochard made it a little easier. He drove her crazy at times with his slick compliments and proprietary attitude, but he was also bright, witty and perceptive. Besides, she wanted some answers of her own.

"John Redmon is my ex-husband," she said uneasily. "I wanted to have a child, but he insisted on waiting until he was a partner in his law firm. The partnership offer came last week, years before anyone expected it would. But for Tracy..." She took a deep breath. Her throat was tight with pain now. "The study she plans to turn into a nursery was my study. The apartment was our apartment."

"Tell me something." His voice was gentle, sympathetic. "Was she his mistress? Did he leave you for her?"

She shrugged. "Of course."

"Of course?" He smiled and shook his head. "Listen to me, Diana. John is a handsome man. Intelligent and ambitious, I suppose. I'm sure you had good reason to fall in love with him and marry him, so I hope you won't be insulted if I tell you that he's also an insecure fool. Girls like your cousin Tracy are a dime a dozen. Women like you are one in a million. He made an extremely stupid mistake, but personally, I'm glad that he did."

Tracy was brighter and more talented than he seemed to realize, but there wasn't a betrayed ex-wife in the world who could have heard something like that from a man as handsome as he was and not felt a little better. "You sure know the right things to say," she murmured.

"I've simply stated the truth. When you know me a little better, you'll realize that I never lie." He paused. "I believe I owe you some answers."

"Yes." She couldn't help smiling. "Honest ones."

"That's the only kind I give. I used to be the sales director for a winery my family owns in Bordeaux. I still am, technically, but only until they can replace me. As for why I bid you up at the auction and insisted on buying the sideboard . . . If I hadn't, you would have ignored me or brushed me aside as someone insignificant. I preferred to be recognized and respected."

Diana had already figured that out. "Yes, but why? Do you want to do business with me?"

He walked over to the oven and took out a loaf of bread. "In a manner of speaking. Let's serve the soup, *chérie*."

The subject was obviously closed.

Chapter Four

Marc was deeply indebted to Tracy Redmon. If she hadn't stolen away Diana's husband, Diana wouldn't have been free to marry *him*. The girl was beautiful, but sadly insecure. She obviously considered Diana a threat, and struck out at her at every opportunity. And most successfully, too, it seemed.

It was a habit he intended to break, but just this once, he was willing to overlook it. Diana's reaction had been very informative. Quite clearly, he'd underestimated the complexity of the situation. He would have to proceed more cautiously than he'd first thought necessary.

It was obvious that she'd been hurt badly. Her husband had left her for another woman, and now she felt inferior and undesirable. That was ridiculous, but it was also entirely understandable. Quite naturally, she was wary of men in general and mistrustful of their motives.

Under the circumstances, the ardent declaration of love he'd planned to make simply wouldn't do. She wouldn't have believed it. She would have thought it was a line, or some bizarre but fleeting infatuation.

Seduction, alas, was also out of the question. As much as he wanted to make love to her, he couldn't afford passion followed by morning-after regrets. He would have to arouse her without frightening her, then hold himself firmly in check and let her set the pace. In time, she would come to trust him. She would see that the future he envisioned would make both of them supremely happy.

In the meantime, he was content to enjoy both her company and the pleasures of the chase. With each minute, she captivated him more completely. He'd loved her and wanted to care for her from the start, but now he found himself admiring her deeply.

His Diana had breeding and class. Life had thrust her into a situation that most women would have found unbearable, but she'd responded with generosity and grace. He was all the more impressed because he'd seen the way she ached inside. Her pain—and her struggle to conceal it—made him all the more determined to protect her.

The trick was to do it in just the right way. She was very proud, very independent. She considered him a stranger, even an adversary, and would resent his interference. But if he rescued her from an unpleasant situation by having her help him with dinner, or spared her from humiliation by steering the conversation into more congenial waters... That she would accept and even welcome.

He seated her, then brought out the rest of the soup and went back to the kitchen for the wine. Everyone was chattering about childbirth and babies when he returned. Diana was valiantly taking part, but he could guess how she must feel.

Her smile never faltered, not even when Tracy gushed about how protective John was now that she was pregnant. "I should hope so," Diana said lightly. "After all, that's my newest cousin he's taking care of."

Marc poured some wine into William's glass as Tracy prattled on about the way John spoiled her. William sniffed it, then took a sip. "Not one of yours, I see," he said.

He'd known because the wine was white, and the Rochard family made only reds. "It's from Burgundy—a Mâcon-Villages," Marc said. "I'll serve you one of ours with the duck."

Babe's ears perked up. "One of yours? Do you own a winery, then?"

"Not me. My family."

"Château du Ciel, near St. Emilion," William said. "They're small, but they make a damn good wine. This is excellent, by the way."

Marc smiled. "Of course it is. I wouldn't have chosen it for you otherwise." He filled William's glass, then served the others.

"Château du Ciel," Babe murmured thoughtfully. She snapped her fingers. "That's it! That's where I saw you. I toured Bordeaux a few years ago and drove into your winery. It wasn't open to the public except by invitation, but the prettiest young girl took pity on me and said she would ask if she could show me around. She said she was the owner's granddaughter."

"That would have been my sister's daughter, Thérèse Corot," Marc said as he sat down.

"She was very charming. She went over to ask your permission—you were talking to some workers by the side of the house—and you glanced at me and then shook your head." Babe gave him a reproachful look. "That wasn't very hospitable of you, Marc, especially when I was a member of the family."

He laughed, enjoying her teasing. "My profoundest apologies, *Madame* Van Slyke. If only you'd told me..."

"If only I'd known, and it's Babe." She sighed dramatically. "Still, it's only what one expects from the French. Insularity, aloofness, xenophobia..."

"We don't dislike foreigners. We simply believe ourselves to be superior to other people, and therefore too exalted to take notice of them. The winemakers of Bordeaux consider themselves a sort of untitled nobility, you know." He poured himself some wine. "Especially my father, who has a fierce attachment to his land and a passion for privacy. Given how aristocratic he is, you'd never guess he was descended from something so disreputable as a pair of pirates. I would have approved the tour if I'd known you through my job, but I didn't, so I didn't dare."

"Your job," Babe said. "I thought you didn't have one."

Marc turned to Diana. His evasiveness had served its purpose and piqued her interest, but it had also tried her patience. Now he could make amends.

"You see how open I'm being?" he asked. "How completely unmysterious? You have my permission to give your aunt an answer."

"Do I, Mr. Rochard? I'm honored." Despite her dry tone, she was smiling. "He's the director of sales there, Aunt Babe, or rather, he was. I established that in the kitchen, and at great personal sacrifice, I might add."

Babe cocked an eyebrow. "Oh? What did you have to do? Give him another Van Slyke heirloom?"

Diana laughed, warming Marc's heart. It was something she did far too little of. That was another thing he meant to change.

"It wasn't quite that bad," she said, "but I don't think I'm going to tell you."

"This gets better and better." Babe looked at her older daughter. "Worm it out of her, Risa, and then call me right away. I won't sleep until I know. About his job, Diana... Exactly what were his duties?"

"He didn't say. In my dealings with Mr. Rochard, I've found that he tells me only as much as he's agreed to and not a whit more."

"But look how much I've intrigued you," he said.

"Irritated me, you mean." She sipped her wine. "This *is* good. So is the bread."

"Only good? Not wonderful?"

"All right, then. Wonderful. And the soup... You already know what I think about the soup. You're forgiven, I suppose, but only partially."

"Then it's fortunate that it's a four-course meal. By dessert I'll have redeemed myself completely."

She gave him a level look. "Food can't make up for the loss of a hundred fifty thousand dollars, *mon ami*. I don't care how good it is. You'll have to provide something more."

"My God, a hundred and fifty grand?" Risa gasped. "That's what he cost you, Diana?"

"A little more, actually," Marc said, feeling pleased with himself. Diana was having a grand time fencing with him. He'd see that she had an even better time later on.

"Actually, I thought I might return it," he continued, gazing at her admiringly, "but you Americans have a saying—there's no such thing as a free lunch. I'm afraid I'll have to charge you at least as much as I did in the kitchen." He lowered his voice, using a tone that made his meaning unmistakable. "Something more than information, *chérie*."

Taken aback, she blushed and lowered her eyes. Her shyness enchanted him. "Let's just say that I reserve the right to negotiate," she murmured. "What about the sideboard? Are you going to return that, too?"

"Not yet. One shouldn't risk all one's chips on the same hand." He looked across at Babe. "To answer your question, when I became director of sales eight years ago, our wine was sold almost exclusively within France. I thought it deserved a wider audience. Each year since, I've made trips throughout Europe and America to bring it to the attention of wine merchants and restaurateurs. Our foreign sales almost equal our sales at home now."

"Your countrymen's loss and our gain," William said.

"Yes, for our Château du Ciel label, but we were able to buy a neighboring vineyard about four years ago, so our total production has almost doubled. Our second wine is called Château Vermeil. My father is extremely conservative by nature and refused to expand at first, but we managed to talk him into it."

"We?" Diana repeated. "And who would that be?"

"My sister, Catherine, and I, but even more important, my grandmother. My mother's mother. She was very wealthy. She threatened to buy the vineyard herself, if my father wouldn't, and give it to Catherine and me to compete with him. He came around rather quickly after that."

"Marc's grandfather made a fortune in auto parts, Diana. An American—from New Jersey, of all places." William took a long swallow of wine. "Conjures up visions of grease and gasoline. Doesn't mix with wine, at all."

"Money mixes with everything," Marc said. "Forty years ago, my father was in desperate need of capital in order to modernize and my mother had an ardent desire for a husband with an impressive pedigree. They met while she was touring Europe with her parents. She was smitten with his position and he was enchanted by her money. It's been a very successful match."

He noticed Diana gaping at him. "What's wrong, *chérie*? Was I too crass for you?"

"Crass?" She blinked at him. "No. It's just that when Daddy mentioned auto parts... Was your grandfather Sam Parisi?"

He nodded. "You've heard of him?"

"In my line of work? Of course I have." She glanced around the table. "Parisi put together one of the first conglomerates—took over half a dozen companies with money from his auto-parts business and then sold everything at a huge profit and retired. Everyone thought he'd get bored and go back to work, but he never did."

"He was too busy enjoying himself. My grandfather had great *joie de vivre*." Marc stood up. "Give me a few minutes, Diana, and then come into the kitchen and help me with the next course."

"I'd be glad to," she said. "What are you making?"

Despite her agreeable tone, he sensed that he'd annoyed her in some way. "Lobster quenelles with a *parisienne* sauce." He picked up a couple of soup bowls and carried them into the kitchen.

Diana followed him with her eyes as he strode away. The mystery might have been gone, but the fascination lingered. For one thing, he was obviously very rich, and she was always on the lookout for people with money to invest. If that was the business he had in mind, she was definitely interested.

For another, she wondered what had prompted him to leave the family business and move to New York. She was curious about his ancestry, too, especially after that mention of pirates. And finally, she wanted a look at his map. She wasn't foolish enough to believe it would lead to buried treasure, but it might have some historical significance. If so, maybe he would donate it to her museum, although God only knew what he would ask in return.

Aunt Nelly and Aunt Babe began discussing the finer points of quenelles, which were a sort of dumpling, while her father complained to his brother about a lurid biography he'd just published. Henry retorted that William would stop grousing when his next dividend check arrived, evoking a scowl and even hotter criticism. Henry was tartly defending himself, when Nelly ordered them to stop ruining her birthday party by squabbling like a pair of children. Both brothers told her to mind her own business, but instead, she announced that neither of them was right and apprised them of what the company should *really* publish.

Risa looked at Diana with a barely suppressed smile. She claimed that fighting kept the Van Slykes young. Trying not to laugh, Diana got to her feet and cleared the rest of the soup bowls from the table.

Marc was standing by the stove when she walked into the kitchen, stirring what she assumed was the *parisienne* sauce. She put the bowls in the sink, then opened the dishwasher to load them inside.

"You can do that later," he said, beating more cream into the sauce. "Come over here and taste this. Tell me what you think."

Although she didn't care for his habit of ordering rather than asking, she crossed to the stove. He gave the sauce a final stir, then cupped her chin and held out the spoon. "Be careful," he said. "It's hot."

He was at it again, touching her like a lover and treating her like a child. He was their guest, though, so she held her tongue.

She tried the sauce. It was perfect and she said so.

He released her chin, then tried it himself. "Not quite. It needs more lemon juice. A little pepper, too."

She quashed the urge to ask him why he'd told her to taste it if he wasn't going to listen to her opinion, and started toward the dishwasher. She hadn't taken two steps before he issued another command. "Take the quenelles out of the oven and turn on the broiler. There's some grated cheese in a plastic bag in the refrigerator. Top shelf. I'll need that and some butter."

She stopped and turned around. "I got the impression you'd never cooked professionally, but maybe I was wrong. You give orders like a head chef."

"And you follow them flawlessly, *mon ange*." My angel, my darling. "I'll need the quenelles now. Turn off the oven and leave it ajar. The duck should sit for a while."

Sorely tried, she switched off the heat and grabbed a pot holder. Then she removed the quenelles from the oven and set them down with a thud. That, at least, got his attention.

"Is something the matter?" he asked. "Are you annoyed with me?"

He couldn't be serious. Nobody was that dense. "You order me around, treat me like a child and fling around empty endearments, and you wonder if I'm annoyed? Take a guess, *mon grand général.*"

He grinned at her. "Turn on the broiler and get me the cheese and butter."

He was teasing her, of course. At least he had a sense of humor, however irritating it might be. "All right, but you'll be lucky if they don't wind up on your exalted head."

"Do you lose your temper this way with your clients, too, or just with me?"

"*Monsieur* Rochard, even the worst of my clients isn't as aggravating as you are."

He turned down the flame under the sauce and switched on the broiler. "At least you're not indifferent to me. The endearments are completely sincere, by the way. I'm crazy about you. Come taste this. You'll feel much better."

Diana rolled her eyes. "Are you this glib with all the women you know, or just with me?"

"I'm not being glib. I'm being honest. I told you—I never lie." He cut a slice of quenelle and dipped it in the sauce. "Here. Taste this. And be careful. It's—"

"Hot. I know." Unable to resist something that smelled so good, she took the spoon from his hand, blew on the food to cool it and took a small bite. It was wonderful—

subtly seasoned, succulent with lobster and light as a soufflé. She quickly ate the rest.

"You may be aggravating, but you cook like an angel," she said. "You were right about the sauce, by the way. It's even better than it was before."

He took back the spoon to sauce the quenelles. "Of course it is. A little cheese, and it will be perfect."

"And so modest about your culinary talent, too!" she said, but took the hint and fetched the cheese and butter.

"It's only one of many, but I wouldn't want you to think I was conceited. I know I have my faults. For example, I was a very indifferent student. I worked just hard enough to get my degree and put my real effort into cooking school."

He sprinkled the cheese on top of the sauce, dotted the dish with butter, and slid it under the broiler. It would be ready in a few minutes, he said.

As they waited, he leaned casually against the counter, looking completely at ease. As much as he sometimes annoyed her, he had two qualities she admired, confidence and competence. He dominated a room in the same way that her boss did.

His comment about school renewed her interest in his background. "If you enjoy cooking so much, why did you bother with college?" she asked after a minute. "Why aren't you a professional chef?"

"Family obligations. I'm an only son, so my father expected me to take over the winery eventually. He's no intellectual, but he wanted me to be well-educated for social reasons. I didn't tell him I was attending cooking school at the same time, or that I was more interested in running a restaurant than a winery. I didn't think it would ever be possible."

So he had a strong loyalty to his family. Given her background, she naturally approved of that. "But something happened to make it possible?"

"Yes, but it's a long story. I'll tell you about it when we have more time." He opened the broiler and took out the quenelles. Not surprisingly, they were browned to perfection. Everything he did seemed to be perfect.

He started out of the room. "Would you bring in the serving spoon and plates, please?"

She did a double take. "Would I? Please? Can I possibly have heard you correctly?"

"Of course. Did you think I hadn't listened to your complaints?"

"I knew you'd listened. I just doubted you'd taken them seriously." She fetched the spoon and plates and followed him into the dining room, thinking that he wasn't as hopeless as she'd assumed. In fact, if he hadn't robbed her blind the other night, she might have begun to like him.

Everyone was so enthralled by the quenelles that if he hadn't already been a relative, they would have adopted him. Diana was amused by his nonchalant acceptance of their praise. As one of the oldest families in New York, the Van Slykes didn't lack for noblesse oblige, but Marc Rochard could have outdone them any day of the week.

Afterward Nelly announced that she was sure everyone wanted to know how Marc had come to seek them out, and he explained about reading the article in *National Geographic* and learning about the pirate Philippe Rochard and his marriage to Anna Van Slyke. Aware of the Rochard family lore about being descended from pirates, he'd searched through old papers and records to see if Philippe might be one of the pirates in question.

A family Bible and a pair of diaries had provided the answer: he was a direct and legitimate descendant of Philippe and his wife Anna through their son, Pierre, while according to the article, Diana was their descendant through their daughter Marie, who had married her second cousin George Van Slyke. To Diana's astonishment, he said that their son Pierre had been survived by a pregnant wife, Simone Saint-Denis, the daughter of a pirate named Louis Saint-Denis.

At that point, William took over. "He showed me the documents this afternoon, Diana. They're the real thing. Read some of Simone's diary, even though I couldn't really spare the time. It confirms what Philippe wrote in his journal—that he and Pierre were sailing back to France when they died, and that he planned to pick up Anna and their two daughters in Cherbourg and move them to an island near Madagascar. Simone was an impudent little thing. Wondered if he planned to move in his native mistress, too."

"It makes one doubt he was in his right mind," Marc said. "From his point of view, he had the perfect arrangement—homes in two different countries, with a wife in one and a mistress in the other. Why fetch his family?"

"And from yours?" Diana asked tartly.

"That depends. If Anna was as enchanting as you are, he was a fool to have taken a mistress, at all."

"And if Philippe was as slick as you are," she replied, "he probably thought he could get away with anything."

"Me? Slick?" He looked wounded.

"After the way you maneuvered me at the auction? Definitely." She paused. "To answer your question about why Philippe went back for Anna... During the late 1680s and 1690s, England and France were at war, and Philippe claimed to be a French privateer preying on English ships. Since India and England were allies of sorts, he was able to justify looting Indian ships, too. But then the war wound down. It ended in 1698. Even in France's eyes, he became a pirate, an outlaw. He was afraid he'd be tried and hung if he stayed, so he decided to move his family to Madagascar." She looked at William. "What else was in the diary?"

"Simone mentioned that last, huge prize he took, and said he was afraid someone would rob him while he was

gone. Claimed he'd dug a booby-trapped pit and buried a
fortune in coins and jewels inside. Pierre made a map of
how to retrieve the treasure and left it with her. Rounding
the Cape was always dangerous, and he wanted her to be
provided for in case anything happened to them.''

"Then she dug up the treasure after she learned about
Pierre's death?''

William shook his head. "No. She was living with her
father at the time, and didn't trust him. She was afraid he
would spend the treasure on himself, if he got his hands on
it. They left Madagascar after the Royal Navy landed in
1699 and put a stop to piracy in the area. She'd given birth
to a son by then, Pierre-Luc. Her father bought a vineyard in France and married into the local gentry. Simone
held on to the map, intending to have Pierre-Luc go back
for the treasure when he grew up. That way, none of it
would go to her father's second family. That's as much as
I had time to read.''

"If Pierre-Luc ever tried to find it,'' Marc said, "it's not
mentioned in his journal. Grapes seem to have been all he
cared about. He built Château du Ciel into a fine winery
almost single-handedly. Louis and his second wife had
four daughters but no sons, so the winery was left to
Pierre-Luc in the end. It's been in the Rochard family ever
since.''

Nelly was entranced. "Isn't that a wonderful story? Just
think, everyone! The treasure might still be buried, just as
the old legends say it is, waiting for us to dig it up.''

"More likely, it was found years ago or never existed in
the first place,'' Diana said.

"You have no romance in your soul,'' Nelly complained. "What about your map, Marc? Surely it tells
where the treasure is located. You could head up an expedition.''

"I could if I knew which island it was on, but I don't.
The map doesn't say.'' He turned to Diana. "There's

something I've been wondering about. According to Simone's diary, she wrote to Anna in Cherbourg as soon as she reached France, but Anna never answered. Why not? And why didn't you know that Simone and Pierre-Luc existed? Aren't they mentioned in your records?''

"Anna must have left France before Simone's letter arrived," Diana said. "We have a good picture of her life in Cherbourg from her letters to her favorite cousin in New York, but she never wrote anything about Pierre getting married. Obviously she never received word of it. There's no mention of it anywhere, even in Philippe's journal.''

"I see." He still looked puzzled. "But why did she leave France in the first place?''

Diana repressed a smile. His tone said that no one in his right mind would have done so. It made her wonder why *he* had. "With all due respect to your homeland, Anna never would have moved there if she and Philippe could have stayed in New York. He was a privateer in the Caribbean when they met and fell in love. He traded with the American colonists, including Anna's father, who was a local merchant. Her father refused to approve the match because of the difference in their religions, so Philippe spirited Anna off to France and married her there. After he died, his shipmates gave her his journals, which he'd kept in his cabin. Until then, she'd thought he was still a privateer, and she was horrified to learn he'd turned to piracy. She was afraid the truth would come out and ruin her daughters' reputations. As far as she knew, there was nothing to keep her in France, so she returned to America. Her parents were dead by then, so she moved in with her favorite cousin. Five years later, her older daughter, Marie, married that cousin's son, George Van Slyke.''

"Thereby saving everyone a great deal of trouble about who should own Van Slyke's Island," William said. "It was supposed to be passed to the oldest son, or to the oldest daughter if there was no son, and Anna was the only child of the previous owner. But she'd been gone for almost twenty years, by then, and her cousin thought of it as his. The male line runs directly from George and Marie's older son down to me."

"And eventually it will be Diana's," Nelly said. She had a dreamy look on her face. "I was just thinking... Philippe's journal is still out at the house, isn't it, Diana? Maybe there's some clue about where the treasure is."

If there was, Diana didn't remember it. Besides, she didn't have time for wild-goose chases. "I'll fetch it the next time I go to the island, Aunt Nelly. Why don't you read it and see what you can come up with?"

"My French isn't good enough. I want *you* to do it." She frowned in concentration. "Or you, Marc. You'd definitely be the best one for the job."

"I'd be glad to translate it. In fact, I'd like to look at whatever records you have. I'm as fascinated by the subject as you are, Nelly." He put his hand on Diana's shoulder. "The duck should be ready now. Would you mind helping me serve it?"

His tone was soft and low, like a proposition. He seemed to know of only two ways to procure her help—either he ordered her around or he tried to seduce her. It definitely said something about his view of women.

She was tempted to point that out, but instead, she nodded and got up. She cleared and reset the table while he made a raspberry sauce for the duck. By the time she'd brought out the side dishes—wild rice, green beans and more bread—the duck was sauced and ready. The wine he'd brought along, a six-year-old Château du Ciel, was as perfect as the food. Whatever else she thought about Marc Rochard, he certainly did things with style.

Her father was utterly delighted with him, and that was unusual for William Van Slyke. It wasn't that he gave his approval reluctantly, but that he was usually too lost in the mists of history to notice his fellow human beings.

"I'm glad you looked us up," he said to Marc, "and I wouldn't say that to just anyone. History and wine. It's a superb combination." He refilled his glass, looking puckish. William only got puckish when he'd had a little too much to drink. "History is wonderful. Always new discoveries to make, and you never know where they'll come from. Better be nice to the man, Diana, because when you come right down to it, it's *his* island, not mine or yours. After all, Anna would certainly have left it to Pierre-Luc if she'd known he existed, and eventually it would have passed down the Rochard line to Marc."

Marc looked delighted by the idea. "Van Slyke's Island, eh? What do you think, John? You're the lawyer in the family. Do I have a legal claim to it?"

"I'd have to look at old documents and family records. Depending on what's in writing, you very well might."

"I believe I'll pursue it. I like the idea of having my own island." He grinned at Diana. "Don't worry, *chérie*. If you're very nice to me, I'll let you visit once in a while."

She didn't take him seriously. As he'd said, he enjoyed teasing her. "If you ever want to set foot in this apartment again," she said darkly, "you'll forget you ever heard of Van Slyke's Island. It's mine."

He blithely ignored her. "I have quite a collection of things you *wish* were yours, don't I? A hundred fifty thousand dollars, a sideboard and now an island. I'm a reasonable man, though. I'm always willing to negotiate. I'll give some thought to what I want in return and then get back to you."

Diana rolled her eyes.

Chapter Five

The talk turned to the November elections. The Van Slyke siblings were all Republicans, but that didn't stop them from arguing about everyone and everything. It was nearly an hour before they even remembered it was Nelly's birthday.

Marc had made the cake, an orange-almond gâteau with an orange butter-cream filling. It was so moist and tangy that Diana would have had seconds if there had been any left to have. Given the calories, it was just as well that there wasn't.

She looked at her watch. It was almost nine, just an hour before she was supposed to call Warren Fielding. Nervous about finishing the party in time, she set down her coffee and got up. "I'll get your presents, Aunt Nelly. I can't wait to see what everyone's bought you."

"I'll give you a hand," Risa said, lumbering to her feet. "I need to move around a bit. It's not good for me to sit still for so long."

Diana suspected Risa wanted to talk privately, not stretch her legs. She shot Diana a quizzical look every time Marc went into his ardent-lover routine. An incurable romantic, she was probably planning their wedding by now.

"My God, the man is smitten with you!" she hissed as they walked down the hall. "The way he looks at you... The tone he uses... Tracy's in a panic. She's afraid that if you get interested in another man, John will become insanely jealous and try to get you back."

"Every betrayed wife's fantasy, huh?" There was a time when Diana would have responded, but it had long ago passed. John had lost her trust, then her respect, then her love. "Tell her she has nothing to worry about. Even if he wanted me back, I wouldn't go. Besides, I'm not interested in Marc Rochard."

Risa was incredulous. "How can you not be interested? He's a total hunk—handsome, successful, intelligent..."

"And a hopeless chauvinist."

"If he is, he's the most charming one I've ever met. Anyway, you can't have everything."

"Why not?" Diana asked. "You do."

"Don't change the subject. We were talking about you, not me." They entered the living room. "All this time, I kept telling myself that if you met someone special enough, you'd stop burying yourself in your work and start living a normal life. But now you have, and he's obviously crazy about you, and—"

"Wait a minute. Time out." Diana pointed to the couch. "Sit. You need to be educated."

Risa sighed and sat down. Diana joined her, then enlightened her about Frenchmen. They were experts at pretty speeches and admiring stares, but it meant nothing. They were wonderful at falling violently in love, but love had a different meaning to them than it did to Risa. It lasted weeks or months, not a lifetime. It led to affairs, not marriage.

"That's ridiculous," Risa said. "I mean, sooner or later they do get married, Diana. The least you can do is give him a chance."

"Yes, they do get married, but they're practical about it, just like Marc's father was. They choose sweet young things from suitable families and keep mistresses on the side. Anyway, I told you before... I'm not interested in Marc that way. I'm just not attracted to him."

"Because you won't let yourself be. You were hurt badly, so you've put up a wall that no man can knock down."

"And both of us know that dozens have tried."

"You might as well wear a sign that says 'Hands Off' for all the encouragement you give them. They do get the message, Diana. Besides, you intimidate most men." Risa wrinkled her nose. "Princess Di. It's a wonder they don't genuflect. And that awful job... When are you going to stop playing Monopoly and do something you really like?"

"You know the answer to that as well as I do." When she'd bought back the last Van Slyke heirloom. When the mansion opened as a museum. Tired of arguing, she began gathering up Nelly's presents. "They'll wonder what's become of us. We should go now."

"All right, but you haven't heard the last of this." Risa started to help her. "When can you have lunch?"

"Not before Friday. I have to call Warren Fielding tonight—to convince him to make some concessions and meet with me in Los Angeles this week."

"Friday, then. I'll come to your office at noon."

"But I don't want you to trek all the way downtown—"

"Given your crazy schedule, it's the only way I'll get to see you," Risa said. "I don't want to be a nag, but I love you and I'm worried about you. Promise me you'll listen to my advice—that you'll give it a fair chance."

Diana promised, but she had mixed feelings about it. In many ways, Risa was smarter than she was. If *her* husband had been carrying on with another woman for two solid years, she definitely would have known. Her life was smooth, predictable and happy.

On the other hand, Risa had a wonderful husband and a sunny, uncomplicated nature. She hadn't been raised to consider Van Slyke's Island her special joy and burden, or been forced to look after herself from the age of nine. Her life had been shaped by security, Diana's by instability and unthinking neglect.

They returned to the dining room with Nelly's presents, which she opened with great ceremony and much delight. Henry and Babe had bought her an exquisite silk blouse, but everyone else had brought along an antique for one of her collections. There was a Swiss Army knife from William, a pair of bifocals from Risa and Graham, and a salt-and-pepper set in the form of a brass violin and cello from Diana, but the gift Nelly liked best was a Christmas water globe from Tracy. It depicted skaters in a snowy Central Park in the late 1800s, and John made sure everyone knew how many shops Tracy had searched in order to find it.

Diana knew Tracy was genuinely fond of Aunt Nelly, but she also suspected Tracy had been determined to outshine everyone, especially her. It was a mark of Tracy's insecurity, of course, but Diana always wound up feeling inferior. The plain truth was that Tracy was more creative than she was and had better taste.

Nelly beamed at everyone. "Thank you all so much. You've made this a wonderful birthday. I'm going to find a special place for each and every treasure."

"Fine, as long as it's not in my bedroom or study," William grumbled.

"Who could even get in them, with the way you stack books and papers all over the floor?" Nelly asked. "Really, Billy, it's a wonder you haven't tripped and broken a leg."

"Why put things away when I'm only going to need them again? Anyway, if I were going to trip and break my leg, it would probably be from tiptoeing through the house trying not to knock over your so-called treasures."

Babe ended their squabbling with a firm, "I don't think we've thanked Marc properly for dinner, everyone. It was simply wonderful, Marc."

"Absolutely delicious," Nelly agreed, forgetting her quarrel with William. There were never any hard feelings among the Van Slyke siblings because they never took one another seriously enough to get upset. "Thank you, Marc, dear." She got to her feet. "Why don't we move to the living room? I'll get us some coffee."

"Diana and I will join you in a few minutes," Marc said. "We have some business to discuss—a small matter of some money I owe her." He turned to Diana. "Is there someplace private we can talk, *chérie*?"

It was nine thirty-five and Diana felt pressed for time, but if Marc wanted to give her a check, she wasn't going to put him off. She led him down to her office, which was in an alcove off her bedroom. The room itself was a large one, and contained a small conversation area around a working fireplace in addition to the usual bed and chests.

They both sat down, Diana by her desk and Marc in a chair he pulled over from the conversation area. "I should have brought Nelly a present," he said. "I was so wrapped up in cooking that I completely forgot."

"Don't be silly. Your dinner was the best gift of all. Nelly would have insisted on cooking otherwise, and we'd be suffering from indigestion now."

"Your father did mention her lack of talent in that area." He lazed back in his chair, making himself completely at home. "She's quite a collector. I've never seen so many knickknacks in my life. I have to admit that I don't blame your father for complaining."

Diana didn't have time to chitchat, but she didn't want to be rude, either. "He's more tolerant than he pretends. It's just that they've been bickering for so many years that it's automatic by now. He knows that each of her collections has a special meaning to her. For example, she worked for the phone company as a girl, so she collects telephones. The Swiss Army knife collection was originally her father's, and she's added to it. And the great love of her life was an optometrist, so she collects antique eyeglasses."

His eyes softened with sympathy. "How tragic that an unhappy love affair should have kept such a charming woman from marrying."

"But it didn't," Diana said. "Nelly's kept company with Dr. Wolfman for over forty years. She says she loves him but can't live with him. He retired to Florida a few years ago. They still visit back and forth, but never for more than a week or two at a time. They're both rather eccentric."

"Having met your father this afternoon, I'm prepared to believe that eccentricity runs in your family," Marc said.

He didn't know the half of it. "Umm. And the older we get, the worse we are. I'm afraid it's in the genes—that I'll be the same way someday." She straightened a little, thinking about the time. "You mentioned a donation to the foundation, Marc. I don't want to rush you, but—"

"It's all right, *chérie*. I understand your eagerness." He removed a check from his wallet and held it up. It was for one hundred sixty-eight thousand dollars. "I thought it was only fair to add an extra ten percent to cover Conable's consignment fees."

"Thank you. That was very generous of you." She reached for the check.

He drew back his hand. "Not quite yet. I'm sure you remember the discussion we had about free lunches..."

She blushed. She'd forgotten temporarily, but his smoky tone had reminded her. "Yes. You said you'd want something more than information. What did you have in mind?"

He folded the check and tucked it in his pocket. "One summer, when I was about eight, I visited my grandparents in New Jersey while the town fair was going on. I remember the animals and rides, but most of all, I remember a pretty girl with red hair who was raising money for the local 4-H club by selling kisses for a dollar apiece." He grinned at her. "It's a time-honored American custom, I believe."

Her face got even warmer. "Yes. How many did you buy?"

"Just one. After all, a dollar was a lot of money to me then. Besides, even at eight, I understood the pleasures of self-control. She kissed me on the cheek and ruffled my hair. I walked on air all night. A second kiss would have been an anticlimax."

If he was working up to a proposition, it was certainly a unique approach. In fact, she was flattered that he was interested enough to be so creative. "But now you're—what? About thirty?"

"Thirty-two. Why?"

She smiled wryly. "Because self-control or not, I imagine a kiss on the cheek just isn't going to do it for you anymore."

"From you it would," he replied, "but I had something a little different in mind. I thought *I* would kiss *you* rather than the other way around. Would that be acceptable?"

She was so astonished that she burst out laughing. "That's it? You're going to give me a check for a hundred sixty-eight grand and all you want in return is to kiss me?"

"That's all," he said. "Anything else would be a breach of a noble American tradition."

She hesitated. It was too good to be true. "Kiss me exactly where?"

"Nowhere that couldn't be shown in a film rated *PG*. Don't be so suspicious. It's just a simple kiss. You might even like it. And it *is* for charity."

She studied him, still uncertain about his intentions. "But you could ask for a Van Slyke heirloom or even for my services as an investment banker. As it is, you're getting the short end of the stick. You do realize that, don't you?"

"Not in my opinion. Besides, I couldn't live with myself if I kept the money I'd cost you."

And that, she thought, was the crux of the matter. He was going to give her the money anyway, and being French, he couldn't resist combining it with a little romance. "In that case, how about throwing in the sideboard?"

"I'm afraid not. As I told you, I'm saving it for another time." He got to his feet and held out his hand. "We might as well make ourselves comfortable. Why don't we sit on the love seat?"

She withdrew a little. "You make it sound fundamentally unpleasant—like going to the dentist or paying your taxes."

"I hope it will be infinitely more enjoyable. Come, Diana. I promise I'm not dangerous."

"I never thought you were," she said, but remained where she was. "I mean, it's just a kiss, right?"

"Right." He took her hand. "Come along, *chérie.*"

Obviously he expected her to melt in his arms the moment he touched her. Given the size of his ego, he no doubt assumed she would offer herself within days. She almost told him he was wasting his time, but actions spoke louder than words. Besides, it would take more than words to discourage the likes of Marc Rochard.

She let him help her up. "All right, since it's for charity."

He kept her hand firmly in his and led her over to the love seat. Since it faced the fireplace, she couldn't help seeing the clock on the mantel. Her thoughts abruptly shifted to the phone call she had to make. It was a quarter of ten, and Warren Fielding was a stickler for punctuality. She didn't dare keep him waiting. Still, how long could a kiss take?

Marc put his arm around her and bent his head. She was too nervous about Fielding to worry about his intentions now. She'd rehearsed what she planned to say all day long, but it wouldn't hurt to go over it one more time.

She was concentrating intensely, mentally reviewing her arguments, when Marc nuzzled her neck quite ardently. She was so startled that she jerked away. He immediately released her, looking concerned and a little unnerved.

Embarrassed to have alarmed him, she hastily apologized. "I'm sorry. I didn't realize that nuzzling my neck was going to be part of the operation. Please, go on with whatever you planned to do. Within reason, that is."

Marc took a deep breath. He had to get a grip on himself, but it was difficult. To finally touch the woman he loved—to breathe in her erotic scent and savor her milky softness... Perhaps inevitably, his body had raced far ahead of his mind.

But, *mon Dieu*, her reaction...! In the thirty-two years of his life, he'd never had such a response from a woman. He didn't know whether to be astonished, insulted or depressed.

Here he was, on fire with passion but determined to show restraint, trying doggedly to make love to his future wife without frightening her, and she'd felt absolutely nothing. Less than nothing. She'd utterly ignored him, then been startled to realize he was even touching her. It was unprecedented, unbelievable.

It was all the more inexplicable because he was sure she wasn't indifferent to him. On the contrary, she seemed to enjoy his company immensely, as he did hers. Not only was she alluring and adorable, gracious and valiant, but she was amusing and provocative. They were perfect together, even a fool could see that, so why couldn't she?

She was staring into the empty fireplace now, seemingly lost in thought. He put his arm around her, but she didn't react. It was as though he were a ghost, without form or substance. Still, he wasn't about to give up.

He kissed her more gently, running his lips along her jawbone and down her throat. Her breathing didn't quicken even a fraction. Her skin was as cool and dry as ever. He might as well have been making love to a statue.

Disappointed but undaunted, he moved closer. He held her more possessively and kissed his way to her ear. He'd no sooner brushed his lips across her lobe than she smiled. Some response was better than none, he supposed, but if he'd had his way, he would have chosen something other than being laughed at.

He nuzzled her ear as erotically as he could, and she twitched and giggled. *Giggled!* Such total failure was unheard of, downright insulting! Baffled and frustrated, he couldn't stop himself from stiffening and asking a little coolly whether she cared to share the joke.

It was a few seconds before she answered. "The joke? What joke?"

"You were laughing at me," he said. Or at something, he suddenly realized. Her mind was so obviously elsewhere that perhaps something other than his lovemaking had amused her.

Diana wasn't so lost in the Parkman-Fielding merger that she failed to notice how offended Marc was. It was obvious that things hadn't gone the way he'd planned, and not surprisingly, he wasn't taking it well.

In retrospect, the situation was sort of funny, but she never would have been so rude as to say so. Meanness wasn't a part of her character. "I wasn't laughing at *you*," she said honestly. "I was just laughing. I guess I'm a little ticklish. On my ear, I mean."

"You guess?" he repeated. "You mean you don't know?"

It never occurred to her to lie. "I really don't. Nobody's ever nuzzled my ear before. John wasn't much for—well, for that sort of thing."

"Wasn't he?" Mollified, he drew her close again. "Then he missed a great deal. You have beautiful ears. Sweet. Delicate. Succulent. Made for a man to taste."

Like a juicy piece of fruit, she thought. Leave it to a chef to compare her to food. "You Frenchmen come up with the most creative metaphors. I spent a summer in Paris when I was twenty, but I never got used to the way Frenchmen flatter a woman."

"We appreciate beauty and say so. Most women find it an attractive trait." He frowned. "These compliments you received... I suppose a great many of my countrymen tried to make love to you that summer."

"A few, but I'd known John for two years and I was in love with him. I wasn't interested in other men. Except for this cute Italian in the next flat..." Paolo Moretti. She'd adored his sense of humor. "Well, never mind about him."

"You had an affair?"

She was shocked he would think so. "Of course not. I told you—I was in love with John. He wanted us to see other people that summer, to be sure we wanted to get married, so I went out with Paolo a few times. But it was never serious."

She glanced at the clock, wondering how the conversation had gotten so personal. She didn't normally talk about herself, and besides, they weren't on the love seat to talk. "I don't want to rush you, but I have some business to take care of," she said. "How much longer is this going to take?"

She realized it was an unfortunate choice of words even before he stiffened and scowled. "That's a question one asks one's dentist, Diana, not one's future—"

He cut himself off, but Diana could supply the missing noun. Lover. She didn't bother telling him he was wrong. It would have been a waste of her breath.

He visibly collected himself. "The point is, you might try to get into the spirit of things a little more."

"I'm sorry. I don't have anything against being kissed. It's just that I have a phone call to make at ten and I can't be late."

He sighed. "Are you always so wrapped up in business?"

"Not always," she said thoughtfully. "Sometimes I'm wrapped up in Van Slyke's Island instead."

Exasperated now, he muttered something in French about knowing it would be hard and keeping his temper in check. Too amused to help herself, she answered in the same language. "My dear cousin, it's going to be worse than hard. It's going to be impossible. But if you insist on trying..."

"I do. And we'll see just how impossible it will be." He put his arm around her and cupped her chin. "The preliminaries obviously bored you. Maybe this won't."

He kissed her lightly several times. His eyes, she noticed, were closed, and his breathing was decidedly uneven. To her surprise, she found his closeness rather pleasant. She wasn't aroused, but for the first time in ages, she felt feminine and desirable.

Then she sneaked a look at the clock, and her thoughts flew back to Warren Fielding. It was five of ten. Fielding would have fits if she were late. It wasn't a good idea to offend a man, when you were trying to convince him to make concessions he didn't want to make.

Marc took her lower lip between his teeth and nibbled it gently. Then he did the same with her upper lip. It brought back such strong memories that she forgot Fielding and said in surprise, "Paolo used to do that, too. Nibble when he kissed, that is. I'd never run into that before. Is it some sort of European thing?"

"*Pour l'amour de Dieu ... !*" He threw up his hands in frustration. "I give up. Go make your phone call. But you're having dinner with me tomorrow night, and I promise you, Diana, I'm going to kiss you until you forget you even have a job, much less what it is."

"I'm afraid you're not," she said firmly. Nothing seemed to discourage him, which left her only one option, a loud and clear *no*. "No more kissing, not even for the sideboard. And I'm not having dinner with you tomorrow, either. Even if I wanted to, I'll be in Los Angeles for the next few days, and I don't want to."

Marc was too agitated to answer. He would have grabbed Diana and kissed her passionately if he'd thought it would do any good, but he knew it wouldn't. Just when he'd begun to make some progress, the woman had switched off completely. She was utterly impossible— wrapped up in some trivial phone call and totally cut off from her feelings.

"I'll get Philippe's journal to Nelly as soon as I can," she added. "She'll let you know when you can pick it up." She stood, implicitly dismissing him.

It was bad enough to be banished like a child, but he damn well wasn't taking the journal from anyone but Diana. She would find that out soon enough, just as she would learn to hunger for both his company and his love-making. He would simply have to bide his time and wait for a favorable moment to approach her again.

It took every ounce of his self-control, but somehow he smiled and got up. "I'll look forward to reading it. I hope your trip goes well." He pressed a seductive kiss into her palm, then took out the check and closed her hand around it. *"Au revoir, chérie. Soignez-vous bien."* Take good care of yourself.

She smiled distractedly and thanked him, then headed for the phone. It wasn't the reaction he'd hoped for. Exasperated all over again, he stalked out of the room.

Rather than go straight to the living room, he decided to stop into the kitchen to gather up his belongings. He needed some time to calm down.

He hurtled through the doors to find Graham washing pots while Risa sat nearby, keeping him company. Although he quickly replaced the scowl on his face with a smile, he wasn't quite fast enough.

"Cheer up," Risa said with a grin. "She does like you, Marc, very much in fact. She just doesn't know it yet."

Chagrined that he'd been so obvious, he raised a cool eyebrow at her. He'd been taught that a gentleman kept his own counsel about matters of the heart. "Oh?"

"That's it? *Oh*?" She rested her hands on her belly and fixed him with a knowing stare. "Obviously I misread you. I thought you had the look of a man who'd just come from a very frustrating encounter with a woman he was crazy about. And if you had, I was going to tell you some things that would help you understand her. But since you're not interested . . ."

He stared back. Risa was Diana's best friend, and a potential ally. But still . . . "Of course I'm interested. It's just that—"

"Interested in what?" Graham interrupted. "In getting her into bed?"

His voice was so icy that Marc laughed and unbent a bit. He needed all the help he could get, and the Morrisons seemed willing to provide it. Besides, people who cared for Diana so deeply were by definition his friends. "You're exactly right, and the sooner the better. I intend to marry her."

"Do you? Already?" Risa sighed. "Love at first sight. How romantic!"

"Maybe so, but I thought it would be a mistake to say so. Thanks to her ex-husband and your sister, I doubt she'd believe me."

Risa looked surprised. "You mean she told you about John and Tracy? That's amazing. She's usually so close-mouthed. It just proves that she likes you more than she realizes."

"Then one of these days she's bound to notice that she's a woman and I'm a man, but much to my regret, it hasn't happened yet. I got nowhere with her just now."

"Give her time. You're probably right that she'd think it was a line if you told her how you feel, so you'll just have to show her. She was hurt awfully badly, and to have it shoved in her face all the time..." Risa shifted awkwardly in her chair. "The thing is, she's enclosed herself in a protective shell. She thinks that if she doesn't let herself feel anything, she can't be hurt again."

"That's completely understandable." He was reassured to learn that he'd assessed the situation so accurately. "Perhaps this is God's way of telling me that it's been too easy for me in the past. I admit that I'm not the most patient man in the world."

"It's a good thing, too," Risa said. "If you were, you might wind up like poor Dr. Wolfman, Nelly's friend. He's been courting her for forty years."

"Yes. Diana told me about that." He crossed to the sink and began drying containers and pots, most of which he'd brought from his house. "Unfortunately, she shares her aunt's stubbornness and independence. Is it a characteristic of all the Van Slyke women?"

Graham turned around. "Absolutely. I keep telling Risa to stop working, but she won't listen."

"Only because I'd die of boredom, or maybe of fat. You try being pregnant and doing nothing all day." She shifted her weight again, vainly trying to get comfortable. "Besides, Marc, this is America, not France. Women are more liberated here. They expect to have careers—"

"I have nothing against something suitable, at least until a woman has children. Being an editor, for example. But not investment banking. It's too difficult. Too time-consuming. And I don't approve of the men Diana works with, either. They're cold and hard. A woman should be protected from that aspect of the world."

He knew a lecture was coming even before Risa opened her mouth. Sparks were flying from her eyes. "Good grief, she was right. You *are* a hopeless chauvinist. If you really want to marry her, you'll have to change your attitude, because she'll never be willing to live with it."

"You mean she loves her job so much?" He found the idea astonishing, incomprehensible.

"Not at all, but it makes her the money she needs for the foundation. Anyway, that's not the point. I plan to go back to work in a year or two because I love what I do. Most women I know feel the same way. Diana's real passion is history, especially Van Slyke's Island. She'd like to teach and run the museum there someday, and she's not going to give those things up even for marriage and motherhood." She paused. "Besides, she lost her mother when she was only nine, Marc. William was always in his own world, and Laura's death didn't change that. Diana was pretty much on her own after that. Eventually she and William moved in with Nelly and her mother, but they were both so scatterbrained that Diana took care of them more than the other way around. She was hungry for their love, but she learned very early that the only person she could rely on was herself. Her experience with John only underscored it. She'll always be extremely independent. And she certainly won't marry anyone who doesn't treat her as an equal."

Marc told himself it could have been worse. Running the museum would be impossible once they'd returned to France, but he could live with a little teaching once their children were in school. As for her independence, what had been learned could be unlearned. Once she understood that he loved her and would never leave her, she would come to rely on him for protection and guidance, as a wife naturally should.

"I see," he said, and began loading pots into a carton. "Thank you for talking to me. I'll remember what you've said."

"Not that you have to follow her advice," Graham told him. "You just have to act as if you are. Play your cards right and Diana will never know the difference."

Risa made a face at him. "Very funny. Do you think I don't know that you only nagged me to stop working so I would compromise, cut back on my hours and take cabs everywhere?"

"It worked, didn't it?"

She laughed. "Yes. It worked."

"I rest my case. When you're ready, Marc, I'll give you a hand taking everything downstairs."

Marc thanked him and said he could use it, explaining that he had a problem with elevators. "When I was four, my grandmother and I were trapped for hours in an elevator inside the Statue of Liberty. I've hated them ever since."

"It's nice to know you have a flaw—other than your appalling paternalism, that is," Risa said. "Did you carry all this stuff up three flights of stairs?"

He shook his head. "I gave the doorman some money to wait a few minutes and then send everything up in the elevator. I don't think of it as a flaw, by the way. It's simply a minor inconvenience. I've learned to work around it."

He was tempted to add that his so-called paternalism wasn't a flaw, either, but he held his piece. Why argue philosophy? He knew what worked between a man and a woman. He knew what Diana needed.

Chapter Six

Diana had been waiting in front of her building for about five minutes when she spotted Risa's taxi. She dashed into the street, opened the back door and slid inside, then directed the driver to an Italian restaurant a few blocks away.

"Hi." She gave Risa a hug. "How are you feeling?"

"Fine," Risa replied, "but *you* look exhausted. How did things go in L.A.? And when did you get back?"

Diana yawned. "Okay. I managed to come up with a deal that Fielding says he can live with, but it took me till eight last night to do it. My plane left at ten and got in at six. I had a meeting with some of Parkman's people at nine, so there wasn't much time to rest. Their initial reaction was positive, though. They're going to study the proposal over the weekend and get back to us on Monday."

Risa was convinced that Diana's heavy schedule was ruining her health. "Does that mean you can take a few days off?" she asked.

Diana nodded. "Umm. I'm sleeping over at your parents' tonight and going to the island first thing tomorrow morning. Two days of solitude and rest is the closest thing to heaven I can imagine."

"Which just goes to show how deficient your imagination is, but we'll leave the subject for lunch." The driver slammed on his brakes, then accelerated sharply and zipped around the car in front of him. "Take it easy, or I'll deliver right in your cab," Risa said to him. "Now where was I? Oh, yes—the island. If it's rest you want, why don't you leave work early and go there this afternoon? After all, there's nothing more you can do on the Parkman-Fielding merger till Monday."

"I'd love to, but I have a meeting with Marc Rochard at four." Just thinking about it made Diana's teeth ache. "I could kill him, Risa. In fact, I *will* kill him, but not till after lunch. I want my seafood fettuccine before they cart me off to jail."

Risa laughed and said she was glad Diana had her priorities straight. Then, as they pulled up to the restaurant, she asked what the meeting was all about.

Diana paid the driver and got out of the cab. "What it's about is, the man doesn't know the meaning of the word *no*." She helped Risa out. "I need a glass of wine before I give you the details. I'll wind up screaming, otherwise. Or asking if anyone knows a hit man I can hire."

They strolled into the restaurant. "In that case, we'll definitely get you some wine first," Risa said. "I wish I could join you, because Graham's been driving me crazy lately. He's a father again. The mountain gorilla had twins. They're endangered, you know, and twins are very rare. They popped right out. I should only be so lucky. He goes on and on about it. You'd think he'd given birth to them himself."

Diana smiled. "Ah! Womb envy!" No matter how bad things were, Risa could always cheer her up. Given her frenetic schedule, it was a quality she valued highly.

They ordered their meals, chatting about Graham's work until their drinks and salads arrived. Then Risa said, "So what's this about a meeting with Marc? Does he want to take a few of the millions he seems to be worth and speculate in pork bellies?"

"Pigs aren't my field, and anyway, Charlie Canfield has bigger things in mind," Diana said, referring to her boss. "When I got back from the Parkman meeting this morning, he called me into his office and told me that Marc had phoned on Tuesday to set up an appointment with me. He plans to open a restaurant in New York and he wants my help. He somehow forgot to mention that we know each other, by the way."

Risa looked puzzled. "What sort of help? What can he possibly want from you?"

"I thought I explained that on Monday," Diana answered tartly.

"Well, yes, there's always that, but what does he want in a business sense? Financing? A list of potential backers?"

"What *doesn't* he want?" Diana sipped her wine. "Help finding a good location. Names of good interior designers and first-rate chefs. And money, I guess, although he's rich enough to finance the project on his own. Charlie had one of our researchers put together some background material on him. His grandmother died last spring and left him assets worth fifty million dollars. That's a conservative estimate, by the way."

Risa whistled softly. "A very tidy sum. Still, it's hardly a fortune in Charlie Canfield's terms, so why is he being so generous with your valuable time?"

Risa was more knowledgeable about Diana's work than Diana sometimes gave her credit for. "Because Marc also mentioned that Château du Ciel is considering a partnership with an American winery and might want our help putting a deal together. It isn't the money we could make—that's small potatoes. It's the contacts. Charlie wants to do more business overseas, and the Rochards are very well connected. The background report reads like a *Who's Who* of European business and society."

"You've lost me completely now," Risa said. "I thought Marc had resigned from the family firm. Why would he be involved in a deal involving the Rochards' winery and an American partner?"

"Exactly. He probably wouldn't." Aggravated all over again, Diana stabbed a piece of lettuce with her fork, regarding it balefully before she sighed and ate it. "The operative word being *probably*. He might have moved to New York, but he's still a Rochard. I'm almost sure that his real agenda is personal, but suppose I'm wrong? Charlie will have my head if I refuse to cooperate and the deal goes to another firm. So I've spent the past few hours on the phone, making calls about Marc's restaurant and wanting to strangle him. I'll probably have to waste another hour on that, and then I have to go to his town house for the meeting. He told Charlie he preferred not to come to my office. Preferred not to, hell! He probably plans to feed me something obscenely good and try to seduce me during the afterglow."

Risa laughed so hard that she almost choked. "Oh, Lord, are you ever off base..." she sputtered. "The look on your face... You haven't been this cross since the fourth time Gertrude Klostermann changed her mind about selling you the chinoiserie chest." She giggled again. "He doesn't want to seduce you, Diana. He wants to avoid your elevator. A sixty-story ride would probably finish him off."

"Finish him off?" Diana repeated with a frown. "What are you talking about?"

"He and his grandmother were trapped in an elevator in the Statue of Liberty when he was four years old and he's been terrified of them ever since. He told me and Graham about it Monday night, while you were talking to Warren Fielding." Risa paused, then added teasingly, "That was just after he'd slammed into the kitchen looking like he wanted to bash his head against the nearest wall. What on earth did you do to the poor man?"

"What did *I* do? How about what *he* did?" Diana supplied an indignant summary, finishing irritably, "He's raised conceit to an art form, Risa. I swear, he expected me to throw myself at his feet the moment he touched me. According to the report Charlie gave me, he's considered a prize catch in Europe, so I guess he comes by it honestly. When they write about men who work hard and play hard, he's the type they have in mind."

"And you think he wants you for his newest toy."

She shrugged. "It certainly looks that way. I suppose I'm a novelty, a challenge. He's used to debutantes and actresses, not workaholic investment bankers."

"And it's never occurred to you that he likes you just for yourself? That he meant the things he said Monday night, in full view of your entire family, I might add?"

Diana picked at her salad. It was as though Risa hadn't heard a word she'd said. Her cousin had evidently decided that Marc was madly in love, and that was that.

"Have it your way," she finally said. "Lecture me about my insane schedule and neurotic insecurities and get it over with. That's what we're here for, isn't it?"

Amused by Diana's show of temper, Risa said cheerfully, "I'm seven months pregnant and I don't have the energy, so I'll cut to the chase. Give Marc a chance. He's not just on the make. He really likes you. He told me so Monday night."

"Some best friend you are," Diana grumbled. "The man's been nothing but a thorn in my side from the moment I met him. First he costs me a fortune and steals my sideboard, then he involves himself in *my* island, and then he maneuvers me up to his town house under false pretenses, and you tell me to give him a chance! If Graham had done all that to you, you would have expected me to run him out of town."

"Graham didn't have to, but Marc did. I know you too well, Diana, and quite obviously, so does Marc. You may hate being outmaneuvered, but you admire someone who can beat you at your own game. Don't try to deny it."

She couldn't because it was true. Besides, she'd had a little too much wine to fib successfully. "Fine. He gets high marks for making a damn nuisance of himself and inflicting his presence on me without my consent."

"That's baloney and you know it," Risa retorted. "You like the man. You enjoy trying to outwit him. You come to life when he's around."

"That's not life, that's aggravation, and besides, you can enjoy fighting with a man without liking him or being attracted to him."

"The hell you can. You're just afraid to admit—"

"And in case you weren't listening," Diana plunged on, "the earth didn't exactly move when he kissed me."

Risa looked skeptical. "Not even a little? I mean, the man is gorgeous, Diana. Come on. Be honest."

"All right, then. There was a moment or two when..." Her voice trailed off. It hadn't been Marc, but the fact that for the first time since her divorce, a man had held her. "Never mind. It didn't last. I wasn't even turned on. It was just nice to have a man close to me again. If you want the truth, I've never been all that—" She reddened and stopped.

"Never been all that what?" Risa said.

She shook her head, too embarrassed to answer. "Nothing."

Risa let the matter drop, and they continued eating. The waiter added more wine to Diana's glass and she absently sipped it. It made her groggier, but it also loosened her inhibitions. She wanted to confide in Risa, but the subject was horribly personal. She didn't know how to begin.

Finally Risa set down her fork and said in a low voice, "I've never mentioned this before because I know how much it hurts you to talk about John and Tracy, but Tracy and I were at Jennifer Andersen's bridal shower last spring—you were out of town at the time—and the champagne was flowing like water, and everyone who wasn't pregnant got a little drunk. We were talking about men and sex, and Tracy started bragging about how she'd taught John everything he knew and turned him into the biggest stud since Warren Beatty. Believe me, it was obvious he'd had tons to learn. So if it was never that great between you and him . . . Well, you know the old saying. There are no frigid women, only clumsy men."

Diana thought about all the conversations that had started with her asking John to slow down and ended with him insisting there was something wrong with her. "So he listened to her and not to me. I guess it figures. I did try to talk to him, but he said I was a virgin who didn't know anything. She'd had a couple of lovers before him, so he couldn't ignore her. So much for the theory that virtue is its own reward."

For once, her anger was actually greater than her pain. "And you know what the clincher is? We didn't sleep together often during those last two years, but when we did, it was the same as always. A few kisses, a little groping, and then slam, bam and it's Diana's fault that nothing happened. The bastard knew better by then, but he never changed a bit."

Risa covered her hand and gave it a gentle squeeze. "It's over, Diana. In all these years, you've never let it poison you. Don't start now."

"I won't. He's not worth it." But she'd never had much confidence when it came to men, and her anger was no match for her insecurities. Tracy probably had qualities she lacked. That was the real explanation.

She suddenly felt small and cold. "But suppose he was right, Risa? Suppose it *was* me? Maybe that's why he never bothered to try. Because I was hopeless. Or because I just don't inspire that sort of—effort."

"Don't be ridiculous. Either he was a selfish jerk or he figured you would get suspicious if he changed. There's nothing wrong with you. Don't you remember the first summer you dated him? When he used to come to the island on weekends and the two of you would disappear for hours?"

Diana did, but it seemed like a lifetime ago. "I guess so. Mostly we just talked, but we kissed and petted a little, too. I know I enjoyed it, but I never came close to losing control. And neither did John."

"Then he was the wrong man. All you need is the right one, and you'll forget the word *stop* even exists." Risa leaned back in her chair and smiled. "Of course, if you doubt that, there's one sure way to prove me wrong."

"By sleeping with Marc Rochard, you mean. You seem to think he's the best medicine since penicillin." Diana screwed up her face. "Thanks, but I'll pass. With all due deference to the doctor's undoubted skills, the cure would be worse than the disease."

Risa laughed. "I wasn't telling you to hop in the sack with him. I know you'd never do that. I just want you to stop running away. Lower your defenses and see what happens. Not only is he smitten with you, but he genuinely likes women. That's a very promising combination."

Despite her glib objections, Diana knew there was some sense in what Risa had said. It was just that she'd never had so many conflicting emotions about someone. Marc was a sophisticated, attractive man and she was flattered by his interest, but only a fool wouldn't have been wary.

Not only was he incredibly slick; according to Charlie's report, he'd been linked with countless women over the years but had never come close to marrying. Of course, their information came from stories in newspapers and magazines. When you worked on Wall Street, you learned that media gossip was seldom worth the paper it was printed on.

But the way he'd behaved ... She'd wanted to kick him clear to Brooklyn at times. His presumption was astonishing. His chauvinism was infuriating. And his ego was so enormous that it was obvious that women seldom if ever refused him.

Still, she respected his intelligence and shrewdness. He'd been sweet and understanding Monday night, and it *had* been sort of fun to fence with him. While she hadn't swooned in his arms, she hadn't jerked away in disgust, either. She was curious about whether she would have felt something more intense if she hadn't been so preoccupied with Warren Fielding.

"I just don't know," she said. "I mean, I admit he has his good side, but I don't have any feelings for him—not romantic ones, anyway."

"You mean you don't have them *yet*," Risa insisted. "You have to give them a chance to develop. You have to spend some time with him. And don't try to tell me you're too busy. You could start this weekend."

The waiter interrupted with their entrées before Diana had a chance to answer. That was just as well, because she'd reached the point where talking only confused her. Her brain seemed to have checked itself at the door.

"I'd promise to think about it," she said as the waiter walked away, "but I think I'm too tired to think. I never should have had so much wine." She yawned. "At the rate

I'm going, I'll fall asleep during our meeting this afternoon."

"So sleep. Marc won't mind." Risa grinned. "In fact, I suspect he'll use it to good advantage."

Diana called the waiter back over. "In that case, I'd better order myself some coffee."

Much to her relief, Risa stopped pressing her about Marc and started talking about her latest find, an elderly woman from Minnesota who'd written a saga set in the time of Christ. By the time they said goodbye, the coffee had taken effect and Diana was more alert. She walked back to her office and finished up her phone calls, then hailed a cab for the trip uptown.

The traffic moved better than it usually did on Fridays, and the motion of the car made her sleepy again. She was twenty minutes early, so she walked briskly around the block to clear her head. Then she knocked on the door.

A tall, shapely blonde answered. She looked to be about fifty and was dressed in green paisley slacks and a matching blouse, probably made of silk. "Hi, sweetie. I'm Tina D'Angelo." She had a warm smile and a pronounced New York accent. "Marc's up in the kitchen, but he'll be down in a few minutes. Why don't we sit down and get acquainted in the meantime?"

Diana introduced herself as they shook hands, but it was obvious Tina already knew who she was. In fact, she acted as though Diana were a friend of Marc's, not a business associate, which meant that he must have described her in those terms. As she'd suspected, she'd been dragooned here under the pretext of business when his real agenda was personal. So much for all the phone calls she'd made.

She schooled her features into a polite smile and entered the house. Her first reaction was astonishment, her second disbelief. The place looked like a bordello. It wasn't the sort of decor that she associated with the very urbane Marc Rochard.

"This is a beautiful house," she said aloud, which it was. Only the furnishings were hideous.

"It sure is," Tina said brightly. "I love living here. It's got everything—tons of space, a great location and a bathroom and fireplace for almost every day of the week."

"I'll look forward to seeing the rest of it," Diana murmured, which was also true, but only because she wondered if it could possibly be as incredible as the foyer.

"I'd offer to give you a tour, but Marc'll want to do that himself. He'll drag you up and down the stairs, though. Elevators scare him silly. I wish they scared me, too, because if I'd been climbing steps all these years, I could have eaten a lot more desserts."

"I know exactly what you mean," Diana said, warming to the woman. She was a bit of a character, but no more so than her own relations. "Then you've lived here for quite a while?"

She nodded. "For twenty years. The Parisis—Marc's grandparents—bought it after they sold their place in New Jersey and moved to France. Their New York pied-à-terre, don't you know? All five floors of it!"

So the town house was part of Marc's inheritance. That gibed with the report Diana had been given, which had mentioned real estate in New York as well as blue-chip stocks. "Then you leased the place from the Parisis?"

"Good heavens, no," Tina said with a laugh. "I couldn't afford a place like this. I'm a starving musician. I've lived here free for all these years and looked after things in return. Tiffany and I go back to the cradle together. That's Marc's mother. I'm sort of his honorary aunt, which means I can tell him he's wrong without him puffing himself up and ignoring me because I'm only a woman."

Diana smiled, liking Tina even more. She was funny and down-to-earth, and she definitely had Marc's number. Still bemused by how garish the house was, Diana followed Tina through the foyer.

She paused by the stairs and sniffed. Something smelled wonderful. "Whatever dinner is, it certainly smells good," she said.

"That's not dinner. It's some mushroom thing Marc's making. I told him you'd like him better if he fed you well. He had the sense to listen to me for once."

Diana would have liked him better if he hadn't cost her hours of valuable time, but Tina was the wrong person to complain to. "You were right there. The dinner he made the other night was one of the best I've ever eaten."

"He loved doing it. Enjoyed meeting your family, too." Tina led her through a library decorated with pictures and statues of horses into a large living room that was even more like a bordello than the foyer. "And the history... All I can say is, if there's really buried treasure somewhere, hand me a shovel and tell me where to dig."

"I'm afraid it's probably gone by now," Diana said. "There are lots of legends about treasure caches, but very few have ever been found."

They sat down on a red-and-gold couch that was as comfortable as it was gaudy. The rest of the furnishings matched, even the romantic paintings on the walls. The only exception was a glorious grand piano in one corner.

Diana set her briefcase on the coffee table. "You said you were a musician...."

"Umm. A rehearsal pianist. I was kidding about the starving part. I'm working on Andrew Lloyd Webber's newest show right now. It's going to knock everyone's socks off."

"I'd love to hear something from it. Would you mind playing for me?" Yawning, Diana settled back on the couch.

"I'd be glad to, honey. Take off your shoes and close your eyes. Have a little nap if you want to."

Diana had been taught never to sleep in sermons or concerts, but when Tina started playing a slow, melodic ballad her eyes drooped closed despite her best efforts to keep them open. She faded in and out after that, never really asleep but never fully awake, either.

She only opened her eyes because she felt someone join her on the couch. Marc. She stared at him groggily. He'd seated himself about a foot away and was watching her intently. It was a little unnerving.

She straightened and reached for her briefcase, which he'd pushed to one side in order to make room for a tray of hors d'oeuvres. He'd also brought in a bottle of wine and a pair of glasses. "I'm sorry," she said with a yawn. "I took the red-eye in from Los Angeles last night and—"

"You work too hard." He sounded annoyed, or at least disapproving. He took the briefcase out of her hands and set it on the floor. "Relax. Have something to eat and drink. We have plenty of time."

Diana felt a stab of annoyance. What he'd meant was, *he* had plenty of time. He didn't know her schedule. "I'm afraid that's not true. Nelly's expecting me for dinner, and then I'm—"

"No, she's not. I called her and told her I was taking you out. We have a reservation at Dulong's at six-thirty."

She gaped at him. "We *what*?"

He calmly repeated the statement, then added, "Nelly thought it was a good idea. She said you've been wanting to try the place but hadn't gotten around to it. You don't get out enough, Diana." He picked up an hors d'oeuvre and held it up to her mouth. "Here. Taste this. It's a mushroom turnover."

Diana was glaring at the turnover in speechless indignation when Tina finished the ballad and stood up. "I'll see you later, kids. I've got some shopping to do. Diana, sweetie, I know he's impossible at times, but he does have his good points. Don't get so angry with him that you can't see the forest for the trees." She winked. "Besides, trees can always be trimmed, y'know."

"He doesn't need trimming; he needs half his trunk cut off and a whole new variety grafted on." She snatched away the turnover and set it back on the plate. "And don't think you can get around me by feeding me, Mr. Rochard. It won't work—not again."

Tina laughed and breezed out of the room, leaving Diana and Marc alone. He filled the two glasses and held one out. She shook her head. With a sigh, he placed it back on the table. A moment later the front door opened and closed.

"Obviously you're angry with me," he said. "Would you tell me what I've done wrong?"

He honestly didn't know. He looked completely baffled. Incredulous, Diana said, "To begin with, you dragged me here for an alleged business meeting when your motives were obviously personal, and just to make sure my boss would order me to cooperate, you concocted a possible merger out of thin air, when you don't even have a connection to your family's winery anymore." Ignoring the coolness that entered his eyes, she took a quick breath and continued, "And if that wasn't enough, you made arrangements for my evening without consulting me first, and when I objected, you all but patted me on the head and told me you knew what was best for me. You're darn right I'm angry. You manipulated me and treated me like a child, and I thoroughly resent it."

By all rights, he should have hung his head in shame and begged for forgiveness, but he looked anything but contrite. "On Monday night, I told you I never lie," he said stiffly. "I'll repeat it. I never lie. You're here for a business meeting. I don't deny that I wanted to see you, or that I requested you specifically, but you're here to help me professionally and I'll be billed for your time as any other client would. As for the possibility of a merger, it's quite strong. I own ten percent of the winery, which is connection enough to be intimately involved. If we move ahead and I ask that we use an American investment firm—your firm—we will."

Diana was flushed with embarrassment by the time he finished. It didn't matter that he hadn't responded to the second half of her tirade; her sins were so grievous that she only hoped her boss never got wind of them. "Oh," she said weakly. "I'm sorry."

His manner softened. "And so am I. I meant dinner to be a pleasant surprise, but I should have known you wouldn't take it that way. Whenever I try to protect you or take care of you, you accuse me of treating you like a child. I suppose spoiling you is a privilege I'll have to earn."

Diana stared into her lap. "I wish you wouldn't talk that way. It makes me—uncomfortable. I'm here for a business meeting, so let's stick to business."

"Given my feelings for you, I would find that very difficult," he said. "Why does it bother you so much that I'm attracted to you and say so? Are you afraid I'll try to force myself on you?"

"Of course not." He hadn't pushed her on Monday, and he'd certainly had the chance. "It's just that . . ." She paused. She found it hard to overcome her embarrassment and put her feelings into words. "If it's a line and you're trying to get me into bed, I don't sleep around. And if you really mean it—if you really care for me so much—I don't feel the same way, so it wouldn't be fair to lead you on. I wish you'd just forget about me."

He hesitated, then said, "You're very tired, Diana. If I'd realized you'd been on a plane all night, I would have canceled our meeting today. Tell me, how did things go in Los Angeles?"

Her head snapped up in disbelief. "How can you ignore what I just said? Do you know how hard it was for me to get all that out?"

"Yes. I think so. I also know that you like me more than you're willing to admit, and that you're far too tired to deal with it right now. You've had a difficult few days and you haven't had a chance to unwind, so let's talk a little and have something to eat. It will do you good."

"You see?" she demanded in exasperation. "That's exactly what I mean. You're always telling me what I feel and what I need, as if I'm too dense to figure it out by myself."

"You're not tired, then? You're not tense?"

To her chagrin, she couldn't help yawning. Marc smiled triumphantly, but didn't say a word.

"That's it," she muttered. "I'm going home." But she didn't leave because she didn't have the energy to move.

"At least have something to eat first." Clearly humoring her, he picked up a turnover. "Just a taste, Diana. After all, I slaved in the kitchen for hours to make these."

"Oh, all right," she grumbled, and took it out of his hand. The aroma had driven her crazy from the first moment she'd smelled it. Why deny herself?

One bite and she was lost. It was exquisite. Sighing in defeat, she finished it and reached for another.

Marc picked up a glass of wine. "You'll like this, too, I think. It's a Château Vermeil. It has a little more Cabernet Franc than a Château du Ciel, which gives it a softer, fruitier flavor. It's very nice before dinner."

She shook her head. "I'll fall asleep. I had two glasses of wine with lunch."

"Not wine like this," he said. "Try it. You won't be disappointed."

She gave in and tasted it. It was everything he'd promised, as soft and smooth as nectar. "That's wonderful," she said, her voice slurred with fatigue. Warmed by the wine, she settled more deeply into the couch. "I was wrong before. I'm the easiest mark in the world. Feed me well, and I forget I was ever angry." She drank some more wine and reached for another turnover.

"I'm glad you have at least one weakness, *chérie*. It makes things a lot easier." He waited until she'd finished eating, then took away her glass and set it on the table. "Take off your jacket. I'll give you a massage."

She blinked at him in confusion. "You'll what?"

"Rub your neck and shoulders." He moved closer. "Don't worry about falling asleep. I won't mind if you do."

Diana might have been groggy, but she wasn't brain-dead. "You want an excuse to touch me. You think it's going to turn me on. That's why you want to do it."

He smiled. "I want to give you a massage because I think it will relax you and because I enjoy taking care of you. I certainly *hope* it will turn you on, but I'll manage to restrain myself if it doesn't. There's nothing to be afraid of. I'd have to be very stupid to do something you don't want me to do and get you angry with me all over again, wouldn't I?"

She hadn't expected such honesty. Avoiding his eyes, she said softly, "But it's not fair to you. You want to—well, you know. And I don't."

"That's my problem, not yours." He unbuttoned the top button of her jacket. "Take a chance, Diana. If you're at all honest with yourself, you'll admit that you like me at least a little. What have you got to lose?"

She thought about her conversation with Risa. Give him a chance, Risa had said. You wouldn't enjoy fighting with him unless you liked him. Find the right man and you'll forget the word *stop* even exists.

She yawned, too tired to keep thinking. What did she have to lose? The answer was nothing. Nothing at all.

Chapter Seven

She was nervous at first. Removing one's jacket didn't exactly qualify as undressing for a man, but it was the closest she'd come in a very long time. She draped the jacket over the arm of the couch, then turned around.

He started with the muscles in her neck and shoulders, kneading out the knots with firm but gentle strokes. It felt good—very good. After a minute or two, she yawned and let her head roll forward. She was so tired, and the massage was so relaxing...

He moved his hands lower and ran his thumbs along her shoulder blades. The tension seeped out of her body. She turned toward the back of the couch, burying her face in her arms as she snuggled against a soft, plump cushion.

Several minutes passed. He began working on her spine and the small of her back, rubbing out the soreness. She drifted, enjoying the soothing sensation of her muscles slackening and warming. For all the physical pleasure of the massage, it was almost as if she were dreaming. She felt as if she were floating weightlessly outside her body.

He moved closer, brushing her back with his chest as he bent to rub her neck. She could feel the heat of his body, but it didn't alarm her. She yawned and burrowed more deeply against the cushion.

The room spun slowly in the darkness. She only realized she'd nodded off when she felt him remove some pins from her bun—the last few pins before he fanned her hair over her shoulders. He massaged her scalp and temples with slow, circular motions of his thumbs and fingers, touching her in exactly the right spots with exactly the right amount of pressure. It was as though he could read her mind. She moaned softly in appreciation.

It never occurred to her to resist when he eased her head from the cushion to his chest. She was much too tired. She wanted—needed—to go to sleep. As he rubbed her nape and temples, she curled her hands into his shirt and snuggled into the crook of his neck. He smelled of cologne and cooking. Trying to get more comfortable, she kicked off her shoes and pulled her legs up underneath her.

He stopped massaging her and simply held her. She sighed, thinking it was exactly what she'd wanted. No distractions, only warmth and quiet. She felt snug, safe and content.

She woke slowly, as she always did, fighting her way through a dream-like fog to wakefulness. It was a moment before she remembered where she was, and with whom, and another moment before the physical reality of the situation really hit. She was on a couch with Marc Rochard, wrapped tightly in his arms, cuddled against his chest and clinging to his shirt.

Blind instinct took over. She withdrew without thinking, jerking away her hands and wrenching herself free. He eased his hold but kept his arm lightly around her shoul-

ders. On some primitive feminine level, she understood the
silent male message. *You're not going anywhere. You're
staying right here.*

Disoriented and embarrassed, she stared blankly at the
wall above the fireplace. There was a portrait of a blowsy
nude there, her flesh white against a crimson background.
She couldn't imagine paying money for such a picture,
much less hanging it in one's home.

Her thoughts were interrupted by a low, amused, "I told
you you were tired. You slept for nearly an hour."

Nearly an hour? In such an intimate position? At a loss
for words, she uncurled her legs and slipped her shoes back
on. Her blouse was wrinkled and a little damp, and her
skirt wasn't much better. And her hair... How was she
going to go home this way?

"I thought about carrying you up to my bed," he added,
"but judging by your reaction just now, it's just as well
that I didn't. The shock of waking up beside me might
have killed you."

She heard the laughter in his voice and forgot about the
blowsy nude and the condition of her clothing. He would
have been startled, too, if he'd fallen asleep in a daze and
wakened not quite knowing where he was! Besides, whenever he teased her, she immediately wanted to pay him
back in kind. Double.

He caressed her neck with a light, proprietary touch, as
if holding her while she'd slept had changed their relationship in some fundamental way. Maybe it had. Now
that her initial shock had passed, she didn't mind him
touching her. He'd been doing it from almost the moment
they'd met, so maybe she'd gotten used to it.

"You have no idea how tempted I am to claim that you
woke up, made violent love with me and then fell dead
asleep again," he drawled. "Totally sated, of course."

Fully alert now, she gave him a skeptical look. "I doubt it. Your ego couldn't abide the thought of a woman sleeping with you and then forgetting all about it."

"It's a matter of simple fact, not ego. When I make love to you for the first time, you'll definitely remember it. After all, one doesn't forget the single most pleasurable moment of one's life to date."

Once she would have blushed, but she knew him too well now. His conceit was too enormous to take seriously. "Even more pleasurable than Monday night, Marc? How can that be possible?"

He grinned at her. "But it wasn't a fair test, *chérie*. You were preoccupied with business."

"Someone with your talents as a lover should have found that a very minor obstacle," she retorted.

His grin disappeared. Tucking a finger under her chin, he said in a husky voice, "If you give me another chance, I promise to do a great deal better."

They stared into each other's eyes. His gaze grew more intense, and the arm he'd draped so casually around her shoulders tightened possessively. With stunning abruptness, everything changed. He was tired of teasing and trading quips; he wanted to make love to her, and not playfully, either.

Her heart began to race. She was suddenly nervous in a whole new way, afraid for reasons she couldn't explain. He wasn't dangerous or threatening, but she felt cold and a little shaky.

She lowered her eyes. "About your restaurant, Marc... I made some phone calls today—"

"Later, Diana." He brushed his lips across her mouth, then murmured in French, "You're so beautiful... All week long, I've been thinking about your eyes, your hair, your mouth... And the things we did in my dreams... Not seeing you for three days almost killed me."

She'd heard words like these before, from the Frenchmen of Paris, but none of them had spoken with such passionate emotion. On some level, that emotion reached her. She didn't respond, but she didn't pull away, either. It was only human to want cataclysmic passion, and if there was the slightest chance Marc could provide it . . .

He kissed her more firmly, then nipped and teased her lips with a restraint and tenderness that went straight to her heart. Her lips softened and parted. She felt a flutter of excitement as he tasted them with his tongue, but it passed as quickly as it had come, like a door slamming shut. She didn't want to tense up, but she couldn't help it.

He kissed her lightly for several seconds more, then eased away. He was aroused and didn't bother to hide it, but he was also very controlled. She turned her head, feeling that she'd failed both of them.

He fondled a lock of her hair. "That's progress, I suppose, but your ex-husband has a lot to answer for." He paused, then added thoughtfully, "Fortunately, *mon ange*, you're in excellent hands. It's in the genes, you know. Something about being French. Take that portrait you were studying so intently before. A masterpiece! Who else but a Frenchman could capture a woman so perfectly?"

She went from guilty to befuddled in no time flat. He'd sounded completely serious. She glanced at him. He *looked* completely serious. How could he think something so hideous was an artistic masterpiece?

Politeness had been bred into her, though, so she never considered saying what she thought. "I, uh, I don't recognize the artist," she mumbled.

"Don't you? But then, his greatest masterpieces weren't executed on canvas, so perhaps that explains it."

She was more confused than ever. "You mean he's more famous for his work in other mediums?"

"Yes. His specialty, I believe, was oil on black velvet." He grinned at her. "Fortunately my grandmother's bad taste never sank quite that low, unless you count the cherubs in the dining room. Please don't tell me you thought *I* furnished this place. I don't think I could survive the insult."

Like Risa, he had a knack for smoothing over awkward situations and making her smile. She hadn't realized that before. "Well, I did wonder," she said.

"But I bought your sideboard. I told you it was my favorite piece." His hand swept the room. "How could you think I was responsible for a travesty like this? Do you know what's behind those repulsive gold drapes? Windows overlooking a garden. Do you think that someone from a paradise such as St. Emilion would prefer gold lamé to flowers and trees?"

He sounded so offended that she was hard-pressed not to giggle. "I'm sure you wouldn't. My profound apologies. I hope you'll find it in your heart to forgive me."

"If you'll have dinner with me, I will." He stood, holding out his hand. "Come. I'll give you a tour. Since Tina isn't here, you can laugh as much as you like. She's lived here since my grandparents bought the place and loves every foot of it. I don't dare redecorate too quickly or she'll be mortally offended. Babe came by on Wednesday, by the way. I doubt she's recovered from the trauma."

Smiling, Diana let him help her to her feet. She wasn't sure about dinner and wondered what had happened to their meeting, but she was willing to take a look around. After the week she'd had, she needed a good laugh.

"Tina mentioned that she and your mother have been friends all their lives," she said as they walked out of the room. "Did she help choose the furniture?"

He shook his head, explaining Tina's history as they made their way upstairs. The Parisis and D'Angelos had lived next door to each other in a working-class section of Newark when Tiffany and Tina were babies. At first, Tina's father, Eddie, had been a butcher in Sam Parisi's shop; later, after Sam went into the auto-parts business, Eddie became his foreman, and both families moved to the suburbs.

Tiffany studied French literature at Vassar and married Louis Rochard, while Tina, a Juilliard graduate, began a career in music. Then at twenty-five Tina met a lawyer and fell passionately in love. Unfortunately he was married, with four children. His wife, an alcoholic, was usually drunk or drying out in some posh sanatorium, but Tina's lover had been too religious to divorce her. Tina had understood and gone along.

"He died five years ago, after a two-year battle with cancer," Marc finished. "Tina was the one who nursed him. His wife was still drinking and his children were too busy with their own lives to bother. All she has left are a drawerful of jewelry and some good memories. Her brother died last year, so she's sixty and alone now, and my sister and I are the closest thing to children she has. It's tragic, really. She would have made a wonderful wife and mother."

"But she has an extremely successful career," Diana pointed out, "and she spent thirty years with a man she loved. What's so tragic about that?"

"A career and a mistress might be enough for a man, but women are made differently," he answered.

He made it sound like the word of God Himself, handed down from on high. It reminded Diana all over again of what a chauvinist he was. "That's ridiculous," she said. "I know women who are perfectly happy—"

"But what about you? Would you want to be in her shoes?"

"I can think of worse things," she said.

Although Marc didn't argue, she could tell he didn't agree. In his opinion, a woman could be fulfilled only through marriage and motherhood. His attitude was so antiquated that sometimes she thought he must have been raised in the wilds of the Alps by wolves.

"Let's not waste time debating philosophy," he finally said. They walked past a powder room into the kitchen. "This is the one room in the house my grandmother didn't redecorate. Her mother died when she was only twelve, and she did the cooking for her family after that. She came to hate it so much that she hired a cook the moment my grandfather became successful, and never set foot in a kitchen again. I assume that's why she left the room alone, but whatever the reason, I'm grateful."

They continued into the dining room. One look and Diana burst out laughing. She'd never seen so many cherubs in her life. There were plaster ones carved into the ceiling, golden ones supporting the glass dining table, brass ones in the chandelier, wooden ones ornamenting the furniture and painted ones on the walls.

"But this is much, much worse than a painting on black velvet," she said. "Did people actually eat in here?"

He nodded. "And no doubt suffered attacks of indigestion that would put your Aunt Nelly to shame. You might have noticed that my grandmother was a great believer in decorating around a theme. As you can see, she tended to get carried away."

"Tended to?" Diana repeated with a giggle. "She must have scoured every street fair and furniture store in Brooklyn and Queens to find this stuff."

"Probably so," he said glumly. "And there's much more."

She was still smiling as they returned to the hallway. The staircase was to their left, the elevator directly in front of them.

A spark of mischief entered her eyes. "I've always wanted to ride in a private elevator," she said. "Could we take it to the top floor and work our way back down?"

He looked at her suspiciously. "Risa told you I don't like elevators. I can see it in your eyes."

"You're right. Frankly, I was very surprised." She managed to sound completely earnest. "After all, you were with your grandmother when you were trapped, and you were old enough to understand what had happened. How traumatic could it have been, Marc? Really, I never would have thought you were so neurotic."

He stiffened a little. "I was with a grandmother I rarely saw and could barely communicate with. My parents had decided that hearing both English and French had caused my sister to talk very late, so they spoke only French to me until I was six or seven. I didn't know any English when I was four and my grandmother spoke very poor French. The elevator was crowded, and we were trapped for hours. A few people got hysterical. If I'm neurotic about it, I think I'm entitled to be."

She'd wounded his Gallic pride, she thought in amusement. Frenchmen felt they had to be invincible in front of women. They didn't realize that a weakness here and there made them more appealing. "That certainly explains it, but it *is* inconvenient. Tell me, have you considered therapy?"

"It's not that big a problem," he insisted. "Anyway, I don't believe in therapy. It's nothing but a lot of talk."

"On the contrary, it's very scientific. Since you associate elevators with something traumatic, all you have to do to cure yourself is substitute something enjoyable." She tried to keep a straight face but didn't quite succeed. "Making love, for example."

He looked startled, then pleased. "So you were teasing me, were you? It was a dangerous game, you know. I might have assumed you were offering to be my therapist."

"Not me! I majored in history, not psychology." Laughing, she darted toward the stairs.

He chased her, catching her by the arm. The desire in his eyes as he pulled her around to face him took her breath away. Within moments, the hallway was suffused with sexual tension. The sensation was completely new to her. It excited her, but it also made her nervous.

"Not so fast," he said. "Your theories intrigue me. Let's explore them a bit further. It seems to me that my attraction to the therapist would be much more important than her academic credentials. A test is obviously in order. I suggest that we start slowly, in a stationary open elevator."

Diana stared uneasily at his chest. "I don't think so, Marc. I'd rather see the rest of the house now."

He released her and took a step backward. She looked at him uncertainly, afraid he was annoyed. The strain in his eyes was impossible to miss.

"You'd rather look at my grandmother's monstrosities than kiss me?" he demanded. "Incredible! I've obviously lost my touch." He took her arm. "Ah, well, my ego will recover in time, I suppose. Come along, *chérie*."

She was grateful he was so sweet, that he never pressed her too hard. She wanted to apologize, to explain, but the words wouldn't come. And then she realized that words were unnecessary. He'd understood without being told.

They walked up the stairs. Thanks to his grandmother, who'd decorated Tina's bedroom and parlor around a theme of Greek mythology, it wasn't long before they were laughing again. The master suite, designed as some sort of indoor garden, was slightly less outrageous, but only because he'd replaced the original bed and carpets. Diana liked the things he'd chosen very much.

The fourth floor contained two baths and three bedrooms. The first was filled with chinoiserie and the others were designed around the circus and the ballet. Diana told Marc they weren't half bad, but he insisted she was simply getting used to the place.

The fifth and final floor, which had been designed to house the staff, contained four bedrooms and another bath. The Parisis hadn't had live-in help, though, so they'd used the larger two rooms for storage and left the smaller ones empty.

Marc opened a door so Diana could look inside. She saw a couch, some tables and lamps, numerous stacks of cartons and several rackfuls of dated but well-made clothing. "One of Nelly's charities runs a thrift store," she said. "These things are in good condition. It's a shame for them to sit here unused."

"I'll talk to her about donating them. Come look in the room next door. I think you'll find one of the pieces there interesting."

Intrigued, Diana followed him down the hall. He opened the door, and her eyes went straight to the center of the floor. Her mahogany sideboard was sitting there, gleaming in the dim afternoon light.

She rushed up to inspect it, wanting to assure herself that it hadn't been damaged during the trip from Conable's. It was in perfect condition, and even more beautiful than she'd remembered. Having touched it again, she couldn't bear the thought of parting with it. She wanted to take it to Van Slyke's Island as soon as possible.

She turned around. Marc was lounging in the doorway, his arms folded casually across his chest. "It would look perfect in my dining room," he said, "but I might be persuaded to return it to you—under certain conditions."

That was only to be expected. After all, he'd once told her that he didn't believe in free lunches. He was smiling, but she didn't miss the steel in his eyes. Whatever he wanted, he wasn't in the mood to negotiate.

She walked up to him. "What conditions?"

"Nelly told me you were spending the night with your aunt and uncle—that the furniture you'd bought at the auction was stored at their house in the suburbs, and that you planned to take it to the island tomorrow morning. She said you'd decided to give the caretaker the weekend off and stay there all alone."

She waited for him to continue, but he simply stood there, looking disapproving. "That's right," she finally said. "Henry and Babe live in New Rochelle, right on Long Island Sound. They have a private dock and several boats. You can see Van Slyke's Island from their property. We'll take the furniture over in their cruiser."

His jaw tightened. "If you want the sideboard, you'll have to let me bring it to the island tomorrow—and stay with you until you leave. I'll bring Tina along if you'd be more comfortable with a chaperon, but I don't want you staying out there alone."

She finally understood what he was getting at. The man was hopeless, completely hopeless. "You think I'm a helpless female who can't look after myself. That I need a big, strong man to protect me."

"I don't think you're helpless, Diana, but you *are* a woman, and the island is very isolated." His tone was very stern. "Something could happen. You might need help."

"So I'll pick up the phone and call," she said. "We do have phones there, Marc—and also lights, heat and even indoor plumbing."

"And if someone suddenly shows up, determined to make trouble?" he asked. "What good will all those conveniences do you then?"

"Nobody's going to show up."

"Oh? Then why do you need a caretaker?"

He had her there. People did trespass now and then, but usually because they were curious, not malicious. "If my family isn't worried—"

"Your family forgot to stand in line when they passed out the common sense," he said curtly. "Do you want the sideboard or don't you?"

What she wanted was a few days of peace. She glanced at the sideboard, then sighed. He wasn't going to bend on this, so it would have to wait. "Obviously I'll have to live without it for the time being."

He put his hand on her shoulder. "Perhaps you should reconsider, *chérie*. If you don't, you might have to live without it for years—or permanently."

She didn't believe that for a moment. He knew the sideboard was rightfully hers and had every intention of returning it. Not in years, either, but in months or even weeks.

She was about to crisply call his bluff when she noticed the heat in his eyes. He was exasperated with her, maybe even angry. She decided it would be foolish to provoke him.

"I think we should go downstairs," she said. "We still have business to discuss."

"Business! *Mon Dieu*, but you're stubborn!" His hand tightened a little on her shoulder. "Stubborn and reckless. If you won't take care of yourself, then I will. Whether you approve of it or not, I'm staying with you this weekend."

It was a struggle to rein in her temper. "Be reasonable, Marc. I'm a grown woman. I can—"

"Then why do you act like a child? You have no more sense than the rest of your crazy family!"

It was the last straw. "Just who do you think you are, anyway? If I want to stay there alone, I damn well will, and if you trespass, I'll call the Coast Guard and—"

"The hell you will!" He scooped her up in his arms and marched her to an old double bed in the far corner of the room. Her heart began to pound wildly, but not with fear. She was too annoyed to be afraid, and—she had to admit it—too stunned by the intensity of the feelings he seemed to have for her. Nobody except Risa had ever cared for her enough to worry about her before.

He laid her on the bed and followed her down, looming over her. "You're about to have your mind changed. Don't bother fighting it. This time, you're going to lose."

His soft but confident tone demanded submission. The fierce desire in his eyes said he'd die if he didn't get it. Needs she hadn't known existed surged through her body. She stared at him, confused by the raw power of them.

And then, so suddenly that she shuddered in reaction, she realized she *wanted* to lose. Shocked by the thought, she watched him in silence, waiting for him to make good on his threat.

He stretched out half on top of her, hooking a leg over her thighs to gently imprison her. His chest was pressed lightly against her breasts and his mouth was only inches above hers. She trembled as she waited for him to kiss her. She was aroused enough to want him, but afraid something would go wrong. It always had in the past.

His eyes grew gentler. "I have a confession to make. It's not just that I'd worry about you every moment. It's also that I'd miss you every moment. Does that make a difference in whether you want me to come?"

She couldn't think straight. She didn't know what to say when he talked that way. "I don't know. I had such a hectic week.... I thought I needed some time alone."

"You can be alone as much as you want to be." He gave her a lingering kiss on the mouth. "I hope you won't want to be."

The kiss made her dizzy and breathless. "I don't know. The way you're making me feel..." She closed her eyes, unable to get another word out.

He nuzzled her neck, and it was like fire licking at her skin. After a few moments, he slipped one of his hands behind her head and settled more heavily against her. Her nipples tightened at the intimate contact. Wanting to touch him back, she put her arms around his waist and arched closer.

He planted soft, hungry kisses on her throat, her jaw and her eyes, making her feel precious and desirable. By the time he reached her lips, they were parted in anticipation. In all her life, she'd never been so eager to be kissed.

He began to tease her, nibbling and tasting till she thought she'd die from pleasure. He could have tortured her like that for hours and she wouldn't have minded. He coaxed her lips farther apart, then slipped his tongue into her mouth and explored it with deep, possessive strokes that were even more wonderful than what had come before. She tasted him back, shyly at first, then more confidently, thinking hazily that she'd never known what kissing was all about until then.

The embrace grew more passionate and breathless. Then, when she tenderly stroked his face, it abruptly ended. He gave her a final, hot kiss and rolled onto his back. She watched through a fog of arousal as he slowly sat up, puzzled about why he'd stopped.

He ran his hand through his hair. It was shaking slightly, and his breathing was harsh and uneven. He might have stopped, but she doubted he'd wanted to. She felt a warmth toward him that had nothing to do with passion.

It was a minute before he looked at her. There was no triumph in his eyes, only tenderness. "Now can I stay with you?"

She sat up. He'd done exactly what he'd set out to—made her want his company—and there was no point denying it. "Yes."

He smiled, then kissed the tip of her nose. "Good girl."

"But Marc..."

"Hmm?"

She flushed deeply. "I hope you liked that even half as much as I did, but I'm not ready for... What I mean is, when we're alone this weekend..."

"Don't worry, *chérie*. You'll never have to tell me when to stop, because I'll be able to feel it in your body." He stood. "Which, incidentally, is enchanting, exciting and only barely resistible. You have no idea how remarkable my self-control is. Why don't you take the elevator downstairs? I'll meet you in the living room."

She nodded. He made her feel so good, so special, that she would have met him just about anywhere.

He joined her a minute or two after she'd sat down. She opened her briefcase and took out a manila folder. "I guess we should take care of this before dinner," she said. "About Dulong's—I'd like to go, but the way my clothes look..."

"You can press them if you'd like, but I had another thought on the way downstairs. When I phoned your aunt, she mentioned that the cook was making a large pot of stew for dinner. She invited me over, but we decided I should take you to Dulong's instead." He paused and smiled. "I've reconsidered. If Tina is going to join us on the island this weekend, it would be nice if she met your family. Do you think Nelly would mind?"

"I know she wouldn't, but why are you smiling that way? What do you—" Diana gaped at him, suddenly understanding. "Not Tina and my father. You can't be serious."

"Why not? He's intelligent, handsome and in good health. The right age, too, I would say."

And a music lover, as well, but still... "He's in his own world, Marc. Women have chased him for as long as I can remember, but it never does them any good."

Marc looked dubious. "You mean he's gone without women from the time your mother died?"

"Well, no," she admitted, "but he never gets as involved as they do. That auction the other night... Gertrude Klostermann was one of his—friends. They were on and off for years. Whenever they were on, she'd offer to sell me back the pieces I wanted and start a round of interminable negotiations. Then my father would ignore her for a while and she'd get angry and change her mind. She was always gleefully malicious about it, as if it were all my fault. She once told me Dad would have to marry her before I got a thing, but there was never any chance of that. He preferred his books to spending time with her."

"I know her type. Hard and selfish—a taker. Women like Mrs. Klostermann are never happy, because their behavior goes against their deepest natures. Women were meant to give freely and generously."

"Is that so!" Diana rolled her eyes. He was making sweeping generalizations again. "And men? What are their deepest natures?"

"We're predators. Our instincts tell us to take whatever women are willing to give us." He curled a lock of her hair around his finger. "Until we encounter perfection, that is. Only a fool wouldn't protect and cherish an angel when she appears in his life."

She tried to ignore the way he was toying with her hair. "You make the most wonderful speeches, but didn't it ever occur to you that people should protect and cherish each other? That most of all, women want to be respected for their intelligence and accomplishments and treated as equals by men?"

"I'm sure they do, but they want a great deal more. They just don't know it. In any event, what matters is the way a woman acts, and you, *mon chou*, please me very much in that regard."

She was about to tell him that she wasn't his little cabbage, much less his courtesan, when he removed the manila folder from her hands. The top page contained the names of half a dozen restaurants in danger of closing and a list of top realtors specializing in small commercial properties.

She forced her mind back to business, which, after all, was the reason she'd come. "This is only a beginning. I didn't have time for more than a few hours of work. I wasn't sure whether you wanted to rent or buy, so—''

"Buy, perhaps the building Ming Chen is in." Ming Chen was one of the restaurants on her list. "The Lincoln Center area appeals to me. I see you've got Elliott Angleton's name on your list. He was recommended to me by several people. I plan to use him."

He glanced at the page beneath, which contained a list of prospective investors. "I recognize a few of the names here, but I'd rather not have partners. I can afford to do this on my own."

It looked as if she'd spent a lot of time for nothing. She bit her tongue as he proceeded to the next page in the folder, where she'd listed the hottest restaurant designers in town. Not only had he already settled on one of them; he had the audacity to compliment her on her good work in turning up the man's name.

The final page contained the names of the most celebrated chefs in the area. By then, it was an effort not to raise her voice. "I don't know if any of them is available, but even if they're not, it wouldn't hurt to talk to them. They might be able to recommend someone they've worked with."

"Actually there's a chef in Los Angeles I'd like to hire. I spoke to him earlier this week, but he's reluctant to leave California. A share of the business might persuade him to change his mind, though." He closed the folder and set it on the coffee table. "If not, you've come up with many of the same names I did, and I certainly plan to speak with them. I can see why your boss values you so highly, *chérie*. Considering what short notice you had, you did a very thorough job."

It was more than she could endure. "Thank you, Marc, but I wonder why I bothered. This might have been your idea of a business meeting, but it wasn't mine."

"No?" He looked puzzled. "Why not?"

"Because you didn't really need my help. You'd done everything already." She remembered the way he'd raked her over the coals and got even more irate. "And you had the gall to sit there and scold me when I accused you of—"

"And you're forcing me to do it again. I'm not arrogant enough to think I'm infallible, Diana. I wanted another opinion. For example, if Angleton's name hadn't been on your list, I would have used someone else."

"I see," she said, only partially mollified. "That's something, I suppose."

He put his arm around her. "I'm not stupid, Diana. If I'd wanted to deceive you, I would have listened to your presentation and said nothing." He caressed the back of her neck, gently and seductively. "You did exactly what I wanted and you did it well. Why are you so annoyed? Isn't it your job to satisfy your clients?"

She didn't want to enjoy the way he was touching her but couldn't help it. His caresses reminded her of the pleasure he'd given her upstairs. Annoyed with herself for responding, she said, "No. Not the sort of satisfaction you have in mind."

He laughed at that. "You've got it backward, *mon ange.* When it comes to personal matters, it's the man's job to satisfy the woman." He kissed her, then murmured against her lips. "Which I promise to do, often and completely."

Diana was torn between longing to kiss him and wanting to kick him. With a flash of insight, she realized that she'd felt that way almost from the start. She'd just been too blind to see it.

Chapter Eight

In Marc's opinion, John Redmon should have been horsewhipped for the damage he'd done to Diana, but fortunately the chemistry between the two of them was so incendiary that nothing short of physical separation could keep them from catching fire. He was pleased but not surprised when she took a quick, unsteady breath and parted her lips for his kiss. Someday soon, the scars would heal and the last barrier would come down. Then she would feel the same overpowering passion he felt and offer herself completely.

In the meantime he was only human, and experienced enough to know his own limits. He kept a firm grip on his emotions as he skillfully aroused her, teaching her to enjoy the sensual side of her nature. She gave and took with delightful enthusiasm, but there was no wild urgency in her response, no frantic invitation to go further. She wasn't ready for more than kissing, not yet. But if his sanity wasn't to suffer, he'd have to see to it that she was before the weekend was out.

He wanted to learn every plane and curve of her body, but instead he slowly withdrew. A few seconds later the front door opened. "There's Tina," he said with a calmness he didn't feel. "Why don't I call Nelly and see if we can come to dinner? If you'd like, you can repair the damage I've done in the powder room upstairs. There's an iron and ironing board in the laundry room next door."

Diana nodded, still under the spell of his kiss. She didn't understand how she could be exasperated with him one moment and helpless in his arms the next, but when he touched her—when he whispered promises of greater pleasures to come—their differences disappeared.

"Yes," she said. "All right. I won't be long."

"The shorter, the better." He handed her her jacket and purse. "Every minute you're gone will feel like an hour."

"Will it?" She smiled distractedly. "I'm actually starting to believe the things you say. I should probably have my head examined."

"But you *should* believe them. I told you. I never—"

"Lie. I know." She got to her feet, walking from the room in a dream-like haze. Maybe she was crazy or self-destructive, but she was glad Marc was coming to the island. No one had ever excited her the way he did, or made her feel so beautiful and desirable. Risa had been right. She'd been half dead before, too busy working to enjoy herself, but Marc had brought her to life.

She stopped in the laundry room to turn on the iron, then continued into the powder room to fix her hair and makeup. Things were coming into focus now, things she would have seen a week ago if she hadn't been so scared to look.

She'd taken Marc's shortcomings too seriously, probably because it was safer to reject him than to risk further pain. It was illogical, she realized, to blame him for being imperious and paternalistic when he'd been trained that way from the cradle, or to fault him for pursuing her so relentlessly when nothing else would have weakened her defenses. Instead of arguing or losing her temper, she had to patiently educate him, just as she did with difficult clients. He was too intelligent not to see the error of his ways and change.

She ironed her skirt and blouse, then went downstairs. He was waiting in the foyer with Tina, who was holding a cookie sheet containing the rest of the mushroom turnovers. He put his arm around her and she moved into his embrace. Tina smiled approvingly.

Twenty minutes later they were sitting in the Van Slykes' living room with William, Nelly and Nelly's friend, Dr. Irving Wolfman, who'd arrived a short time before and was staying until Monday. Diana almost wished Tracy had been there, too, because Marc was sitting close beside her and toying with her hair, looking every bit as smitten as John ever had.

It wasn't just a matter of pride, though. More and more, she enjoyed it when he touched and held her. She looked forward to showing him her island—to being alone with him in her favorite places and telling him about her family's past. It was hard to believe that she'd felt almost nothing the first time he'd kissed her.

The group discussed history during dinner, telling Irving about the Rochard branch of the family and the possibility of buried treasure. William had finished Simone and Pierre-Luc's diaries by then and spoke of them with all the enthusiasm and eloquence of the first-rate historian he was. Tina looked utterly fascinated.

So did Nelly, but as much by Marc and the thought of a treasure hunt as by the contents of the two diaries. She made Marc promise to read Philippe's journal that weekend and report back to her on Monday. Then she began questioning him about his past.

To hear him tell it, his life had been supremely boring, a quiet country upbringing followed by college and a job in the family business. Much to his chagrin, Tina was quick to disagree. She described the mischief he'd gotten into as a boy, usually to the detriment of the vineyard's best grapes, and the narrow escapes he'd had as a man, inevitably from predatory women whom he vehemently denied having encouraged. William had a habit of ignoring social chitchat and retreating into his own private world, but Tina was such a good storyteller and Marc such an entertaining victim that even *he* listened and laughed.

Eventually Diana noticed that her father couldn't take his eyes off Tina, and that Tina was looking at her father far more often than at anyone else in the room. Playing matchmaker, she asked Tina to play some Mozart after dinner. Her father considered Mozart the world's greatest composer. To her astonishment, he followed Tina to the piano and sat down beside her on the bench. It was the first time in her life that she'd seen him pursue a woman.

She and Marc settled down on one couch, Nelly and Irving on the other. As Tina began to play, Marc cupped Diana's ear and whispered, "So, *chérie*? Was I right about introducing them or wasn't I?"

"You were right," she admitted. Brilliantly so.

"I should have suggested a bet." He nuzzled her ear, lightly exploring it with his tongue. "You would have lost, and there's no telling what you might owe me right now."

She wasn't ticklish this time, only aroused. "If you're going to be conceited about it—" He cut her off with an erotic nip that made her want to turn into his arms.

"It's not conceit. It's extraordinary perceptiveness." His lips trailed lower. "God, I want to kiss you."

Diana felt the same way, but it was hardly the time or place. She glanced at Nelly and Irving. They were talking quietly, probably eager to be alone but too proper to leave.

Babe and Henry were due at any time. "Marc, please...
Nelly and Irving—"

"Barely know we're alive, but very well." He put his
arm around her and coaxed her head onto his shoulder.
After a moment, she sighed and snuggled closer.

"This is very nice," he said, absently petting her hair.
"Remember what I said about leaving you alone this
weekend? You can forget it. I'm not letting you out of my
sight."

She smiled at his imperious tone. "No? Not even at
night?"

"Is that an invitation?"

"Don't flatter yourself. It's just that you're so arrogant
that it's hard to resist teasing you."

"And you, *mon ange*, are hard to resist, period. Tease
me too much and you'll find yourself naked in my bed tomorrow night."

"Is *that* an invitation?" she asked coyly.

"Definitely."

She sighed. "I'm afraid I'll have to refuse. Maybe in a
few months, Marc."

"A few *months*?" He gave her hair a gentle tug. "At
that rate, you'll turn me into a frustrated wreck of a man.
If you think you'll get off unscathed, you're crazy."

She'd never known what fun it was to flirt. How exciting, either. "Oh? And what will you do to me?"

"Torture you until you beg for mercy," he said softly.
"Like this."

He cupped her waist under the closed jacket of her suit,
then moved his hand higher, tracing the full, soft curve of
her breast with gentle up-and-down strokes of his thumb,
going closer and closer to the sensitive peak but never
reaching it. She'd never been touched so seductively before, and her nipples throbbed violently in response.
Within seconds, she was warm and flushed, especially her

cheeks and neck. This was nothing like John's hurried fumbling. Nothing at all.

She tried to squirm away, but Marc's arm tightened around her shoulders to prevent it. Then he slid his hand from her breast to her belly and caressed it with light, teasing strokes that made her tingle all over. "All right," she said hoarsely. "You win. I'm begging."

"An empty victory, *mon chou*. I'm in agony." He glanced up, then smiled. "My apologies, Nelly. I thought you were too preoccupied with Dr. Wolfman to notice the fact that I was trying to seduce your niece."

"Not at all, dear. I wish you the best of luck." She winked at him. "Just don't set my couch on fire."

Diana groaned and turned her face into Marc's chest. Everyone burst out laughing. Then, to make matters worse, Tina stopped playing and asked what the joke was all about.

"Marc can't keep his hands off my niece," Nelly answered blithely, "and she's blushing to beat the band. She doesn't know how lucky she is, but then, she's always been somewhat backward in that department."

This time, all five of them chuckled. It was more than Diana could take. She mumbled something about packing for the weekend and escaped to the privacy of her bedroom.

Babe and Henry had arrived by the time she returned with her suitcase. Her father was nowhere to be seen, but Tina had joined Marc on the couch. "I'm ready any time you are," she said to her aunt and uncle.

"We're waiting for William," Babe replied. "He's going with you."

"You mean to the island?" Diana asked.

"Of course to the island," Nelly said. "That's where you're going, isn't it?"

Unlike Diana, William had no attachment to Van Slyke's Island and seldom went there except to use the library. "But he isn't researching an article right now."

Nelly snorted. "Really, Diana, don't be dense. The tree may be older, but the sap hasn't stopped running yet."

The tree? The sap? "I beg your pardon, Aunt Nelly?"

"It's my sister's quaint way of saying that you're a damn good matchmaker," Henry explained.

"Actually, it was Marc's idea," Tina said. "Your father's a real charmer, Diana. A little slow on the uptake, though. Nelly had to hint around like crazy before it occurred to him to invite himself along."

"Well, I certainly don't want him *here*," Nelly grumbled. "I see Irving rarely enough as it is, and then the two of them start yammering about history and chess—"

"Drives Nelly nuts," Irving said to Tina. "She can't stand either one."

"I'm crazy about both of 'em," Tina said.

Marc looked incredulous. "But you don't know a thing about either."

She smiled. "So I'll learn."

Diana always felt a sense of renewal when she came to Van Slyke's Island. It was exceptionally lovely there, and her memories of the place were mostly happy ones. As children, she and Risa had played in the eerie hollows that the sea had cut into the cliffs ringing its fine white beaches, and camped in the central stand of oak and pretended it was a primeval forest. Most of the island's five hundred acres had been cleared centuries ago, leaving rolling green meadows, once farmland, dotted with old wooden buildings and crisscrossed by meandering dirt roads.

The grandest of these roads, which was two lanes wide and several hundred feet long, led from the beach to the main house through a break in the cliffs. Henry had phoned the caretaker early that morning, just before they'd left, and asked him to meet them with the island's small pickup. It took two trips in the cruiser to bring all the furniture to the island, and more than twice that many trips in the truck to transport everything to the front yard, but finally around nine o'clock they started carrying pieces of furniture inside.

Diana felt a burst of pleasure each time an heirloom was restored to its proper place. Slowly but surely, the empty spaces in this house were filling up. More and more, it was becoming the magical home of her childhood.

As soon as they were done, William mumbled something about checking some records and disappeared into the library. Diana drove Henry and the caretaker back to the dock, arranging to meet the caretaker at five on Sunday at the Van Slykes. There were two boats moored at the island, a small racing craft and a midsize cruiser for transportation.

It was ten-thirty by then, and the early morning chill had left the air. She walked briskly across the island, drinking in the sun and sea, wondering how her father could stay inside on such a glorious fall day. He was such a cerebral man that he sometimes seemed disconnected from the world of the senses. Even his enjoyment of wine, music and chess were rooted in logic and intellect.

She circled back to the dock along the shore, then took off her sneakers and waded in the surf. Every now and then she checked her watch, wishing Marc and Tina would arrive. They'd had to shop for groceries and rent a van big enough to hold the sideboard before driving to New Rochelle.

Her heart gave an erratic leap when she spotted Henry's cruiser. Marc was standing on deck, his hair blowing wildly in the wind. Thinking he looked wonderful, she ran onto the dock and waved. He blew her a kiss and waved back. It suddenly struck her that in all the years she'd dated John, she'd never been this thrilled to see him.

Happy, yes, but not emotionally exhilarated. Not physically excited.

As Henry pulled slowly up to the wharf, Marc hopped out, caught Diana by the waist and lifted her high in the air, laughing as he swung her around. Then he eased her down, sliding her flush against his body so she could feel his sinewy strength. The kiss he gave her wasn't the sort of perfunctory peck she'd always gotten from John, but full, deep and hot. Although it embarrassed her to be kissed so passionately in front of her uncle and Tina, she didn't pull away. It felt too good.

Henry and Tina stepped onto the dock as Marc released her. "It's beautiful here," Tina said breezily, as if she hadn't just witnessed a scene straight out of *Gone with the Wind*. "I'm a city girl, but I could really learn to love it."

Diana tried to sound just as natural. "Then maybe you can do something with my father. He's never had any affinity for the place. He's up at the house, with his nose in a book."

"Not anymore." Marc pointed inland. William was trotting down the road.

Diana could hardly believe her eyes. Her father, who never let anything interfere with his work, had obviously been watching for Tina from the window. "And they say you can't teach an old dog new tricks! You're a miracle worker, Tina."

"Yes, well, love is grand and all that," Henry grumbled, "but an author I'm trying to steal away from Viking is coming to lunch, and I should have been back ten minutes ago. Give me a hand with the sideboard, Marc."

As the two of them walked to the boat, William jumped onto the dock and strode up to Tina. Taking her hands in his, he said, "Welcome to my island, my dear. I look forward to showing it to you."

Diana stiffened, but held her tongue. He'd never done a damn thing for this island but rape it. Yanking her sneakers back on, she hopped onto the cruiser and grabbed a bag of groceries.

For once in his life, her father noticed her feelings. "My daughter's never forgiven me for selling off antiques to support my journal," he told Tina, "but I've always considered scholarship more important than physical objects." He paused. "I was wrong about one thing, though. I never should have sold the harpsichord. I'd give anything to hear you play it."

"Diana will get it back someday, and then I'll play it whenever you like." Tina took his arm. "You can start the tour right now. I want to see absolutely everything." They strolled down the wharf and continued inland.

Henry left for home as soon as the sideboard and groceries were safely on the truck. Marc slid into the driver's seat as if, being male, he rightfully belonged there, and drove to the house. He wanted to wait until William returned to unload the sideboard, but Diana pointed out that she'd helped with far heavier pieces that day, and he reluctantly gave in. She was strong for someone so tiny, he admitted as they carried the sideboard inside, but a woman had to be careful about what she lifted.

"Because she'll strain her back and won't be able to pleasure her lord and master?" she asked tartly.

"I hadn't considered that aspect of it, but it's a valid point." They eased the sideboard into place against the wall. "I was thinking in terms of having children. You could injure—"

"Of all the ridiculous old wives' tales! If women's insides were really that fragile, the human race would have become extinct during the Stone Age."

"All the same, when you become pregnant with—" He pressed his lips together.

"Yes?"

"Never mind. Let's unload the groceries."

Her eyes widened in mock surprise. "But the bag I carried to the truck was so heavy, Marc! I suppose you think it's woman's work if it's groceries, but still..."

"I think you're deliberately provoking me." He gave her an erotic little swat on her backside. "Do as you're told, *chérie*, and I'll reward you generously later on."

"Of all the egotistical, conceited—"

"I was talking about cooking you dinner, not making love to you," he said with a laugh, "but I might do both if you're especially obedient."

"I'm afraid it's not in my nature," she retorted.

He gave a long-suffering sigh. "I know. Willfulness is your worst fault. It's going to be the greatest challenge of my life to reform you."

She had the damnedest reaction when he teased her that way. As much as she wanted to shut him up with a clever comeback, she would have surrendered on the spot if he'd taken her in his arms. "I'm not the one who needs reforming around here," she muttered, and marched out of the house.

He followed her, telling her it was a delight to walk behind her. "I love the way your jeans cling to your body. Your derriere is utterly delectable. And that sweater you're wearing... Your breasts are even more exquisite than I realized. I can't wait to undress you and kiss every inch of them...to take your beautiful red hair out of that very adorable ponytail and bury my hands in it. They'll have to commit me if you make me wait months, *mon ange*, because I'll be stark, raving mad by then."

Diana felt his words in every bone of her body. Nobody had ever said such things to her before, or wanted her so desperately. By the time they reached the truck, she wondered why she'd ever been annoyed with him.

"Why don't you show me around the house," he said as they put the groceries away, "and then I'll make us a picnic lunch. We could eat in the woods."

Diana didn't have to ask why he'd suggested the woods. They were isolated and private. "That sounds wonderful. We might run into my father and Tina, though."

"Locked in a passionate embrace, you mean. If we do, we'll chase them inside. Unlike us, they're too old to be rolling around on the ground."

She blushed. "Is that what we're going to do after lunch? Roll around on the ground?"

He came up behind her and kissed the nape of her neck. It made her hot and shivery at the same time. "Would you like that?"

She closed her eyes to intensify the feel of his mouth. "Yes."

"Then I think it could be arranged." He pulled her around to face him. She expected him to kiss her, but instead, he took her hand. "Come, Diana. Show me around. Tell me about your work here."

Her eyes lit up with pleasure. She loved talking about Van Slyke's Island and was thrilled he wanted to listen. John hadn't, not really, although he'd been polite enough to pretend otherwise.

She took him from room to room, pointing out the most important antiques and telling him about the pieces that were still in other hands. Van Slykes had first settled in the New World in the 1630s, she explained, acquiring property in the Bronx in the 1650s and Van Slyke's Island some ten years later. Anna Van Slyke's grandfather, a merchant, had built the first house here, a crude little cottage where he'd stored his smuggled goods, a practice continued by his son, Anna's father.

The first real home on the island had been built in 1712 by Anna's daughter, Marie, and her husband, George, who had cleared a few dozen acres, planted some vegetables and

stayed here each summer. When a hurricane had damaged the building four decades later, their son had pulled
it down and erected the central portion of the current
mansion in its place. There were a parlor, dining room,
kitchen and study downstairs, and three bedrooms and two
baths—once four bedrooms—upstairs, with an attic
above. Over the next fifty years, various owners had added
two graceful wings. One contained a library and ballroom, the other more bathrooms and bedrooms. Various
outbuildings had been constructed as well.

"By 1800, this was a prosperous farm and Van Slykes
lived here all year round," Diana said as she led Marc into
the ballroom. "The family also owned land on the Sound,
including the property where Henry and Babe live. The
mansion is basically the same as it was in 1800, except for
the modern plumbing and electricity. Most of the Van
Slykes were conscious of its historical importance and
made an effort to leave it alone, but they repainted and
repapered constantly over the years, and every now and
then some wife took it into her head to rip out molding or
add paneling, and there are also two centuries of ordinary
wear and tear to repair. My goal is to restore everything to
the way it looked in 1800 and turn the island into a working farm of the period."

"I didn't realize your plans were so ambitious—or so
fascinating." Marc glanced around the ballroom, which
was empty except for some drop cloths on the floor and
some tools and a ladder in one corner. "I see that you're
restoring the ceiling. Was it difficult to find the proper
craftsmen?"

"Yes. I had to wait my turn in line." The plasterwork,
an intricate series of pastel moldings, was badly damaged
in spots and needed extensive reconstruction and a good
cleaning. She pointed to the largest gap. "Uncle Henry was
playing stickball in here with his friend one day when he
was thirteen, and that's the result. We know how most

things looked originally from written descriptions and paintings. My father kept them all, thank God. He considered them history—as if the rest of the furnishings weren't."

Marc put his arm around her and said gently, "After all these years, you're still angry with him, hmm? It doesn't do much good, you know."

Diana did, but she could never forget how helpless she'd felt as a child, when she'd raised anguished objections to his actions, only to be scolded or ignored. "He was raised to cherish this place. His mother told me so. But instead, from the moment his father died and he inherited it, his only concern was restoring some moldy historical journal to its former glory. It came out only once or twice a year in those days, but it was still called *The Manhattan Island Quarterly*. He said it was a matter of honor, because Van Slykes had founded the damn thing and edited it ever since, but Van Slykes built this house, too."

"And selling off antiques was the only way he could pay the publishing and promotion costs for four issues a year?"

She nodded. "Yes. There's a trust fund that pays most of the upkeep on the island, but he couldn't legally touch that. His only personal income was from teaching and writing, and we needed that to live on. He taught at City College back then. It's part of the public university. But after fifteen years of effort, the *Quarterly*'s prestige was so great that Columbia offered him financial support for the journal and an endowed professorship for himself. It's ironic, really. Dr. William Van Slyke, the prizewinning colonial historian, thinks that words read by a few thousand scholars are more important than living history that tens of thousands of people will be able to see and touch."

"And you?" Marc asked. "Your devotion to this house didn't come from your father, obviously, so who was responsible?"

"My mother. She died when I was nine—of a massive stroke." Diana's eyes welled up. She still missed Laura keenly, still ached because they'd never said goodbye. "I left for school one morning with a loving mother and returned that afternoon to find myself a virtual orphan."

Marc drew her closer. It felt warm and comforting, like being eight again and safe in her mother's arms. "I know how hard it was for you. Risa told me that William wasn't much of a father or Nelly much of a mother."

"They did their best." Diana brushed the tears from her eyes, impatient with her loss of composure. As much as she wished they'd been different, she knew they hadn't deliberately hurt her. "Mom was an ordinary girl from Buffalo, who came to the big city to work as a secretary and married her boss, but she loved this island as much as any Van Slyke ever did. I was the child she'd never expected to have, because my father had a fertility problem. She thought of the house as mine from the day I was born. My earliest memory is of walking through the parlor with my hand in hers while she told me a story about the figures on the chinoiserie chest. When I come here, I can feel her presence everywhere."

"So you really are a princess, not of Wall Street, but of your own private island." He lifted her face to his and kissed her. "A very beautiful, very noble princess. Your kingdom is lucky to have you, *chérie*."

The world was suddenly a warmer, happier place. Unlike John, Marc really liked this house. He really understood her devotion to it. "You Frenchmen say the loveliest things. I think you must be the world's best talkers."

"Since it's time for lunch, it's lucky that we're also the world's best chefs."

"I won't argue with that," she said. "You've proven it conclusively."

He took her arm and led her from the room. "And the world's best lovers, too. I'd be happy to prove that as well, whenever you'd like."

She giggled. "Maybe in a few months, tiger."

He looked crestfallen.

Chapter Nine

If Marc had really believed he would have to wait months, he would have bowed to the inevitable and checked into the nearest asylum. It would be a week or two at the most, he thought—perhaps even tonight. Diana wasn't as hungry as he was, but he was sure he could make her that way if only she would give him the chance.

Tonight or next month, though, he was lucky and he knew it. It wasn't often that a man fell violently in love with a woman who pleased him so completely. His Diana had great depth and feeling, great spirit. Her love for her island proved it. She would be a good wife and mother, and given her deep respect for the past, a fitting addition to the illustrious Rochard family.

As for her temper, he looked forward to transforming it into passion. He smiled at the thought. The right mixture of petting and teasing would turn her into a wildcat in bed.

She noticed the smile and frowned. "You're plotting something," she said. "What?"

"Not plotting. Anticipating." They entered the kitchen. "You have a habit of losing your temper when you think I'm being protective or dominating. I was wondering what you would do if I said something you objected to while I was making love to you."

"Deliberately, you mean? Said it just to provoke me?"

"Of course. You know how much we enjoy trying to get the better of each other."

She rolled her eyes in exasperation, but he knew it was only an act. She was blushing enchantingly. "Kick you out of bed," she said.

"But I wouldn't be foolish enough to say it too soon. I'd wait until you were naked in my arms and desperate to have me inside you." He chose his words with diabolical care. "And then I'd do something totally despicable, like forbid you to drive if it was snowing that day, or order you to bed early if you'd worked especially hard. You'd be angry, but remember, I'd have aroused you so completely that stopping would half kill you. What would you do?"

He didn't know what he'd expected—more blushes, perhaps, or an outraged lecture—but it certainly wasn't a stricken look and a nervous withdrawal.

"I don't know." She crossed to the refrigerator. "About lunch... Should we make some sandwiches or just pack everything up and take it outside?"

He watched in bewilderment as she pulled out packages of cold cuts and stacked them on the counter. She was very anxious, very upset. Obviously he'd gone too fast.

"I've made you uncomfortable," he said. "Mentioned things you weren't ready to think about. I'm sorry."

She didn't answer, just kept pulling out containers and bottles. He tried again. "I told you last night, Diana—I would never push you. We'll make love when you're ready to, not before. Please don't be afraid of me."

"I'm not. It's just that—" She stopped and shook her head. "It doesn't matter. You must be starving. I'll—"

"It *does* matter." He strode up behind her and turned her around. She was frighteningly pale. "Tell me what's troubling you. Whatever it is, I promise that it's not half so bad as you think it is."

She stared at his chest, trembling now. Something had distressed her deeply, but what? He tried to think. He'd been teasing her about making love, about the passion she would feel... She seemed to be afraid of that, afraid of too much intimacy. It had to be Redmon's fault. He was the only other man she'd been with.

He took her in his arms and held her close. She hesitated, then put her arms around him and laid her head against his chest. His heart contracted. She was so damn independent, but what she really needed was someone to take care of her.

He smoothed back her hair and said gently, "We'll be fine together, you know. You're too sweet and passionate for us not to be." She clung a little more tightly, and he swallowed back the lump in his throat. "I want very much to please you, *chérie*. I admit I was almost insufferably self-confident about my ability to do it, but I'm not anymore. You frightened me just now. If there are things I should know—things about you and Redmon—I wish you would tell me."

A week ago, Diana couldn't have pictured herself talking comfortably with Marc Rochard, much less confiding her most painful secrets to him, but listening to his soft, emotional words, she felt there was nothing she couldn't tell him. A few more speeches like that, and she'd be half in love with him. Maybe she already was.

"What you said before—about stopping half killing me... I never minded stopping. I never—it never mattered to me one way or the other."

He tensed. "Did Redmon hurt you? Is that why?"

"Sometimes. A little. He wasn't—brutal or anything. He was just—in such a hurry." Or maybe it had been her.

Just because Risa said otherwise, that didn't make it true. Her voice dropped to a whisper. "Or maybe I was hopelessly slow. Hopelessly cold." She swallowed hard and rushed on, "If I sleep with you... The things you expect from me... They won't happen, Marc."

"Because they didn't with Redmon?" He slid his hand under her sweater and gently rubbed her back. "Did he kiss you the way I kiss you? Touch you the way I touch you?"

"No," she admitted, soothed by his caresses. "He was in too much of a rush to get to—well, you know."

"Yes, although it's hard for me to imagine such stupidity." His touch grew more erotic, and she shuddered with excitement. "Your body is exquisite. It was made to give and receive pleasure, slowly and very thoroughly. Don't you enjoy the things I do to you? Don't they arouse you?"

He knew the answers as well as she did. He could probably feel them right now. "You're right. You *are* insufferably self-confident. But I haven't exactly attacked you, you know. If it had been up to you, we would have spent the night together last night, but I wasn't even close to wanting to." She paled. "Maybe I won't ever be."

He eased her out of his arms and cupped her face. "Would you care to make a friendly bet about that?" he asked with a smile.

"No." Her eyes settled on his mouth. She wanted him to kiss her. That seemed to be happening more and more lately. "I'd never bet against what I want to happen."

He pecked her on the forehead and released her, and she felt a stab of disappointment. "Then it will," he said. "I guarantee it. Let's throw everything into a sack and take it outside. You and I have a great deal of talking to do. I don't know nearly enough about you."

Diana fetched a blanket from her bedroom while Marc packed their lunch. A few minutes later, as they walked to the door, she asked if the talking would work both ways,

and he replied that he certainly hoped so. She could ask him whatever she liked; he didn't want to have any secrets from her. It was ironic, but for all his overprotectiveness, he paid far more attention to her feelings and opinions than John ever had, and John had paid lip service to women's equality from the day they'd met.

They went outside, meeting William and Tina in the front yard, strolling hand in hand toward the house. "I see you're about to have a picnic," Tina said. "Where are you going?"

"Into the woods," Marc replied.

"Good choice, kids. It's very romantic." She winked broadly. "We'll be sure to stay inside."

Diana was too busy staring at her father to be embarrassed. He looked moonstruck. The sap wasn't just running; it was racing wildly. She was pleased, and not just for him. She'd never cared for the society types he usually went around with, but she liked Tina very much.

Tina and William continued into the house while Diana led Marc to her favorite spot in the woods. The sun was almost directly overhead, warming them as it filtered through the trees. They sat close together on the blanket, eating and talking quietly.

She'd met John at City College, she told Marc. He'd been her first real boyfriend, the son of a salesman from Queens, and she'd fallen in love with his ambition and intelligence. He'd wanted to be a lawyer, she a teacher, but she'd known by then that her career would be on Wall Street. Her family background had given her terrific contacts, and M & A—mergers and acquisitions—was the one place where she could start out with nothing and make a bundle.

During the first years of her marriage, she'd learned her trade and worked her way up, earning enough to put John through Columbia Law School and start buying back antiques for Van Slyke's Island. She hadn't liked her job—it was extremely stressful, the hours were brutal and she'd questioned the social value of ripping companies apart or trading them like baseball cards so a few people could make a killing—but the future had come first. She'd had a life to build with John. She'd had a mansion to restore.

All in all, she'd been happy. It was true that she'd wanted to cut back on her hours and have a child once John had gotten a good job, but she'd gone along with his plans to buy an apartment in Manhattan first, and then build up a good-sized nest egg. Throwing herself into her job had helped ease the disappointment.

"I was blind," she admitted. "He married me because I was his ticket to law school and his entrée into a prestigious New York firm, but I never saw it. I was too busy working. He worked hard, too, but I earned much more money than he did, and I guess he felt threatened by that. Abandoned, too. It never occurred to me to wonder why Tracy suddenly started dropping by our apartment all the time. She'd gotten friendly with John while she was a sophomore at Columbia and he was in his last year of law school, and besides, she was my baby cousin."

"Who was trying to seduce your husband," Marc said, sounding offended by the idea.

"Yes." She stared at him without seeing him, lost in a fog of painful memories. "I came home a few days early from a business trip and found them in bed together. I went crazy—shouted and threw things, cried hysterically and then fled to Risa and Graham's. I didn't want the divorce. I still loved him. I thought we could work things out. But he said he wanted to marry Tracy, and admitted that they'd been sleeping together for two years, so I got out of the way as quickly and graciously as I could. He said she made him feel like a real man. He thinks she's the perfect woman. The ideal wife."

"Submissive. Adoring. Catering to him completely." Marc shook his head in distaste. "On the surface, anyway. She runs his life completely without him even knowing it. I could see it the other night.''

He was right, but Diana didn't say so. It would have sounded bitchy. "And you? You're not the type to let anyone run you, but don't you want the exact same things in a wife?''

"Obviously not,'' he said in a soft, emphatic voice. "If I did, I wouldn't have fallen in love with *you*.''

For a moment or two, she was too stunned to speak. It hadn't been another of his lighthearted comments about being crazy about her, but an impassioned statement of fact, an implicit proposal of marriage. "But we hardly know each other. It's only been a week . . .''

"A week is long enough to have seen your warmth and grace, your honesty and goodness, but if you want the truth, I've loved you from the first moment I saw you. *Un coup de foudre, mon ange.* Right between the eyes.''

Diana didn't believe in thunderbolts. She was too practical by nature, too wary. "I don't know what to say,'' she mumbled.

"You don't have to say a word.'' He smiled roguishly. "Fortunately, there are other ways to communicate.''

When he smiled that way—used that husky tone of voice—she was hard-pressed even to think, much less talk. A flush stole over her face and her heart sped up in anticipation. He was dressed much as she was, in slacks and a sweater. She suddenly wanted to touch him as he'd once touched her, to learn the feel of his bare flesh and see the desire in his eyes as she caressed him.

An hour ago she would have been too shy, but being told she was passionate and exquisite had boosted her confidence. She slid her hand under his sweater and ran it from his belly to his chest. His firm, warm skin and lean, muscular build were as intoxicating as any wine. Her touch grew bolder, more provocative.

His smile gave way to a look of fierce desire. If he hadn't been so controlled in the past, she might have panicked and pulled away. Instead, trusting him not to rush her, she felt for his heartbeat and fondled his nipples. His heart was racing just as hers was, and his nipples, like hers, were erect.

Still staring at her, he unhooked the clip from her ponytail and fanned her hair over her shoulders. "God, but you're beautiful," he said in French. He used *tu*, the familiar form of you. That was only for family...for dear friends...for lovers. In its way, it was even more intimate than the passionate kisses they'd shared.

"*Et tu, aussi*," she whispered back. And you also.

It was a promise of future intimacy, and his response couldn't have been any more emotional if she'd stripped off her clothes and offered herself then and there. He thrust his hands into her hair and lowered his mouth. His kiss was scorching, an unspoken claim of possession that started slow and hot and got wilder and more demanding with each passing moment.

She slid her arms around him, tasting him only to teasingly withdraw, then sliding her tongue past his and exploring eagerly. For the first time since they'd met, she asked for more than kisses, pressing her breasts against his chest in an invitation he couldn't possibly misconstrue. She wasn't the same woman with Marc that she'd been with John. Instead of passively letting him take her, enjoying it in a distant sort of way, if at all, she was involved down to the tips of her toes.

He kissed her until she melted and clung to him, then groaned and pulled away. "And you thought you were cold. Or slow. My darling Diana, if you were any more enthusiastic, I'd die of pleasure. You kiss like an angel."

She was thrilled that she'd pleased him so completely. "And *you* kiss like the devil," she said. "I feel as if it's a hundred degrees out here."

"Only a hundred? So cold?" He eased her onto her back and stretched out beside her. "I'll have to warm you up."

Supporting himself on an elbow, he slipped his hand beneath her sweater and felt for the hooks on her bra. She turned to make them easier to reach, catching her breath as he deftly unsnapped them and moved his hand slowly back to her chest. The warmth of his palm on her breast was so exciting that she closed her eyes and blindly reached out, pressing herself against his hand as she twined her arms around his neck.

He caressed her with a light, sensual touch, exploring her as if she were infinitely fragile and precious. After a few moments, he began to playfully nibble her lips, arousing her until she parted them in a silent plea for his tongue. He tasted her gingerly, sparingly. She wanted more, but he was holding himself too far away for her to take his mouth and refused to let her pull him any closer.

He traced the contours of her breasts with warm, sure fingers, provocatively skirting her nipples, then lightly stroking them until they were pebble-hard. Hazily aware that he was deliberately teasing her, she moaned his name and feverishly caressed his back. The pleasure—and torment—were so intense that she couldn't decide whether she wanted him to keep teasing her or put her out of her misery.

But if her brain wasn't sure, her straining body was, and that was what he listened to. He took a nipple between his thumb and forefinger and gently massaged it, and a pulsing ache spread through her body. He increased the pressure, and she surrendered to him completely. He could do as he pleased. He knew what she needed even better than she did.

"I love you," he murmured in French. "You're so sweet, so enchanting..." He pushed up her sweater and eased himself on top of her, yanking his own sweater out of the way as he settled himself against her. She'd felt half crushed when John had done that, but Marc, who was even bigger, was careful not to make her take his weight.

His chest, hot and a little slick, rubbed excitingly against her breasts. She loved the texture of his naked skin, loved lying beneath him. He was power, life and warm male shelter, and she wanted—needed—much more of him.

Holding him tightly, she shifted her weight to make the contact more intimate. His maleness was so arousing that her hips began to rock seductively, almost without her conscious consent. Her boldness shocked her. She'd never taken the initiative with John, never even wanted to.

Then Marc responded to her movements, and everything changed. She was aroused and eager, but his excitement far outstripped her own. She could feel the wild urgency in his fiery kisses and hard, insistent thrusts. Deep down, it frightened her. He wanted her so much he was shaking. In another minute or two, he would undress her and take her. She knew she'd invited it, but she didn't want it.

She was torn between needing to give and wanting to stop. She couldn't bring herself to push him away, or even to withdraw her mouth, but she did stiffen slightly. That was all it took. He rolled onto his side at once, and breathing hard, buried his face against her neck.

She lay there feeling guilty, waiting for his breathing to slow and his body to still. Finally he raised his head and sought her eyes. "I'm sorry," he said softly. "I shouldn't have—"

"No. It was all my fault. I wanted to—to be closer to you. To feel you. But I should have realized it would—"

"You did, hmm?" His voice was teasing now, almost devilish. "And did I meet with your approval, *chérie*?"

She lowered her eyes. "You know you did. But John was right about me. I'm—"

"Sheer perfection." He kissed her and sat up. "It wasn't your fault, at all. It was mine. I want you very much, but I shouldn't have let it show. I frightened you. You thought I would rush ahead the way John did, but I wouldn't have. I'm too selfish to deny myself the pleasure of sucking your beautiful pink nipples or caressing your very alluring derriere."

The things he planned to do seemed even more intimate than raw sex. He would see and touch every inch of her. She didn't reply.

"No response, hmm?" He caressed her hair. "You don't think you'll like it, I suppose, but you will. I promise."

"It's not that." She sat up, hooking her arms around her knees and resting her chin on them. "You keep saying I'm beautiful and perfect, but I'm not. Compared to the women you're used to—"

"One look at you and they ceased to exist." He paused. "I'm an acknowledged expert, so when I tell you you're perfect, you have to believe me."

She smiled at the mixture of ego and gallantry in that statement. "I don't have to do any such thing. The fact is, I love to eat. Every spoonful of cream sauce and pasta goes straight to my hips and thighs, and since I'm hopeless at dieting—"

"Lose a single pound and I'll feed you until you gain it back," he said with a laugh. "For the tenth time, you're perfect the way you are. A man wants soft, warm flesh to caress, not skin and bones."

He circled her thigh with his hand and playfully kneaded it. She started at first, but quickly began to enjoy it. "You see?" he said. "Not a bit of fat. Very firm and smooth."

"I walk a lot," she mumbled.

"And you have the muscles to prove it. When you wrap your legs around my hips while we're making love, I'll be powerless to leave. Your complete prisoner, *mon ange*, to be enjoyed however you wish. I'll like that very much."

He kept mentioning things she'd never experienced, never even contemplated. "I wish you wouldn't be so graphic about it. You're embarrassing me."

"But I was only trying to educate you," he protested.

"You were trying to tease me, you mean. The truth is, you get a kick out of how naive I am."

He stood and held out his hand, but she refused to take it. "Very well. You're enchantingly innocent and I enjoy seeing you blush. I enjoy teaching you the things you don't know. After all, you have such a passion for learning."

"Which you attribute to your incredible skill as an instructor, I suppose."

"And to the sensuality of my prize student. I'm looking forward to tonight." He took her hand and pulled her up. "But right now, it's your turn to be the teacher. Show me the rest of your island. Tell me about the buildings here and explain how everything will eventually look."

Diana did as he wished, but her mind was on that night. She wondered what he would do and how it would feel. She worried he'd lose patience with her the way John always had.

In time, though, her passion for the island won out. She reminisced about the caves and cliffs where she and Risa had played pirates and smugglers as children, described her plans for the tumbledown bunkhouse where the farmhands had once lived, and insisted that the graceful old windmill was the loveliest on the coast. Then, afraid that she'd rambled on and bored him, she asked about his own past and plans. They visited the weathered barn and the carpenter's and blacksmith's sheds, the family graveyard and the caretaker's cottage, and finally the splendid garden that had been restored only that summer, and he told her everything she wanted to know.

He'd had a wonderful childhood, growing up in a happy and loving family, a royal prince among the elite of Bordeaux. Both sets of grandparents had spoiled him, as had his mother and older sister. If his father had been less indulgent, that was only to be expected. Louis Rochard was every inch the French patriarch, the ruler not only of his household but of a distinguished French winery, and he'd seen his son as an heir to be disciplined and instructed.

Marc, meanwhile, had fallen under the spell of the family cook, a local widow who might have been the toast of Paris if she'd taken a job there but preferred the beauty of St. Emilion, where she had a nice little house and family to help her with her children. Besides, everyone who was anyone eventually came to dinner at the Rochards', so her talent hardly went unappreciated. Marc had loved watching her and learning the intricacies of cooking and, in time, loved helping her create new recipes.

As for winemaking, he'd learned a great deal about that, too, and loved it as well, but not with the same passion as haute cuisine. His sister, Catherine, older by six years, had been the one with wine in her veins. By all rights, Marc said, she should have married a local vintner and become the chatelaine of his winery, but instead she'd chosen a wealthy dairy farmer from a neighboring province. They'd had children at once, Thérèse and Jean-Luc, now eighteen and sixteen.

When the children entered school, Catherine began driving to the winery several days a week to help her mother with the paperwork and offer her opinions about aging, mixing and bottling. Her father didn't entirely approve, but he recognized that she had a nose to rival his own and grudgingly listened to her advice. Besides, her husband had given his permission, so who was a mere father to object?

Marc was at school in Paris by then, taking cooking lessons behind his father's back but resigned to the idea of running the family winery eventually. After all, it was unthinkable that the business should pass out of the hands of the Rochards. As Louis's only son, he was the most suitable person to take over.

But over the next few years, after he'd finished school and become the winery's sales director, it had slowly dawned on him that there was someone equally suitable, his sister, Catherine. She didn't have his talent for business, but she was definitely the better winemaker and, unlike him, dearly wanted the job.

In time, they broached the subject with their father, but Louis wouldn't hear of anyone but his son succeeding him. He claimed he would work himself to the grave before he would hand the reins to a female. Given Marc's devotion to his family, he'd felt he had no choice but to stay.

"But I was hardly a silent martyr," he said as they walked into the house. "The whole family knew how I felt—that I thought my father was being unreasonable. My mother supported her husband, which was only proper, but my grandmother agreed with me and my sister and didn't hesitate to say so repeatedly. He always answered that she was a meddlesome old woman who should have been sent to a convent years ago. She never paid the least attention. You would have liked her, *chérie*. She was almost as independent as you are."

Diana ignored the teasing smile on his face. "You're speaking of your mother's mother, I take it."

"Yes. My father's parents had died by then, and Sofia was a widow. She spent most of her time in France, in the house she and Sam had bought when my parents married. Nobody could tell her what to do. She had the will of a mule. I suppose she had to, to raise four younger brothers and sisters from the time she was twelve."

They went into the kitchen to put away the leftovers. "Sofia owned forty percent of the winery at that point," Marc continued as they worked. "Sam had originally bought fifty percent. That was more than my father wanted to sell him, but he was a tough businessman and he'd insisted. Family or not, he'd wanted an equal say in his investment and my father had needed the money too badly to refuse. But he did manage to extract a promise that Sam wouldn't interfere as long as the winery made a profit, and that the Parisis' fifty percent would be returned to him or his heirs eventually."

Diana remembered Marc saying that he owned ten percent of Château du Ciel. "Then the missing ten percent was given to you over the years?"

"Yes. Half when I was born, half when I turned eighteen. Sofia had always said she would give me the rest when I married, but I was still single when she died." He put the kettle on to boil and ground up some beans for coffee. "Everyone assumed she would leave it to me in her will, but she fooled us all. She left it to my sister instead, along with her house in St. Emilion and some property in Paris. The rest went to me."

"And nothing went to your mother?"

"Not a dime. I suppose Sofia knew my mother would always be taken care of and wasn't worried about her, but Catherine and I were a different story. I think she wanted to make our dreams come true—Catherine's to run the winery, mine to own a restaurant. Between the two of us, Sofia and I owned fifty percent of the stock and could have challenged my father at any time, but she was almost ninety by then and I doubt she had the stomach for open warfare."

"And besides," Diana pointed out, "someone who owned nothing and depended upon the generosity of her brother and grandmother to give her what she wanted would be in a very weak position. As a forty percent owner, Catherine speaks with a great deal more authority."

"Spoken like a true banker," Marc said. "I've told my father that I intend to vote with Catherine every time they disagree, unless he accepts her as his successor, but he refuses to believe me. It's evolved into a cold war by now. She still works there, but they barely speak. Things go along as they always have, but God help us the next time a difficult decision has to be made."

And that was why he'd left France, he explained as he made the coffee. His father was sixty-eight now, and his stamina wasn't what it once had been. Louis knew he couldn't go on indefinitely, but he was holding out, telling himself Marc would reconsider. By removing himself from the scene and getting on with his life, Marc hoped to prove him wrong and force him to accept Catherine.

They carried their coffee into the parlor and sat down on the damask-covered settee that Diana had reclaimed the previous Saturday. "This must be difficult for your mother," she said. "She's caught in the middle."

"Not at all. She's my father's wife. She supports him completely. That's only proper."

He'd made an almost identical comment before and she'd let it pass, but now she said what she really thought. "But she's also your mother. Surely your happiness matters to her."

"Yes, but my father's happiness matters more. She even tried to get Yves—Catherine's husband—to put his foot down and order her to stay home, but he wouldn't."

Again, the first time Marc had mentioned Yves's role in this, Diana had swallowed her objections and politely kept listening. Now, suspecting that Marc thought Yves would have been well within his rights to refuse to let Catherine work, she found it impossible to remain silent. "You mean Catherine would have obeyed him if he had? She would have forgotten her dreams just because her husband wanted her around to fetch his pipe and slippers?"

"To look after his home," Marc corrected, "and naturally she would have. Her husband and children come first. She wouldn't have considered running the winery if Yves had disapproved, or if Thérèse and Jean-Luc still needed her full attention. It's much too demanding a job."

"Then it's fortunate that she has such a tolerant husband, isn't it?" Diana asked sweetly.

Her sarcasm went right over Marc's head. "Yes, very. He was generous about it from the start. He didn't need her to help with his own business and felt that working at the winery would keep her busy and happy. Of course, Catherine is an exceptional woman. She has as much knowledge about wine as any man does, and such incredible energy that she's able to put in a full day at the winery and still look after her family. Fortunately, they have a good housekeeper. Otherwise, with all the entertaining they do, she would never be able to manage."

God forbid Yves should help out, Diana thought sourly. He only approved of his wife's working because it didn't affect his life. Chauvinism wasn't just alive and well in France, it was thriving.

Somehow she managed to hold her tongue. After all, losing her temper would accomplish nothing. "So you support your sister because she's exceptional. If she weren't, you'd have given up your dreams and taken over, no matter how much she wanted the job and you didn't."

"I'd have had no choice. It would have been my duty as the only son." He sipped his coffee. "In any event, Catherine won't be running things forever, and I hope that alone will bring my father around. Her son Jean-Luc takes after his mother and grandfather when it comes to wine. In another ten years or so, once Catherine's taught him the business, she'll be able to retire."

Diana stared at him. "But she'll only be forty-eight. That's the prime of life for an executive."

"I'm sure she'll still be involved, *chérie*, but she and Yves will want to travel and enjoy each other once the children finish school and leave the house. That would be very difficult to arrange with two demanding schedules to take into account. Besides, she'll probably be a grandmother by then. She'll want to spend time with her grandchildren.''

The explosion that Diana had so staunchly repressed finally took place. ''Oh, of course! She'll have gotten all that nonsense about running a winery out of her system by then, won't she? She's only a simpleminded female, so she won't have plans that she's excited about and wants to implement. She won't care about improving her wines each year, or be thrilled by each new vintage. Oh, no! She'll turn everything over to her big, strong son and devote herself to knitting booties for the rest of her life.''

His reply was so calm she could have slugged him. ''I said she would still be involved. There's no reason she would also want to be in charge. It seems to me that she'll have the best of both worlds.''

''But if she were a man instead of a woman—your older brother instead of your older sister—you wouldn't expect her to step aside for her son when she was only forty-eight. Never in a million years.''

He set down his cup. ''Catherine and Yves are reasonable people who love each other very much. When the time comes, they'll settle the matter to their satisfaction. How they do it is none of my business.''

In other words, he disagreed completely but didn't want to argue. ''You didn't respond to what I just said,'' she persisted.

''Because if I answer honestly, you'll tell me I'm chauvinistic or prehistoric and stay angry with me for the rest of the weekend.'' He smiled. ''I'd rather make love than war.''

Diana reined in her temper. At least he'd supported his sister, which was more than most Frenchmen of his background would have done. She just wished he'd been able to see that, exceptional or not, Catherine deserved the same opportunities as he did, and that being a woman didn't make her any less ambitious or dedicated than a man would have been.

She sighed. Rome hadn't been built in a day.

Chapter Ten

Diana checked her watch. It was half past five, so she suggested in a cool tone that they should forget about making love or war and think about making dinner. Marc's response was the same as it always was when she got annoyed. He told her a good meal would improve her mood and then recited the menu, which Tina had insisted should be reasonably healthy: an Italian dish, scallops with a lemon-and-garlic sauce, accompanied by pasta, a tossed salad and French bread. There was fresh fruit for dessert, along with an orange custard sauce that he swore wasn't too fattening.

The mere thought of it improved her mood, but that didn't mean she'd forgotten his faults. The fact was, she was falling for a man who belonged more to George and Marie Van Slyke's time than to her own. For all her resolve to change him, she wasn't sure it was possible. It was only sensible to pull back before she got in too deep.

They picked up their cups and left the parlor. As they walked through the hall, she noticed that Tina's suitcase, which Marc had left at the foot of the stairs along with his own, was gone. "Dad probably put Tina upstairs, in the room next to mine," she remarked. "You can sleep in the south wing. Remind me to turn on the heat after dinner."

He looked amused. "We haven't seen Tina and William all afternoon. I doubt he's been teaching her chess in the library. I also doubt he intends to have her sleep anywhere but in the master bedroom. *I'll* sleep in the room next to yours—unless you'd like me to share your bed, that is."

He was at it again, doing his best to make her blush. "Keep teasing me, and you'll wind up sleeping in the caretaker's cottage," she said. She paused and frowned. "About Dad and Tina—do you really think they...? I mean, already?"

"Of course. They're crazy about each other. What would be the point of waiting?"

"I guess you're right." The two of them had clicked immediately, as if they'd been waiting for each other all their lives. "It's just that my father is so ascetic. It's hard to picture him being swept away by passion."

"Only because you're his daughter. Besides, there aren't many women like Tina. She's open, generous and great fun to be with."

"Which makes me wonder what she sees in Dad."

"He's handsome and brilliant, and when she plays for him, he looks at her as if she's a goddess." He took her arm. "Come help me cook. You can earn your dinner by doing all the most disagreeable chores."

He was as good as his word, asking her to make the salad and prepare the fruit, but she didn't mind. Given their respective skills, it was a fair division of labor. William and Tina, showing an impeccable sense of timing, strolled in just as they finished cooking and offered to help. It was obvious they'd spent the afternoon in bed; they were intimate and relaxed in a way that only lovers are.

They ate at the old wooden table in the kitchen, discussing the show Tina was playing for and current books and movies. Afterward, Tina reminded Marc of his promise to read Philippe's journal and dragged everyone into the library. There were seven volumes, all of them filled with small, spidery script, but mercifully, they were relatively thin.

They would have to read all seven, they agreed, because if they stopped at the first or even the tenth mention of some island, it might turn out to be the wrong one. An unenthusiastic William suggested dividing the job up, but Diana's French was rusty and Tina's depended heavily on the fact that she was bilingual in Italian. Even more important, they might miss a crucial clue due to the lack of continuity. In the end, the men took turns reading, translating aloud into English as they went along.

Within minutes, Diana was dragging out maps and spreading them on the floor, including Marc's map of the unnamed island where Philippe had allegedly buried his last haul. There were hundreds of islands near Madagascar, and at times it seemed that Philippe must have visited them all. He'd had a thirst for exploration rare among the men of his trade.

Tina kept notes, jotting down details about each island he referred to. St. Mary's Island, now called Nossi-Boraha, and Bourbon island, now Réunion, had been important ports of call in those days and appeared frequently in his journal, but neither resembled the island on Marc's map. At times he mentioned only groups—the Comoros, perhaps, or the Amirantes—leaving them to wonder exactly which island he'd visited. Even more frustrating, sometimes there were no names at all, just vague references to stopping to take on supplies or make repairs.

They worked till midnight, finishing four of the seven volumes before calling it a night. Marc didn't bother asking Tina where she was sleeping; he simply picked up his suitcase and walked upstairs. Up in the hallway, Tina and William hurriedly said good-night and disappeared into the master bedroom, leaving Marc and Diana alone.

Marc set down his suitcase and lazed against the railing above the stairs, obviously waiting for Diana to invite him into her room. She was sorely tempted. He was so damn handsome, and the warmth in his eyes could have seduced a vestal virgin. It wasn't fair.

Squaring her shoulders, she reminded herself of her decision to be sensible. "Why don't you go ahead and use the bathroom first?" she said. "I'll see you in the morning. And, uh, thanks again for dinner. It was delicious." She walked briskly into her room.

Marc sighed as she closed her door, not so much disappointed as puzzled. He knew she was annoyed about something to do with his sister, but he couldn't imagine what. Hadn't he supported Catherine when most men wouldn't have? Hadn't he agreed that she was as capable of running the winery as any man was?

Diana kept denying that there were differences between men and women, but that was nonsense. Women were gentler, more vulnerable and more emotional. Family was the center of a woman's world. Even Diana herself admitted how strenuous she found her job and how much she wanted a child. If she were honest with herself, she would see that her anger was a defense mechanism, a way to keep him at a distance until the scars left by her marriage had healed.

He straightened. Physically, at least, she wanted him more than ever. Tomorrow was another day.

* * *

Diana groaned and buried her face in her pillow. Some-one was knocking on her door. She hoped that if she didn't answer, they would give up and go away.

Instead, the door opened and someone walked inside. "Diana?" Marc murmured. "Are you all right?"

She grunted. "Go away. I'm sleeping."

"But it's half past ten. I was worried about you."

She rolled over and peered at the clock. It *was* ten-thirty. She never slept this late, but then, she never tossed and turned half the night agonizing over some man, either—reliving how good he made her feel only to brood that she'd never respond completely, or marshaling brilliant arguments that would utterly transform him only to de-cide dejectedly that thirty-two-year-old men didn't change.

She squinted at him. He was holding a breakfast tray, looking incredibly sexy in a black turtleneck and well-worn jeans, regarding her with obvious concern. "I'm just tired," she said. "I didn't sleep well."

"I know the feeling." He leaned closer. "So they're gray with blue-and-green flecks. Very beautiful and unusual. Plain green suddenly seems exceptionally boring." He held out the tray. "I made you some French toast. Your father and Tina are out boating, by the way. They promised to be back by lunchtime so we can finish reading the journals."

A little more awake now, she realized that her hair was a tangled mess and her pajamas as sensual as an old sweat suit. "Oh. Thanks. Put the tray on the night table, would you? I'll be down in about half an hour."

He did as she'd asked, but instead of taking the hint and leaving, he pulled over a chair and sat down. "Obviously you're too nearsighted to have noticed that there are two cups on the tray. I'll keep you company while you eat." He paused. "Don't just lie there; run along to the bathroom and then come have breakfast. It won't taste very good if it's cold."

She frowned. "Did it ever occur to you that maybe I don't want you here?"

"It occurred to me last night, when you slammed your door in my face."

"I didn't slam my door—"

"I was speaking metaphorically, Diana. The least you can do is explain why you're angry and give me a chance to respond."

At least he cared. That was something. She nodded and got out of bed, feeling horribly self-conscious as she crossed to the door. Regardless of her mixed feelings, she wanted to look her best when he was around.

She washed her face and brushed her teeth, then combed the tangles out of her hair. The pajamas couldn't be helped, so she returned to her room. Marc was sitting with the tray on his lap, sipping some coffee. She slipped into bed and pulled the covers up under her arms.

Without a word, he gave her the tray. She took a sip of orange juice—it was fresh-squeezed—and then removed the cover from her plate. He'd made the French toast with some sort of fancy bread and topped it with sliced almonds. Ignoring the syrup, she cut and tasted a piece. It had a delicate almond flavor and was wonderfully light and moist.

She took another bite. "This is wonderful. Now I'll never be satisfied with the way I make it. It used to be my favorite breakfast, too."

"All the more reason to forgive me for the heinous crimes I unwittingly committed yesterday afternoon," he said. "Marry me, and I'll make you French toast whenever you like."

Despite his light tone, he obviously meant it. She couldn't cope with that, not first thing in the morning. "You're too patriarchal to marry. Couldn't you just give me the recipe?"

"I'd be glad to, but it would be a lot easier to marry me. The bread is homemade. That's why it's so good. Do you want the recipe for that, too?"

She conceded defeat. "No. I've never baked bread in my life. I'd only mess it up. You'll just have to live with the fact that I'll never enjoy my own French toast again."

"I can handle that. I'll fight as dirty as I have to." He smiled. "Food, sex, abject apologies ... I'll use whatever weapons I can."

"Will you?" She looked at her plate, suddenly and desperately hoping he meant it. "How about really listening to how I feel?"

"That goes without saying, Diana. You should know that by now. Finish your breakfast before it gets cold, and then we'll talk."

She nodded and continued eating. The room was uncomfortably quiet at first, but he started talking about sailing after a while and the tension dissipated. He loved the sport—the speed, the freedom, the hint of danger—and had raced competitively in France whenever he'd had the time. She told him she enjoyed it, too, and had crewed for her uncle since her early teens. Their differences faded as they boasted about their triumphs and laughed about their near disasters.

"Perhaps your uncle would let me borrow his boat some weekend," he said as she finished her French toast. "I'd love to take you out."

She ignored the fact that their future was very much in doubt. When they talked and laughed this way, she couldn't imagine breaking things off. "And I'd love to go, but it'll be a tough sell. That boat is his most precious possession. You'll have to prove how good you are before he'll trust you with her."

He lifted the tray off her lap and set it on the floor. "I understand how he feels. I wouldn't entrust my most pre-

cious possession to another man, either, unless I was sure
he would take proper care of her.''

He meant *her*. Judging by the way he was looking at her,
boating had gone straight from his mind. ''I'm not your
possession,'' she said uneasily. ''Women don't belong to
men, not even wives to husbands or daughters to fa-
thers.''

''Don't be so literal.'' He moved from the chair to her
bed, sitting down by her waist. ''I simply meant that I love
you very much—that nothing is more important to me
than you are.''

She edged away, putting some distance between them.
''I don't know what to think when you talk that way.
You've only known me a week. I can't be more important
to you than your family or the restaurant you want to
open.''

''Thank you for telling me how I feel. I didn't realize
how confused I was.'' He toyed with a lock of her hair.
''Right now, I'm dying to kiss you, but it's probably all in
my mind. Tell me, *chérie*, what do I really want to do?''

A flush rose up her neck. When he was this close, this
teasingly seductive, kissing seemed like a wonderful idea.
But it wasn't. ''Take the tray downstairs and wash the
dishes,'' she said.

He brushed his mouth across her lips, and a wave of
warm, moist desire rippled through her body. ''I don't
think so,'' he said, pulling the covers down to her hips.
''Try again.''

He gazed at her breasts, and her nipples tightened in response. ''Read Philippe's journal?'' she asked weakly.

''No.'' He kissed her more firmly, coaxing her lips to
relax and part. ''Try tasting every inch of you. Kissing you
absolutely everywhere. Caressing you until you explode
with pleasure.''

She pressed herself back against her pillow. ''Marc, I
really think we should—''

"That's your whole problem. You think too much."

He kissed her again, hard and deep this time, arousing her with his tongue and teeth until she was too excited to fight him, even mentally. What little willpower she had left evaporated completely when he stretched out beside her, slid his hand under her pajamas and cupped her breast. His gentle fondling quickly gave way to a possessive, wildly erotic kneading that frustrated as much as it satisfied and left her hot and submissive in his arms.

Still kissing and caressing her, he slid on top of her and wedged his leg between her thighs to part them. Once she would have panicked and pulled away, but he'd conditioned her to anticipate pleasure, to crave more and more of it each time he touched her. She twined her legs around one of his and hugged him closer.

Then wanting to please him back, she pulled his shirt from his jeans and ran her fingers up his naked spine. He tensed and stilled, but only for a moment. When he resumed making love to her, he was gentler, exerting such tight control over himself that she could feel it in his body. She felt a surge of tenderness, then even hotter passion. His restraint had somehow liberated her, freeing her to give herself up to the sensual delights of touching and being touched.

Finally he broke the kiss and eased away. She opened her eyes, gazing at him through a fog of need and desire. Smiling tenderly, he smoothed back her hair, then unbuttoned the top button of her pajamas. The other buttons quickly followed, until her naked breasts were exposed to the cool morning air—and to his warm blue eyes.

He pulled off his shirt, then traced the fine blue veins that led outward from one of her nipples. She shivered as much from delight as from the cold. "You're magnificent," he said in French. "Exquisite."

She ran her hand over his chest. He had the sexiest body she'd ever seen, muscular, powerful and lean. "And you, also," she whispered.

"Then all those hours in the gym are worth it." He took a nipple into his mouth and sucked it. Trembling with pleasure, she twined her hands into his hair to keep him close. She loved what he was doing. It was sweet and gentle, she thought as her eyes fluttered shut. It warmed rather than burned.

Then he sucked a little harder, and tongues of flame licked at her skin. He gave her a gentle nip, and then a second and third, and the fire spread downward, making her moist and achy. After another minute or two, he raised his head and murmured that he loved her, then kissed and nipped her other breast. She moaned softly, overwhelmed by the sensations tearing through her body.

She was so dazed that she barely reacted when he moved his mouth to her belly and gently nuzzled her, but when he grasped the waistband of her pajamas, her head began to clear. He slid her pajamas slowly downward, his lips following. Her embarrassment was immediate and excruciating. She needed to be touched there, but not like that— not with his mouth.

She went rigid. "Marc, no... Don't."

He paused. "Hush, *chérie*. Just relax."

"But I don't want you to—"

"Of course you do. I can feel that you do." There was a quiet amusement in his voice. "Don't worry. You'll love it. I promise."

When he continued undressing her, she pushed wildly at his shoulders and twisted away. "No. Just stop."

He took a quick, harsh breath, then released her and sat up. "All right. Just take it easy. Nothing's going to happen unless you want it to."

Shaking, she rolled onto her side, turning her back to him. He massaged her neck, clearly trying to calm her.

"I'm sorry, Diana. I wanted to please you, that's all." He paused. "And myself, as well, if you want the truth. I've been dying to kiss you that way...to enjoy your taste and scent."

She didn't reply. She was worldly enough to know that she was the one with the problem, not he. She was awkward and repressed and he'd probably lose patience with her eventually. God knew John always had.

Neither of them spoke for several seconds. "Come back into my arms," he finally murmured. "Let me take care of you."

She shook her head. "No. I mean, I'm fine, Marc. It's so late...I should be dressed by now."

His hand moved to her back, massaging her with slow, deep strokes of his thumb. Her anxiety began to fade. He'd always been sensitive and understanding. He was Marc, not John.

"You're not fine," he said. "You're tense and upset. Only a bastard would arouse you and leave you in such a state, and my lineage, *mon ange*, is impeccable."

He lay down beside her and gently but firmly pulled her into his arms, cuddling her against his naked chest. Her cheeks felt so hot she figured they were scarlet.

"Tell me something," he said. "Did Redmon ever satisfy you?"

"Do we have to talk about—"

"Yes. Did he, Diana?"

He wasn't going to let it drop. "I guess so," she mumbled, then bit her lip. That wasn't totally true. "Sort of. I'm not sure."

He lifted her chin. "You'll be sure with me, I promise you that. I know you think you're not in the mood anymore, but I'll bet I can have you that way in two minutes flat." He smiled. "Of course, you'll have to let me touch you eventually. I'm good, but I'm not a magician."

She lowered her eyes, more embarrassed than ever now. The truth was, she wanted to know what she'd missed. She was dying to know how it felt. But if she messed up again—if nothing happened . . . "I'm not sure I want you to."

He laughed softly. "I should have bought the chinoiserie chest the other night. It would have given me something to bargain with. But since I didn't, I have a proposition to make. Say yes to me now, and if you change your mind, I'll stop right away."

She remembered how she'd felt a few minutes before, when he'd kissed her with such passion and sucked and nipped her so erotically. She thought about how warm and strong he was right now, and how safe she felt in his arms. "Yes," she whispered.

She expected him to pick up where he'd left off, but instead, he massaged her until she was relaxed and a little sleepy. In time, his hand wandered to her breasts and thighs and the massage became more seductive. A lovely warmth stole through her body, then a growing desire, and she sought his mouth. She couldn't have said whether two minutes or ten had gone by, but after the first hot kiss, stopping was the farthest thing from her mind.

She came to life after that, as if she'd been poised on the brink and needed only his hands and mouth to push her over. The tension skyrocketed until she was exactly where she'd been before—hot and wet, wildly kissing and caressing him, longing to be touched.

At first, he stroked her through the fabric of her pajamas, teasing her with a deft, light touch that left her pliant in his arms. She began to want more—to move in time with his hand, to strain for a more intimate embrace. He caressed her more firmly, but the wanting only got worse. She wasn't just eager now, but desperate, moaning helplessly with every sensual stroke.

When he slid his hand under her pajamas, she arched her hips to meet it. After a minute of gentle exploring, he touched her where the ache was most intense, but only briefly. Then he began to probe her, slipping a finger inside her and mimicking the act of love as he cupped and stroked her.

She was beyond embarrassment by then, beyond rational thought. Panting, she dug her nails into his back and writhed against his hand. Finally he found her again, staying a little longer before he eased back inside her. His palm alternately skimmed her lightly and pressed her more firmly, his fingers going gradually deeper. He was teasing her, keeping her at a fever pitch of need, and the pleasure was so shattering that she wanted it to last forever.

Then he touched her again, and a violent tension took hold of her. She pulled away her mouth. "Please, Marc—don't stop again. I can't stand it."

He stiffened, then said roughly in French, "Easy, darling. I won't." He began caressing her again. "Just enjoy it."

Enjoy was the wrong word. It was torture and ecstasy, all rolled into one. And then the spasms began, rolling on and on until she couldn't bear it a moment longer and had to push away his hand.

She was utterly spent afterward, unable to move or even to speak. And then giddiness set in, and she smiled. He was wonderful. It had been incredible.

"He didn't," she said.

He looked down at her. "Who didn't what?"

"John. He never satisfied me. It was like the difference between a cap gun and an atomic bomb."

"An atomic bomb, eh?" A self-satisfied smile spread over his face. "I'm glad he never reached you the way I can. You're mine in a way you were never his."

For once, she found his Gallic possessiveness rather endearing. "I am, am I?"

"Yes." He stroked her cheek. "Just as I'm yours in a way I've been waiting all my life to experience. Does that meet with your approval, my overly liberated angel?"

She was about to inform him that a woman could never be too liberated when she realized how selfish she'd been. She'd been so caught up in her own needs that she'd forgotten about his. "Yes. It does," she said shyly. "Uh, Marc... You must be... That is, I'd really like to make you—happy."

He burst out laughing. "My darling Diana, as great as my self-control is, it isn't infinite. What with you clawing at me and thrashing around..."

"Oh." She pulled herself up and inspected his back. "Oh, God. I really did, didn't I? I'm sorry."

"Sorry? *Mon chou,* I would have been disappointed if you hadn't. There isn't a man alive who doesn't relish scratches inflicted in the heat of passion—or find them almost unbearably exciting." He paused. "If I stay in this bed a moment longer, I'm going to keep you here all afternoon. And then I'll catch hell from Nelly for not finishing the damn journal." He cupped her breasts and kissed them. The nipples swelled and hardened. "I'll drive you home tonight. We'll spend the evening together, all right?"

He meant in bed, and this time, she'd probably let him do whatever he pleased. Her pulses raced at the thought, and she nodded.

Chapter Eleven

William coughed to clear his throat and turned to the next page of volume six of Philippe's journal. The year was 1697, and Philippe was complaining about the heat and rain, the scarcity of good sailors and the decline of the pirate trade with America due to the appointment of an overly zealous royal governor in New York.

His life on Madagascar no longer pleased him. His mistress was too demanding and he missed his wife and daughters. His son Pierre, who was yet to turn sixteen, had fallen head over heels for some provocative little wench and was mewling about wanting to marry her. In retrospect, Diana realized that the wench was Simone and that the marriage had eventually taken place.

"December twenty-sixth," William translated in a bored voice. "Returned from Baldridge's yesterday. Marquette was visiting, too."

Baldridge was the pirate Adam Baldridge, the virtual king of St. Mary's Island, which was several hundred miles up the coast from the port where Philippe had made his home. Marquette was Father Marquette, a priest who irritated Philippe no end. Diana knew from Marc that Marquette had married Pierre and Simone the following February, but Philippe hadn't mentioned the marriage in his journal. The pair had evidently wed in secret, over his objections.

William continued to translate. "He's still wandering from place to place trying to civilize savages like me with his talk of burning in the fires of hell. I told him hell couldn't be any worse than listening to his damnable speeches. Otherwise it was an agreeable two weeks. I envy Baldridge his kingdom. I'll have one of my own someday, but somewhere more remote, where pests like Marquette won't bother me. Not too remote, though. A vessel every few weeks would suit me, for company and news. I'm weary of fighting and death. Afraid of the hangman. Getting old, I suppose."

William yawned, then went on, "January first. A new year, the same as the old one. Fear and loneliness. I had a dream last night. I was on an island. My family and servants were there, and a few dozen settlers. A vessel arrived. The captain was lost and asked me where he was, but I couldn't tell him. I didn't know. The island was small but beautiful, with thick woods surrounding a clear blue lake. A paradise. I recognized it when I woke, of course. The dream was an omen. One great prize and I swear I'll go there."

"My God, that's it," Tina said. "Look at Marc's map."

The island on the map had a lake surrounded by trees, too, but there was no indication of its size. "Even if it is, that isn't much to go on," Diana said. "Dozens of islands could fit that description."

"But obviously it was a place Philippe knew well," Marc pointed out, "and it was within a reasonable distance of Madagascar. Remote but not too remote, he says. Besides, he mentions a ship stopping by."

"But only in his dream," William said. "It doesn't prove anything. We'll need a lot more to go on. I wish I could remember if he refers to this paradise of his again, but it's been too damn long since I read the journal. We'll have to keep going." He held the volume out to Marc. "Here. You read for a while."

The next entry was on January fourth, a grizzly account about a native who'd met a sickening end while fishing in the area's shark-infested waters. It wasn't until six months later, in the final volume of his journal, that Philippe mentioned his paradise again.

The first entry in several weeks, it began with a lengthy description of the attack and capture of two rich merchantmen off the west coast of India. "Our hold is full," Marc translated, "and we're going home. But in my mind, home is no longer France or Madagascar. Another few such prizes and home will be a fragrant forest and a crystal lake. A beach to build on and a reef swarming with fish. And beyond, green shadows in a bright sea, not too close, not too far. Home will be paradise."

Marc looked up. "There it is again," he said. "There's apparently a coral reef around the island. I assume the green shadows he pictured in his mind were neighboring islands."

Diana studied a map of the general region. "Then the island must be part of a chain. The strongest candidates are the Comoros, the Amirantes, the Mascarenes and the Seychelles. That's a lot of islands, and the description is too vague to be of much help. It's almost as if he couldn't resist writing about the place, but was afraid someone would read the journal and beat him to it."

"Poor guy! All those plans, and he was dead five months later," Tina said. "Keep reading, sweetie. Maybe there's something more."

Marc frowned. "That description... It's familiar for some reason, but I can't put my finger on why."

"It's pretty generic stuff," William pointed out. "A forest, a lake, a reef... A thousand different novelists must have described islands like that."

"I don't read novels," Marc said.

"Travel books, then."

"I don't read those, either."

William rolled his eyes. "What *do* you read?"

"Books on cooking and wine. On business. On history."

"History, then. We historians have been known to describe how things look, you know."

Marc looked dubious but didn't argue. "June twentieth," he continued. "A fight broke out between Higgins and LeClerc..."

Everyone settled back to listen. Those final few months had been busy and lucrative, with successful raids in the Gulf of Aden and the waters around Madagascar. And then, in late September, a fortune had dropped into Philippe's lap.

Some of his men, content with the riches they'd already acquired, had skipped the voyage, so Philippe had sailed with a smaller crew than usual. He'd gone north to the mouth of the Red Sea, where, during an early storm, he'd come across a large Indian merchantman that had become separated from her convoy. He and his men had struck with lightning boldness, taking her so quickly that they'd plundered her and sailed away before help could arrive. Their prize was a fortune in spices, silks and ivory, in silver and gold coins, and in jewels and damasks. Even a single share of it, Philippe wrote, would keep a man in comfort for the rest of his life.

There was nothing in his journal about burying any loot on an island, but in the middle of October, after several weeks without an entry, he'd written, "Pierre and I returned today from a pleasure cruise in my sloop. The rumors are evidently true. The war with England is over. The Royal Navy will be after us soon. Time to fetch my Anna and settle down in paradise.''

''That was no pleasure cruise,'' Tina said. ''They went to bury a fortune on his island. The treasure really exists.''

''Or it did once,'' Diana said.

''Well, I'm all for seeing if it's still there, sweetie. His paradise is probably in one of those four groups, right? So all we have to do is find the island that matches the one on Marc's map, and we're home free.''

''Maybe there's something more,'' Marc said. He read the last few pages, but the island wasn't mentioned again. Philippe wrote of his plans to return to Madagascar with his family the following spring, after the storm season had passed, and described the weather on the last few fateful days of his final cruise.

Diana gathered up the maps and put them away. Their scales were too large to be of any help, showing all but the biggest islands as dots or tiny circles. ''We'll have to find something more detailed,'' she said. ''I'll be too busy working to look, but maybe someone could check the public library or the collections at Columbia.''

''Actually, I've got some British Admiralty charts that should do the trick,'' William said. ''Used them when I was researching my history of American piracy. I'll dig them up and take a look.''

William was famous for his lack of organization. His research materials were filed or stacked helter-skelter in three different locations—in his journal office, his academic office and various rooms in the apartment. The charts could be in any of the three, providing he hadn't loaned them out and forgotten all about it.

Still, if the treasure had been buried for three centuries, it would still be there even if it took them a few extra weeks to track down where. Not that Diana believed it was, of course. As much as she wished otherwise, she knew that if Philippe's men hadn't found his share of the booty after his death, some lucky explorer had probably stumbled across it years later. There was no point getting excited about how important it was historically or daydreaming about the work it could pay for on Van Slyke's Island. It was probably long gone.

They packed and straightened up the house, then took the cruiser to Henry and Babe's place, arriving about half past five. Nobody was there except the caretaker, who was waiting impatiently on the dock. Marc handed him the keys to the boat, then led the way to his van.

They were back in the city half an hour later. Nelly had given the cook the night off and gone out with Irving, and there wasn't much in the apartment to eat. Marc offered to make everyone dinner in his town house, but everyone felt he'd done more than his share already. They wound up going to Tina's favorite Italian restaurant in the Village.

Now that Diana was back in Manhattan, the two days on Van Slyke's Island felt like a weekend out of time, as unreal as a movie or daydream. In twelve hours she'd be back at her desk, working on the Parkman-Fielding merger. That was real life, and making a success of it was vitally important to her. A huge amount of money was at stake, not to mention the prestige of bringing together two of the most important communications companies in America.

Without consciously deciding to, she mentally shifted gears. The Parkman people had Fielding's latest proposal. They wouldn't accept it as is; it didn't work that way. What objections were they likely to make? What counterproposals? How could she see to it that the two sides got together as quickly and painlessly as possible?

Much to her distress, the answers wouldn't come. In two short days, a host of important details had slipped from her mind. Either she reviewed her files that night or she'd never be prepared when the Fielding people got back to her the next day.

Talk and laughter swirled around her, but she barely noticed. It was all she could do to offer an occasional polite comment or smile when someone made a joke. It seemed to take forever before the meal finally ended and everyone decided to leave.

"You were very quiet tonight," Marc said as they drove uptown. Diana was sitting in front, and William and Tina were in back. "What's the matter? Are you tired?"

"Just preoccupied," she said. "I have a long week ahead of me. I'm working on a big merger, and it's— crunch time."

"Crunch time?" he repeated, sounding mystified.

"It's a sports metaphor. The final few minutes of a close game, when everything's on the line. My brain is going a mile a minute. I hope I can get to sleep tonight."

He massaged the back of her neck. "You will. I'll see to it personally."

She didn't need to ask what method he planned to employ. If Tina and William hadn't been in back, able to hear every word, she would have explained that she needed to work, but it was just too personal. She didn't reply.

Marc dropped everyone off in front of her building, then left to park the van. She excused herself as soon as she got upstairs and went straight to her room. She was sitting cross-legged on the bed amidst a sea of files when he finally joined her.

"If you don't move all those papers, they're going to get very rumpled," he teased.

She hesitated. "Marc . . . I wish I could ask you to stay, but I can't. I have an important meeting tomorrow and my grasp of the details isn't as good as it should be. If I don't review this stuff tonight, I could miss something crucial and blow the whole deal. It's one of the biggest media mergers in history—Parkman Publishing and Fielding Communications.'' She managed a smile. "I had a wonderful weekend, though. Next weekend can't come soon enough."

"What do you mean, next weekend?" He pushed aside some folders and sat down on the bed. "I'd assumed you would take some time off this week. Or if that was impossible, combine business with pleasure and work with me on my restaurant."

Far from having any free time, she'd probably work straight through till Sunday. She'd only mentioned the weekend because she didn't want Marc to be angry and hoped she could manage at least a few hours off. "I wish I could, but I'm just too busy," she said. "I'm sorry."

"Evenings, then."

She shook her head. "I can't, Marc. I'll be working."

He looked unhappy but resigned. "Very well, but you still have to eat. Come by my house after work tomorrow. I'll make you dinner."

"I'd love to, but if I'm not in some meeting, I'll be plugging away in my office. If I'm hungry, I'll grab a bite at my desk. I could be there half the night."

He frowned. "I won't have you working in an empty building or hailing a taxi in the middle of the night. It could be dangerous."

"There are security guards in the building," she said in her most reassuring tone. "One of them always walks me downstairs, straight into Charlie Canfield's limo. Door-to-door service." She paused. "I'm not any happier about it than you are, but I won't be able to see you this week. If things go well, the Fielding people will be flying in from the coast and I'll be negotiating nonstop. If not, I'll probably go to L.A. for another round of talks."

He wasn't just unhappy now, but downright disapproving. "You'll exhaust yourself and get sick. Let someone else handle some of the work."

She prayed for patience. "But it's my deal, Marc. I'm the one who put it together and knows all the details. No one else *can* do it—not half as well as I can."

"I see," he said, but it was obvious from his brusque tone that he didn't see at all.

In his world, Diana thought to herself, women weren't entrusted with such important responsibilities. A female was expected to stay in her proper place—to be a wife and mother, a giver and nurturer. If she did, she was respected and protected, but God help her if she strayed. Even Catherine, whom Marc had labeled extraordinary and made an exception for, was expected to return to her former role once a suitable male was available to take over.

She didn't want to fight, so she said none of that. "Thanks for being so understanding." She pecked him on the cheek. "Good night, Marc."

"That's it?" His eyes narrowed. "You're so busy with your precious deal that you can't spare me even a few more minutes of your time?"

His sarcasm was the last straw. As much as she cared for him—as good as he made her feel—she wasn't returning to the Dark Ages for him or anyone else. "Tell me, do you think women are equal to men?" she asked coolly.

"Of course I do. Just because I've said there are differences, that doesn't mean I believe women are inferior." He smiled his most winning smile. "Don't be too hard on me, *chérie*. I didn't mean to snap, but I'm disappointed and frustrated. We agreed we'd spend the evening together, and I was thinking about it all through dinner. No matter how busy you are, I hope I'm important enough for you to want to spend at least a few more minutes with me."

She ignored his cajoling tone. If he started making love to her, it wouldn't be a few minutes, but all night. Besides, if she gave in now, he'd never take her seriously.

"I see," she said. "You assign women a certain role and you say it's different from a man's but just as important. I'm sorry, Marc, but that's nonsense. A woman should be free to try whatever she wants to—to succeed or fail on her own merits, just as a man can. She shouldn't have to be extraordinary, the way you say your sister is, to have the same opportunities as a man would."

She took a quick breath, then continued firmly, "I happen to be damn good at what I do. That's how I've gotten where I am. You wouldn't tell a man to let someone else do his job, so don't tell me to. You'd be scathing if a man took time off to make love when he had crucial work to do, so don't ask me to. In fact, if I *were* a man, you probably would have asked me about my job by now, but for all your supposed interest in business, you've barely bothered to learn a thing about it. I told you I was working on one of the biggest media mergers in history, and it's as though you never even heard me."

There was a long, uncomfortable silence. Finally he said, "You're right. If you were a man, I would have asked for the details. But you're a woman and I love you, so I had other things on my mind. That doesn't mean I'm not interested, or that I consider women inferior."

"But you do," Diana said. "Look at your attitude toward your sister."

"And what's wrong with it?" He was visibly nettled now. "The fact is, I supported her when most men wouldn't have. She's grateful for that. I doubt—"

"Grateful! I like *that*! Why should she be grateful when you only did what was sensible and fair?"

"It might be sensible and fair in your world, but not in mine," he retorted. "Instead of giving me credit for my actions, you attack me for my alleged thoughts."

"There's no 'alleged' about it," she insisted. "You think I'm weak and impetuous—that I need a man to protect and guide me." She raised her chin. "Let me set you straight, Mr. Rochard. I survived when my husband ran off with my cousin and I've worked my way to the top of one of the hardest fields there is. I'm tougher than ninety percent of the men you'll ever meet, and don't you forget it."

"Are you really?" His annoyance faded, giving way to a tender smile. "Then who was the woman whose eyes filled with tears over a chest she wanted to buy? Who was hoarse with pain over the child she'd never had? Who fell asleep in my arms from pure exhaustion?"

He was hitting below the belt, pointing out every little slip and weakness. "So I get a little emotional at times," she said irritably. "So I get tired when I haven't slept. What does that prove?"

He put his arm around her. "I know you're strong, *chérie*. You had to be after your mother died, and also during your marriage to Redmon. You work at a job you don't really like because you're devoted to a special cause, and you're obviously very good at it, and that takes strength, too. But strong isn't the same as tough or hard. Deep down, you're gentle and vulnerable. I realize you don't need a man to take care of you, or even think that you want one to, but that's only because Redmon hurt you very badly and you're afraid to give yourself again."

He drew her closer. She stiffened, but only a little. There was too much truth in his words to stay angry—too much understanding of who she really was.

"You don't have to be afraid with me, though," he added softly. "I've waited thirty-two years to find you, so I'm not about to let you go. Let me share some of the burden. Give me the right to worry about you and look after you."

Given her insecurities, she couldn't picture herself inspiring such total devotion, but she never doubted that he meant what he said. He was honorable in a way that had gone out of style years ago. He truly believed he loved her. He thought it would last forever.

Still, she doubted he knew his own feelings as well as he thought. How could you fall deeply in love in only a week? Certainly she didn't love him—not yet, anyway. Even thinking about it made her uneasy.

She was as honest as she knew how to be. He deserved nothing less. "A lot of what you say is true. People think I'm strong, but sometimes it's just an act, a show I put on when I'm dying inside or scared half to death. And when that happens..." She sighed and relaxed against his shoulder. "At times, I want to stop being so brave or dignified. Stop being Princess Di, who can pull off any deal you can name. Have some man charge in and take care of me. And I'm ashamed to admit it. It's not very liberated of me."

He nuzzled her hair. "Men have moments like that, too, you know. Times when we're in pain and need comfort. I would come to you in a moment for that, and I wouldn't feel the least bit ashamed."

He was talking about suffering a personal tragedy. That wasn't the same as being weak with exhaustion or rigid with fear. She doubted he'd ever been either.

"But I'm not you," she said. "I'd have to love you to turn to you for help, and it's just too soon. I don't know you well enough. I need time, Marc."

"I know that. I've accepted it." He moved away from her. "I'm tempted to stay and make love to you, but if I do, you'll be up for that much longer, studying those damn files. You'll be exhausted tomorrow morning and it will be all my fault. I'd better go."

"I never realized how seductive sensitivity could be," she said suspiciously. "You know it, too, don't you? It's a ploy to get me to relent and ask you to stay."

He laughed. "What a devious mind you have. It never even occurred to me." He gave her a quick, hard kiss and stood up. "Promise me you'll call me if you have some free time. I'll do anything to see you short of climbing up sixty stories to your office."

"I promise," she said.

She wished him good-night, then watched him walk away. Once he'd gone, she wished he could have stayed. Sighing, she picked up a folder and got down to work.

Chapter Twelve

The Parkman counteroffer was so promising that Charlie Canfield could barely contain his glee until the meeting was over and he and Diana were alone in his limo, heading back downtown. A few days of hard bargaining, he said, and the deal would be nailed down tight. They'd make tons of money and grab away the headlines from their competitors. The Parker-Fielding deal would be the biggest thing since the Time-Warner merger.

Diana called Warren Fielding as soon as she got back to her desk. He agreed to leave for New York that morning with his top assistants and legal advisors, adding that he would contact the key members of his board and ask them to join the discussions. The Fielding team would negotiate with the Parkman camp beginning on Tuesday, working out of a hotel a few blocks from Parkman Publishing's midtown headquarters.

She spent three or four hours ironing out various details, then worked late into the night on projects that would have to be put on hold until the merger negotiations were complete. The next morning, she, Charlie and a group of the bank's technical experts sat down with Fielding and his team at his hotel.

In deals like this, the principals from each firm stayed put while the lawyers and bankers, nearly a dozen on each side, shuttled back and forth. They worked through a catered lunch until two, then walked to Parkman Publishing. Several reporters, having gotten wind of the merger earlier that month, had learned that Fielding was in New York and stationed themselves outside the Parkman building in search of a story. Diana told them as much as she properly could, then went inside.

The two sides spent the afternoon bargaining about share prices, shareholder dividends and management structure. The talks went well, the two companies moving measurably closer. Eventually the bankers and lawyers returned to the hotel for a dinner meeting with Fielding, breaking for the night at two in the morning.

Diana dragged herself into a cab for the short ride home. She found a note on her bed saying that Marc had called, but she didn't call him back. She was too busy, and besides, she couldn't afford distractions.

Wednesday and Thursday proceeded much as Tuesday had, with a series of tough but fruitful bargaining sessions over catered meals that she only picked at and questions from a growing crowd of reporters that she dealt with as honestly as she could. The meetings started so early and ended so late that she saw neither her father nor aunt, but she found roses on her night table on Wednesday and a box of Swiss chocolates on her pillow on Thursday. Both had accompanying notes from Marc saying he'd seen her on the news and missed her very much. She thought the gifts were sweet, but she was too wrapped up in business to miss him back.

Then on Friday morning, the last nettlesome problem was resolved and the negotiations came to a successful end. Led by a smiling Warren Fielding, everyone trooped past what was now an army of reporters into the Parkman building, where they went over the details of the merger one final time. An hour later, the two chairmen approved a press release announcing the creation of Parkfield, Inc. There were still some formalities to take care of—finalizing the language in the contract and securing approval from the boards and stockholders—but that didn't stop everyone from celebrating over a champagne lunch.

About twenty minutes into the meal, a security guard slipped into the room and walked over to Gregory Burnside, the chairman of Parkman Publishing. The guard whispered something in Burnside's ear, and Burnside looked at Diana. "Do you know someone named Marc Rochard?"

"Yes. He's—a client of mine." And if he'd shown up at Parkman Publishing demanding to see her, she was never going to live it down. "Why?"

"Seems he sent something over to the Hilton for you— a package of some sort. They had the deliveryman bring it here." He nodded at the security guard. "Todd wanted to check it out before he brought it upstairs."

Charlie Canfield smiled. "Rochard is worth millions, Greg—he's Sam Parisi's grandson. I think I can assure you it's nothing dangerous." He paused. "I'm intrigued, Diana. Why don't you open it right now, so all of us can have a look?"

"Sounds reasonable to me," Burnside drawled.

Warren Fielding frowned thoughtfully. "Marc Rochard. Handsome guy in his thirties, right, Diana? His family owns a winery in France?"

"Yes," she said in surprise. "How did you know?"

"I saw him in a restaurant in L.A. last year—a show-business hangout. He was with an actress I know. With his looks, I figured he was an actor, so I called him over and offered him a screen test with our studio." Fielding laughed and shook his head. "It was one of my better faux pas. He declined politely and had a bottle of his wine sent to my table. It was so good I bought a couple of cases for my cellar. Let's get this mysterious package up here and see what's inside it."

Diana was worried the contents might be personal, but there was no gracious way to refuse. The security guard left, returning a few minutes later with a large carton. She pulled off the sealing tape and opened it up. It was filled with smaller boxes. There was a folded piece of stationery on top, presumably a note from Marc.

Charlie, who was sitting next to her, snatched it away before she could pick it up. "It says, 'Hope this improves everyone's mood and gets things moving.' Better late than never, I guess. It's signed, 'Love, Marc.'" He grinned at her. "'Love, Marc,' huh? Doesn't sound like just a client to me."

She blushed. "A friend, then. You know how flowery Frenchmen can be."

With as much aplomb as she could muster, she took out a box. "One more thing about Marc—he's a trained chef. If I'm not mistaken..." She opened the box up and breathed in deeply. "Oh, God. Eclairs. I hope your caterer won't mind if we skip his dessert, Greg, because everything Marc makes is absolutely delicious."

There weren't only éclairs, but also cream puffs and napoleons. If Marc had meant to remind her of his existence in the way that was dearest to her heart, he'd succeeded. The pastry was wonderful. She thought he was a prince to have sent it over. After barely thinking of him all week, she suddenly could think of little else.

She got teased about their relationship, but once she'd admitted they'd gone out a few times, everyone lost interest and started discussing business again. Eventually the two chairmen retired to Burnside's office for a series of interviews with reporters, taking along some of the pastry to serve. Diana parceled out the rest of it, making everyone promise to credit the chef.

Back in her office, she spent the next few hours on the phone, giving interviews of her own. Now that the initial exhilaration had passed, she felt at loose ends. After over two years, her work on this deal was almost finished, and there was nothing equally challenging to replace it.

At half past five, Charlie poked his head around her door and told her to go home, but she pointed to her overflowing "in" basket and shook her head. "I want to sort through this stuff before I leave tonight. Get it organized for Monday morning."

"I hope that means you plan to relax this weekend, because frankly, you look beat." He walked into the room. "In fact, why don't you take some time off? Go to Europe or the Caribbean. I can't even remember the last time you had a vacation."

She shrugged. "Neither can I, but you know me. I won't be happy until the *i*'s are dotted and the *t*'s are crossed on the merger. Besides, I have to touch base with the people I've ignored all week."

"So spend a few days doing that, and then go. The world won't come to an end if you're away for a while."

"Maybe I should." It did sound appealing.

"Never mind the maybes, Diana. Consider it an order. If you need to feel you're working, take your friend Rochard along and discuss his winery merger over dinner some night." Charlie chuckled to himself and strolled out of her office.

She grimaced and picked up another letter. By Monday, the gossips in this city would have her embroiled in a torrid affair. She was too private a person to take that totally in stride but consoled herself with the thought that, in time, they'd find someone better to talk about.

Over the next few hours, she worked her way through both her "in" basket and half a dozen pastries. She was bone-tired by the time she finished, ready to fall into bed and sleep till noon. But when she got home, she found her whole family in the living room, and also Tina and Marc. There was a sign on the mantel reading, "Congratulations, Diana."

As usual, Tracy and John were tangled together on a couch, but for once she wasn't hurt or jealous. She simply didn't care. She smiled and said hello to everyone, her eyes lingering on Marc. She didn't have to be told that he'd arranged this. Her family had never celebrated any of her successes before.

He strode up to her and pecked her on the lips. "You missed your own party. Sit, and I'll bring you some dinner."

"This was really sweet of you, but I'll skip the food. I'm not hungry." She slipped her arm around his waist. "I've been eating your pastry all night. It was a huge hit, by the way. Thanks for sending it over."

"You're welcome." He pointed to the coffee table. "We have something else to celebrate tonight. Your father finally found those Admiralty charts."

"In a carton on the top shelf of one of his closets," Nelly said tartly. "Can you imagine?"

"We can't all be as organized as you are," William retorted. "Besides, if I had even a third as much space in this apartment as you do—"

"You'd be drowning in dusty papers, sweetie," Tina said.

He looked sheepish. "You're probably right, darling."

The two of them were as smitten as ever, Diana thought. She sat down between Marc and Risa, then peered at the chart on the coffee table. Marc's map was sitting next to it.

"It's this one here," he said, pointing to an islet in the Comoros. It had the same shape as the island on the treasure map, right down to the lake in the middle. "It's called Pamanzi. When I saw the chart, I realized why the description sounded familiar. A childhood friend of mine—a naval officer—told me about it. He was stationed at the French base on Mayotte at the time. That's here."

He pointed to the southernmost island. While the four main islands in the Comoro group were spaced quite far apart, Mayotte and the islet of Pamanzi were separated only by a narrow strait. "The lake, the forest, the coral reef around Mayotte—he described them in detail," he continued. "He said Pamanzi was totally unspoiled, a tropical paradise."

Diana felt a rush of excitement. Pamanzi was the right island. It fit perfectly. The thought of standing where her ancestor had once stood—of visiting the place he'd so loved—thrilled her.

As for digging for buried treasure, given the local politics, she wondered if it would even be possible. The Comoro Islands, once a French colony, had become an independent Islamic nation after a referendum in the 1970s. The residents of Mayotte and tiny Pamanzi had voted to remain under French protection, though, and France had responded by declaring them an overseas territorial community. Now both countries claimed them, but France, with its greater power, had easily enforced its will.

"France and the Comoros have been arguing over Mayotte for years," she said to Marc. "It's not the most stable area of the world. The authorities might not welcome treasure hunters."

He nodded. "We were talking about that before. Still, I think I could get us permission to dig there."

"Could you really!" She smiled. "Charlie did mention that you're very well connected in France."

"Of course. I'm the president's godson."

Her eyes widened. "You're kidding."

"Yes," he admitted with a laugh. "I do know him, though. He's been to dinner a few times. As have various admirals, government ministers, museum officials—"

"Museum officials?" she repeated in alarm.

He put a comforting arm around her. "I know you feel that anything to do with Philippe belongs on Van Slyke's Island, but the French government might not agree. We'll probably have to promise them a share in any archaeological artifacts we find before they'll grant us permission to dig, but I'll make the best deal I can. I thought I'd go to Paris next week. Why don't you come along?"

"I wish I could." Diana explained about the work that had piled up, adding that she planned to take a few weeks' vacation as soon as she'd cleared her desk. Rather than have Marc wait for her, she preferred to save her time off for the dig and have him handle the negotiations on his own.

The talk turned to the conditions they'd probably face, and she relaxed in his embrace. She'd forgotten her exhaustion in all the excitement, but now it returned in full force. After a few minutes of trying to listen, she yawned and closed her eyes.

The conversation swirled around her, William grumbling that he was too old to live in a tent and eat canned food, John telling an eager Tracy that joining in the dig was out of the question due to her pregnancy, and Henry saying he was too busy to go chasing treasure halfway around the world. The three older women were more enthusiastic, but only Nelly could get away, and she reluctantly admitted that the dig would probably be too strenuous for a woman of her age.

Diana was dozing lightly when Marc suddenly eased her onto his lap and stood up, taking her with him. Too sleepy to be startled, she put her arm around his neck for support. He was warm, strong and impossible to resist—not that she wanted to.

"Say good-night to everyone, *chérie*," he ordered softly. "You're exhausted. I'm taking you to bed."

She obediently mumbled good night. Tracy, she noticed, was gaping at her. She smiled to herself. Her cousin was jealous. John was never this romantic.

As Marc carried her into the hall, she unbuttoned the top few buttons of his shirt and nuzzled his throat. "That was an interesting choice of words," she said.

"What was?" His voice was soft and hoarse. "Don't stop kissing me. It was very nice."

She ran her lips along his collarbone. "You said you were taking me to bed."

"I am. You're half asleep already."

She finished unbuttoning his shirt as he walked into her room. "It has another meaning besides tucking someone in for the night, Marc."

"Does it? It must be some American expression I'm not familiar with." He laid her on the double bed and turned on a lamp, then locked the door. He was grinning from ear to ear as he returned to her side. "Why don't you explain?"

She sat up, tucking a pillow against the headboard for support. "You were teasing me," she said. "You know exactly what it means."

"True enough." He stripped off his shirt, tossing it onto a chair. "You were supposed to glare at me and refuse to do as you were told. Then I would have had the pleasure of seducing you into a more obedient frame of mind." He took off his shoes. "The last thing I expected was that you would start ripping off my clothes."

"I didn't rip—"

"Start undressing me, then. Either you missed me this week or you were too tired to know what you were doing."

"A little of both, maybe." Her pulse sped up when his hand went to his belt. "What are *you* doing?"

"Finishing what you began. Unless you'd rather I didn't, that is."

He was going awfully fast, but she hated to disappoint him. "I don't know."

"Just trust me, all right? Things will be fine. I promise."

"Yes. All right." She watched with a mixture of excitement and anxiety as he stripped to his briefs. He had a beautiful body—just looking at him made her desire him—but he was also fully aroused. He was ready to make love; she wasn't.

He sat down on the bed. "You associate making love with pain and failure. I understand that. But it's not going to be that way between you and me. Okay?"

She swallowed hard. "Yes. Okay."

"You're obviously very nervous." He hesitated, then stroked her cheek very tenderly. "Perhaps we should wait a while longer."

Diana didn't know what to say. She looked into her lap. "Whatever you think, I guess. Whatever you want."

He loosened her bun. "I want to hold you naked in my arms. I want you to desire me as much as I desire you. I want us to love each other and give each other pleasure." He combed out her hair with his fingers. "Sexual relations can wait. You'll tell me when you're ready, all right?"

She felt a rush of relief. He was the sweetest man in the world. "You're very understanding. I'm sorry to be so—I shouldn't have started and then changed my mind."

"I love you very much, so naturally I'm dying to sleep with you, but in my saner moments I do realize that we've known each other only a few weeks. It's not unreasonable for you to need more time." He tipped up her chin and smiled. "Just promise me you'll sleep with me on our wedding night."

She stiffened. "Marc, I really can't—"

"I know. Marriage terrifies you even more than making love does." He removed her jacket, then unbuttoned her blouse. "It won't be all that horrible, you know. I'll cook your favorite foods, give you pleasure every night, give you beautiful children... In time, you may even come to enjoy it."

When he put it that way, it didn't sound horrible at all. "I think you could talk the devil into attending Sunday school."

"And talking isn't even my greatest talent." He removed her blouse and bra, then lowered his mouth to her breasts. "Enjoy your freedom while you can, *mon ange*, because I'm going to seduce you into total enslavement." He nuzzled her nipples. "I've been there since the moment I saw you. It's time you joined me."

Diana shivered and closed her eyes. She could hardly believe this was happening to her—that someone so wonderful loved her so passionately, excited her so intensely and wanted her in so many different ways. He suckled her breasts until she moaned and pressed herself closer, then turned off the light and stretched out beside her.

Maybe it was sheer exhaustion, but she felt as relaxed as she was aroused. As he kissed and caressed her, she moved her fingers languidly over his shoulders and back, enjoying the warm, firm feel of his skin. Then she slipped them beneath his briefs and lightly massaged his buttocks.

His mouth got more fiery and his breathing a little more strained, but he made no further demands. Instead, his touch grew gently seductive, as if to tell her that her pleasure mattered more to him than his own. At that moment, she felt such a surge of gratitude and happiness that her only thought was to pleasure him back.

The thought grew into an aching, overpowering need. She pulled away her mouth and trailed it down his body— to his neck, his nipples and his belly. He stiffened for a moment in surprise, then rolled onto his back.

She was surprised, too. John had always been after her to satisfy him this way, and wanting to please him, she'd usually agreed, but she'd never volunteered. In time, she'd gotten used to it, but she'd never really liked it.

John had, though. From what she'd heard, all men did. She slid down Marc's briefs, her lips following. He groaned and thrust his hands into her hair as her mouth closed over him. Obviously he was no exception.

She enjoyed his excitement where she'd eventually come to resent John's, but even more shocking, she enjoyed what she was doing. She'd never dreamed that the scent and taste of a man could be so erotic. The more aroused he got, the more she teasingly slowed him down, until he moaned in French. "Have mercy, Diana. You're killing me inch by inch. My God, but I love you..." Her mouth closed over him again, and he tensed. The little death, the French called it.

It was a long minute before he'd recovered enough to take her in his arms. "Well, well, well," he said softly. "You're full of surprises, aren't you? I'm glad I didn't know, because I would have gone insane just looking forward to it."

She was glad it was dark in the room; his praise embarrassed her as much as it pleased her. "I *was* married for six years," she mumbled.

"To an incredibly selfish man. Only a bastard would let you give him that sort of pleasure and not move heaven and earth to please you back."

She blushed even harder. "To be honest, I don't think I was as—I didn't—" She shook her head. "It was different with him, that's all."

"You mean you were less passionate." He laughed softly, a sound of pure delight. "Less—inspired."

"Yes." She paused. "Was it really that nice?"

"Fishing for compliments, eh? I'm sorry, *chérie*, but for once, words utterly fail me." He unbuttoned her skirt and pulled down the zipper. "If you want to know how nice it was, you'll have to let me show you."

She started to pull away. "But I told you before—"

"Hush, Diana. This time, I won't take no for an answer. You had your way with me, you know. It's only fair that you should return the favor."

Half an hour ago she wouldn't have understood what he meant, but she knew now that the pleasure went both ways. She allowed him to undress her, fighting the urge to bolt away. It made her feel horribly vulnerable to lie naked and passive in the darkness.

He ran his hands down her body, caressing her with a light but possessive touch until she relaxed and responded. Then his mouth closed over her breast and gently suckled her, and heat began to build between her legs. He fanned the fire with playful strokes of his fingers, pausing now and then to whisper a graphic compliment in French about how beautiful she was. Words that would have embarrassed her in English were somehow intensely erotic in French.

He kissed her belly and thighs, then explored her intimately with his tongue and teeth, arousing sensations more intense than any she'd ever experienced. She knew now what he'd meant by killing him inch by inch; he was teasing her just as sweetly, keeping her breathlessly at the edge. She fought the pleasure much sooner this time, struggling to control it because she knew he'd eventually satisfy her. And he did, sensing the right moment without being told, tenderly prolonging the ecstasy for second after magical second.

If he'd wanted to enslave her, he'd succeeded. He was giving her a taste of heaven, and she adored him for it. Still writhing beneath his mouth, hardly aware of what she was saying, she moaned, "Oh, Marc...I love you so much... Please...Oh, yes..." Then the pleasure tapered off, slowly fading until she lay motionless beneath his mouth, utterly sated.

After a few moments, he freed the bed covers and covered them both up. "I've never been so happy," he said as he took her in his arms. "I didn't know it was possible."

"Neither did I," she said. "That was—incredible."

He kissed the tip of her nose. "You and I, *mon ange*, are going to have a perfect life together."

"Are we?" She traced an aimless design on his chest. Suddenly the thought of marriage was downright seductive. "Tell me about it."

"There is one bad part. You'll have to endure a big wedding. My parents will insist on it."

"In France, I suppose. In your local church."

"If you don't mind. I realize there might be problems—"

"No, there won't." In the eyes of his church, she'd never been married. "They say converts are the most devout," she teased. "You'd better watch out. I might drag you to mass every day."

"You would convert for me?" His voice was tight with emotion.

"Not just for you." She explained that she had a great deal of faith but no particular religion, and that his had always attracted her. "About this perfect life of ours..."

"Umm. We'll discover a fortune on Pamanzi and you'll buy back the rest of the heirlooms your father sold off. I'll be busy with my restaurant, and you'll be bearing and raising our children. In a year or two, when my sister is in firm control of the winery, I'll take you back to France and open a restaurant in St. Emilion. It's the only civilized place to live, you know. You'll love our château. It's a wonderful house to raise children in."

Diana felt as if someone had taken a sledgehammer to her enchanted new world and smashed it to bits. There were so many impossible assumptions in Marc's plans that she hardly knew which of them to challenge first. How did you deal with a chauvinism so ingrained that the man in question had no idea it even existed?

"We need to talk about this," she finally said.

Marc knew at once that something was wrong. Diana had sounded frightened, almost despairing. It didn't make sense.

Then again, he told himself, like all women, she was highly emotional. She'd probably seized on some trivial wrinkle in the grand fabric of his plans and blown it all out of proportion. "Tell me what's troubling you," he said. "I promise we'll work it out."

"It's—a lot of things. What you said about finding a fortune, for example... The odds are against it, but you based all sorts of plans on it."

He smiled to himself. She worried about the silliest things. "And if there's no fortune? What will change?"

"Everything," she said. "You're assuming I'll leave my job to be a full-time wife and mother, but—"

"And work on your museum. I know it's important to you. Once you leave your job, you'll have far more time for it."

She sighed. "Marc... You saw the island. You know how much work it needs. Even with all the money I make—with all the donations I get—it could take nine or ten years to pay for it. The only way I can quit my job is if we find a fortune on Pamanzi, and we probably won't."

He fondled her breasts, not seductively, but to remind her that she was his now, and that he would always cherish and protect her. She had to learn that she wasn't on her own anymore—that she would soon have a husband to look after her. "You're marrying a wealthy man, *chérie*. There's no need for you to work at a job you don't like in order to raise money I can simply give you."

"But you want to buy the building your restaurant will be in. You want to pay for everything yourself, without taking in partners."

"Fifty million goes a long way, even in New York. I can spare twenty or twenty-five of it."

There was a long pause. "That's very generous," she finally said, "but Van Slyke's Island is my responsibility, not yours. I can't let you spend your inheritance on it."

He marshaled his patience. She was as stubborn as a mule, as blind as a newborn kitten. "You're refusing my help because you've been hurt in the past and you're afraid to rely on anyone but yourself, but you can rely on me, Diana. I'll be your husband soon, and that gives me the right to take care of you. Besides, I'm a Van Slyke, too. If Pierre had lived, the island would have been mine. I think I'm entitled to spend my money on it if I want to."

"But you *don't* want to, not really. It's nothing but a bribe, so my principles won't complicate your plans."

His jaw tightened. "I don't bribe people, Diana, least of all my own wife. I'll be giving you a gift for your museum, so you can concentrate on your work there. I want you to be happy."

She pulled away. "You act as if it's some cute little hobby I've been dabbling in all these years. It's not, Marc. It's my joy and passion—my duty to history—and it's just as important to me as having a restaurant in St. Emilion is to you. I'm not going to leave in the middle of restoring it and go waltzing off to France for the rest of my life."

She was getting hysterical, he thought. It was pointless to keep talking. "Please, Diana, just calm down. I'm sure we can work things out."

"How? New York is my home. It's where my family is. I don't *want* to move to France. You seem to think I'm your personal property, to be indulged and commanded like a child, but I'm an intelligent adult who's capable of making my own decisions. I don't need some man to tell me what I should do with my life."

He cursed himself for a fool. He'd raised the subject too soon, when she was exhausted from her job and had barely begun to accept the idea of marrying him. "You've had a long day," he said. "You need some rest. We'll discuss this later."

"You see? You're doing it again! Deep down, you think I'm overly emotional and totally unreasonable. You believe a woman should follow her husband wherever he goes, and that her family should be her whole world. You plan to feed me and make love to me until I'm so addicted to you I can't think straight, then whisk me off to France and train me to be a proper wife." Her eyes welled up. "It's no good, Marc. It won't work. I can't be what you want me to be or live the way you want me to live. Oh, God, why didn't I just accept that a week ago instead of telling myself..." She gulped for air, then burst into tears.

He pulled her into his arms and settled her head on his chest. She clung to him, sobbing as if her heart were breaking. It saddened him to see her so unhappy, but a woman cried that way only when she was deeply in love, so he couldn't be *too* sad.

He massaged her back until she'd quieted, then said gently, "Perhaps both of us have some thinking to do. I love you too much not to find a way for us to be together. You finish up your work in New York, and I'll go to France and Mayotte and make arrangements for the dig. Then, when I come back, we'll talk about this again."

She tearfully agreed, just as he'd known she would. In time, she'd follow her heart and put herself in his hands. It was inevitable.

Chapter Thirteen

Diana told herself she was the biggest coward in the world, or maybe the biggest fool. Ignoring all logic, she'd done exactly as Marc had wished and finished up her work while he'd arranged for the dig. She'd even allowed herself to hope his attitude would change while he was gone.

Even worse, instead of asking about the future when he'd returned, she'd stood passively in his embrace as he'd kissed her hello, neither withdrawing or responding. He'd quickly released her, apparently no more eager to discuss the subject than she was. They'd circled each other like wary boxers after that, politely discussing their plans and avoiding anything personal.

It was tearing her apart, but she didn't let it show. She knew what he was up to. He was biding his time, waiting for her to give in, sure he could turn her into an obedient little housewife who would follow him around like a puppy and jump to do his bidding.

He was wrong, though. She'd missed him terribly while he was gone, and when he'd come back, she'd longed to be in his arms, but she had more sense than to resume a love affair that threatened to end in heartbreak. If she'd had any guts she would have confronted him with her demands, and if she'd had any brains she would have refused to go away with him, but she'd found it impossible to do either one.

It took two days of travel to reach their destination—to Nairobi and the island of Grande Comore on commercial airlines, and to the territory of Mayotte via charter. Charles Lemonde, an archaeologist representing the French government, had already arrived by then. Not coincidentally, he was also a good friend of Marc's.

They spent the night in the capital, a little town on the west coast of Pamanzi called Dzaoudzi. The next day they collected the supplies and equipment Marc had ordered the previous week and loaded everything into a rented boat. The remaining three members of their party joined them soon afterward.

Diana didn't like any of them. The first two, a pair of brawny laborers who made lewd jokes about having a woman along, were probably harmless, but the third, an oily territorial official named Robert Sabatier, kept looking at her in a way that made her extremely uncomfortable. Unfortunately there was no law against staring. Sabatier had the authority to stop the dig, at least temporarily, so she had no choice but to be civil to him.

After lunching in Dzaoudzi, they cruised to the northern tip of Pamanzi. According to Marc's map, the treasure was located directly inland, well inside the woods.

Standing on a thin strip of gleaming white beach, Diana could see why Philippe had loved it here. Pamanzi was peaceful and lovely, a tiny dot of life amidst a seemingly endless expanse of sea. The woods were thick, verdant and redolent with ylang-ylang, a fragrant nectar used in French perfume. Lake Dziani, though it was invisible from the coast, had been described to her as a pristine gem. With its fresh water and abundant supply of fish, this beautiful island would have provided everything Philippe had wanted.

They picked up some of their gear and headed toward the woods, looking for the clearing where Philippe had supposedly dug his booby-trapped shaft. It was easy to find the proper spot. The map showed various signposts, most notably a large outcropping of rock directly to the north, that guided them right to it.

Diana felt a surge of excitement. The clearing was slightly higher than the surrounding terrain, but the ground in the center had caved in a little, forming a noticeable depression. Philippe's shaft was almost surely beneath.

Lemonde, the archaeologist, studied the area, taking photographs for the historical record. "It could be a case of natural subsidence," he said in French, "but I doubt it. Somebody probably dug here once. More than once, perhaps."

If so, they wouldn't have found anything except dirt. According to his diary, Philippe had expected to be gone the better part of a year. He'd obviously worried that his associates or competitors would become greedy and search for his share of the Indian prize, because he'd gone to a great deal of trouble to throw them off the track.

The shaft, which was only a decoy, was linked to an underground stream by means of a horizontal tunnel located some fifteen feet beneath the surface. As soon as a digger reached the tunnel, the shaft would begin to flood. A logical man would conclude one of two things—that he'd encountered a mysterious natural obstacle, or that the shaft had been booby-trapped to protect something valuable. In either case, he would probably persist with what would prove to be an impossible excavation.

In fact, the treasure was buried at the ends of twin tunnels that Philippe had dug off the main shaft some five feet above the flood tunnel. These treasure tunnels, which he'd later sealed off, sloped gradually upward, so that the chambers holding the booty were some thirty feet from the main shaft but only five feet below the surface. According to Lemonde, pirate treasure vaults similar to this had been reported in Haiti, Madagascar and Oak Island in Canada.

Marc's map showed the tunnels' approximate locations, but the treasure couldn't be retrieved by digging straight down. The chambers were well beyond the clearing, beneath thickly wooded land, and the authorities didn't want any trees to be removed or damaged. Their best alternative was to dig along the edge of the clearing until they found a tunnel, then have someone crawl his way to the chamber at the end.

Having located the main shaft, they retrieved the rest of their gear and returned to the clearing. News traveled fast in a place as small as Mayotte, and Marc didn't entirely trust the local members of their party. He wasn't about to leave the site unprotected each night and invite them to steal the treasure from under his nose.

Diana set out for Lake Dziani with some plastic containers while the men set up camp. They'd be sleeping in tents in the woods, but the conditions would hardly be primitive. Marc had obtained everything from a propane stove to a portable toilet.

The lake was only a short walk away, and as beautiful as everyone had said. Several boats were on the water, their occupants enjoying the perfect weather. She watched for a while, then filled the containers and returned to camp. She was taken aback by what she saw there. There were only three tents, and they were all quite small.

She approached Marc, who was standing with Charles Lemonde. "Can I speak to you for a minute?" she asked in clipped English. "In private?"

The two men exchanged an amused look. French was the group's lingua franca, but she had the feeling Charles had understood her perfectly. He was Marc's friend, so maybe he even knew why she was annoyed.

Marc led her to the edge of the camp. "Yes, *chérie*? Is something the matter?"

"Those tents," she said. "They're very small. Three grown men would be a damn tight squeeze."

"But there are six people and three tents." He smiled ingenuously. "I fail to see the problem."

She was in no mood to be teased. "I'm not sharing a tent with you. Things between us are too unsettled."

"I see. You're afraid I'll lose control of myself and force my despicable attentions on your very enchanting person."

"I didn't say that. It would be—uncomfortable. You know it would."

"Perhaps, but it's also necessary. Charles is my friend, but I don't like the way Sabatier looks at you, and those other two are rough men." He folded his arms across his chest in a gesture she'd come to recognize as a prelude to laying down the law. "I want you beside me at night, where I can protect you."

His concern wasn't totally unreasonable, but she didn't care for his solution. "So I'll take the boat back to Dzaoudzi every evening. I can stay in the hotel—"

"No. Some of the people here are very poor, and desperate men get crazy ideas when a fortune is involved. Somebody could kidnap you and hold you for ransom. You could be hurt or even killed."

She rolled her eyes. "Talk about crazy ideas . . ."

"It's not crazy, at all. Don't waste your breath arguing. I won't touch you if you don't want me to, but you're sleeping in my tent. If you refuse, I'll have you expelled from Mayotte and escorted back to New York."

She glared at him. "I'd have to be insane to marry you. You're arrogant, high-handed and tyrannical. You don't want an equal partner. You want—a cross between a courtesan and a lapdog!"

"It's the tent on the left," he replied evenly. "Your duffel bag is already inside."

He had her and he knew it. He was a Frenchman with excellent connections on a French island, and she was an American nobody. If she wanted to stay—and she did— she would have to play by his rules. Too irate to surrender gracefully, she stalked into the tent and started blowing up an air mattress.

A few minutes later she heard the roar of their gas-powered jackhammer, loosening up the soil where they planned to dig. Her temper began to cool. Marc had been overprotective from the night they'd met. You couldn't expect a tiger to turn into a tabby. Besides, it was too beautiful a day to stay in the tent and sulk.

She blew up the second air mattress, then went outside. Marc and the two laborers were digging an arc-shaped trench along the edge of the clearing, while Charles shoveled away dirt and Sabatier lazed against a tree, watching. Sabatier noticed her and beckoned her over. She waved halfheartedly, then walked over to Charles and asked if she could help.

"Sure," he said. "If you clear, I can dig."

Marc looked up. He was stripped to the waist and glistening with sweat. Annoyed or not, she felt a rush of warmth.

"Be sure to take a break when you feel tired," he said. "Sit and have something to drink."

She nodded and fetched a shovel. Although she was careful not to push herself too hard, she was exhausted after only a few hours of work. She sat for a while, then changed into her swimsuit, grabbed her soap and towel and walked to the lake. The water was soothingly warm, the bath a sensual delight. Then Sabatier arrived to take a swim and she reluctantly returned to camp, hating the fact that she lived in a world where men could intimidate women so easily.

The men had quit for the day and were lazing under a tree, complaining good-naturedly about the roots that had snaked into the soil beneath the clearing and slowed their progress. Diana dressed, making dinner while they took a swim. There was no cooking involved, just opening cans and heating up the contents.

The meal provided her with her first real laugh of the day. Marc was too hungry not to eat heartily, but never in her life had she seen him look so offended. Canned stew was obviously an insult to his refined French palate.

The men left her to wash the dishes, and she wearily cleaned up. Five male chauvinists were more than she could handle just then. She didn't join them afterward because she wasn't interested in their conversation, which was about soccer, and wasn't made to feel welcome. Instead, she visited the camp's makeshift bathroom, a pair of sheets looped over some branches for privacy, and then retired to her tent for the night.

She changed into pajamas and took out her contact lenses. Given the conditions here, they were more trouble than they were worth. Fortunately, though, she'd brought a pair of glasses along.

She was nestled in her sleeping bag when Marc finally came in, reading by the light of a battery-powered lamp. Without a word, he started to undress. She resisted the urge to watch—to give herself the pleasure of looking at him—and rolled onto her side facing the other way.

She heard him get into his sleeping bag, which was about a yard away from her own. A wave of anxiety hit her, as if she were sharing the tent with a stranger. She tried to keep reading but couldn't concentrate.

After about five minutes, he said, "I missed talking to you while I was gone."

She didn't answer. There was no point to it.

"I missed holding you, too," he continued softly. "Tell me you missed it, too. I won't sleep, otherwise."

She couldn't remain silent after that. There had been too much pain in his voice. "Of course I did. But nothing's changed. You don't take me seriously. You want to cut me off from everything I love, move me to France and turn me into a carbon copy of your mother. I can't do it. I'd be miserable, and I'd make *you* miserable."

"That's not fair, *chérie*. I love you just as you are. I don't want to change you." He paused. "I'd never cut you off from your home. We'll visit as often as we can, during Christmas and over the summer. If your museum isn't finished by the time we move to France, you can hire a curator and supervise the work from St. Emilion. It's not so far from New York that you can't fly there whenever you need to."

He was honestly trying, but his offer reflected a total lack of understanding of who she was and how she felt. "Please try to understand . . . From the time I was a child, that island's been my heart and soul. And then—after my mother died—it became my tribute to her memory. I can't turn it over to someone else. I have to see it through no matter how long it takes. There's only one Van Slyke's Island, but you can own a restaurant anywhere. Would it be so terrible to stay in New York?"

"But you can't honestly like it there—crammed in like a sardine, breathing filthy air, fighting traffic and worrying every minute about your safety."

"We wouldn't have to live in the city. We could buy a place in the country—five or ten acres, with gardens and woods and lots of space." Her enthusiasm grew as she spoke. "You could open a restaurant in the area, so you wouldn't have to commute. Buy an old house or inn and restore it. It would be warm and charming. With your cooking, people would flock there."

"Yes. I might enjoy that." Diana's hopes soared, but only for a moment. "For a few years, anyway," he went on. "Eventually we'll have a family to consider. American children are spoiled and selfish. They have no sense of sacrifice or responsibility. How can they, when your culture teaches them only to want more and more? Besides, I won't have them raised in a country where drugs, violence and sexual promiscuity will surround them each time they walk out my door."

"That's a ridiculous exaggeration." The French were impossible at times, she thought—sure they had a monopoly on virtue. "We have our problems, but we're not Sodom and Gomorrah. Besides, parents raise children, not countries. And what about American freedom and opportunity? No country on earth can match us there. I don't see people from all over the world desperate to get into France, Marc."

"But it's my home," he said with quiet emotion. "My family has been there for at least a thousand years. The sight and smell of it are in my blood. I could tell you I'd live in America with you forever, but in time I would need to go back. Not just want to—need to. Even now, there isn't a day I don't miss it."

He was telling her he would shrivel and die anywhere else, and listening to him, she had to believe it. That was the real problem, and nothing she could say would solve it. She felt drained, despondent.

He touched her shoulder, and she flinched. "I want to make love to you," he murmured. "Don't say no, Diana."

She shook her head. "I'm sorry. I can't."

"But it would bring us closer. Make us happy."

"No." Her voice was tight with pain. "It would hurt too much afterward."

Neither of them spoke again.

The next day, after several more hours of work, Charles Lemonde's shovel struck a hard object near the west end of the trench. It wasn't a root or a rock, but a piece of rotting lumber. It turned out to be part of the bracing inside Philippe's tunnel, which was about two and a half feet square and lined on the sides and top with timber. An inspection of the ground above the tunnel's path showed no signs of digging, but the evidence of intrusion could have been erased by time.

They broke for lunch, then excavated a hole in the top of the tunnel, making sure it was large enough for someone to maneuver himself inside. Diana was smaller than the men and the logical one to go, but Marc wouldn't hear of it. He said he would go himself.

Charles laughed at the idea. "My friend, you panic inside elevators that are ten times larger. You'll never be able to slide twenty feet on your belly inside a tunnel, much less take the proper photographs and search for artifacts. Anyway, I'm skinnier than you are."

"My problem is elevators, not claustrophobia," Marc replied, "but I'll bow to your professional experience. Go get dressed. I'll get the oxygen."

Charles put on protective clothing while Marc positioned the breathing equipment, a mask connected to a tank by about forty feet of hose. Diana was so giddy with impatience that she could have used some of the oxygen herself. Still, when it came right down to it, she wasn't sure she would have had the courage to slither through a black and ancient void braced only by rotting wood.

Charles returned with a powerful flashlight and slipped on the oxygen mask. Picking up his camera, he lowered himself into the trench. After taking a few photographs, he maneuvered himself inside the tunnel.

He went at a painstaking pace. The bracing was at best precarious, and he didn't want to miss any half-buried artifacts. Every minute or so he raised his mask and shouted a report of his progress. Since the treasure chamber was only about twenty feet from the opening, they hoped to be able to hear him till the very end.

When he yelled that he'd found some coins, Diana's heart began to thunder. Sabatier, who'd left his usual spot against a tree to observe, drawled that she was about to become a rich woman. Ignoring him, she moved closer to Marc, who gave Sabatier a hard look and put his arm protectively around her waist.

Several more minutes passed. It seemed like an hour. Then there was another muffled yell: "A few more coins." Her throat went dry with anticipation.

And then, a few minutes after that: "Some pearls, I think. Loose ones." The excitement became almost unbearable. He had to be close to the end.

And finally, a message that sent her crashing back to earth: "That's all. I'm coming back."

Someone had beaten them to the treasure, scattering bits of it as he crawled back out. "At least Charles found *something*," she said dejectedly. "Maybe we'll have more luck with the second tunnel."

"Maybe," Marc agreed. "I'm sorry, *chérie*."

She nodded, trying to be optimistic. Charles emerged, then started down the tunnel the opposite way, toward the main shaft. He found a few more scattered coins about four feet along, then nothing but dirt.

He cleaned the pearls and coins as Marc, Diana and Sabatier watched. The pearls were quite large, with tiny holes indicating they'd been part of a necklace or bracelet once. The coins, about a dozen in all, were gold from the seventeenth century, minted in the Middle East and Spain.

The two Comoronians, meanwhile, had resumed work, filling the first trench with dirt, then starting work on a second. Having located one treasure tunnel, they expected to find the other much more quickly. According to the map, the two tunnels were directly opposite each other off the main shaft.

They stopped for the day when the trench was about five feet deep. Everyone headed for the lake, Charles taking the pearls and coins with him. After they'd bathed, Diana again made dinner. Marc helped her this time, grumbling about the quality of the food, making her laugh. Afterward, she sat by his side as the men talked.

She left when the conversation began to wind down. Now that she and Marc were on good terms again, she felt more awkward than ever. His every look and touch announced how much he desired her. She could tell herself a million times that sleeping with him would be a mistake, but that didn't stop her from craving his company and desiring him back.

She tried to take the easy way out, turning off the lamp and pretending to be asleep, but it didn't work. The moment he came in, he went right to her side and sat down. "Dead to the world, eh?" He caressed her hair. "No matter. You'll enjoy being seduced out of a sound sleep. It's very erotic."

She burrowed further into her sleeping bag. "Okay, so I'm awake. Go away."

"But I'm tense, *mon chou*. It's been a hard day. I need to unwind." He pushed down her sleeping bag and gently massaged her shoulders. "How's that? Does it feel nice?"

It felt wonderful. "No. Go to sleep."

"Liar." He laughed softly and went right on kneading her shoulders. "You were happier today, even after the disappointment with the treasure. You can't help it when we're together, any more than I can. I know you want to make love. I saw it every time you looked at me. By the way, your glasses are adorable. All day long, I've wanted to take them off and kiss you."

She began to weaken. Any more of this and she'd fling herself into his arms. "Dammit, Marc, you promised not to do this. You're not being fair."

He sighed theatrically and removed his hands. "Now you've done it. Appealed to my sense of honor and shamed me into stopping."

"Because nothing's settled. There's no solution."

"Of course there is. We love each other, so there has to be. We just haven't found it yet." He kissed the back of her head. "Good night, *chérie*."

Diana said good night, wishing she had even half his confidence.

They found the second tunnel late the next morning. Once again, Charles crawled cautiously inside, but this time, he was stopped about eight feet along by a cave-in. He immediately crawled back out, saying he wanted to clear out the dirt and proceed. Had the blockage been further in, it might have been too dangerous to try, but he had oxygen to breathe and would be close enough to rescue if the earth should give way and trap him.

After lunch, armed only with gloves and hand tools, he returned to the tunnel. He tossed the loosened dirt onto a sheet, which Marc periodically retrieved and emptied, then dragged back inside. Both jobs entailed crawling partway into the tunnel, something the Comoronians had wanted no part of. Marc, who was more claustrophobic than he'd admitted, found it difficult but not impossible.

Diana's heart rose to her throat every time he disappeared. Though he was close to the opening, and the first section of bracing appeared to be in good shape, Charles had oxygen and he didn't.

After some thirty minutes of slow but steady progress, Charles called out, "My God, there are bones here—like a human hand, but smaller. A primate, perhaps." And then, a few minutes later: "I've found a skull. I'm coming out. I want a better look."

Diana stared in horror as Marc pulled out the sheet. There was a small pile of bones on top of the dirt, including what looked like a human skull. Charles, while not an anthropologist, had seen enough human remains in the course of his work to make a tentative identification. It was a young child, he said, perhaps eight years old. He'd evidently been sent into the tunnel to retrieve the treasure—and suffocated in the subsequent cave-in.

The thought made Diana physically ill. History fascinated her, but it was also full of brutality and cruelty. Hundreds of years ago, a child had died. She wondered if his murderer had even cared.

She didn't want Charles and Marc to continue after that. One lost life was enough. But Charles vehemently insisted on looking for what the child had died trying to retrieve, and Marc agreed to help him.

They continued working. Charles found more bones, and then, wedged so deeply into the tunnel floor that he almost missed it, a priceless golden dagger with a handle encrusted with gemstones. For an object of such beauty, it conjured up a singularly hideous image—of the child grabbing it as the earth gave way, then frantically trying to claw his way out.

It took almost an hour to clear away the rest of the cave-in. Everyone hoped for another spectacular find, but the only object Charles unearthed was an ancient wooden chest, now partially decomposed. The child had evidently been dragging it along behind him when he'd died. It was empty now except for some dirt, the treasure it had once contained long gone. The tunnel beyond was empty, as well. Diana had the answer to her question now. The boy's murderer hadn't cared at all. On the contrary, he must have dug down from the surface to retrieve his prize after the cave-in, not even bothering with the dead boy. As a result, he'd missed the dagger which had become trapped under the boy's body as he'd died.

It was late afternoon when Charles went back in the tunnel for the final time, to check the ten-foot section leading down to the main shaft. He was tired now, and wise enough to be extremely careful. He didn't bother with photographs, but quickly scanned the area with his light and, seeing nothing, crawled back out.

There was no treasure, no fortune in coins and gems to pay for the work on Van Slyke's Island. Diana fought down her disappointment. After all, it was only what she'd expected.

Charles had his choice of artifacts on behalf of France, and selected the dagger. She would get the coins, pearls and chest, and also the boy's skeleton. Along with copies of Charles's photographs, they would make a fascinating exhibit for her museum.

The two Comoronians filled up the trench while the rest of the group broke camp. They were going back to Dzaoudzi for the night, and then home.

Chapter Fourteen

Diana heard a knock on her hotel-room door and groped for the lamp by her bed. She'd gone upstairs hours before, leaving Marc and Charles to talk over a bottle of brandy. Too keyed up to sleep soundly, she'd been tossing and turning ever since.

She turned on the light. "Who is it?"

"Marc. I need to talk to you. Can I come in?"

Yawning, she got out of bed and walked to the door. He'd sounded serious, but not upset. She let him in, wondering how much he'd drunk. Not a lot, evidently. He looked completely sober.

He closed the door. He was wearing his bathrobe now, so obviously he'd stopped by his room to change. She had her usual modest pajamas on, but his gaze stripped her naked. It aroused her to be regarded with such passion—to be alone with him in the dead of night, knowing he would take her in his arms if she gave him the slightest bit of encouragement.

"I couldn't sleep," he said. "I was thinking about you and me." He put his hands on her waist. "Actually, that's something I do constantly. The last two nights have been hell. Sleeping only a few feet away from you, knowing I could make love to you if I pushed you even a little..."

She stiffened, fighting the growing warmth in her veins. "Don't, Marc. You promised."

"Yes. I promised. But we're not in that damned tent anymore, Diana."

Her heart began to race. The touch of his warm, strong hands reminded her much too keenly of the pleasure they'd so often given her. "We're not engaged yet, either," she said. "Nothing's been settled."

"I disagree. You're going to marry me eventually. The living arrangements are just a minor detail."

"Not to me." She felt herself losing control of the situation. "Please—just leave."

"No. You're being unreasonable." He looked exasperated with her now. "For God's sake, Diana, we love each other. You know we do. Eventually we'll work things out. In the meantime, it's crazy for us to suffer when we could be making each other happy. Let me make love to you."

His arguments were starting to make sense, and that frightened her. She was afraid that if she gave in, she'd do whatever he asked of her afterward. "No." She turned around. "I don't want to."

"Of course you do." He slipped his hands under the top of her pajamas and slid them upward to cup her breasts. "You see? Your nipples are hard for me already."

He took them between his thumbs and fingers and gently massaged them, sending hot curls of pleasure through her body. She tipped back her head and closed her eyes. Two long weeks without his touch had made her almost painfully responsive.

She couldn't pull away. It felt too good. "Please, Marc. You're making me too crazy to stop you, and I know I'll be sorry afterward."

"Of course you won't. You'll only wonder why you waited so long." He pressed himself closer, letting her feel how aroused he was. "Your body is a total delight—so hot...so moist...so eager for me."

He was right about her being eager. She tried desperately to pull back from the brink. "You're not being fair. You know the effect you have on me and you're using it against me." But she let him go right on touching her.

"*For* you, and you've brought it on yourself. The effect you have on me is at least ten times stronger." He nuzzled her neck, and she trembled. "Turn around," he murmured. "Let me kiss you."

It was useless to keep fighting him; she wanted him too much to win. "No," she said irritably. "You can't expect me to conspire in my own seduction."

He laughed softly. "So you want to be persuaded, do you? Very well, then. It won't take long."

"You're damned arrogant, do you know—" His fingers tightened demandingly on her nipples, sending a fiery burst of pleasure to her loins, and she breathed in sharply. "Oh, God. You're totally unscrupulous. I never should have gotten involved with you."

He moved rhythmically against her and, helplessly aroused, she answered with seductive motions of her own. "Again, *mon ange*, you've brought it on yourself. You're enchantingly passionate. You can hardly blame me for taking advantage of that." His lips returned to her neck. "Are you ready to give up yet?"

"No," she said. She liked this too much.

"Ah, well, you always were stubborn." He slid his hand beneath the waistband of her pajamas and caressed her belly. "You're forcing me to be ruthless, you know."

His fingers slid downward, stroking her until she moaned his name and arched against his hand. She wanted his mouth so badly that she twisted her head around and blindly sought his lips. He kissed her deeply, dominating her mouth, caressing her until the mounting tension took her completely in thrall. She wanted to turn into his arms but couldn't seem to move.

Finally, breaking the kiss, he picked her up and carried her to the bed. After settling her under the covers, he took off his robe and tossed it over the headboard. Everything was foggy now, almost unreal.

He sat down beside her. "You always looked frightened before. You don't now."

"I'm not." The sight of him made her desire him even more. She wanted to tell him how aroused she was, how eager she was to have him inside her, but she was too shy to get the words out.

He reached into the pocket of his robe, took out a condom and gazed at her solemnly. Her blood cooled a little. It was as if he was waiting for her to object, to say it wasn't what she had in mind.

It was, though. He'd won completely, just as he'd known he would. He'd even prepared for it. "Did anyone ever tell you that you're obnoxiously overconfident?" she asked.

He smiled. "Obnoxiously overconfident would be making love to you without protection, because I expect to have my ring on your finger within days. Unfortunately, I have the feeling I'm in for some hard bargaining first, and with a real expert. If it's all the same to you, we'll take precautions until we're married. I'd rather our first child be born at least nine months after our wedding."

"And it never occurred to you to try to get me pregnant—to force the issue?"

"I considered it," he admitted, stretching out beside her, "but it's no way to begin a marriage. I want you to trust me as well as love me."

At that moment, she trusted him completely. He was too honorable to talk about hard bargaining unless he'd begun to take her aspirations more seriously. Surely they would find a solution.

"I do," she whispered. "You're the best thing that's ever happened to me."

He took her in his arms. "It's about to get even better, *chérie*."

He'd always gone slowly in the past but seemed incapable of that now, undressing her with almost clumsy haste. She helped him, impatient to feel flesh against naked flesh.

Lying side-to-side, they kissed lightly, then more passionately. The feel of his chest against her breasts—the intimate thrust of his maleness—excited her wildly. Their caresses, hot from the start, grew almost violent in their intensity, as if, having denied themselves for so long, each feared the other would vanish into thin air if they didn't take each other at once.

As they feverishly aroused each other, she realized that now she knew what real passion was. It wasn't just physical, but an emotional hunger so great that it could be satisfied only by becoming a part of the one you loved. After only a few weeks, she felt closer to Marc than she ever had to John. She'd had a merger once; now she wanted a marriage—a husband, a home and a family.

She hooked her leg over his hip, silently offering herself. She knew how much pleasure he could give her; now she wanted to experience it while he was deep inside her.

He stiffened, then groaned and pulled away. "I'll just be a moment..."

She bent her head to his chest and teased one of his nipples with her tongue. "We don't have to stop. I was thinking... It would be nice to make a baby."

"After we're married," he insisted raggedly. He shuddered as her mouth moved lower. "Diana, for God's sake, how am I supposed to do this—"

She nuzzled his navel. "You'll manage."

He pulled her on top of him only moments later. "Take me inside you," he said softly. He slid his hand intimately between them. "Let me visit paradise."

She felt a heady sense of control in that position, a wanton sensuality. She moved seductively on top of him, gradually drawing him deeper as they kissed and caressed. There was no fear or discomfort, only intense emotion. Soon he filled her in every way, not just her body but her heart and soul.

She wrapped her arms around his neck and let him take command. Caressing her more firmly, he teased her with slow, erotic thrusts that pushed her relentlessly higher. Finally, desperate for release, she frantically increased the pace, and their lovemaking raced out of control. In the end, there was shattering physical pleasure and a joyful sense of oneness. And best of all, there was the fiercely possessive way he held her as he exploded in her arms, and the fulfillment she felt in giving herself completely.

Afterward, content and drowsy in his embrace, she murmured, "Now I know what making love is. Thank you for showing me."

"We showed each other. You're an angel in bed. You can call me an intolerable chauvinist, but I'm glad you never shared this with Redmon."

"Me, too." She paused. "And you? Did you—"

"No. How could I? I hadn't met *you* yet." He toyed with a strand of her hair, wrapping it gently around his finger. "You'll get very little sleep tonight, *mon ange*. I'm going to make love to you until we both collapse."

It was a delicious thought. "You're very presumptuous," she teased. "Maybe I won't want to."

"You'll want to, all right. I'll make sure of it."

"And I suppose you're prepared to go on all night. It probably never occurred to you that you might not get what you came for."

He laughed softly. "Not seriously, no. And yes, I did prepare for it. If you doubt it, you're welcome to check the pocket of my—"

"Talk about obnoxious overconfidence!" Her desire for him stirred anew, and she fondled him with a lightly seductive touch. Like her, he was eager to make love again. "You're shameless, coming here half naked and claiming you wanted to talk. I never should have let you in."

"But I did come to talk. Then I saw the look in your eyes—the helpless passion, the terrible frustration—and I decided talking could wait. It would have been cruel not to put you out of your misery first."

She rolled her eyes. "Were you always this egotistical, or do I bring out the worst in you?"

"Not the worst. The best. Come, Diana, admit it. You wanted to be seduced."

He was probably right. "That's ridiculous. It was the farthest thing from my mind."

He rolled her onto her back and slid on top of her. "The hell it was." He cupped one of her breasts. "You loved every minute of it, too."

She put her arms around him. "Did I? I've forgotten, darling. You'll have to remind me."

He parted her thighs and teased her with his body, watching her face to see her response. Aroused and a little frustrated, she twined her legs around his hips to coax him deeper. "Oh, no," he teased. "First you have to admit that you loved it."

Enjoying the game, she lay motionless and silent for as long as she could. Then he eased himself fully inside her and began to move, and she surrendered completely. "I did. It was wonderful. Oh, God, Marc..." She thrust her hands into his hair and pulled his head down to hers.

"Not yet," he murmured against her lips. "Next you have to ask me what I wanted to talk about."

"Talk? I don't— Oh. That. What?"

"I'm going to France tomorrow." He nibbled her lower lip. "I want to show you off to my family—to show you my home and village and introduce you to my friends. Say you'll come along."

She was in no fit state to refuse.

A Frenchman to the core, Marc regarded his native province as perfect in every way. As they boarded the train to Bordeaux, he told himself that once Diana saw it, she would agree that it was the only possible place to live. It was inconceivable to him that her museum would prove a serious obstacle, not when he was willing to do anything within reason to indulge her.

Women, after all, were creatures of emotion. She'd shown him her love in too many ways to refuse him—in her willingness to embrace his faith, in her longing to bear his child and in her passionate gift of her body. She would come to love his home as much as she loved him, and that would settle the matter.

Diana, who was shrewder than Marc gave her credit for, had realized what he was up to even before they'd left Dzaoudzi. She wasn't annoyed; two more nights in his arms, in Nairobi and then in Paris, had opened her mind on the subject. She hoped she would like St. Emilion and want to live there, because she couldn't bear the thought of giving him up.

In fact, it was love at first sight. His home, Château du Ciel, was smaller and more intimate than she'd expected. A nineteenth-century gem, it had a whitewashed central facade that was flanked by twin turrets and topped by a gray slate roof. It sat in a cobblestoned, tree-lined courtyard surrounded by acres of vines on a limestone escarpment overlooking St. Emilion.

The village itself was as charming as it was old, a delight of golden limestone buildings with rust-colored roofs, narrow, winding streets dating to the Middle Ages and wonderful little shops that sold crafts and foods of all sorts. It was bustling and friendly, too. If you lingered for a few hours in one of its cafés, half the world would come by to greet you.

She expected to stay a day or two, but their visit stretched into a week. Much of the time she was alone with Marc, enjoying long, lazy picnics in the countryside and exploring the local towns and vineyards, but there were also glorious meals at Château du Ciel and visits with the Rochards' friends and neighbors. Marc was loved here, and, as the woman of his choice, Diana was greeted with typical French curiosity and treated with great warmth. Of course, it didn't hurt that she had a hearty appetite and spoke very good French.

Marc's parents were much as she'd pictured them, an aristocratic and patriarchal father who expected deference and respect, and a beautiful, vivacious mother, as French as pâté by now, who seemed completely content with her role as chatelaine and helpmate. Despite their dissimilar personalities, both of them lit up with joy when they first saw their son. Over the next few days, it became obvious to Diana that they'd missed him very much and were thrilled to have him back, if only for a short visit.

She also met his sister Catherine, seeing her at the winery most days and dining with her family twice, once at the Corots' and once at Château du Ciel. In most ways, Catherine was a traditional Frenchwoman, submissive to her husband, respectful to her parents and solicitous of her family. When it came to business, though, tradition went straight out the window.

During both meals, Catherine, Marc and their father, Louis, engaged in spirited discussions about the winery that threatened at times to dissolve into fights but never quite did. When Louis addressed his daughter, Diana sensed a grudging respect colored by condescension, but Marc treated Catherine as a complete equal, both in matters of business and during more personal moments. More often than not he took her side, something that, much to Diana's surprise, didn't seem to anger Louis so much as exasperate him. It was as if he knew he was going to lose but couldn't bring himself to give up.

Still, the reason for Marc's absence was never mentioned directly until the morning they left for Paris. They were standing in the station with Marc's parents, saying goodbye, when Louis mumbled, "You know, St. Emilion could use a first-rate restaurant." He sounded as if the words had been torn from his mouth. "Perhaps you'd like me to do a little work on it after you leave. Look around for a good location."

Marc was openly astonished by the offer. "Running a restaurant takes a great deal of time. I wouldn't be able to involve myself very deeply in the winery."

Louis shrugged. "Your mother misses you. Soon you'll marry your beautiful Diana and give your mother more grandchildren. She'll be desolate if they're thousands of miles away."

"And Catherine?" Marc asked warily. "Where does she fit in?"

"She's capable, I suppose. Not much of a business-woman, though."

"She's more than capable, Papa. She's as good a wine-maker as you are. She deserves—"

"Fortunately, Jean-Luc has a talent for business," Louis interrupted, referring to Catherine's son. "Of course, it will be years before he finishes school, and I'm not getting any younger. Your mother worries about my health. She wants me to take it easier, and I suppose I'll have to indulge her. When the time comes, perhaps you'll teach the boy what you know. And it wouldn't hurt if you gave your sister some help in the meantime. If she asks you to, that is."

Marc nodded. "Of course, Papa. I'd be happy to."

A moment later, the two embraced. The estrangement between father and son, so difficult for all of them, was over. Marc had won, and more quickly than anyone had dreamed possible.

Diana was moved and pleased, but she knew their reconciliation would complicate matters. There was no reason for Marc to stay in New York now—no reason except her.

They said their final goodbyes and got on the train. She was as frightened of the future as she'd been in New York, but she couldn't bear another moment of uncertainty. Even heartbreak was better than that. They would have to talk.

"I'm glad you patched things up with your father," she said as they settled into their seats. "I think your mother engineered it. She looked very pleased with herself afterward."

"Umm. One way or another, you women get what you want." He smiled teasingly. "You certainly will. There's no reason for me to open a restaurant in New York now, so I'll have more money than I know what to do with and plenty of free time. With an unlimited source of funds and the two of us working full-time on your museum, we should be able to open it very soon. Then we'll move to France. If you'd like, we can spend a few weeks in New York each summer, so you can make sure things are going the way you want them to."

Diana fought to keep her emotions under control. His proposal, though obviously made in good faith, was miles from fair or workable. Still, if she flew off the handle as she had in the past, they would never reach a compromise.

She told herself to treat it as just another business negotiation. She was good at those. "Even with unlimited funds, it will be a long time before the museum can open as a working farm. At least six or seven years, I would say. You can't hurry restoration work. You should know that from your château, Marc."

He frowned. "Six or seven years is too long, Diana. I have a life, too, and it's not unreasonable for me to want to get on with it. Two years would give the project a solid foundation. Surely, in all of New York, there's someone capable of supervising the work to your satisfaction while you're in France."

"It seems to me that I'm doing all the compromising," she replied. "I'll accept your money if you insist, and I'll move to St. Emilion, but it's only fair that we spend more time in New York. After all, it's hardly a sacrifice for you to leave for a few weeks when the restaurants in the area all close for July or August anyway. And as far as when we actually move goes, we'll have forty or fifty years together. It's not unreasonable that we should spend the first six or seven of them in New York."

"So you're telling me you want to stay in New York until your museum opens, and then... What? Go there for the whole summer each year? Spend a few weeks there each winter?"

"Something like that." She thought for a moment. "You wouldn't have to come for the whole time. I'd manage just fine on my own, even after we have kids. Other women do."

He looked appalled. "You expect me to allow you to take our children and—"

"*Allow* me to?" she interrupted incredulously. "Excuse me, but I don't recall agreeing to take orders from you. I thought we were equals."

"I'll be your husband." He folded his arms across his chest and regarded her sternly. "Wives should live where their husbands have to live and—"

"*Have* to? Since when do you *have* to?"

"And consider their husbands and children the most important thing in their lives. My suggestions are completely reasonable—more than reasonable, in fact. No other man I know would be so generous."

"Generous?" she all but sputtered. "Is that how you see it? As a gift you're giving a troublesome, irrational wife?"

He had the grace to look a little sheepish. "Of course not. I know your feelings are sincere. But once we're married—once we have children—they'll change."

Diana didn't reply. He wouldn't have understood. As much as they loved each other, the cultural barriers between them were too great to be overcome.

Chapter Fifteen

Back in New York, Marc bought Diana a magnificent diamond ring and kept proposing, repeating the same basic arguments till she thought she'd go mad. He couldn't or wouldn't see that she could love him with all her heart and still refuse to marry him, and all because of what he considered an eccentric, irrational crusade. In his experience, women simply didn't behave that way.

After a week of arguing back, she decided it was pointless to keep seeing him. He disagreed, but there was nothing he could do. Her office was sixty flights up, and though he came by her apartment most evenings to talk to her, he was too well-bred to follow her into her room if she walked away or stand on the other side of her closed door and shout at her.

That left the members of her family to cope with, all of whom thought she should marry him first and bargain with him later. After all, Nelly said, he could hardly haul her off to France without her consent. Since he loved her too much to leave her, the game was as good as won.

Besides, added her father, nothing was more important than love. It was a remarkable sentiment, coming as it did from a man who'd always put his career first. As for Tina, she admitted Marc was a chauvinist but insisted he would eventually see the light. Diana ignored the pair, telling herself they were too besotted to think straight. They were planning a grand wedding and thought she and Marc should be doing the same thing.

Even Babe got into the act, claiming there wasn't a woman alive who couldn't outmaneuver a poor, dumb male if she really put her mind to it. Maybe that was so, but Diana had always regarded manipulative women with contempt and wasn't about to become one of them.

Finally—mercifully—there was Risa, who listened sympathetically and kept her opinions to herself. Eventually, sensing that Diana was cracking under the strain of Marc's nightly visits and everyone else's nagging, Risa invited her to stay in the Morrisons' East Side apartment temporarily. It was on the thirty-ninth floor, higher than anyone but a madman would attempt to climb.

Diana could barely eat or sleep by then, much less work. She was so miserable that she'd begun to weaken, and that frightened her. She had promises to keep, promises to herself, her mother's memory and posterity. How could she turn her back on them and maintain her self-respect?

There was only one consolation, she decided at the end of her second week back from France. Things couldn't get any worse. Then her secretary buzzed her to say that her cousin Tracy was waiting to see her, and she realized she'd been wrong. Talking to Tracy would be the absolute nadir.

"Tell her I'm with a client," she said.

She was too late. The door opened and Tracy strolled in, plopping down in the chair across from her desk. "God, what a great office. Great view, too." Tracy frowned. "These windows don't open, do they?"

For one of the few times in her life, Diana couldn't bring herself to be civil. Tracy had barged in for God only knew what reason and Diana's only concern was to get rid of her. "No," she said. "If you were worried I might jump, don't be. The thought never entered my mind—until you walked in, that is."

Tracy stared despondently at the floor. "That wasn't very nice. I came to offer my help."

Diana wasn't impressed. Other than John, the only one Tracy ever listened to was Risa. "Help? You mean the way you helped me five years ago, when you stole away my husband?"

Tracy's head snapped up. "I only took what you didn't want, and if you're honest with yourself, you'll admit it. You never loved John half as much as you love Marc, and he knew it. He wouldn't have even looked at me, other-wise."

"Of all the self-serving bull . . . !" Diana was livid now. "He was my husband. Of course I loved him. I never stood a chance against someone like you."

"A manipulative little bitch who built up his ego in bed and everywhere else, you mean."

Diana reddened. She'd been thinking of Tracy's youth, sensuality and stunning blond beauty. "Among other things," she said.

"And was John the kind of husband you really wanted? Brilliant, perfect Diana Van Slyke?" Tracy gave her a brittle smile. "He's fine for me. I'm good at being the adoring wife of a well-to-do, successful man—at catering to his insecurities—but he would have aggravated you to death eventually. Marc is much better for you. He knows exactly who he is and what he wants. You should marry him."

"Because he'll make me happy," Diana said scornfully. "You're only thinking of me."

"As a matter of fact, yes. I'm not afraid of losing John, if that's what you mean. A part of him might still want you, but you're not interested now that you've met Marc, so why should I worry?" She paused. "Actually, the reason—"

"You shouldn't," Diana interrupted. "I stopped loving John years ago. I won't thank you for coming, Tracy. If you'll excuse me, I have work to do."

"Dammit, will you listen to me for a moment? You love Marc now, and he loves you. From what Risa says, you'd be willing to move to France except for Van Slyke's Island. Well, I'm a Van Slyke, too, and I love the island as much as you do. John would have a fit if I went to work, but I'm sure he'd let me help you with the museum—"

"Isn't it enough that you stole my husband?" Diana asked incredulously. "Do you have to steal my island, too?"

"It's always been *your* island, hasn't it? No one but you has the right to care about it!"

"You can care as much as you want, as long as you keep your nose out of my museum."

"Your museum. Your island. Your husband." Tracy raised her chin belligerently. "And *my* sister, except that she was *your* best friend. The two of you were inseparable. You were always telling me to get lost. So I—"

"That's ridiculous. We made a point of including you."

"Sure. Once in a blue moon. And while you were playing your private games and trading secrets, I was all alone. I spent hours and hours just looking at things—pictures, furniture, gravestones, even balusters and moldings. They were my companions as a kid. Van Slyke's Island was the reason I took so many art and architecture courses in college. I used to wish it would be mine someday, instead of yours."

"And that's why you went after John? Because you were jealous of my friendship with Risa? Because I was going to inherit Van Slyke's Island and you weren't?"

"No," Tracy said vehemently. "I fell in love with him when we were both at Columbia. I went after him because I wanted him much more than you did. I know I was callous and dishonest, but I was young and selfish and I didn't care who I hurt." She stood up. "I'm sorry about what I put you through, and about what a bitch I've been at times, but I'm not sorry about how things worked out. John wasn't right for you. Marc is. Marry him, Diana. Move to France and let me help you with Van Slyke's Island. No one but you could love it as much as I do. Besides, if you want the truth, I'm bored being a social butterfly."

So after all these years, Diana thought, Tracy had finally apologized. She wasn't indifferent to that, but her cousin had asked more than she could give. "No. There's too much bad blood between us. Working with you would be more than I could stomach."

Tracy looked stricken, as if she truly hadn't expected Diana's rejection. "You really hate me, don't you?" she asked hoarsely.

Diana shrugged, too hostile to deny it, but guilty about the hurt she'd evidently inflicted. After all, Tracy *was* family.

"Then cut off your nose to spite your face!" Tracy snapped. "See if I care!" But her eyes had filled with tears, and she ran out of the office as if she was afraid she'd break down completely if she stayed a moment longer.

At six that evening, Diana let herself into the Morrisons' apartment and looked around for Risa, wanting to tell her what had happened. She found her cousin in bed, watching TV. "You'll never guess who came by my office—"

She cut herself off. Risa had winced and tensed. "What's wrong? Does something hurt?" Her cousin stared at the wall, breathing in a peculiar way. "My God, are you in labor already?" Her due date was over two weeks away.

Risa nodded. "It started about five. Just a minute."

"But where's Graham? Does he know?"

It was twenty seconds before Risa answered. "No. I called his office at five-thirty but he'd already gone, so I phoned his service and left a message for him to call as soon as possible." Graham carried a beeper for emergencies at the zoo but didn't have a phone in his car. "I still haven't heard from him, though. There was a huge accident on the Bruckner Expressway, so he must be stuck in traffic."

"What happened? Was anyone hurt?"

"Not seriously—at least that's what they said on the news. A truck overturned and spilled some sort of toxic chemical onto the road. All lanes are blocked."

Relieved, Diana said, "Call the service back. Have Graham meet us at the hospital. I'll help you pack."

Risa pointed to the suitcase by the door. "I'm all set, but we don't have to go yet. My contractions are almost twenty minutes apart. Besides, you know how I feel about doctors and hospitals. I want to wait until Graham can be with me."

Diana could understand that, but she still thought Risa should leave. "Don't worry—I'll run interference for you. Premature twins aren't exactly routine, Risa, and—"

"Two weeks early isn't premature, and anyway, the doctor says they're big for twins. The hospital's only ten blocks away. Believe me, there's plenty of time." Risa clicked off the TV. "By the way, Marc called around five. He said to tell you that you'd brought him to his knees— that he's desperate to see you. I promised I'd try to convince you to call him back."

"Don't waste your breath," Diana muttered, pulling over a chair. "I've been through this a dozen times before. Marc's definition of being brought to his knees is deciding we can spend four days in New York at Christmastime instead of three."

"Fine. At least I can tell him I tried. Now what were you saying about someone coming to your office?"

"It was your sister." Diana repeated the conversation, then admitted, "If you want the truth, I'm ashamed of how nasty I was. I guess I want you to tell me I shouldn't be."

"You shouldn't be," Risa said promptly. "You had three years of anger bottled up inside you, and it was only human to let it out." She gave Diana a level look. "Of course, that's not to say Tracy wasn't right in a lot of ways. Oh, damn, here comes another one."

Diana looked at the clock. She hadn't noticed when the last contraction had started but was certainly going to time the interval till the next one. "Can I do anything? Get you anything?"

Risa shook her head and concentrated on her breathing, returning to the subject of Tracy as soon as the contraction eased off. It hadn't been easy for her sister these past three years, she pointed out. The family had accepted her relationship with John because they wanted peace at all costs, but that didn't mean they approved of it. Not only did Tracy feel their disapproval keenly; she considered herself inferior to the woman she'd supplanted, seeing Diana as smarter, more successful and more respected than she was.

"Tracy's grown up a lot in the past few years," Risa added. "Whatever her faults may be, she's finally admitted how badly she behaved, and she's sorry she caused you so much pain. Personally, I think her suggestion about Van Slyke's Island makes a lot of sense for both of you. I know you hate the idea of giving her something she wants so badly, but she'd do a good job."

Diana grimaced. "I do recognize her talents, Risa. She's artistic, bright and a terrific fund-raiser. With some training, she'd do a first-rate job." She sighed and shook her head. "If it were anyone but Tracy—but it's not."

"She hasn't had the happiest life," Risa replied gently. "We were rotten to her every summer—included her two or three times a week and acted like we were saints to do it. She was always hearing how wonderful we were—what good athletes, what gifted students, what successes in our jobs—and she felt she could never match up. Somewhere she got the idea that all she had to offer were her looks and sex appeal, and nothing anyone said could change that. But she's finally gotten some self-confidence, and it would make a huge difference in her life if she had something worthwhile to do. Couldn't you bring yourself to work with her? It would help you, too, you know."

Diana did know, but she couldn't stand the thought of lolling around in France while Tracy took over *her* museum and got tons of attention and praise. "I'm sorry," she said. "I'm not that generous."

"Of course you are. You always have been." Risa flinched. "Here comes another one."

Diana checked the time. Seventeen minutes had gone by.

Risa tried to relax but looked more and more uncomfortable as the pain swelled and peaked. The moment the contraction was over, though, she started talking about Tracy again, trying to convince Diana to give her a chance. Quite naturally, Risa loved her sister and wanted her to be happy. Diana didn't fault her for that, but she wasn't as charitable as Risa supposed.

Still, Risa was her closest friend and had done more for her than she could repay, so she tried to keep an open mind. And gradually, almost despite herself, she softened. It was hard to hate someone so insecure, and besides, Tracy had probably been right about Diana and John, and also about Diana and Marc. If the future worked itself out, the past might make a lot less difference.

Thirty minutes dragged by, then an hour. Risa's contractions came closer together and lasted longer and longer, but there was still no word from Graham. Diana forgot about her problems with Marc and started brooding about Risa. She was afraid something might go wrong, but held her tongue because she didn't want to nag.

Then a contraction came only nine minutes after the last one and quickly grew wrenchingly intense. "That's it," Diana said. "I'm calling Graham's service, and then we're leaving for the hospital."

"Where my labor will probably—stop dead," Risa panted.

Diana ignored her and reached for the phone, only to be stopped by a loud pounding on the front door. "Oh, God, what now?" She got up. "I'll just be a minute. Don't go anywhere."

"That wasn't—funny," Risa gasped. "Hell. This—is— the pits. I hate—pain. You win. I'll—call Graham."

"When it's over, call your doctor, too. I'll be back as soon as I can."

Diana raced to the front door and peered through the peephole. Marc was standing outside, looking winded, sweaty and irritable. It was just what she needed—another tedious, repetitive argument. Sighing, she let him in.

"How long have you been here?" he demanded.

She shut the door. "Since six. Look, Marc, Risa is—"

"Did she tell you I called? That I wanted to see you?"

"Yes, but—"

"Then why didn't you call me back?"

She glared at him. "Would you stop interrupting me? It's not my fault you're in a rotten mood from climbing up forty flights of stairs. I don't have time to talk to you right now. Risa—"

"Then you'd damn well better make time!" He backed her against the door, then grabbed her hand and pushed his engagement ring onto her finger. "You're going to marry me, Diana. I'll do anything within reason to make you happy, but I won't be avoided or ignored and I certainly won't bow to a mulish, all-or-nothing demand just because I'm miserable being without you. We're going to compromise."

Pregnant cousin or not, Diana was too outraged not to respond. "Oh, right. Your definition of compromise—"

"Has changed radically." Smiling now, he stepped forward, trapping her between his body and the door. "I told Risa—you've brought me to my knees. Like my sister, you're an extraordinary woman." He cupped her chin and lifted her face to his. "It complicates matters," he added teasingly, "but I've decided to make allowances."

He moved closer, pressing himself intimately close, and her pulse rate soared. She hadn't let him touch her in weeks, and despite her irritation, her physical hunger for him was almost overwhelming. "What allowances?" she asked suspiciously.

"Major concessions." He nuzzled her lips, making her ache to be touched and kissed. "We'll talk about it later."

"But what concessions?"

"I said later, Diana."

He gently nibbled her lips, teasing away her objections. She couldn't help but start to respond, but then she remembered Risa. "But Marc—"

"Hush, *chérie*. I'll go crazy if we don't make love now." He slid his tongue into her mouth and gave her a scorchingly erotic kiss. With a convulsive shudder, she put her arms around his waist and moved sinuously against him. A minute's delay wouldn't matter.

Within seconds, though, the kiss flared out of control, turning into an exchange of feverish, impatient caresses. He finally tore away his mouth and lifted her into his arms. "Where's your room?"

"At the end of the hallway. But Risa—"

"Will understand completely."

"Is in labor," she managed to sputter as he strode through the foyer. "*Hard* labor."

He stopped dead, looking comically unnerved. "You mean here? In the apartment?"

"Yes. Graham's stuck in a traffic jam. Risa wanted to wait for him, but I finally talked her into going to the hospital. We were just about to leave."

Without another word, he went straight through Risa's door to her bedside. She was noticeably paler now, her eyes glazed and frightened and her skin slick with perspiration.

Diana went cold with alarm. "What happened? Did the pain get worse?"

"Yes. I tried—to get up." Risa was panting, not to ease a contraction, but because she couldn't seem to catch her breath. "To go—to the bathroom. I had to stop. The pain—was so awful. And everything—started spinning around." Her eyes welled up. "I should have left—when you said. If anything goes wrong—"

Marc set Diana down. "It won't," he said with a reassuring smile. "You're a little nervous, that's all. You're hyperventilating, and it's made you dizzy and shaky. Try to calm down and breathe more slowly. I'll carry you to the bathroom, then phone for an ambulance. All right?"

Risa nodded, and he gently picked her up. "That's it. Slower still, *chérie*. Just relax. Everything will be fine."

Murmuring words of comfort, he carried her into the bathroom. She was still pale and shaky as he carefully set her down, but she looked a little less frightened.

She swayed, and Diana took her arm to steady her. "It would be faster to take a cab," she said to Marc. "The hospital's only a few blocks away."

"Fine. I'll buzz the doorman and tell him to have one waiting. If you need me, just yell."

The next contraction came only moments after he'd closed the door. Risa seemed to be in terrible pain, even after it ended, but Diana managed to help her relieve herself and then get her back to the bedroom.

"You'd better carry her to the elevator," Diana said to Marc. "I'll take a chair so she can sit on the way down. The doorman can help us on the other end."

Marc lifted Risa up. "He would probably drop her. He's twice my age and half my size." He started toward the hall. "I'll ride down with you."

Diana grabbed Risa's suitcase and the chair from her dressing table, and followed. "In a high-rise elevator? Thanks, but we'll manage. If she still can't walk, we'll find someone to carry her."

"You think I would allow some stranger to look after her?" He shook his head. "There's no way. I'm staying with her until I turn her over to the doctors."

Risa smiled wanly. "Marc, please. Don't put yourself—through that. One person in a total panic—is enough."

"I'll be fine," he insisted. "It's something about being in a crisis. The elevator won't bother me at all."

Diana opened the front door. It was useless to argue with him when he got protective. "Okay, but if you faint, I'm leaving you in there."

He grinned. "I might be tempted to scream or claw at the walls, but I promise you I won't faint."

Risa actually laughed. Some color returned to her face and her breathing began to slow.

The elevator was open and waiting when they reached it; the doorman had ridden upstairs and held it for them.

Marc carried Risa inside and settled her on the chair, turning toward the front as the doors slid closed. He acted completely at ease, but Diana could see the tension in his body and the anxiety in his eyes. She took his hand and gently squeezed it, and he smiled sheepishly.

The elevator stopped twice to pick up passengers, then continued down to the lobby. Marc, who was a little green by then, was visibly relieved when the doors finally opened.

He took a shaky breath, then picked Risa up and carried her to the cab. By the time they reached the hospital, her contractions were six minutes apart and longer than ever.

Once the paperwork was taken care of, Marc went to the lobby to watch for Graham while Diana accompanied Risa to her room. The hospital had single-room service, so if everything went well, she would be able to stay in the same place through her delivery, recovery and eventual discharge.

Diana waited outside while Risa was examined, then joined her. According to the monitor, the twins were doing beautifully. Reassured, Risa quickly calmed down, accepting a painkiller to dull her contractions. Since Graham wasn't there, a nurse acted as her breathing coach. After all the rushing and worrying, her labor stabilized, the contractions coming five minutes apart.

Diana told her what had happened with Marc, and they joked about his incredible timing. Laughing seemed to relax her, so Diana dredged up funny stories from their childhood in an effort to keep her entertained. Her obstetrician showed up at eight-thirty, checked her out and predicted the twins would be born within hours. She promptly picked up the phone, saying she wanted to pass on the news to her family.

Ten minutes later, just as she finished talking to her mother-in-law, Graham rushed into the room. Diana,

who'd never seen him look so harried, teased him about
being a nervous first-time father, but he blamed it on being
stuck in traffic for three hours. "I'm an old pro," he said
as he kissed Risa hello. "Been through dozens of deliver-
ies. It'll be a piece of cake."

"A piece of cake, hell!" Risa said woozily. "I'd like to
see you give birth—" She suddenly clutched his hand.
"Oh, God, Graham . . ."

The contraction had come less than four minutes after
the last one, but Graham helped her through it with a tenderness that touched Diana's heart. Although it lasted a bit
longer, Risa seemed to handle it much better. Graham's
presence had comforted her and given her strength. Diana
thought it must be wonderful to be so close—to be so
completely in tune that words became unnecessary.

"I'm not doing this again," Risa said afterward. "If you
want more kids, *you* can have them."

She was smiling, but Graham didn't smile back. Her
pain had left him visibly shaken. "Two is a good number.
I'd give up sex before I'd put you through this again."

"It's not *that* bad, honey. Well, actually it is, but fortunately, women are much stronger than men." She looked
at Diana and winced. "Forget I said that. Don't let this
stop you from having kids."

"I won't. With my hips, why should I worry?" Diana
sponged off Risa's face with a cool, damp cloth. "Actually, I was about to thank you. Being with you—watching the two of you together—has put things into
perspective for me. I'm selfish, I guess. I want to be happy.
I want what you two have. Van Slyke's Island just isn't
going to do that for me, is it? Not all by itself, anyway."

"Then talk to Marc. Meet him halfway." Risa touched
her hand. "That's much too fabulous a ring to give up.
Much too fabulous a man, too. He was terrific before, and
I know it wasn't easy for him. Riding down the elevator, I
mean."

"No. It wasn't." Diana paused. "I'll be back in a little while—with Marc, I hope. Would that be okay?"

"Of course," Risa answered. "After all, he's going to be a member of the family."

Marc wasn't in the lobby anymore, so Diana tried the cafeteria. She found him in a quiet corner of the room, bent over a cup of coffee, lost in thought. A little nervous now, she sat down across from him.

"Risa's doing fine," she said. "All she really needed was Graham. It shouldn't be more than a few hours."

He nodded solemnly. "And tell me ... Will you be as nervous as she was?"

"Not unless my husband gets stuck in traffic for three hours." Her love for him was shining in her eyes. "We won't be living in the city, so there's not much chance of that, is there?"

"Then you've resigned yourself to marrying me?" He looked relieved and a little surprised.

"Yes, assuming we can work things out." In truth, she would have accepted his most recent terms, but the seasoned negotiator in her wanted to get as much as she could. "You mentioned concessions. I'd like to hear about them."

He took her hand. "Like my sister, you have a special calling, *chérie*. Unique talents. The husband of such a woman has to make allowances for that—for the benefit of society, that is. He has to share her."

"I see," Diana said, fighting the urge to smile. She was never going to turn him into a feminist, but since he seemed to make "allowances" for every female he cared about, it hardly mattered.

"We'll stay here for three years," he continued crisply. "We'll buy a place in the country and I'll open a restaurant in the area. You'll leave your job and work full-time on your museum, and start training someone to take your place. At least four times a year we'll visit France for several weeks. We'll keep our home here after we move to St. Emilion, and spend a week here in the winter and a month here every summer."

"The *whole* summer," Diana said, "and also a week in the spring. If you can't get away, I'll stay here by myself."

He frowned. "But we'll have children by then. At least I hope we will."

"So do I, and if we do, they'll stay with me. I want them to be close to their American relations."

He stared at the table for several seconds, then sighed. "All right. I suppose that's only fair. But not for the whole summer, Diana. I'd miss you all too much. Two months at the most."

"Okay. Two months." In truth, she was amazed he hadn't ranted about her staying in New York without him.

The tension drained from her body. She'd expected an all-out battle and wound up with a minor skirmish. "That's settled, then. I'm so glad." She broke into a relieved smile. "The past few weeks have been awful, Marc. I was so torn. I knew I'd never be happy without you, but I couldn't walk away from the promises I'd made. I was afraid we'd never work things out."

"I knew that we would, but I thought it would take much longer. You said you were irreplaceable... that you needed six or seven years here. I expected to have to bargain with you half the night." He paused. "What changed your mind, Diana?"

"I found someone to help me. Someone bright and capable, who loves the island as much as I do." She shook her head, bemused by the strange turns life took. "Tracy Redmon, of all people."

He looked startled. "How on earth did that come about?"

She explained about Tracy's visit to her office and described her long conversation with Risa, then admitted that she'd found it hard to accept the truth about her and John and even harder to let go of her resentment. "Now that I finally have, though, I feel incredibly free. All the bitterness is gone. I feel like I could tackle the world and win." She squeezed his hand. "If it hadn't been for you, I would have wound up a cranky, eccentric old millionaire and missed most of what I truly wanted in life. I do love you, Marc."

"I'd like you to show me how much, but I suppose it will have to wait." He leaned forward and kissed her. "I love you, too. Run along now. Go check on your cousin."

"You can come with me if you want. Risa would like you to be there." She paused and grinned. "It's on the fifth floor, but now that you've gotten over your phobia about elevators—"

"The hell I have. I did what was necessary to help Risa, that's all. Unless there's another emergency, I'll stick with staircases from now on."

"Then I'll walk upstairs with you." They both got up, and she took his arm. "I'm going to be in great shape, married to you."

"You will once I've fed you some decent meals. You've lost weight these past few weeks. I'm going to spend the weekend making love to you and feeding you."

"That sounds perfect," Diana said with a smile.

They took their time climbing the stairs, stopping every now and then to kiss. When they finally got upstairs, they found a small crowd gathered outside Risa's door—Graham's parents, Babe and Henry, and Tracy and John.

"One down, one to go," Babe said. "A boy. He was over six pounds."

"Already?" Diana asked. Only about an hour had gone by.

"Umm. Things just took off, and the next thing we knew, she was ready to push. She didn't want anyone but Graham there, so we all cleared out." She peered at

Diana's hand. "What a gorgeous ring! It's about time you two got together. Who gave in?"

"We both did. We're going to live here for three years, then move to France." Diana looked at Tracy. "The island will need lots of love and hard work. Do you still want to help me?"

"Risa *said* you were going to ask, but I didn't quite believe it." Tracy looked as happy as a kid on Christmas morning. "Yes. I do. When can we start?"

"Not before Monday," Marc said. "I have plans for her this weekend."

Tracy laughed. "I'll just bet you do! Take good care of her, Marc. She deserves to be happy."

"You're right. She does." He put his hand on Tracy's shoulder. "It took courage for you to go see her, and to ask if she would let you help. You have my thanks."

"You're welcome," Tracy said with a blush, "but it was more like sheer gall."

"Whichever you choose to call it, you and Diana—and your whole family—will be happier for it. And I know you'll do a wonderful job with the museum." He dropped his hand and looked at John. "You'll support your wife's work there, of course, even though it will mean she'll have less time for you. After losing one Van Slyke, you wouldn't be foolish enough to risk losing a second."

"No. I wouldn't. I've learned a few things over the years." He kissed Diana on the cheek. "Congratulations, babe. I should have been as good to you as he is."

"We both made mistakes," she murmured.

"Maybe." He held out his hand to Marc.

As the two men shook hands, there was a wail from inside Risa's room. "It's another boy," Graham called out. "Just as big, too. Give us another minute or two..."

But it was ten minutes before he opened the door, and by then, everyone had planned Marc and Diana's wedding for them and invited themselves to visit the Rochards' château. Marc and Diana stood with their arms around each other's waists, smiling absently while they listened with half an ear, thinking no further than later that night.

The babies, of course, were beautiful. Risa held one and Graham the other while everyone studied them and argued about whether they were identical. "Graham and I were talking about godparents," Risa finally said. "Tracy and John, Diana and Marc... We'd be honored if you'd take on that responsibility."

"But who goes with which?" Tracy asked.

"We thought it would be nice if the four of you could go with both," Risa answered. "That wouldn't be a problem, would it? I mean, now that we're all one family again?"

Diana and Tracy exchanged a smile. It wouldn't be a problem at all, they said.

* * * * *

Double your reading pleasure this fall with two Award of Excellence titles written by two of your favorite authors.

Available in September

DUNCAN'S BRIDE
by Linda Howard
Silhouette Intimate Moments #349

Mail-order bride Madelyn Patterson was nothing like what Reese Duncan expected—and everything he needed.

Available in October

THE COWBOY'S LADY
by Debbie Macomber
Silhouette Special Edition #626

The Montana cowboy wanted a little lady at his beck and call—the ''lady'' in question saw things differently....

These titles have been selected to receive a special laurel—the Award of Excellence. Look for the distinctive emblem on the cover. It lets you know there's something truly wonderful inside!   DUN-1

Take 4 bestselling love stories FREE

Plus get a FREE surprise gift!

PASSPORT TO ROMANCE
SWEEPSTAKES RULES

1. **HOW TO ENTER:** To enter, you must be the age of majority and complete the official entry form, or print your name, address, telephone number and age on a plain piece of paper and mail to: Passport to Romance, P.O. Box 9056, Buffalo, NY 14269-9056. No mechanically reproduced entries accepted.
2. All entries must be received by the CONTEST CLOSING DATE, DECEMBER 31, 1990 TO BE ELIGIBLE.
3. **THE PRIZES:** There will be ten (10) Grand Prizes awarded, each consisting of a choice of a trip for two people from the following list:
   i) London, England (approximate retail value $5,050 U.S.)
   ii) England, Wales and Scotland (approximate retail value $6,400 U.S.)
   iii) Carribean Cruise (approximate retail value $7,300 U.S.)
   iv) Hawaii (approximate retail value $9,550 U.S.)
   v) Greek Island Cruise in the Mediterranean (approximate retail value $12,250 U.S.)
   vi) France (approximate retail value $7,300 U.S.)
4. Any winner may choose to receive any trip or a cash alternative prize of $5,000.00 U.S. in lieu of the trip.
5. **GENERAL RULES:** Odds of winning depend on number of entries received.
6. A random draw will be made by Nielsen Promotion Services, an independent judging organization, on January 29, 1991, in Buffalo, NY, at 11:30 a.m. from all eligible entries received on or before the Contest Closing Date.
7. Any Canadian entrants who are selected must correctly answer a time-limited, mathematical skill-testing question in order to win.
8. Full contest rules may be obtained by sending a stamped, self-addressed envelope to: "Passport to Romance Rules Request", P.O. Box 9998, Saint John, New Brunswick, Canada E2L 4N4.
9. Quebec residents may submit any litigation respecting the conduct and awarding of a prize in this contest to the Régie des loteries et courses du Québec.
10. Payment of taxes other than air and hotel taxes is the sole responsibility of the winner.
11. Void where prohibited by law.

COUPON BOOKLET OFFER TERMS

To receive your Free travel-savings coupon booklets, complete the mail-in Offer Certificate on the preceeding page, including the necessary number of proofs-of-purchase, and mail to: Passport to Romance, P.O. Box 9057, Buffalo, NY 14269-9057. The coupon booklets include savings on travel-related products such as car rentals, hotels, cruises, flowers and restaurants. Some restrictions apply. The offer is available in the United States and Canada. Requests must be postmarked by January 25, 1991. Only proofs-of-purchase from specially marked "Passport to Romance" Harlequin® or Silhouette® books will be accepted. The offer certificate must accompany your request and may not be reproduced in any manner. Offer void where prohibited or restricted by law. LIMIT FOUR COUPON BOOKLETS PER NAME, FAMILY, GROUP, ORGANIZATION OR ADDRESS. Please allow up to 8 weeks after receipt of order for shipment. Enter quickly as quantities are limited. Unfulfilled mail-in offer requests will receive free Harlequin® or Silhouette® books (not previously available in retail stores), in quantities equal to the number of proofs-of-purchase required for Levels One to Four, as applicable.

PR-SWPS

OFFICIAL SWEEPSTAKES
ENTRY FORM

Complete and return this Entry Form immediately—the more Entry Forms you submit, the better your chances of winning!
- Entry Forms must be received by **December 31, 1990**
- A random draw will take place on **January 29, 1991**
- Trip must be taken by **December 31, 1991**

3-SSE-2-SW

YES, I want to win a PASSPORT TO ROMANCE vacation for two! I understand the prize includes round-trip air fare, accommodation and a daily spending allowance.

Name_____

Address_____

City_____ State_____ Zip_____

Telephone Number_____ Age_____

Return entries to: **PASSPORT TO ROMANCE**, P.O. Box 9056, Buffalo, NY 14269-9056

© 1990 Harlequin Enterprises Limited

COUPON BOOKLET/OFFER CERTIFICATE

Item	LEVEL ONE Booklet 1	LEVEL TWO Booklet 1 & 2	LEVEL THREE Booklet 1, 2 & 3	LEVEL FOUR Booklet 1, 2, 3 & 4
Booklet 1 = $100+	$100+	$100+	$100+	$100+
Booklet 2 = $200+		$200+	$200+	$200+
Booklet 3 = $300+			$300+	$300+
Booklet 4 = $400+	____	____	____	$400+
Approximate Total Value of Savings	$100+	$300+	$600+	$1,000+
# of Proofs of Purchase Required	4	6	12	18
Check One	____	____	____	____

Name_____

Address_____

City_____ State_____ Zip_____

Return Offer Certificates to: **PASSPORT TO ROMANCE**, P.O. Box 9057, Buffalo, NY 14269-9057

Requests must be postmarked by **January 25, 1991**

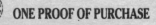

ONE PROOF OF PURCHASE   3-SSE-2

To collect your free coupon booklet you must include the necessary number of proofs-of-purchase with a properly completed Offer Certificate   © 1990 Harlequin Enterprises Limited

See previous page for details